Hunters

· · · · · · · · · · · · · ·

WHITLEY STRIEBER

TOR

A TOM DOHERTY ASSOCIATES BOOK
NEW YORK

This is a work of fiction. All of the characters, organizations, and events portrayed in this novel are either products of the author's imagination or are used fictitiously.

HUNTERS

Copyright © 2013 by Walker & Collier, Inc.

This novel was previously published in 2013 under the title *Alien Hunter*.

All rights reserved.

A Tor Book
Published by Tom Doherty Associates, LLC
175 Fifth Avenue
New York, NY 10010

www.tor-forge.com

Tor® is a registered trademark of Tom Doherty Associates, LLC.

ISBN 978-0-7653-8832-2

Our books may be purchased in bulk for promotional, educational, or business use. Please contact your local bookseller or the Macmillan Corporate and Premium Sales Department at 1-800-221-7945, extension 5442, or by e-mail at MacmillanSpecialMarkets@macmillan.com.

First TV Tie-in Edition: March 2015

Printed in the United States of America

0 9 8 7 6 5 4 3 2 1

This book, and the Alien Hunter series, are dedicated to the people who work behind the scenes to keep our world safe.
Thank you.

ACKNOWLEDGMENTS

I would like to thank Anne Strieber, who always insisted; my editor, Robert Gleason, who always understood; and Eliani Torres, whose attention to detail extracted my story from my prose.

Beware the bearers of false gifts and their broken promises. Much pain but still time. There is good out there. We oppose deception.

—message in a crop formation found on a farm in the United Kingdom, August 2002

Hunters

·················

CHAPTER ONE

2002

Flynn reached for her and she wasn't there. Her side of the bed was cold and he was a detective, so he came immediately awake.

"Abby?"

He rolled out of bed, slid his feet into his slippers, and set off into the midnight house. It was November 16, 2002, the time was twelve-forty, the house was cool but not cold, there was no obvious sign of foul play.

"Abby?"

Hurrying now, he went downstairs, turning on lights as he passed the switches. By the time he reached the kitchen, he knew that she wasn't in the house and that there was no point of entry that would suggest a forcible kidnapping. In any case, he couldn't imagine why she would be kidnapped or by whom. But he'd been a cop for six years, a detective for two. In that time, he'd made a couple of hundred very bad people very mad, and some of them were people who might do just about anything.

Going back over his cases in his mind, though, he

couldn't see a revenge kidnapper, at least, not one that was presently at large.

Just to be thorough, he checked the basement. They were in the process of finishing it, and it was full of boxes of ceiling tiles and Pergo flooring.

She wasn't there.

All doors were locked, all windows were locked. The alarm system was armed. So nobody could've come in here, not without all hell breaking loose.

She'd gone out. Had to have.

He called her cell—and heard it ringing upstairs. He went up. It was on the dresser but not in its usual place in her purse. Her purse was gone.

The first cold tremble of fear passed through him. Something was obviously very wrong here. Abby didn't get up in the middle of the night and go out. Never, not without telling him.

Following the rules, he dialed 911. "This is Detective Errol Carroll. I'd like to report my wife, Abigail Carroll, missing. Probable foul play."

The 911 operator responded, "We have a car moving, Flynn."

Next he called his boss, Captain Edward Parker. "Eddie, it's me, I'm sorry about the time. Abby's gone missing."

As the reality set in, a terrible, frantic urgency swept him.

"Okay," Eddie said. "Okay. Any evidence of an entry?"

"The alarm system is still on. Nobody broke in."

Silence. Flynn could practically hear Eddie thinking. They'd known each other since they were kids and they'd both known Abby almost as long. Both had dated her. Flynn had won.

"You guys doin' okay?" Eddie asked. It was his way of broaching the question that was going to be on everybody's mind.

"Eddie, this isn't a marital thing. Somebody got Abby." He knew that every word had to be measured tonight, because if he wasn't careful, this would get knocked down to an adult missing person real fast. "Look, I can't stay in here. I gotta roll."

"Wait for the uniforms. I'm sending a detective right now. Mullins. Tom Mullins, he's duty."

He didn't much like Tom and Tom didn't much like him. But Tom did his job. Sort of. "Okay, I'm gonna back him up, though. He's not gonna drop this down to an MPA because it's not an MPA, Eddie."

"You got it."

There came a knock at the front door. Decisive, loud, the way cops knock.

Where are you, baby?

He disarmed the alarm system and let the uniforms in. It was Willy Ford and a deputy sheriff he didn't know, name of Menchaca. "Hey guys, thanks for doing it so fast. I got a missing wife. Almost certainly a kidnap."

"Jeez, Flynn, Abby's been kidnapped?" Willy had flirted with Abby at the Memorial Day barbecue last year. Lots of laughs.

"Looks like it."

"Is there a point of entry?" Menchaca asked.

"Not that I can see."

A car pulled up and Eddie got out. He hurried up the walk, his belly bouncing, his gray hair fluttering in the night wind. His fly was down. You could see pajamas in there. Flynn had a damn good friend in Eddie.

"Anything?" he asked as he came in.

"We need prints out here," Flynn said. He shuddered.

He was freezing cold on a hot night. "Look, I can't stay here. I'm gonna drive."

"No you aren't. I got the troops moving. Every car's on, everybody's looking."

Eddie was right. Flynn's going off into the night wasn't going to help anything.

"Who comes in through an alarm system?" Eddie asked.

"A professional."

"You drop time on any professionals? Time that they may have served?"

Cops were routinely informed when their collars were released from prison. "Nobody."

"What about ever?"

"You know my collar history."

"Yeah, you got a fair number, buddy. Some bad'uns."

"Nobody special, Eddie. Nobody—" He gestured toward the emptiness of the house. Another wave of fear was hitting him. He imagined Abby being tortured, buried alive, raped.

He wanted to run through the streets calling her name. He wanted to drive and drive, searching every crack house, every flop, every crib he knew. She was out there right now. Abby was out there and suffering *right now*.

Detective Charlie Mullin came in. "Where are we?"

"Doing an APB," Eddie replied. "Get me a picture."

Flynn strode across the living room and grabbed the photograph that stood on the mantel. It was a studio portrait taken two years ago, for her father while he was dying in St. Vincent de Sales, choking out his lungs, poor damn guy with his cigarettes and his unfortunate opinion that the dangers were overblown.

Eddie put the picture down under a lamp and took a

few shots of it with his cell phone. He then took a verbal description from Flynn and inside of three minutes the all-points bulletin was appearing on police computer networks all across the state.

Flynn knew the statistics. Every hour that passed, it was less likely that she would be found.

"You have any idea when this happened?"

"I might." He went to the side table in the hall and dug out the alarm system's instruction book. "The system might tell us the last time it was disarmed and re-armed." He glanced at Eddie and Mullen. "He had the code. Had to have."

"Who had it?" Mullin asked.

Flynn shook his head. "Me and her, far as I know."

"Parents? Brothers and sisters?"

"No brothers and sisters. My mom and her folks have passed. My dad doesn't have it."

"You're certain?"

"Unless she gave it to somebody, which I very much doubt."

"She didn't," Eddie said. "She was way too smart and too careful."

Flynn input his code, then followed the instructions. In a moment, the answer appeared on the system's LED screen. "Three thirty-two," he said. Then the next figure flashed, the time it had been re-armed. One minute later. "This can't be right," he said.

"What time?" Mullen asked.

"Within the minute. Three thirty-three."

There was a silence. Then Mullin said, "We need an inventory, Flynn."

"She was kidnapped!"

"Somebody came in here and took her in under a minute? Who would that be?"

"Hell if I know!" He turned to Eddie. "For God's sake, don't cancel that APB, don't cancel anything!"

Eddie held out his hands, palms up. "Hey, I got the county choppers up. I'm goin' all out, Flynn."

This was a small police force in a small city, with a compliment of just thirty personnel. They liked to think that they were good, but at the same time, there were a limited number of challenges. A murder every six weeks or so, a meth lab or crack house a week on the south side, a thin but steady stream of family disturbances, assaults, burglaries and robberies.

"I gotta admit, I can't remember the last time we had a kidnapping," Eddie said.

"Nineteen ninety-six. Kid named Angela Dugan, fifteen years old. Turned out to be her boyfriend. They were brought back from Tijuana—married."

"So, you got any ideas yet?"

He didn't. "Let's canvas," he said. "Before people take off for work."

"It's five."

"Let's canvas."

It was cool and still outside, the silence broken only by the busy clatter of lightbars left running. The morning star hung low in a blood-red eastern sky. Up and down the street, lights were coming on. Across the street, Sarah Robinson stood on her front porch in her robe, her arms crossed on her chest.

Flynn gazed across at her. "She and Abby are planning to have their babies together."

"Abby's pregnant?"

He started across the street. "She hadn't said anything."

In times of extreme stress, details come crowding in, the crisp scent of the air, the soft crunch of grass under your sneakers, the distant pumping clatter of one of the county choppers patrolling above the silent streets.

"Are you guys okay?" Sarah asked, her voice constricted, her smile choked back into her face.

"Abby's missing."

"Oh, Flynn, oh my God."

"Did you see or hear anything?"

She shook her head. "The cars woke me up. Let me get Kev."

"I'm here," Kevin said, coming out from behind her. "Same story from me. Nothing."

They did the Monteleones, got nothing but sadness from this gentle, elderly couple.

"The next house is Al Dennis," Flynn said. "He's often up at this hour. I've seen his lights on when I come in off night duty."

"Good."

This time, though, Al had been sound asleep, and he came to the door bleary and blinking, pulling a terrycloth robe on over his pajama bottoms.

"Flynn?"

"Al, Abby's missing. She's been kidnapped. We're trying to find out if anybody noticed anything unusual during the night."

"Unusual?"

"Lights, voices, a vehicle passing the house more than once, anything like that."

Flynn saw him look into himself, a sign that detectives come to know, that somebody is genuinely searching their memory.

"Lights about three. A car out there." He gazed at Flynn. "I thought it was you, Flynn."

"Why was that?"

"I just assumed it was you coming off duty. I guess it

was like, you know, the car stopped there. At your place. I didn't hear your garage opening, though. I do remember that."

"Did you see the car?" Eddie asked.

Dennis shook his head. "Sorry. I just—a car came up and stopped."

"Did you hear it pull away?"

Again, he shook his head. "I got the impression the lights had gone out. Like I said, you coming home. That's what I thought."

"A time, Dennis?"

"After three. In there."

He'd heard the car but hadn't seen it. "Do you remember anything about the engine noise? A large car, maybe? A truck? Could you tell?"

"God, Flynn, I am so sorry. I wish I could help."

As he thanked Dennis, he realized that he was beginning the rest of his life, and it would be a time of wondering and suffering and the pain of love that has been stolen, but not lost.

As he expected, the rest of the canvas turned up nothing.

Late in the morning an FBI agent came up from Austin to Menard, a kid named Chapman Shifley. Agent Shifley wore a suit, cheap but carefully pressed. He had a burr haircut and the fast eyes of someone who might have a special forces background. He introduced himself, jamming his hand out and pumping Flynn's arm, the gesture an unconvincing parody of manly sympathy.

Only one assignment mattered to the FBI in Texas, and it wasn't this. Either you were on drugs and gangs or you were essentially nowhere. This assignment was nowhere.

The first thing he asked for was an inventory.

"I haven't done that. Except that her purse is missing."

"Could we just do a little looking around," Shifley said, not unkindly. He wasn't insensitive.

"Please be my guest."

The house was filling up with forensics personnel, "Lady" Christopher with her careful hands, her supervisor Jamie Landry, who hailed from the Evangeline Country over in Louisiana and made remarkable crawfish bisque.

It would take hours, but the two of them would methodically work over the entire house, looking for fingerprints and subtle evidence of some kind of skilled break-in.

As he climbed the stairs, followed by Eddie and Shifley, Flynn found that he didn't want to go back into their bedroom. He never wanted to go back in, not until Abby was safely home.

The cheerful curtains, the soft blue wallpaper, the sleigh bed—it was all as familiar as ever, but it now seemed miraculously beautiful, like a room from some past world found in a museum.

Landry came up and handed out latex gloves. "Don't move things more than you absolutely have to," he said.

Nobody replied.

Flynn rolled on his gloves and opened Abby's top drawer.

Immediately, he saw that clothes were gone, two or three bras, socks, underpants.

"Everything in place?" Shifley asked.

"I'm not sure."

"Because that looks like somebody took stuff outa there."

"It sure does."

In the closet, he found her backpack missing. Also, her white sneakers were gone, and some shirts and jeans.

If he'd been working this case on a stranger, he would have said that they'd left voluntarily.

"Flynn," Shifley said, "were you guys doing okay? I mean, the marriage?"

"She didn't run out on me."

"I have to ask."

"Yes, okay! *Yes*. We're happy."

"Because that's not what this looks like."

"Then it's a setup! She'd never walk out on me. She—we—we're in love. It's a happy marriage."

He knew the Bureau. He knew that they were going to back this down to an adult missing person, probable walkout. That would give the case maybe two more days of search time.

Eddie said, "They're happy."

"Yeah, I get it."

His tone said that Flynn was right, and in that terrible moment, he could almost feel her soul flying away from him.

Of course, the locals didn't quit. Eddie didn't quit. But police forces live in a strange sort of a straitjacket. A local Texas police force has access to information from other Texas authorities, but not other states, not other countries. To really pull down a sophisticated kidnapper, you need the reach of the FBI with its connections around the world, and the co-operation of Interpol. The motive for stealing beautiful young women, if it was not perverted, was often nowadays for sale into slavery abroad. A twenty-two-year-old blond like Abby could bring big money in hidden slave markets.

By the time Landry and company had finished, Flynn

had been awake for more than fifty hours. He was not in grief, but desperation. It wasn't as if Abby was dead, it was as if she was waiting for him. Abby trusted him. She would believe that he would do anything to find her. She would have faith that he would come.

By sunset on the third day, the house was empty and quiet. Not a single trace of useful evidence had been found. Abby, her backpack, her purse with her ID and a little money in it were all gone, along with three changes of clothes.

His wife had not walked out on him. His wife was out there somewhere, in the hands of a monster. He chose not to consider the possibility that she might be dead, and in so doing joined many thousands of people waiting every day of their lives for closure that never comes.

He had nightmares that she had been buried alive.

He had nightmares that she was being starved.

He had nightmares that she had been sold to some Arab prince.

On and on and on it went.

Every morning at five, he ran. He ran through the quiet streets of his neighborhood and down into the Railroad District where the great grain elevators stood, past their ghostly immensity, past the long lines of hopper cars dark in the early dawn, past the heaving engines with their great, staring lights, past the café with its warm windows and steaming coffee. He ran like a man under threat. Over time, he became narrow and hard, his body steel cable.

He became a master of the handgun, he learned fast shooting and target shooting and he became known among the shooters of West Texas as a competitor to be aware of. He learned tae kwan do and karate, and learned them well. He went beyond the normal investigative skills of a police detective, venturing into areas as diverse as wilderness tracking and the use of sophisticated bugging devices.

His colleagues admired his skills and feared his obsessive dedication to his cases. When he was on a kidnap, he routinely worked twenty-four hours at a stretch and slept three. He could have risen in the department to a captaincy, but he prevailed on Eddie to leave him a lieutenant so that he wouldn't get sucked up into administration.

As the years wore on, he gradually turned his den into what became known on the force as the Abby Room.

Even though the FBI had abandoned the investigation before it was three days old, Eddie did not abandon it. Far from it, he hid Flynn's case time for him, allowing him to continue looking for his wife for two more years.

Finally, he quietly and sadly eased it into the cold case file. This meant that nobody could be assigned to it without his personal approval.

Still, though, Flynn's investigation continued. He became the most knowledgeable expert on kidnap in the State of Texas. Every force in Texas consulted him. The Texas Rangers consulted him. He solved case after case after case. But the Abby Room only grew more full of clippings, of clues, of false leads. He slid his unending search for her ever deeper into his caseload, accepting Eddie's silent compliance with equally silent gratitude.

Their bond of friendship deepened. Eddie had loved Abby, too. He had sat on the summer porches of youth with her, also. He had never married. Instead, his love affair with her had continued down its own lonely path, and he had watched with pain and joy as she and Flynn made their life together. When he went to their house for cop nights, he'd watch her out of hooded eyes. She'd had a dancing heart, had Abby Carroll, and looks and ways that no man could ever forget.

Not often—maybe once or twice a year—Flynn ran into a case similar to Abby's, an apparent walkout that seemed to him to be something else. Time and again, the FBI abandoned these cases after a few days.

Flynn did not abandon them.

Somebody was out there taking people, he knew it, somebody very clever and very skilled.

Somebody was out there.

CHAPTER TWO

The Night had come and gone, November 16, as always, the worst night of Flynn's year.

As he always did on the anniversary of Abby's disappearance, he had spent it in the Abby Room, pouring over files, seeking some new lead hidden in some record he hadn't considered before.

As always, he'd found nothing. Her case was dead cold. Still, though, she lived on within him. His side of the conversation of life continued.

Sarah Robinson's little girl Taylor was in grade school now. He had never asked her if Abby, also, had been pregnant, but every time he saw Taylor, a question came into the edge of his mind: were there bones somewhere of the woman he had loved, and tiny bones tangled within them?

He'd never remarried, never even considered it. After seven years it would have been legal, but he would never do it, not until he knew for certain that she was no more.

Eddie came out of his office and headed his way. His gut was rolling, his dark glasses bouncing in his breast pocket. He was coming fast, his scowl as deep as a grave.

Flynn was hoping that he was headed anywhere else, but he did just what it looked like he was going to do, and dropped down into the old chair beside his desk.

He said, "Special Agent Diana Glass wants to talk to you regarding an investigation you've been pursuing."

"The Mercedes case? The meth lab on Fourteenth Street?"

"The Carroll Case. Abby."

Flynn said nothing.

"She even knows about the Abby Room," Eddie continued. "She knows you were interviewing Charlie Boyne again yesterday."

The Boyne case was one of the other disappearances that were mirror images of Abby's. "I wasn't."

" 'Course you were."

"Dallas PD and the FBI closed the Boyne case years ago. So I wasn't interviewing him, as there is no case on the books."

"Then let's say you were pursuing your hobby of refusing to drop closed cases."

"Who the hell told her?"

"Not me. I just sit in my office and wait for the parade to go by. Which it never does."

"There was a parade. When the Tomcats won the semi-finals."

Eddie looked blank.

"The Tomcats. Menard High's football team on which you once served as a wide receiver. Last year they reached the semi-finals and the school decided on a parade. You were there. You rode in the lead pickup. In a uniform with a big cap. Very impressive."

"Is that sardonic or sarcastic?"

"Both. Anyway, where is Agent Glass from, Dallas or San Antonio?"

"She emailed me for permission to talk to you about disappearance cases in general. Pick your brain, be my guess."

"Okay."

"Could be a break, Flynn, if the Bureau's gonna finally do something." He paused. "Thing is, she's got a Gmail account."

That was odd. "So she's not the Bureau? Did she name an agency?"

"She did not."

But who else would it be? ATF? No, no interest in missing persons there. Border Patrol? Possibly. "I've looked for evidence of border transport for years. So maybe she's Borders."

Eddie Parker said, "You're gonna find out. Right now."

A woman in a suit stood in the doorway of the squad room.

"My God," Flynn muttered.

Her hair was so dark it made her skin look as pale as marble. She wore a black, featureless suit that shimmered like silk. Her eyes moved to Flynn, then to Eddie, then to back to him again. Then the most beautiful woman Flynn had ever seen in his life strode through the dead-silent squad room. She stopped at his desk.

Eddie had taken off. His office door was already closing.

"Lieutenant Errol Carroll?"

He stood up and shook an unexpectedly powerful hand. Her eyes, emerald green, drilled into him. She was all job, this woman. Beauty, yes, but in service to a cause, which was very clear.

"Lieutenant, we need to talk."

He gestured toward his chair.

"Privately."

Silently, he led her toward the conference room. He could see Eddie lurking way back in his office, watching through the blinds, not wanting to get anywhere near this. He didn't want a single thing to do with this ice sculpture, either. She might as well have "Bad News" tattooed on her forehead in big red letters. Expensive clothes like hers did not go with garden variety FBI personnel, or any ordinary personnel at all. No, this lady came from way up high where the dangerous people lived.

After they were in the conference room, she shut the door. She turned the lock with a decisive click. He hadn't ever seen that lock used before.

"Sit down, please."

"What's this about?"

She reinforced her statement with a sharp gesture, and he found himself dropping into one of the old wooden chairs that were scattered around the scarred conference table.

She went into her briefcase and pulled out a tablet computer. She tapped a couple of times and he could see a file appear. Like many a detective, he was good at reading upside down. He saw his own name on it, and his picture.

She began flipping through the file, touching the screen with a long finger every time she turned a page.

"Do I need a lawyer?"

She stopped reading and looked up. "You have investigated twelve of them, starting with your wife. Each time, you've put in a request for more investigative support. May I ask you why?"

"May I see a cred?"

"You're suspicious of me?"

He did not reply.

She held out an FBI credential that identified her as Special Agent Diana Glass.

"Satisfied?"

Not in the least, but that was beside the point. First off, the credential could be rigged. Second, he would never know the truth—at least, not until it was too late to save himself from whatever dire fate she had in mind for him.

"What do you want from me, Agent Glass?"

"First off, you're not in any trouble. And I'm Diana, Errol."

"Flynn. People call me Flynn."

"Flynn? That isn't in your file."

"Errol Carroll? My folks had a tin ear. Flynn is a joke, as in Errol Flynn."

She gave him as blank a look as he had seen in some time. His guess was that she'd never heard of Errol Flynn.

"Just call me Flynn without the joke."

"We want you to help us nail the bastard whose been doing this, and we want you to start right now."

"Sure," he said carefully. "I'm ready to start any damn time. But why the change of heart?"

She got up and went to the door. "Tomorrow morning at eight. Be prepared to travel."

"Travel? Where? For how long?"

She froze. She turned. "This is going to happen

again, Lieutenant, and soon. With all the effort you've put into your investigations, the expertise you have developed, we believe you can help us prevent the next crime. So to answer your question, we'll be going wherever we need to go, and it's going to take however long it takes."

She left.

He stood staring at the door. What the hell had just happened? As he walked out into the squad room, he saw her striding toward the front lobby.

Guys were being careful, pretending not to be absolutely fascinated with whatever had just gone down.

"I don't know," he said into the silence. "I have no idea."

Eddie burst out of his office. His neck was pulsing, his face was crimson. This was not a man with a temper, but he was on full burn right now.

"What in goddamn hell's the matter with you," he snarled.

"Nothing."

He held up a fax. "They're telling me you've requested an indefinite leave. Thanks for this, ole buddy, ole pal. Next time just damn well tell me. Discuss it with me. Because we've been friends for years, jerkoff that you are." As he talked, he waved the fax.

Flynn snatched it from him. And his jaw nearly sank out of sight.

"I didn't know about this."

"You didn't ask for a leave?"

"'Course not. Why would I? I like to put creeps in jail. It's my damn vocation."

"So if I tear this up, you're back here in the morning?"

At that moment, his phone vibrated with an incoming

text. He read it. "You have a chance to catch the man who kidnapped Abby."

Her timing was excellent, he had to say that.

"No, Eddie, actually the request is good." He could hardly believe what he was saying, but he was doing it and as he did so, his conviction was growing. "The request is good."

"I can't pay you. I'd like to but I can't."

He didn't spend much money, hadn't since Abby. So he could handle the absence of a salary. "I'm sorry, Eddie. I have to do this."

"Yeah, I get it. But clean out your locker. If the janitor has to scrape any rotted doughnuts outa there, you're gettin' a bill."

Their eyes met. His friend was there for him and nothing more needed to be said. Eddie turned away and Flynn did the only thing left for him to do. He gathered up his few personal items and left the way cops always left on their last day, with a cardboard box in their arms and a few good-byes. A police force is like a lake. When you get out, you don't leave a hole.

By the time he was unlocking his car, another guy would already have his current cases. But not the Abby Carroll case, of course. Not the Boyne case, and not any of the other missing persons cases that had gone cold.

He drove home in the quiet of the midday. This was all insane, of course. He never should have done this.

"Abby," he said into the rattling of his old Malibu, "I'm coming, babes, I'm coming."

CHAPTER THREE

As soon as he got home, Flynn texted Diana Glass that he was ready to go, but received no reply. He did an Internet search on her and found nothing. No Facebook page for a Diana Glass that looked like her. No Twitter account. A check of the National Law Enforcement Roster also turned up no Diana Glass, meaning that she'd never been in a local or state police force. His access to FBI records was limited, of course, but he'd emailed their personnel department a verification check on her from the office. Usually, you got an answer in a few minutes, and usually it was "verified." FBI creds were not easy to come by and not easy to forge. If hers had been false, he would have gotten an urgent call, he felt sure. They would investigate an imposter immediately.

So she was for real, but for whatever reason, they weren't going to be releasing any information about her.

He went into the Abby Room. He'd spend the rest of the day looking over his cases. Of course, there had been many thousands of adult missing persons in the years since he'd lost her, but only twelve fit the precise criteria that interested him: an apparent walkout without any sign of forced entry, and a spouse or loved one who insisted that there had been no motive for the person to leave, and had credible support for the assertion.

It was a surprisingly rare situation, so rare that to Flynn it was an M.O.

On the walls were pictures of Abby, of the house as it was then, photographed in methodical detail, of the neighborhood, all the cars, all the houses.

There were maps of the other cases, blueprints of each house from which a victim had been abducted, with all the information from every crime scene intricately cross-referenced.

Abby smiled down at him, her hand shielding her eyes. The shot had been taken at Kitty Hawk in 1999, the summer of their courtship. She had been wearing her blue shorts and tank top. She'd been laughing and you could see it in her face. Later, back at their rental, he would unsnap that tank top and slip it off and stand on the tan carpet in the bedroom. She would seem, when she came close to him, to move with the lightness of a woman made of air, and the moment he had looked down into her eyes on that warm afternoon would remain engraved in his memory forever.

Sitting in meditation, he closed his eyes. "To study the self is to forget the self," he whispered into the silence. That was where he always started. Then he took his attention out of his mind and placed it on his body.

He felt his heart rate slowing until the beating seemed almost to stop. The cool of the room touched him so closely that it felt as if fingers were caressing him, fingers that were both intimately alive and as stiff as death.

He had understood the deep message of martial arts training: you cannot gain the freedom to fight at your best until you make friends with your death.

Beyond fear lies the balance that enables the blow to be perfectly struck, or deflected with perfect grace.

You never quite reach that spot, but you never quite fail.

He sat among his records, a naked man in a cold room.

He sat for a long time, letting go of his thoughts, his concerns, his questions.

As the stars made their nightly journey, he traveled deep within himself, sitting and flying at the same time. His heartbeat was now little more than a memory.

Other names and other faces came back to him: Claire Marlow, Hank Feather, Lucinda Walters, Gail Unterwager, George Nathan Chambers, Kimberly Torgelson— the list that haunted his dreams.

All had disappeared at night. All had taken a small number of personal belongings. Gail Unterwager left three young children and a devastated, uncomprehending husband. So had Lucinda Walters. George Chambers had two sons and a seven-figure bank account, a wife that loved him and a flawless life. Kimberly Torgelson's little boy had been two and her husband had been completely shattered.

Yeah, buddy, I get it. Welcome to hell.

Three o'clock came. Outside the wind whipped the big old trees that surrounded the house, causing skeletal shadows to dance on the lawn. In the distance, an owl hooted, its voice flying in the gale.

When the hour grew late and still sleep did not come,

he did what he always did at times like this, and walked through the house thinking and remembering, trying to understand how somebody could have come in and taken her out of bed like that and then carried her off, and all without her police officer husband noticing a thing.

Flynn was not a heavy sleeper now and he hadn't been then. So how had it been accomplished? To this day, he didn't even have a theory, not for any of them and especially not in Abby's case.

Once or twice, he had dreamed of her so vividly it was as if she was back. Once, the kitchen door had opened and he'd heard her voice calling up, "I'm home," her tone bright. He'd run downstairs, run like the wind, to find her standing in the dining room. "I'm all right," she said, and there had been a mixture of sadness and love in her face that had made him ache.

He had woken up, then, still in his bed.

Just before dawn his cell rang, startling him so thoroughly that he almost dropped it and lost the call.

It was Diana Glass.

"Can you come to a meeting?"

"Now?"

She gave him an address in the warehouse district near the grain elevators. He agreed to go and ended the call.

He called Eddie. It rang. Again. Again.

"Whassa matter?"

"It's me. Glass just called. She wants me to meet her on Avenue Twenty."

Silence.

"A warehouse, Eddie, at four in the morning."

"So you called to wake me up?"

"I did."

"You want a squad car? Protection?"

"I want you to know where I went and when." He gave him the address.

"Okay, got it."

"In other words, if I disappear, it is not voluntary. You got that? *Not* voluntary."

"If you have reason to be suspicious of this woman, don't go alone."

"I ran a verification check on her and I'm not sure what to think. The Bureau never came back to me."

"That is odd."

"Yeah, and she said eight in the morning. It's four in the morning."

"I noticed."

"So don't send anybody, but watch my back for me."

"You're gonna carry, I assume."

"Oh, yes." He headed upstairs, pulled on some jeans and a sweatshirt, then strapped on his gun and threw a jacket over it. He splashed his face, but didn't take the time to shave. Then he took an equipment pack off its shelf in the closet and took it with him. It was all stuff he'd put together himself, a manhunter's kit.

It was still deep night, and colder than he'd thought it would be, with wind coming steadily down from the north. As he opened the garage, the rattling of the door echoed through the silent neighborhood. No lights came on, though. Everybody knew that he kept irregular hours.

The predawn air was icy silver, and the tires crunched on frost as he backed down his driveway. The Malibu's heater screamed.

Cold, hot, his body could absorb whatever came its way.

He had worked himself into a new man, as hard as stone, as quick as the air, a man too silent inside to feel fear. He'd practiced with his pistol until it seemed an extension of his body. He did not push, he did not heel, and hours of exercise ensured that his wrist would never break in anticipation of recoil. He was comfortable with the standard issue Glock, but also with the .357 Magnum, and, of course, with the old Colt Positive, known as the Police Special.

He did not go straight to the warehouse—never that—but rather made his way through the streets of Menard, the pretty, average city that had been his born home and would always be his home.

He passed Abby's girlhood house, now owned by the Dickson family. Along with Eddie and half the other guys in town, he'd courted her on that porch. He'd come to it at midnight, his adolescent body filled with desire, and swung alone on the old porch swing until her dad had come out and swung with him. Bill Baumgartner had understood a lot of things. When he gave Abby away, tears had touched his eyes as a smile had wreathed his face.

Good people, Abigail and her folks.

Bill and Amy were in Menard Memorial now, and when he went to see them on Sundays, he always told them the same thing, "I am searching."

For the kidnapper and killer.

For Abby's soul.

For the unlived life of the child she might have been carrying.

For the truth, cold and clean.

The warehouse was one of the tin-siding jobs that looked like a gigantic barn. On its side was a faded sign, unreadable.

He pulled his car up and got out. There were no other vehicles around.

This was looking more and more wrong. Very wrong. But if she wasn't law enforcement, who could she be? Surely the kidnapper wasn't a woman—this woman.

He been a detective long enough to know that the unexpected is usually the thing most to be expected.

He walked up to the door, which was unchained, the locks thrown back.

There was danger here, no question.

He went in.

CHAPTER FOUR

The air was cold and thick, smelling of mold and wet cardboard. His eyes were good in darkness, but not this good, so he put on the infrared glasses he had designed himself, cutting the lenses from a couple of Hoya RM9s. Then he pulled out his infrared illuminator and methodically swept his surroundings. A sodden mass of cardboard boxes appeared like a distant mountain range. Closer, he saw a jumble of ruined bicycles. Behind them were rows of dead Christmas poinsettias in plastic pots, also dry aquariums.

There used to be light manufacturing here in Menard, little factories that used wetback labor to make cheap goods that would be sent out to California on the railroad. No more.

Debris was what he had expected. It was what he did not see that was troubling him. The sense of abandonment had changed. Now, he felt the presence of watchers. So far, he hadn't spotted them, but he knew that this was only because he hadn't looked in the right place.

With a movement as smooth and natural as taking a breath, he slipped his gun into his hand. Out of habit, he'd brought his Glock. Should have taken the Magnum instead. He was off duty and officially on leave, so it had been his choice.

"Hello," he said. "My name is Flynn Carroll. You asked me to come here."

Then he knew that somebody was behind him. It wasn't a hunch this time, or an instinct. He'd heard the whisper that jeans make when they rub against each other.

Sucking in breath, then slowly releasing it, he went deep into himself, blanking his chattering mind by concentrating his attention on the sound. In another moment, he was going to need to move very, very fast. He would have one chance only.

Another sound came, this time off to his right. So there were at least two of them, and they were maneuvering to place him in crossfire.

"Let's stop this right now," he said aloud. His words were followed by a silence. Were they surprised? He thought not. He thought they were very far from surprised, because he could see a third one off to his left, a figure that was more slight than the other two. Could be Diana. "Look, I'm gonna end up using this thing if somebody doesn't show themselves real soon."

Outside, the wind shook the thousand windowpanes and made the tin roof jump and rattle. The massive late season blizzard that was bringing the arctic to Montana was now also plunging southward into Texas.

"Flynn, listen carefully."

Diana's voice filled the room, a whisper from everywhere.

"Everything is good, Flynn. We're all friends here.

We just need to be very, very careful. This is all routine safe practice in this unit."

"You'll get used to it," a male voice drawled.

A hand came down on his shoulder—and he took the guy down with a standing grapple, a simple jujitsu maneuver for which his assailant was, to Flynn's surprise, entirely unprepared.

"Keep back," Diana snapped. "Don't challenge him."

The guy he'd taken down got up. His face was hard to see in the darkness, but Flynn sensed a scowl of rage.

"Sorry," he said.

All he could see of the eyes were shadowy sockets, but he could feel the anger.

"Flynn," Diana said, "please give Captain Larsen your pistol."

"No."

"Flynn, you've come in here heavily geared and with a drawn weapon. Of course we're being careful. Now, calm down. Give him the gun."

Flynn thought about it. He didn't move.

"We need to fly before dawn. We have a long way to go and time is of the essence. If you want to help prevent another disappearance and maybe stop this perp, now's your chance."

"I don't like total strangers coming up on me in dark rooms."

"This is a special unit, Flynn. We're operating under our own set of protocols. We've set up an orientation for you downstairs." She turned on the lights.

He lost his night vision equipment. Nobody else was showing a pistol, so he put his away. But he did not give it up.

"Thank you," she said.

At the far end of the space there was an old iron spiral

staircase that had probably been ordered from the Sears Catalog a hundred years ago. He followed the rest of them down, and found himself in a basement that was just as dark as the floor above had been, but felt smaller. Not for long, though. A match flickered as Diana Glass lit a gasoline lantern—and hung it on the barrel of some kind of old tank. The thing wasn't in US livery and it was dusty, but it looked like it had never been driven.

"The Korean War," she said, waving a dismissive hand toward it. "They were on their way to San Diego when the conflict ended. Great shielding if you worry about listening devices."

"Which you do?"

"That would be correct. Flynn, first off, I want you to understand that there are many things that make this unit special. The first of these is that we're all just the same as you. We all have a missing loved one."

"None of 'em walked out," a male voice said. "My Cindy did not walk out."

"Louie Lander, LAPD," Diana said. "Just like you, just like the rest of us, he's done a hell of a job on a lot of missing persons cases."

Louie Lander had a tight-to-the-skull faces and a hard, sad smile. "Just like me," Flynn thought, "I smile like that."

"Can you explain this security, because this is the most unusual damn unit I've ever come across."

"Flynn," Diana replied, "we're dealing with the most unusual damn thing that's ever happened. Mike, why don't you tell him your story?"

The second of the three guys standing in the light said, "Sure, Diana." He regarded Flynn with eyes full of pain. "We were having a cookout. It was just after dark. My wife and my little boy were out in the back-yard playing hide-and-seek. I was cooking on the grill. I noticed it was kinda quiet." He paused. "That was in 2008. I never saw them again."

Flynn thought about this. "You were there? Right there?"

"I was standing twenty-three feet from my wife when it happened. My boy was playing near the back fence. Forty feet. I heard nothing, saw nothing. Finally I ran out into the alley. Up and down. Went to the neighbors." He stopped. "Called the precinct." He looked toward Diana Glass. His voice dropped. "A missing roller bag did the investigation in. Plus, the way they disappeared. No sign of an intruder. The local Bureau decided it was a walkout."

"Your son—his case wouldn't have been abandoned."

"He's on goddamn milk cartons," Mike muttered. "Nothing."

The same thought came into Flynn's mind that must have come into the mind of every investigator on the case: she left and took the boy with her, open and shut. No way could they have been abducted right out from under the nose of the father.

Mike's grin was eloquently bitter. "I can see what you're thinking," he said. "We were very much in love." He sighed heavily. "We still are. At least, inside me. Inside me, my family goes on."

"I hear that loud and clear," Flynn said. He looked to the third guy. "What about you?"

"First, my wife's sister, six years ago. She was a talented woman, a violinist with the St. Louis Symphony. We all thought she walked out on her life, all except her boyfriend. The locals did a good workup. Went nowhere. Then, two years ago last month, I got hit. My Lynn. She comes out of the Costco near our place at ten at night—she worked there nights—gets in her car. *And it just sits there.* Eleven, I can't get her on her cell so I drive over. There's the damn Altima, empty. I call in the troops but nobody can find her. We get the security video. Two cameras. She crosses the parking lot, gets in the car, and it just sits there. Except."

"Yeah?"

"There was a power failure at the store. One minute after she got in. Lasted twelve minutes." The locals—my buddies—figured that's when the kidnap took place. But when the Bureau found that a couple of changes of clothes and six hundred dollars in cash were gone with her, they got a different idea."

"So we're all in the same situation. Cases abandoned as walkouts. The operative word here is 'abandoned.' These are dead cases. So why are we here?"

"Last year, the Bureau finally upgraded its relational databases," Diana said. "The first thing I did was to look for cases similar to my husband's." In the hard light of the gasoline lantern, her face had taken on a startling brightness, as if her skin was on fire inside. "What I discovered is that he wasn't alone. Real walkouts are common, but almost always associated with domestic disturbance. Some of them are genuine, some of them are murders. There are a number of them like our cases, with no domestic trouble, and the spouse insisting that he or she would never, ever do this."

"How many?"

"Flynn, over the past ten years, I've found eight thousand unsolved disappearances, two hundred thirty-six of which involve people who continue to claim that their loved one was kidnapped, despite all evidence to the contrary."

"Anything linking them?"

"Nobody was a criminal, nobody was sick, nobody was disabled. Everybody had some sort of notable talent—musician, artist, electronics expert, you name it. It's a highly functional group of people."

"Abby was a musician." He sighed. "So the FBI finally realized that something was up. A serial kidnapper. But why organize the unit now? Just because they got a new database?"

She glanced at her watch. "We need to move. The reason we pulled you in now is we've got the best case we've ever had, and we want the best team that can be deployed."

"Where are we going?"

"There's always an element of risk in this work, Flynn. We don't want to talk about it until we're off the ground."

"You're saying we're not secure?" He looked around. "You're not sure of these guys?"

"There could be extremely sophisticated surveillance," Mike said.

"We've set a trap for the perp," Diana added. "He's taken two sisters. The third sister has moved in to live with her father. It's an easy stakeout, and we intend to be waiting, starting tonight."

"How long? Do you know when he's gonna show up?"

"We think he'll use the blizzard to cover his tracks."

"So it's in Montana. And we're sure he'll show?"

"Nothing is certain, obviously. But this is the most talented of the three sisters. She plays the piano and the violin, she's a novelist, she's a dancer. We have a target profile, and she's way up at the top. Her sisters were good, but she's outstanding." She strode to the rickety spiral stair and went pounding up, oblivious to its creaking and swaying.

What the hell was going on here? What kind of a perp were they dealing with, who could steal this many people and do it so well?

They had an ancient minivan, white and caked with dirt, its side panels scratched deep from a lot of overland work. The interior had once been luxurious, but the leather was now full of scuffs and tears, and the windshield was intricately cracked.

He sat behind Mike, who drove, consulting a hand-held GPS as he maneuvered through the empty pre-dawn streets. If they didn't want to ask the local guy for directions, that was their business.

It was six, shift change, and he saw a cruiser heading toward headquarters, the uniforms inside sipping coffee. Quiet time, six o'clock. The druggies have crashed, the citizens are just waking up, the whores are in the diners or in their motels. Quiet, good time, the eastern sky glowing with promise, dew gleaming in the summer, frost in the winter, here and there a jogger. Your city's most intimate moment.

"You aren't gonna get a flight at this hour," he finally said. "You're gonna need to take the Southwest at eight to Denver, then there's probably a United up to Billings. Assuming anything's flying." The late news had mentioned that the blizzard was setting records for snowfall and wind speeds. They'd called it a snow hurricane.

She drove toward the low buildings of the Menard Airport, now called Menard International since the Mexico City flight had been added. As a teenager, he'd come here to watch the planes taking off. In those days, there'd been a United 737 that headed for San Francisco at seven in the evening, and he and Abby had watched it and dreamed of what it would be to live there in a house in the Marina District or Nob Hill, and listen to the mourning of the buoys and watch the rolling fog. One night she'd said, her voice soft and shy, "What do you want first, a girl or a boy," and he had slipped his hand into hers and replied with silence, and known that she was to be his wife, and it would be good.

They passed the main terminal, which was unchanged from the way it had been all of his life, two low wings and a central tower. Inside were the six gates, now crushed behind a wall of security, but the Airflight Restaurant was exactly the same, and still served the chicken fried steak dinner on Thursdays, and you could watch the planes while you ate.

Down at the end of this road was the hangar where Donald Douglas had once repaired an early Cloudster, and which now sheltered the ten or twenty private aircraft that called this place home.

"You have your own plane?"

"Yes."

"So somebody's a pilot?"

"I'm a pilot," Charlie said. His tone reminded Flynn more of a funeral director.

They pulled around to the small parking area beside the hangar and got out. They moved as a team, he had to give them that. There was a practiced smoothness that he liked to see in a team.

As Diana entered the hangar through the weathered side door, she turned on the interior lights. Mike trotted over to the main door and rolled it open, revealing the empty concrete apron and equally empty runway.

There were two planes in the hangar, one a gleaming turboprop, the other a twin engine thing that was just that—a thing. Old. Grease on its landing gear. Bald tires.

Charlie hopped up onto the wing and opened a door.

"We can't fly into a blizzard in that," Flynn said.

"Charlie can," Diana said.

Flynn was normally an unconcerned flyer, but this situation was not reassuring. "You're looking at seventy-mile-an-hour winds in that storm," he said.

Charlie, who was standing on the wing, said, "It's got new engines compliments of the US Air Force, plus a classified antifriction coating and the most advanced avionics in the world."

"It's too light. No way. I thought you guys had Gulfstreams and things like that. Real planes."

"This is the real world, not TV. I had to fight like hell for this. We're travel-rated for commercial only."

Flynn was the last to climb in.

He saw cracked insulation along the doorframe. He smelled gasoline. Mike and Louie had pulled the hangar door back and the morning sky was red with menace, the north wind already brisk. Billings was a thousand miles away, deep in the vastness of the storm.

CHAPTER FIVE

The more he saw, the less he liked. The little curtains on the windows were threadbare. Under his feet, the carpeting was worn through to bare metal. "I have to say, I don't think this thing is airworthy on a good day. And this is not a good day."

"If Charlie says he can take it into the storm, he can. Now, I want to brief you in procedures, because they're not Bureau standard."

That mattered little to Flynn. He was only vaguely aware of standard Bureau procedures anyway.

Charlie began turning on the electrics. His doubts seething, Flynn strapped himself into his seat, the rearmost in the plane.

Beside him, Diana sat paging through a file on her iPad.

When he realized that the plane was moving, he was shocked. He hadn't heard the engines start or felt the slightest vibration, and yet they were heading out onto the apron.

"Boy, this thing is quiet," he said.

"New engines," Charlie said.

They moved swiftly across the apron. Charlie spoke into his mike, and after a moment the tower's clearance crackled through the confined cabin. The controller's voice, sharp with surprise and concern, made it clear that he'd been taken by surprise.

"Have you filed a flight plan?" came his voice, sharp in the silent cabin.

"We're not required to."

"Sir, if you're heading north, I'd advise filing."

Charlie's reaction was to click off the radio.

"You oughta file a flight plan," Flynn shouted over the engine noise, which was rising as they taxied onto the runway.

"Flynn, we can't afford to leave tracks. Please understand that."

"*Tracks?* It's a flight plan, for God's sake! The perp doesn't have access to FAA records, surely."

She dropped her iPad down on his lap. "You need to do a little studying on the way up. See what you make of the cases. Try to form in your mind an idea of the kind of capabilities the perp possesses. I guarantee you, they are awesome."

The takeoff pressed Flynn back into his seat. In under five minutes, they were leaving ten thousand feet behind.

"This is the damnedest thing," Flynn said. "What is this? Because it sure as hell ain't no fifty-year-old Piper Apache."

"The friction-free coating makes it a different airplane. And the turbos. The airframe's been strengthened. And the avionics, like I said—you can't find better. Plus, it's pressurized. Convenient in a storm. We can do forty thousand feet."

"It's not a Piper Apache, is it? It's camouflaged as a Piper Apache."

She smiled. "I could answer that question for you. But if I did, I'd have to kill you."

There had been humor there—a little. It was clear, though, that Diana Glass really would kill to keep her secrets. It was understandable, though. This was a crack unit. These people were dedicated. Maybe people like this could actually win, even against a genius psychopath . . . assuming they lived through the damn flight.

He watched home slip away beneath the speeding plane. Ahead, the sky was big and dark and mean, and the distant purr of the engines meant that he could hear the wind screaming around the airframe, like a voice from another world, mad and wild.

As the land slid past far below, it became more and more snow-choked. The silence that had settled over the cabin spoke to him in a clear voice. These people were all doing the same thing most people in police work do when they're heading toward danger. Each one considers his life and wonders what will come, and grows silent, seeking within himself for his deepest strength.

Half an hour passed in this silence. Flynn read case files, one after another, more than he'd ever had access to before.

"I notice a pattern," he said. "The same articles of clothing every time. Three changes of underwear, three shirts or blouses, two pairs of pants."

"Interesting," Mike commented.

"Damn interesting," Diana said.

"I wish we could access Behavioral Science resources, Diana."

"Louie, no."

"I know—'until we know what we're dealing with, no leaks.'"

Flynn said to Charlie, "You came out of Behavioral, so what can you add?"

The engines drummed. The plane, now enveloped in grayness, was being steadily buffeted.

"Charlie?"

"I gotta fly an airplane," he said at last.

Soon the snowy fields below disappeared into a gray gloom. Flynn could hardly see the strobes on the wingtips. He craned his neck, looking up at the instrument cluster and seeing gleaming flat panel displays. An autopilot was operating, the plane banking and changing altitude on its own. Charlie didn't even have his hands on the stick. The plane, on its own, was navigating its way through the storm.

These avionics were ten years ahead of the airlines, maybe more.

Flynn thought he should feel safer, but he really wished that Charlie had his hands on the controls instead of reading files on his own iPad. And what about "I gotta fly this plane?" Apparently what it really meant was, "I decline to answer your question."

He watched the wing strobes disappear into the muck. Then the wings.

He leaned forward. "Shouldn't you descend into visual?"

Charlie didn't react.

"Hey, Charlie, I can fly a damn airplane well enough to know we need visual."

Again no answer. Flynn turned to Diana. "Look, this is dangerous. No general aviation aircraft is up to this kind of flying, no matter what kind of avionics it has. What about deicing equipment? It has to be minimal."

"I just did a statistical analysis on the cases," Charlie called back, "and he's right. There's a very fixed pattern to the things that are taken."

"We know our perp has a team. He has to," Diana said. Then, to Flynn, "Just relax, let him do his thing. We wouldn't be up here if the plane couldn't do its job."

"What the hell is it, a drone with seats?"

She laughed a little. "The military's got some very good autopilots, obviously. Look, the computer's a lot better pilot than he is, right, Charlie?"

"Right. I'm looking at the site on the looksee. Snow's really building up around the house."

"What's a looksee?"

"We have surveillance cameras deployed around the target's home," Diana said.

As he paged through case after case, Flynn wasn't seeing a single indication that any witness had ever identified any person, vehicle, sound, or light that seemed to them to be unusual during the times the kidnappings had taken place. "My case is the only one with any sort of witness at all?"

"It is."

Flynn tried to relax. He hadn't slept much and he was tired. Looking at a rough day ahead, probably a stakeout tonight. Stakeout in a blizzard. Lovely. He closed his eyes—and immediately felt a sensation of falling. Then the stall horn howled.

"Jesus!"

"No big deal," Charlie yelled. "I'm on it."

The horn warbled a last time, then stopped.

Flight became steady again, the engines now droning, the wingtip strobes faintly visible. Flynn had not realized until this moment how tired he actually was. Still, though, he clung to the arms of his seat.

More time passed. Finally, he found himself once again closing his eyes.

What seemed just a few moments later, he heard Diana saying, "Good morning."

"I've been asleep?"

"Deep. Three hours."

It felt like three minutes. "I can't believe that."

"Big changes, lotta stress, it's natural. Healthy."

The plane was still deep in the storm system, but flying smoothly, banking gently from time to time.

He saw that Diana had a readout of the plane's position on her iPad. "What's our ETA?"

"About twenty minutes," she said.

"We've made good time, then."

"The autopilot has an intelligent seek function. It finds the smooth air, so we don't have to cut back our speed."

When he was younger, he'd flown his dad's plane between ranches, taking the old man from one of his properties to another. He still had his license and kept up with the field. "A hell of a nice toy."

"That it is." She raised her voice. "ETA upcoming, gentlemen. Just to be on the safe side, let's do a weapons check."

Flynn knew the law, and the law said that he wasn't a police officer in Montana or anywhere except Texas unless in hot pursuit, and flying in to a town and looking for a bad guy was hardly that.

"If you're asking me to check my weapon, that means you're expecting that I might need to use it. So I need to know where we are in the chain of command. Am I legal here?"

"We're not in the Bureau's chain of command at all. Me and Charlie are FBI, but this unit is seconded to the National Security Council."

"*Seconded?* And since when did the NSC have any enforcement powers?"

"Okay, now I'm gonna tell you something that's classified. You need to sign, though." She took her iPad back from him, turned a few pages, then handed it back. "Electronic signature. Use the keypad."

He read the letter, which was under the logo of the National Security Council and signed by the chairman. It granted him a Sensitive Compartmented Clearance under the code name Aurora. It was listed as a Human Intelligence Control System clearance and seemed to have something to do with the National Reconnaissance Office.

"I don't understand this."

"It's an above top secret designation. Officially, we're part of the National Reconnaissance Office, but that's not where our actual chain of command runs."

"Okay, so when you send a memo, who do you send it to?"

"My boss."

"Not good enough."

"All I can tell you."

"And if I sign?"

"A little more."

"Not a hell of a lot," Louie said over his shoulder.

"Look, people, this does not look like a police unit to me. National Security Council? I was looking for a serial kidnapper and probable killer. Where's the national security issue?"

"And the answer is the same, sign and find out."

"Do it, buddy," Mike said. "You need this. Heart and soul, man."

"First I want to know if I discharge my weapon in Montana, what happens?"

Diana explained, "We're operating under a National Security Letter. You fill out a discharge report and forget it."

"A National Security Letter? For a serial killer? How? Why?"

She pointed at the iPad. "It will make sense, Flynn. It really will."

He brought up the keyboard and signed his full name, then added his police ID number and his social security number in the blanks provided.

"Okay, so what have I done to myself?"

The airframe creaked loudly as the plane banked. The wing roots crackled. He could practically feel the tail torsioning, sense the metal weakening, the whole assembly getting ready to come to pieces. No matter how juiced up a small plane was, weather conditions like these were dangerous.

Snow seemed to gush at them. Charlie continued his maneuvers. He hadn't even turned on the wipers, so he was still relying on full IFR. That was absolute confidence, or absolute stupidity.

The ground suddenly appeared below them, a spreading, featureless vastness of snow. When they banked again, Flynn could see roofs buried in the white desert, smoke whipping away from their chimneys. Nearby was a single dark line that looked like runways look when you should definitely not land there.

They banked yet again, and as they did, Flynn saw that there was a sign on the roof of the larger of the two hangars that marked the airport. It said, "Ridge, Montana."

As they lined up on the runway and began to descend, he stopped asking questions. No time for that now.

In the end, he'd discover every secret thing about

this damned operation, he was confident of that, but not just now. Just now, it was time to let this thing unfold and hope that the blood that would fall in the snow on this day would not be his own. There would be blood, he felt, most certainly.

CHAPTER SIX

They taxied to the smaller hangar. There wasn't anybody around, of course. Why would there be on a visual flight rules airport during IFR weather?

Moving with lubricated precision, the team got out and pulled the plane into the shelter of the hangar.

"Diana, I need to talk to you."

"We're behind schedule."

"Look, I want to know what we're dealing with and I want to know right now."

"No problem," Diana said, "when the time is right."

The others began unpacking weather gear, warm jackets, hats, boots.

"You didn't get airsick, Texas," Charlie said. "I'm impressed."

"Flight was smooth. Anyway, I slept."

"And yelled."

"A little."

"We need to move," Diana said.

"When do we meet the local cops?" Flynn asked. Silence fell.

"Five personnel can't run a stakeout in a blizzard!"

Diana continued as if he had not spoken. "What we're looking at is a relatively isolated house. About a mile from the nearest neighbor."

"Hey. You don't go past the locals."

"Lieutenant Carroll, I'll tell you what you need to know. That's all I can legally do. Read your secrecy agreement."

"I thought there was going to be a big reveal when I signed it."

"As soon as possible."

Impasse. He had no choice but to accept the situation.

"They're in a house about four miles outside of town. Armed to the teeth. Scared shitless."

"In weather like this, that's total isolation," Flynn said. "Do we have a read on the local power grid? Because if they don't have power, that's going to look like a real vulnerability to the perp."

"Exactly," she said. "Which is why we're going to cut their power at some point if he doesn't show up. Use their helplessness as a lure. We hope it'll prove irresistible."

"Why is he going after sisters, anyway? Explain that."

"He got the first two, so we're thinking he could try the third. What his motive is, we don't know. There is a selection process, though. High-functioning people, that's clear. Not too old, not too young."

They began putting on the warm jackets, gloves, and boots that they'd pulled out of the plane's rear cargo bay.

"I need gear."

"There's an Army-Navy outlet," Diana said.

"Good stuff, I hope." In weather this cold a stakeout would get dangerous fast.

"Far as I know. Let's pull out the electronics, guys."

Mike and Louie opened the plane's nose cargo bay and Mike drew out a black, hard sided briefcase. Mike carried it to a workbench and released the elaborate lock that sealed it.

Flynn recognized night vision equipment and in-ear radios. But there were five blunt black wands, devices he could not place.

"Ranger equipment," Diana told him. "Mike will check you out on one."

Mike said, "First, you gotta know that it has a self-destruct system built in. And a fingerprint reader. Once you're printed to it, if it gets more than ten meters from your body, acid's going to spray all over its interior. So you don't want to forget your little friend, and Uncle Sam really does not want you to do that. You're holding a million dollars worth of his computing power in the palm of your hand."

He pressed a button on the side, then pointed the narrow end of the device at Diana. A moment later, a reading appeared on a tiny screen.

"First, any reading at all tells you that a human being is out there somewhere, whether you can see him or not. Now, let's evaluate the state of the *commandante's* beautiful mind."

"Careful," Diana said.

"She's reading eighty-four," Mike said. "Anything over fifty is telling you the target's awake. Over seventy, the target's alert. Over ninety, the target has an elevated heart rate and high-level brain activity. In other words, your target is probably aware of your presence and your day is shortly going to be ruined."

He thrust it into Flynn's hand. Flynn looked down at it.

"It's a sensitive radio receiver and a computer that can read and interpret what it picks up. The thing draws a couple of milliamps and has the computing power of maybe a hundred thousand laptops. The receiver is tuned to pick up brain wave frequencies. It works the same as a garden variety electroencephalograph, only without leads. It has an effective range of ninety meters line of sight."

Flynn said, "Police departments could really use this."

"And it's also why we're not going to be calling in the locals. It's as classified a piece of equipment as the United States of America possesses. MindRay saves lives but it's easily defeated. Word gets out, no more trick pony."

"Defeated how?"

"Headgear that suppresses radio frequencies kills it. Embed a copper grid in a cap, and this device cannot read you."

So cops couldn't have it. Word would get out. He saw that. But he also had a question that he didn't ask: did this thing make them more effective than the addition of some local bodies would?

"What's to say the perp won't be wearing a hat like that?"

"The classification of this item is very, very strict," Mike said.

"Okay," Diana came back, "we need to move right now."

Flynn thought that they would have been better off leaving these things behind and going in with local support. If he was in command of this operation, the

MindRays would be headed straight back to the Pentagon.

Outside, the wind was now howling down the runway, blowing a sheer white torrent of snow. They'd gotten in just under what was exactly what the weatherman was predicting: a snow hurricane.

Transport was a weathered Cherokee with chains, a tight fit for five people, especially when one of them was as big as Flynn Carroll.

There was no visible road. The only sign of any activity was a light, faint in the distance, appearing and disappearing as the snow gusted.

Charlie drove, Flynn navigated with the handheld GPS that was part of each equipment pack.

"He has a team," Flynn said to Diana. "You indicated that."

"Has to. At least one accomplice, probably more."

They came out onto a plowed road. Now there were more lights, a snow-clad Motel 6 sign, beyond it a place called The Swashbuckler, a bar of the kind that grew like mushrooms in little places like Ridge, one mushroom per town. Inside, there'd be a bartender and a waitress snapping gum, in the back a cook. Along with the customers, they would have grown up here. In small towns, everybody had everything on everybody. Bitter places. Could also be murderous, especially on hard winter nights when you couldn't escape from those you loved and despised.

They pulled up at a big tin structure lit by a barely visible sign: "Rosen Surplus."

He got out and pushed his way into the store, which turned out to be cave-like. There was an elderly woman with a tight gray bun sitting in a chair in front of rows of surplus fatigues. Hunter stuff.

"I need some warm clothes," Flynn said.

The old woman looked up at him. "You sure do," she said. Her face blossomed into a big, open smile. "Where'd you come from in that stuff, anyway?"

"Nowhere close by."

She didn't inquire further. She was too old to be curious about strangers anymore. She wanted his money, not his story.

"We got parkas on sale, thirty-six bucks. US Army mountain gear. Good stuff."

He bought a parka, found a pair of boots that almost fit, some lined gloves, a hat, and an olive drab scarf that knew the services of moths. She showed him a dressing room behind a curtain where he put on two pairs of long johns and the rest of the clothes.

"Now you might live a while," she said when he came out.

"Let's hope." He paid her a hundred and sixty bucks in cash and got a receipt for his expenses.

It was warm in the Jeep. Nobody spoke. Charlie backed out into the snow-swept street.

Flynn could feel the mission closing in. The absolute silence in the truck told him that these people sensed a whole lot of danger. Not sensed, knew. They *knew* that they were in great danger.

They drove off into a rampage of snow.

CHAPTER SEVEN

Louie was stationed a hundred yards away from Flynn, but he might as well have been in another state for all the good it did in this hell. The others were on the far side of the Hoffman house. The storm had come on even stronger than the Billings weatherman had said it would, and the snow rushed in the sky, pelting Flynn's parka and hood and working its way in under his scarf.

They'd been watching the house now since seven fifteen, and it was pushing nine o'clock. It was an excellent night for a perp who suspected he was under observation to make a move.

He had proven, however, that he could take them any time of year, from any kind of a dwelling, and never leave a trace of himself behind.

Off to his right, Flynn heard a distinct sound. A throaty growl.

It came again, and this time he thought maybe it was a tree scraping. Or could it be a car on the road, its engine straining?

The wind roared around him and the cold invaded his sleeves, the seam of the hood, anywhere it could get in, and that was pretty much everywhere. The scarf was a joke, the socks were a joke. The boots were waterproof, but no boots could keep out cold like this. It made him worry that he wasn't feeling enough pain from his feet, it numbed his hands and made his face burn.

When it comes to cold, after the pain ends is when death begins, and it is a line you can cross without ever knowing it.

The Hoffman place was a prairie Victorian with lighted windows downstairs, looking as warm and inviting as it could be. From time to time, he caught a whiff of oil smoke from what had to be a blazing furnace. In the living room, he could see a fire flickering in the fireplace, and that smoke would drift this way, too. Professor Hoffman, Gail's father, sat in a wing chair before the fire, from time to time sipping at a mug that stood on a small table beside him.

Gail was cleaning up in the kitchen, moving elegantly about, her long arms putting away dishes. Girl-perfect, she reminded him powerfully of Abby.

Flynn was a snow-covered bulge in the earth and that was good. He was well concealed from the road, and the snow would insulate him a little. From time to time, he raised a stealthy, gloved hand and blew into it to warm his nose and face. He rocked from side to side, dipped his knees a little, keeping moving just enough to avoid becoming stiff.

If they weren't properly cleaned and oiled, guns could freeze solid in weather like this, even in your pocket. So he gripped his pistol. He also tried the Mind-Ray. Once, he might have picked up a signal from the direction of the house. Another time he might have detected Louis. Out here, though, the display that had been clear and steady in the hangar flickered and changed so quickly that it meant, essentially, nothing. He was sure now that the thing was high-tech junk. Maybe the Rangers trusted it and maybe they didn't. He didn't.

He also tried the beautifully compact night vision equipment, only to find that the snow made it crazy. All he saw were flashes. He would've been better off bringing his own homemade scope.

He kept old-fashioned naked eye watch and nursed his Glock.

About fifteen minutes later, the living room went dark, then a front bedroom lit up. Professor Hoffman was heading up to bed at nine twenty-five.

Flynn had about decided to make an approach. As far as he knew, the Hoffmans didn't even know they were being staked out, and that was ridiculous. Also, the decision not to involve the local police was wrong, especially when the reason given was to protect the secret status of a piece of equipment that belonged in the garbage. The whole plan was borderline incompetent.

Flynn's worry was that the perp was already in the Hoffman's lives, someone they had come to trust. Was that how he worked—he was the grocery clerk, the night man at the convenience store, getting under the skin of the vic so skillfully that there was never a flicker of suspicion?

He shook the snow off and started toward the house, but there was motion to his right, at about one o'clock. Something low and big. A car? No, impossible off the road in this snow. Anyway, it was living movement, stealthy and low to the ground.

Almost on its own, his gun came out. He stayed

where he was, though. Don't move until you understand.

A minute passed, then another.

This perp had once taken a forty-year-old woman who'd weighed two hundred pounds out of a farmhouse in Oregon on a rain-soaked night and left not even a footprint. He had taken mothers from shopping mall parking lots, fathers from backyard barbecues, nurses from their rounds, priests from their rectories.

He had killed them all, Flynn believed. Of course he had, killed them without remorse, lost as he was in whatever fantasy drove him.

Now there was another sound. What the hell was that? Something tinkling.

No, it was music. It floated like a spirit on the storm. There were windows downstairs with drawn curtains, and he thought that was where the music was coming from. It stopped, then started again. Soaring out above the roar of the storm, the hiss of the snow. Dear God, she could play that piano. What was it? Beethoven, maybe? Beautiful, anyway.

Rocking from side to side, checking his feet, blowing into his hands, Flynn began pressing forward again.

Another sound came, this time to his left. This was a very strange sound, a muffled sort of whistling. It went on and on, this sound, a kind of noiseless screaming.

Finally, it ended and did not repeat. The music swelled and the wind moaned in the eaves of the old house. Low clouds plunged out of the north. The only light was from the house and the glowing snow.

He was going down to that house and he was going to announce himself to those people. He was well under way, slogging through drifts as deep as six feet, when he observed the moving shape again. It came from the right this time, and therefore had crossed his field of vision without him seeing it. So there must be a low area between him and the house, probably the snow-covered road. But it wouldn't offer more than a couple of feet of protection, so whatever that was out there, it wasn't a man.

He called on the reserves of inner silence that twenty years of intensive martial arts training had given him. "All things come to him who waits." The defender has the advantage, always.

He watched as the wind picked up a long stream of snow and blew it off into the darkness. The eaves of the house wailed, the music swelled, and bright scars of moonlight whipped across the desert of snow. Behind the storm would come brutal cold and behind that, they said, another storm.

The moonlight revealed a low form with a long back and tail—an animal. The instant the light hit it, it became so still that many people wouldn't have noticed it. A moment later, though, darkness engulfed the shaft of moonlight, and the animal with it. He fought to control his breathing, fought to stay where he was and not follow the flight-or-fight instinct, which was telling him to get the hell out of here.

He tried the night vision goggles. They hadn't been adjusted to work in snow.

Activate the radio, then? No. The others were all armed professionals, too, and a single spatter of communication could cause the perp to pull out—assuming, of course, that he was here.

The house was still dark. When the moon broke out of the clouds, it stood still and silent. Were they asleep?

Could they sleep? He could see an LED in there, glowing red in the downstairs hall. They had an alarm system. Certainly guns, too. So they probably felt safe.

The snow was now coming down in long, howling flurries punctuated by periods of driving wind. He waited, his hands clutching his gun. He'd stuffed the MindRay into his backpack. The equally useless night vision binoculars hung around his neck.

He was peering into the dark and thinking about trying them again when the moon appeared and he found himself looking into the face of a goddamn puma, which was not ten feet in front of him.

He gasped, choking back a shout of alarm.

How in the world had it gotten this close this fast? A certainty: it was the master of conditions like this. A possibility: it saw him as prey.

The eyes were steady. They were careful. To his amazement, they followed his stealthy movement to his pistol. Since when did pumas understand pistols? But this one sure did.

He wished that he had an Anaconda or a Model 29, because it was going to take some accurate shooting with the Glock to stop this creature if it charged from this close. Worse, it was a Glock Nineteen and not an Eighteen with its greater capacity and automatic fire option. He needed a perfect head shot or the animal would still be very much alive when it connected with him.

Carefully, he tightened his hand around the pistol and began to pull it up into firing position. If the animal leaped before the gun was aimed, he was going to be torn to pieces.

Its eyes shifted to his face, then back to the rising pistol, which was uncanny. How smart could it be?

It pulled its shoulders forward. It was about to leap. But then there was a slight hesitancy.

The eyes—so steady, so alien—returned to his face. In the stare Flynn could see a raw lust to kill. But then they flickered again, and in the next instant the animal was gone. He had gotten the gun into position just in time, and it had clearly understood that it had been outmaneuvered.

Amazing. He'd never seen anything like it. No animal was that smart.

The puma's tracks faded into the snow.

CHAPTER EIGHT

Louie was approximately two hundred yards to his right, covering the house from an angle that gave him a different view. Flynn wanted to warn him on the radio, but he didn't want to be the one to blow this mission, misconceived though it was. He had to warn the guy, though, so he'd go over there. This would leave the house uncovered from this angle for a few minutes, but it had to be done. It was one damn smart cat, and the guy needed to know this.

The piano had started again, the music slipping and sliding in the wind. Abby, also, had played. His dad had played. He'd tried to learn, but he hadn't inherited that gene. What he could do well with his hands was shoot. He could turn even an old snub-nosed Police Special into a useful weapon. A good pistol felt like an extension of his hand. Any pistol, for that matter.

Pushing through the snow, he was tempted to call Louie's name, but even that might destroy the stakeout. Many a cop had wrecked a good collar with an ill-timed whisper.

He was sweating under his layers of clothing when he began to ask himself if he'd gone in the right direction. But he had, no question. So where was Louie?

The snow seemed less, so he tried the night vision goggles again. He could see a little better, but they didn't reveal Louie ahead. Instead, what Flynn saw was a strange, formless shape in the snow.

Was that a rock? A gnarled bush?

He tried working with the goggles, increasing the magnification.

The material was jagged, gleaming darkly. He still couldn't tell what it was.

Another patch of moon glow sped by. In it, he could make out a pale ripped edge protruding from the shape. Bone, maybe? If so, then that was a chunk of something the lion had just killed—a deer, hopefully.

As a precaution, he got his pistol back out and held it alongside his parka. If that was a kill, then the lion was protecting it, and that's why it was hanging around.

As he crunched along, he stepped on something just beneath the frozen surface. It was hard and irregular and it shifted under his foot.

He bent down and pushed away the snow.

What first appeared was a pallid slickness. He kept brushing. Something just below it, hard tufts of material. Frozen hair, he thought. So this was a kill and that was why the puma had menaced him. It had been worried about having its food stolen.

It took all of his training not to cry out when he found the staring eyes and gaping mouth of Louis Hancock looking back at him. The eyes flashed with moonlight when there were rips in the clouds.

The guy had been taken down by the mountain lion, which was about the damnedest thing Flynn could imagine happening. As he pushed more snow away, he discovered that Louie had been hit from behind and thrown forward, then—incredibly—ripped in half.

The legs and abdomen were nearby, a knee and booted foot jutting up from the snow. So the lion must be big. Huge.

This stakeout was over. He reached up and pressed the call button on his radio. "There's been an accident. Detective Hancock is dead. Come in, please."

Silence.

"I repeat, Louis Hancock has been killed, apparently by a mountain lion. We need to close this thing down, we have a dead officer here."

Silence.

He was coming to really not like these people. "You can't continue the stakeout, you have a dead officer! I repeat, *dead officer*!"

The hell with it, he'd go in himself. He'd been on his way anyway, interrupted by this horror show. He went plunging toward the house.

The going was extremely hard, and he had to fight his way through some flurries so high that he was forced to lie forward and push himself ahead.

Every time he was forced to do this, he was very, very aware that he was entirely helpless.

He moved slowly, guided by the music. There were no lights showing in the house. When he finally stumbled out into the road, the going was a little easier, but not much. The house loomed ahead of him, tall and completely dark except for a single strip of light leaking from around the curtains of the room where Gail Hoffman was playing.

He was going up the snow-choked front walk when he saw the lion again. It was standing on the porch, back around the far edge, where it curved around under the living room windows. It was absolutely still, and it was watching him.

Once again, it had maneuvered brilliantly. He thought to back off, but any movement whatsoever was going to be a major risk. The animal could react a whole lot faster than he could. Certainly, trying to turn around and run would get it on him in an instant.

The puma was not protecting its kill. It was still hunting, and he was its quarry.

He calculated its distance from him at fifteen feet.

Its eyes were as still as glass. If the nostrils hadn't dilated slightly as it breathed, it would have appeared frozen. The jaw hung slightly open, the enormous incisors visible.

Was that the face of a mountain lion? He didn't know enough about big cats to tell, but it seemed somewhat longer and narrower. He decided that his best move was to edge in close enough to guarantee a fatal head shot. With luck, it wouldn't react in time.

Another step, then another, as he slowly came up out of the snow and into the compact front garden. Gail played on. The lion watched him.

He saw its eyes close for a moment, then come open again. The message conveyed was clear and it was shocking: the animal was so sure of itself that it was *bored*.

Again he stopped, because he had understood why. The game was already over. It had been since before he'd started his maneuver. The animal was waiting for him to realize that he was caught. No matter what he did, it was going to make its move while he was still too far away for a reliable shot.

Bored did not mean careless. The face remained a picture of attentive patience.

He noticed a flickering light in the sky. Lightning, he thought, which would mean that the blizzard was about to intensify. Could that help him? Would a really powerful flurry give him a chance to return to the road, perhaps to make his escape?

Then he heard a noise even more inexplicable than the earlier one, which had obviously been Louie's death whistle. This was a whispering sound overhead, a big, rhythmic whisper of wind, too regular to be part of the storm. As he listened, it slowed and then settled, dropping down behind the house.

The rhythm was that of a helicopter blade, but it was too quiet. Way too quiet.

A moment later, the light in the front yard changed, and he saw why. The curtained room had just gone dark. The piano had fallen silent.

The lion, also, was gone, slipping away in absolute silence.

He stood still, listening, watching. Could it have jumped up on the roof? Carefully, moving slowly and as little as possible, he raised his head. There was no telltale shadow along the roofline. So it had retreated, backing down the porch until it was out of sight.

Was it trying to escape him or was it still hunting him? Since he couldn't know, he had no intention of going around the corner of that porch. He needed some spot where he could still see the house, but which would give him protection for his back.

Fifty feet to his left was a tree, its trunk thick enough to enable him to lean against it, making attack from behind much more difficult. The lion would have to charge him from some point that he could see, and it would need to start far enough away to make the pistol useful.

The snow in the yard looked deep, and the slower he

had to move, the greater the risk. But if he stayed here, the lion could get behind him.

He raised his gun up beside his shoulder where it could be aimed and fired in just over a second, then plunged off the snow-covered sidewalk and into the deeper drifts of the yard itself. He was at his most vulnerable now.

An enormous splash of snow hit him in the face, temporarily blinding him. He pulled a gloved hand across his face to clear his eyes.

The lion was beside the tree and it was already crouched, ready to leap at him.

Once again, it had outmaneuvered him. Yet again, he was too far away to risk a pistol shot. It, however, was close enough to take him.

Years ago, Menard had recorded a case of a mountain lion stealing a three-year-old out of the bed of a pickup, but he'd never heard of anything like this.

He'd probably been damn lucky to have seen it when he had, or he would have suffered the same fate as Louie.

He took deep, careful breaths, centering his attention on his body, letting his emotions race off down their own frightened path. "You're here, you've survived so far," he told himself. "You can win this."

How had the lion ever gotten over to the tree? How had it concealed itself in the snow? He was having a hard time believing that an ordinary puma could function like this.

Once again, he had to fight the impulse to turn and run.

The lion moved off past the tree, carefully keeping the trunk between itself and Flynn, and once again he had the uncanny sense that it understood guns.

He asked himself, "Do I have any chance at all of getting to the house?"

From where he now stood, the tree was thirty feet away, the porch and front door twenty.

The door had a glass window in it backed by a curtain. Breaking in would take ten seconds.

When a path looked easy, that was usually because it wasn't.

The moment he started back up onto the front walk, he had to assume that the lion would know his intentions.

He made a quick survey of the scene. The house was now completely quiet and completely dark.

Could it be that the lion was trained? Because another way of looking at this situation was that it was not only trying to kill him, it was also trying to keep him from getting to the house.

No, don't even go down that road. The perp didn't have a damn pet lion with a genius level IQ. The creature was bad luck, nothing more. Had to be.

Nevertheless, his cop's intuition screamed at him: secure your position. You don't know where that animal is and you don't know *what* it is, not really.

Once again, he tried the radio. Once again, there was no response, which was completely unacceptable. When this stakeout was concluded he was going to file a red hot report with whoever was in charge of this outfit, about its leadership and its shitty procedures and its worthless equipment.

Six feet to the left of the front door, the porch ended. Beyond it were lumps along the side of the house that indicated the presence of a flower bed. Behind the house, just visible, he could see the dark bulk of what must be the garage.

Somewhere back there Diana and Charlie and Mike were deployed—unless, of course, their radio silence was unintentional.

He would need to find them, but not right now. There was another thing that had to be done, which was that the Hoffmans needed to be warned and they had to be offered the close protection they should have been given in the first place.

Angrily jabbing the transmit button on his radio, sending out call after unanswered call, he approached the house.

He pushed his fist through one of the small panes of glass midway up the front door. Working fast because he had lost track of the puma, he pulled the remaining shards of glass out of the bottom of the frame, then leaned in, twisted the deadbolt, and opened the door.

The alarm sounded its warning buzz, but he didn't even try to cut it off. He wanted it to trigger. Surely that would bring Diana and Mike and Charlie in on the run—assuming, of course, that they were still alive. But surely—*surely*—they were. No matter how clever, a mountain lion simply could not slaughter four police officers. Someone was going to get to his gun in time.

The buzz of the alarm rose to a warble. Thirty seconds to go. "Miss Hoffman, Doctor Hoffman, police! Please disarm your system! Police!"

No reaction. They could have retreated to a safe room. They could be waiting there, guns at the ready. Hopefully, they were calling the locals.

His first order of business was to find such any safe room they might be in. It would most likely be in the basement, so where was that door?

He went into the living room. In the big stone fireplace, the fire that had blazed up earlier still sparked and muttered. Beyond this was the music room. With its drapes still closed, it was pitch black. Inside, he could see the darkly gleaming surface of a grand piano, its keyboard a pale grimace.

The alarm triggered, its horn blaring up from under the stairs. Returning to the front hall, he opened the door of the understairs storage, then waited another full minute before disconnecting it. If it was set to make a distress call, he wanted to make sure that happened before he disabled anything. Finally, he pulled out its power line. Silence followed.

"Is anybody here?"

He detected not the slightest sense of movement, not the whisper of a footstep or a breath or the faintest creak of shifting weight from upstairs.

The wind rose in the eaves and snow swept past the windows.

He examined the alarm system's control box and was horrified to see that the jack socket was empty. It had no phone connection.

Stepping into the hall, he tried his cell phone, but there wasn't even the hint of a bar. In the kitchen he snatched up the receiver of a wall phone, but there was no dial tone. Lines were down, of course, in weather like this.

If that flash of light had been the perpetrator in some sort of helicopter, no matter how incredible it seemed, the brilliant puma had been part of it, deployed as an assassin and a decoy.

He looked out the kitchen window, across the bleak pale desert of the backyard.

He shifted frequencies on the radio, emergency calling again and again, but nobody came back. Field communicators like these were adjusted to a range of just a couple miles. You didn't want them being picked up on bad-guy scanners.

To be certain that he was right about the Hoffmans, he went through the house checking bedrooms, closets, bathrooms, even under the beds.

He pulled down the attic door. As soon as the stairs unfolded, though, he knew they weren't up there. Nobody had trod on these dusty steps in a long while. Still, he shone his light up. "Doctor Hoffman, police! Miss Hoffman!"

No reply.

He climbed the old steps, feeling the slanted ladder give under his weight. "Doctor Hoffman, I'm a police officer. I'm here to help you."

If he was wrong and they were up there, he might be about to get his head blown off. "Doctor Hoffman!"

Shining his light ahead of him, he went up two more rungs. He spotted a couple of cardboard boxes, but mostly the space was filled with loose insulation. Turning, he shone his light to the far end. The house had two wings, but there was no point in crawling any deeper. Anybody coming up here would have disturbed this insulation.

He backed down and closed the stairs, then spent some time in the master suite. The bed had been slept in, but it was cold now. The master bath revealed that this had been Doctor Hoffman's room. It also revealed missing items. There was no toothbrush in the holder and a shelf of the medicine cabinet was empty.

There were too many clothes in the closet to tell if any were missing, but the way that the hangars had been pushed back, it looked possible. He observed no luggage, so that was another question.

He went down the hall to Gail's room and found a

similar situation. The bed was undisturbed, but there was evidence that cosmetics had been removed from the bathroom.

In the hallway, he found a closet that held luggage, but it was unclear if any had been taken.

Still, the evidence was sufficient to at least suggest that these people had left of their own accord. Nobody was going to believe that, though, because their cars were still going to be in the garage and there were no tracks around the house.

He knew damn well what had happened here. The Hoffmans had been taken. No question, it was exactly the same as all the other cases. So the kidnapper had managed to take the third sister right out from under the noses of a stakeout team, which was damn well amazing.

That most criminals were stupid was part of the shorthand of police work. The vast majority of them were going to be too dumb to get away, but also too dumb not to shoot. Catching the average crook was like herding a bull—dangerous, but not exactly what you'd call an intellectual challenge.

What they had here was a lurid genius with a bizarre imagination. To even think of training a big cat the way he had was extraordinary. To succeed was phenomenal.

He went downstairs and looked out the back door. He needed to locate the remaining members of the team. He observed the snow-packed back garden carefully, but saw no sign of any human presence. But he wouldn't, not from here. They'd be back in the tree line.

That damn cat was probably still out there, but he had to do this. He unlocked the kitchen door and drew it open.

The wind-driven snow slammed him so hard that he lurched off balance and had to grab the doorframe to keep from being swept backward.

There were major gusts in this thing, fifty, sixty miles an hour.

Lowering his head, he pushed his way out into the storm.

CHAPTER NINE

The brief shafts of moonlight that had helped him earlier were now gone, replaced by scudding clouds and a literal wall of snow being driven directly in his face by the brutal wind. Out much more than five feet, he was blind. So what about the cat? Was it blind, too?

Despite this, the perp had come in here and taken his victims. Flynn knew when, too. It had happened just after Gail had stopped playing the piano and just before he'd entered the house—when Flynn had been dealing with the puma. It had disappeared because the kidnap had been accomplished and the perp had called it back.

The whole thing had taken roughly ten minutes and had been accomplished without a sound, without a trace of anything being left behind and without a hitch. *In this.*

He reached the garage and shone his light through one of the small windows that lined the two doors—and felt a shock with the power of a fist in the face. There was blood everywhere, blood and ripped clothing. He saw a hand, a leg—pieces of two people, maybe three.

The Hoffmans? The team? All of them?

He raised one of the doors, which came up with a massive creaking and a tinkle of shattering ice.

This door hadn't been opened in at least an hour, and the other one was caked with ice. So who were these people?

Stepping in, gun in one hand and flashlight in the other, he went to where a bloody jacket lay against the door of an old pickup.

North Face, black. High-intensity penlight in the right pocket.

Mike had worn a black North Face. The light was the same one all the team members carried.

Against the back wall, there was an old-fashioned pitchfork. On it was a rounded mass of bloody hair. It was Charlie, his distorted face just barely recognizable in the mess.

The perp may have originally intended to take the Hoffmans in the usual way, leaving behind evidence that they'd departed on their own. Flynn's best guess was that these two men had somehow succeeded in surprising him—whereupon they had paid the same price as Louie.

So this was now a major crime scene. There could be forensic studies done here. Maybe there would be prints, bits of hair, even blood. DNA, even.

Looked at one way, this was a scene of extraordinary violence and tragedy. Looked at another way, it could be a treasure-trove of evidence, the first one in the history of this case.

A quick survey of the remains turned up evidence of only the two men. Diana was not here. He made a quick decision to report this crime first and worry about her later. His guess was that she was beyond saving anyway, probably back there in those woods right now, in the form of frozen remains.

His duty was very clear. He had to get out of here alive and give the state criminal investigators all the help he could.

But how to accomplish that? The perp was going to definitely want him dead. He had effective weapons, including the lion, and probably skills and capabilities that Flynn knew nothing about. Given that he was able to train a wild animal to near-human hunting skills, it had to be assumed that he was well provided with extraordinary assets.

Could Flynn manage to walk out of here? No, the perp would not let that happen. At some point, the lion would reach him or something else would reach him.

Even if he did reach the Cherokee, which was half a mile back along the road, he didn't have keys. So he would need to wire it. Not difficult, but it would take a few minutes that he was unlikely to have.

He was trapped here, that was clear. But he wasn't going to give up. That was also clear. The odds were against him though, seriously against him. In fact, he didn't really think he had any measurable odds. So what he had to do was to leave a record behind, giving all the details of the crime as he had observed them.

A moment's thought brought him an idea. He set about searching the ruins of the two men for a phone. He could use it to record a detailed account of the crime as he had seen it unfold. He'd return it to the pocket it had come from. At some point, forensics would find the recording and listen to it.

Handling the corpse of a person who has just died is

as intimate an experience as there is. Not many people do it—nurses, policemen, emergency medical service personnel—and those who do never get used to it. It's as if a living person has surrendered himself to you so completely that he is lost to your touch.

Largely because Charlie's corpse was the least maimed, Flynn approached it first. He'd taken a shattering blow to the head and sustained deep gouges. A man had delivered the blow, but the rest of it had been done by the lion.

The body lay at a twisted angle, its face turned away as if in some eerie excess of modesty. One arm lay across the chest, the other angled backward, obviously broken. Long gouges had reduced his heavy parka to rags that bulged with tufts of white wool insulation. Mike felt in the pockets, soon coming across the familiar shape of an iPhone. Grasping it, he withdrew it and turned it on.

It took a long time, but finally the opening screen appeared. Charlie didn't use a password, which was useful but not smart for a man who obviously dealt with a lot of classified material.

As Flynn pressed the logo of the recorder app, he found himself watching the battery indicator with increasing amazement. The phone got hot, quickly becoming almost painful to hold. He tried to turn it off but it was no use. He watched helplessly as the battery indicator moved across the face of the thing, reducing it in a matter of seconds to a dead, useless brick. Immediately, he pulled out his own cell phone and found it to be hot, also, its battery drained.

He went to Mike's shattered remains, dug his fingers into a blood-soaked pants pocket, but did not find his phone. He patted the other pocket. Same result. Had it been lost in the battle that had taken place in here? He shone his light around the room.

Mike's jacket was so badly ripped apart that the contents of the pockets had been strewn all over the room. After a few more moments of searching, he found his MindRay under the truck. On the far side of the vehicle was a small black object, which proved to be not his cell phone, but an old Police Special. Flynn pocketed it.

At that moment, he heard a sound, a fluttering in the rafters.

He braced his pistol, but saw nothing. He used his flashlight. Still nothing. Could have been a possum or a coon. Not a lion, though, thank God, not up there.

Continuing his search, he soon located another pistol, this one a Magnum. At least one of these guys had been decently armed. The pistol had been fired until it was empty.

Charlie and Mike had fought for their lives in here. He hadn't heard the shots, so the battle must have taken place while he was still on the rise overlooking the house. That would have been at least half an hour ago.

He thought the situation over. Louie had been done by a big cat that had been expertly trained. Best trained animal in the world, no question. It hunted like a master tracker of the human kind, not like an animal. What had happened in here was that the lion and its human minder had worked together.

The shadow dropping down from above was almost on him by the time he saw it. There were eyes—huge, glaring—and he was firing his pistol again and again, aware that he was emptying it just like Mike had.

Then silence. Nothing was there but a wreath of smoke.

He took a long step toward the truck—and saw

something moving on the far side. Reflex made him brace the empty pistol.

No more movement. No sound.

He went closer, then around to the front of the truck. Shining his light into the darkness between the vehicle and the wall, he saw a mass of something on the floor. A closer look revealed that it was feathers.

"Shit," he said quietly. He'd shot at a poor damn barn owl. Fortunately for the owl, all he'd done was to separate it from part of its tail.

It was time to get out of here. He had one hell of a dangerous journey ahead. Reluctantly, he approached Mike's body again and felt for a reload for the Magnum. He didn't find one. He'd never know if the guy failed to bring extra bullets, or used more than one cylinder. Not that it was that important. Dead is dead, and they certainly hadn't been killed by any barn owl.

It was time to do this, maybe lose his life and maybe not, but the longer he waited the more certain he felt that whoever had done three experts to death would find a way to kill a fourth—or was that a fifth? Diana had yet to be accounted for.

He turned out his light, went to the door, twisted the handle, and raised it onto the storm.

The wind was roaring steadily now, the snow gushing out of the sky in a horizontal cataract. He took his compass out of his pocket and oriented himself, then turned and closed the door.

He started off, pushing his way through snow that was two feet deep at a minimum. When he reached the road, he consulted his compass again, then turned and headed toward the town.

He'd find the Cherokee. He'd survive. He'd get this perp and see him take the needle.

The wind howled around him, clutching him, shaking him with the full power of nature at its most wild.

He struggled off toward the town, his compass his only guide.

CHAPTER TEN

Flynn's struggled to stay on the road, to see any possible attacker, to somehow make progress against a storm that was like a living creature. He timed himself, hoping that he could get at least a rough idea of when he might be approaching the jeep. He also watched as best he could for the puma or for any other sign of danger.

When a flicker lit the snow, his first thought was that it was lightning. There was no thunder, though. Then, for the briefest moment, a neat pool of light crossed a drift to his right.

He reacted by dropping and rolling off the road. He let himself sink into the snow. Face up, he lay absolutely still, breathing as lightly as possible. Heat sensing equipment worked particularly well in conditions like this and he did not want his breath to reveal him to infrared detectors.

He reached for the Glock with his right hand, Mike's Special with the left. He'd worked for years to shoot effectively with his left hand, and was able to hit targets firing from it at eighty percent of his right-handed proficiency.

If anything came at him, he was going to do his best to shoot it and the hell with the police self-identification mandate, this was kill or die. As always in moments like this, he took his attention away from his mind and even his problem, and concentrated it on his body. You'd think that paying attention to the problem was what you needed. But what you needed was a hunter's form, and that was a physical discipline. As he emptied his mind, cocked silence filled him. His breathing became deep, his heartbeat slowed.

After a moment, a more intense light appeared, growing at first brighter, then slowly dimming. It was moving up the road, and it seemed to be coming from above, like a searchlight shining down from a helicopter.

As had been the case at the Hoffmans', there wasn't the slightest sound of an engine. A helicopter produces noise in two ways. There's the engine sound, but the distinctive chopping is caused by the rotor, or wing, breaking the sound barrier for a moment each time the engine drives it forward.

There was no engine noise. There was no chop. So could this be one of the rumored silent wing choppers the air force had been working on? *Was* it the air force, then? Could it therefore mean safety?

No, this same type of aircraft had been used to kidnap the Hoffmans.

So the perp had a trained lion and a helicopter with a silent wing.

He waited, breathing evenly, letting the snow settle around him. He was freezing cold but must not allow himself to shiver. His face burned from cold, but he would not move to push the snow away.

The light flashed down again and again, continuing on past him, growing slowly fainter until it was finally absorbed by the darkness.

Did the possession of an advanced helicopter mean a defense connection of some sort?

If he got out of this alive, that would be another line of inquiry worth pursuing. Right now, though, it was all he could do not to let his mind frantically game survival options. From long experience and study, he knew that in conflict the body is a better master than the mind. He concentrated his attention on his senses, mostly his hearing.

From yoga, he'd learned a practice of containing his body heat, and he regulated his breathing carefully. He needed to remain here for an unknown amount of time, but without intense physical discipline he was going to have to move in a few minutes or be frozen.

He took in breath, held it deep, then expelled it slowly, retaining as much heat as he could.

The light returned, brighter this time. It was definitely coming from above, no question about that. If he had a helicopter with a silent wing, then maybe he also had a MindRay, maybe even a better one. Certainly heat sensors and night vision equipment. But would any of it register the presence of a mind in deep trance?

He concentrated his attention on his inner silence. His mind became totally quiet. He waited. They might get him, but there would be death among them.

Slowly, the light faded once again. Whatever equipment they had, they hadn't found him. Unless, of course, they were waiting for him to stand up into an ambush.

If they were certain that he was here, they might realize that the snow was concealing him from their detectors. Therefore, he had to remain hidden until they concluded that he was dead.

He couldn't see his watch and dared not bend his arm, so he began to count. He needed to stay here at least half an hour, but how was he going to do that without freezing to death?

The cold penetrated deeper and faster than he'd thought possible, coming in through his double ply of long johns, making his bones ache and his skin go numb.

Time passed. He remained still. Methodically, he moved his fingers and toes.

When he'd heard nothing for what he hoped was at least fifteen minutes, he moved slightly.

No light flickered, no sound came but the wind.

He moved more, lifting his head until he could hear the intimate whisper of snow as it slid out of the sky.

As he came to his feet, he did an immediate reconnaissance up and down the road. It appeared that he was alone. To the east, the sky was slightly brighter, but darkness still dominated. He glanced at his watch. Five fifteen. He had not been under the snow for ten or twelve minutes. He had remained here for more than two hours.

He struggled back up onto the road and turned south, then resumed plodding.

Walking was hard work and extremely slow and even without his pursuers to capture him, it was clear to him that he might not make it out of this. If he didn't find the jeep and then also missed the crossroads and therefore didn't find the town, he would die within the hour. In fact, unless everything went perfectly and he had luck, one way or another, he was going to die in this place.

Ahead, a frozen road sign danced in the wind. It was caked with ice and unreadable, but he could see that it contained an arrow pointing to the right.

It was the way to the town. Even better, sometime in the past two or three hours, it had been plowed. Snow was blowing again, but when he put his feet down they hit tarmac, not crunching ice. He was able to safely increase his speed, which he did, forcing more and more out of himself, but at the same time getting his body into the same kind of rhythm that enables animals to lope for hours, checking his breathing, his heart rate, going for the long pull.

He began to allow himself to think that he might have escaped.

The road, though, seemed to go on forever. How long had they driven to get from the town to the Hoffman's turn off? He recalled ten minutes at most. The snow had kept them to twenty miles an hour, perhaps a little faster. So his best guess was that he had about five miles to go. He set his walking speed at four miles an hour, very fast for these conditions, but possible. He knew how each speed felt, from two to six miles an hour. The fact that the road had been plowed was a major plus. If he'd had to slog through the same depth of snow that had choked the side road, he wouldn't have made more than two miles an hour at best.

By the time he could finally see the town's streetlight, putting one foot in front of the other had become a struggle. Beyond it was the Motel 6, a strip of twelve rooms, two cars in front, most likely salesmen sheltering from the storm. He needed to inform the local authorities about the disaster at the Hoffmans', but he had no idea where the police station was located. He headed for the motel. They'd have a phone.

The office was lit by a single storm candle guttering in a saucer on the counter. The room was empty and it was cold. So they'd lost power.

"Hello?"

Nothing.

There was an area map glued under plastic, beside it a stand with brochures promising hunting, fishing, and hot-air balloon rides. They touched him with a strange nostalgia, and he found that he understood the look he'd seen in the eyes of cops who had seen carnage. They longed for the time before, and now so did he.

"Excuse me? Hello?"

Still nobody.

He went around the counter and leaned into the office. An ancient woman sat slumped behind a weathered old desk.

"Excuse me, ma'am?"

When she still didn't respond, he went around the desk and touched her shoulder. Her blouse was dank, the bones beneath dry and light.

Finally, there was a sort of subsurface shudder and she slowly unfolded. She looked up at him out of eyes that had once been tiny with cunning, but were now tired old beads of suspicion. She blinked. Blinked again. Then her face lifted itself from its wrinkled depths, the eyes suddenly full of flicker, and he saw ancient loves reflected there.

"Well, what do I have but a fine-looking young man in here," she said, then she smiled and the whole room lit up. "My God, where'd you come from?"

"Broke down 'bout a mile out."

"Lucky it wasn't more. Lucky we got room, night like

this." She unfolded from the desk, her face briefly rigid with pain. Then the smile came back and she glided into the front like the dancer she must once have been.

He followed.

"Can't run a card till we get the juice back. You good for forty bucks?"

He pulled out his wallet. "I've got the cash."

"Well, that's fine then."

"Where's the local police station?"

"You in trouble?"

"I'm a policeman from Texas. I need some information."

"You lookin' for the rustlers, aint'cha? It's Mexicans, I'm tellin' you. Them illegals. They got trucks, Texas. Big trucks. And guns, too. Big'uns. You're carryin' two pistols, Texas. Ain't enough."

The eyes were sharp, no question there. "Where's the station?"

"There's no police here in Ridge, we got about fifty people living around here is all. You'll have to go on down to the town of River City. There's a state police barracks there. Four fellas. This is Montana. We ain't got a lotta police."

"Is there a bus through here?"

"Eight in the morning, if it's on time. Stops at the café. But you're gonna sleep like an old dog, you lie down on a bed, boy. Want a call?"

"Yeah, that would be good."

With no computer, she didn't record the registration, which was just as well. The more he thought about it, the less sure he was that he would stop at that barracks. He really did not want to explain the Hoffman place to the state cops, how he had gotten there, what he had been doing, any of it. What he wanted to do was to get to an FBI office, and that would mean going all the way to Billings on that bus.

Somebody had to have a record of the men who had died on this operation, who they reported to, who they were, for that matter. Because he didn't think he'd been told a straight story, not any of it. But somebody would know in Washington or wherever, and the FBI office in Billings would be the place to start locating that person. He didn't want to try to involve the locals anymore, not when he was the only survivor. God only knew where things might go, when some smart detective realized that he was the only witness and the only person who had come out of there alive.

"Look," the old lady said, "I can't get the keycard machine to print a key, so here's a maid's key. It works on all the rooms but please don't take advantage of that."

"No ma'am."

"All we got here is a meat broker, some kinda pesticide salesman, and a couple of them gay cowboys keep comin' around here since that damn movie. Ten years and they're still comin'. Gay cowboys, my God, how could there be so many?"

"It's a solitary life," Flynn said.

He left her shaking her head as she negotiated the snow-swept walk that fronted the line of rooms. It was ungodly cold. If his cell phone had been working, he would have pulled up the weather app, but he made a guess that it was no more than zero, and probably below.

There was no heat in Room Seven, but also no wind and no snow. He did not undress, but wrapped himself in the thin blanket and stretched out on a mattress that wasn't long enough for him.

He lay there, his mind turning over what had happened. But what *had* happened? A lion, a helicopter in a raging windstorm?

"Oh, Abby," he said in the privacy of the inner dialogue that he carried on with her, "what secrets do you know?"

CHAPTER ELEVEN

He slept like an animal sleeps, with just enough awareness left behind to rouse him if there was trouble. Sometime toward dawn, he heard the snarl and clank of a gang of plows passing outside. Later, a woman sang to herself on the other side of one of the cardboard walls. Or was that Abby come to him?

A little after seven, thin light woke him. He was washing his face in a chilly memory of hot water when the old lady called. He thanked her and headed out.

The sky was ribbed steel, cold and low, and the wind was blowing what felt like a pretty steady forty miles an hour out of the northwest. There was no snow falling, but streams of it rose from the drifts and pummeled his parka and face. His two-day growth of beard provided welcome insulation.

The café was closed. "No Juice," said a sign scrawled on the door. He needed to eat. There were pies in a case on the counter, bags of Fritos on a stand. He could drink raw eggs without a problem. Plus, the lock was simple. The problem was, if he got caught, there'd be a ridiculous hassle to deal with, and more trouble for him if those bodies had already been found.

He stood on the stoop of the café, looking for the bus. He didn't know where it was coming from or where it was going. It didn't really matter, though. Away from here, that was all that mattered.

He was stomping and blowing on his hands when it finally showed up at nine twenty. It was like an angelic apparition, the big, muddy, slab-sided Greyhound. It had been in a war with the elements, but it was here, rumbling and clattering and shaking, brown ice dripping along its windows, shadowy travelers within.

When he got on, he found it packed. Probably a lot of people were cold. Probably they were looking for shelter in Billings. Well, so was he.

He went to the back where there were still a few seats, and took one beside a huddled red parka.

With a hiss of air brakes and a rumble from the engine, the bus started off. A few minutes passed, and the red parka stirred. "How long to Montana?" its occupant asked as she raised her head.

"We're in Montana," he replied. He turned to her.

It was Diana, and he was too surprised to speak.

"Help me," she said.

"Of course. I thought—"

"I don't know how I escaped." Her hand came toward his. He looked down at it. She withdrew it, entwining it with the other, twisting them together.

"What happened?'

She glanced toward the seat in front of them. "Not now."

"I understand. Where are you going?"

"Billings. I've got to make a report and I want a secure line, not a cell phone." She took a long breath.

"This is unprecedented." She returned to her previous hunched posture. "How did they do it?"

"That's not my question to answer." She'd sent three men to their deaths. How they had been killed or by whom were not the issue. The fact that they'd been exposed to the danger, that was the issue. Her issue.

She turned to him. "You don't want to talk about it?"

"No."

"But you would have handled things differently?"

"Yes."

"You need to know more. Then you'll understand more."

"Who's going to tell me?"

He felt her cold fingers brush his wrist. He did not react, but he also found that he did not move away. "I don't have that authority," she said.

"Then there's something wrong in your chain of command, lady. I'm what you got left on the front line, and you can't tell me my mission? That's poor."

"You're furious."

"Too goddamn much secrecy. Lives wasted. So, yeah."

"And I wasted them?"

"If I get to submit a report, that's part of what I'll say. You shouldn't be doing this work. Sorry."

She sucked in breath. There was anger in her eyes, a flush in her cheeks. Not used to criticism, that was clear. "I didn't know he had a tiger," she said. "Nobody could know that."

"It was a lion."

She whirled in her seat, eyes now flashing. "That was a Siberian tiger."

"Oh?"

"Gray with darker gray stripes. It was a Siberian tiger in its winter coat."

He thought about that. He hadn't seen the flanks. The face had been strange. She could be right. "If that's true, we might be able to use it to track him down."

"How?"

"A Siberian tiger is an endangered species. A zoo had to get a license to import it. If it was sold, that had to be approved. A rare animal like that, there's gonna be a paper trail, and it's gonna lead to our target, or damn close."

"What if it was born here?"

"Whatever, the animal has papers. This could be a break."

The bus wheezed along. Tough buggies, these Greyhounds. He leaned his head back and closed his eyes. Not tired anymore. Ready for action, but sitting in a damn bus.

Once again, he went over in his mind the details of what had happened, the tiger, the helicopter, the carnage in the garage.

"After they entered the garage, what happened?"

"Mike went in. Then we heard him firing his pistol. Charlie was nearest, so he ran after him." Her voice dropped to a near-whisper. "When nobody came out, I went in. The smell of blood was so strong that I knew they were dead before I saw them." She fell silent.

He felt for her. This was a conscientious officer and she was suffering. You lose a man, you're changed forever. You lose three, and you are left in an agony of self-doubt and self-blame. If you're good, that is. Still, though, he couldn't change his opinion, not only of her but also of whatever organization she belonged to. Bad planning, bullshit electronics, excessive secrecy—it was not a workable system.

The bus crossed the great American distance, crawling through the endless, featureless snowscape with its big engine roaring and its windshield wipers creating a hypnotic rhythm.

Diana sat in silence. From time to time she turned to the window. He assumed that she was crying. He said nothing.

"What about the Hoffmans?" she asked. "Do you know?"

"They're gone. I checked the house. A helicopter took them. I saw its lights."

"More traceable than an animal."

"You'd be surprised. Radar coverage out her isn't gonna go much below six thousand feet. Stay under it, then the FAA isn't gonna find out jack about you."

"Homeland Security, surely."

"You come up off of one of these ranches, you stay low, you're free and clear."

"You heard it?"

"Yep. It did not sound like a helicopter. But that's what it had to be."

The bus pulled into another small town. Nameless place. Flynn watched the comings and goings of the passengers. Two left, three got on. He wasn't expecting a problem, but the last of them seemed to check folks out a little more carefully than would be normal.

"You see that?"

"No."

"The guy in the camouflage. He's got busy eyes."

She lowered her head.

He pressed her. "What do you think?"

"I don't know. How would they know we were here?"

"That's not the right question. The right question is,

'Do they want us dead?' I think we both know the answer."

The bus started off. From back here, Flynn couldn't see much of the other passengers. He flagged the guy in the camouflage, though. He was wearing a khaki cap with fur earflaps. When he took it off, his burr haircut was sprinkled with gray. Forty-five years old, maybe. Flynn watched the back of the head, which never moved. "That's a professional up there," he said.

"What kind of a professional?"

"Don't know. But whatever he's doing, he's on duty." Flynn took a breath and released it slowly. Contemplating. He needed to evaluate the situation, so he got up and went to back of the bus. As he stood, he got a chance to take a better look at the man, who was sitting two rows ahead of them. He could just see his profile. The man's eyes were closed but his body language said he was nowhere near asleep.

Flynn stepped into the toilet, waited a short time, then emerged. Returning to his seat, he nudged Diana, then pointed with his chin. Her only response was another slight touch to his wrist.

"We have to assume that he's a threat," Flynn said.

"I agree."

The bus rumbled on, the snowscape outside so total that Flynn could have easily believed they were on another planet.

The guy could be anybody, an insurance salesman, who knew? Except that was not what he was. Flynn had known such men, quiet like that, contained. You couldn't see him watching you, but you could feel it.

"He's here to kill," Flynn said.

"I know it."

You talk about a high-grade hit, what had gone

down back at the Hoffmans' was that and more. It was certainly the most exotic hit he'd ever seen, and one of the most effective.

The bus pulled into a town called Waco like the town in Texas except this was in Montana. Waco was basically a cluster of hills of snow with an occasional neon sign sticking out. There was a grain elevator and a gas station. The gas station was the bus stop. There wasn't even a place to get a hamburger. Or no, there was. You could buy a microwave burger in the gas station.

The bus hung there for a minute. Nobody got off or on. Another minute. Still no action. The driver's hand went for the door lever. The air brakes hissed.

Flynn grabbed Diana by the wrist and pulled her down the aisle. "Sorry," he called out to the driver, "didn't recognize it."

They got off and the bus pulled out, and Flynn saw the face of the guy staring out at them, a face as blank as a tombstone.

"What are we doing," Diana said, "we can't stay here!"

"What we're doing is surviving. Buying time. We're clean now, for a while."

They went into the gas station. "When's the next bus through?" he asked the guy behind the counter, a lanky kid with the swift, unsure eyes of a dog that can't figure out why it gets kicked.

"Two hours, but it's going the other way. Next one through to Billings is gonna be tomorrow."

"We're going the other way. Our car broke down. We flagged him and had him drop us here."

"I got coffee. The meatball hero over there's not gonna kill you, you're hungry. Avoid the burger."

"What about the Philly?"

"I wouldn't eat it."

The kid's eyes flickered away, and Flynn turned, following them toward Diana.

Snapshot: Diana's eyes, staring straight at him.

Snapshot: the guy from the bus coming in behind her. Camouflage. Professional movements. He'd gotten the driver to stop a second time. Flynn dropped his hand into his pocket, closed on the Glock. Behind Diana, the assassin's hands came up toward his chest. He was going for a gun, going into action.

Flynn threw himself at Diana, hurling her to the floor with so little room to spare that he felt the heat of the bullet sear the back of his head as it passed. Maybe an eighth of an inch, maybe less.

He rolled, pushing over a shelf of candy, sending Snickers bars and Kit Kats and PayDays flying.

The killer was bracing his weapon, a big long-range pistol with a laser sight. A red dot appeared in Diana's hair. Flynn pulled her into the heap of candy and shelving as the second round smashed into the floor where she'd been lying. Cement shrapnel ripped at them.

He got the Glock out, felt for the trigger, found it, and fired through the parka.

Then he had the guy. And the guy had him. Gun to gun, the guy with the Glock was going to have to be good. Real good.

Gun fighting is speed and math, but mostly math. Flynn was good at math. Instead of dropping his pistol, he changed his angle of attack. An iffy head shot became an easy heart shot.

The guy had done the same. Heart to heart. Impasse.

But then the guy backed off a step.

Flynn couldn't see Diana, but she had to be the reason. The clerk was hiding behind the counter hammering at the keypad of his cell phone. Not gonna work today, Flynn thought. Cell towers need power, too.

The assassin turned and ran. Flynn followed immediately.

"Stay together," Diana cried. "That's an order!"

The hell. He took off across the pump island and out into the highway. The guy was running hard, about fifty yards ahead. Flynn continued after him, letting the long hours of endurance training he'd done propel him forward despite the wind and the blowing snow. Ahead, the guy's back was visible as a dark smudge in the sea of snow.

"Stop! Police!" Except he wasn't the police, was he, not in Montana, and maybe not even in Texas if he'd pissed Eddie off enough to get himself fired.

The guy did not stop, of course, so he quit wasting breath. He could get off a shot, but there was no chance it was going to connect. He ran harder but did not gain. In fact, the smudge became more and more indistinct. Finally, it was gone. Flynn ran on for another minute, but in the end he did the only logical thing he could and stopped. He stood staring out into the gloom of the storm. He had maybe two hundred yards of visibility. Even as fast as he'd been running, the guy had continued to outstrip him.

Diana came up, her breath surging out of her nose in blasts of fog. "We gotta get out of here."

"How could he run like that? How could anybody?"

"I don't know."

He turned to her. He took her collars. He pulled her close to his face. "Yeah, you do. You've killed three men with this bullshit secrecy, so why don't you give me some kind of goddamn chance and come clean. Tell me what you know."

"What I know? That we're up against a team. That they have excellent equipment and skills."

"They have a helicopter with a silent rotor."

"A silent rotor exists. It can be retrofitted to a number of different helicopters, including some general aviation models."

"So they've been able to steal classified equipment. What about their victims? What's the point of all this?"

"We don't know where they take people. We don't know why. The third sister was the closest we've ever gotten to one of their operations." She gestured. "Obviously, we weren't ready."

They began walking back toward the gas station. "How many of them are there? What's their maximum area of activity? US? Other countries as well?"

"Primarily US as far as we can tell. Concentrated in rural areas near urban population centers where there's lots of turnover and lots of young, well-educated, healthy people. They favor low-density suburbs like you live in. Like we did, me and Steven."

"Your husband?"

"Yes. But let's not go there right now."

"No."

The cold was so intense that the sweat he'd generated running was now flaking off him like an icy powder.

"Okay, one useful face. We've got the Siberian tiger involved. That's traceable."

They had reached the gas station. The clerk had closed it down and gone home, so they stayed close to the front window, using the station to shelter them from the wind and the pumps to interrupt the sightlines of possible snipers. Flynn didn't like it, but it was what they had.

"We're way too vulnerable here," he said, "so keep

low and keep watch." Then he asked her a question that had been troubling him. He already knew the answer, but he asked it anyway. "You're not a field officer, are you?"

After a moment, she shook her head. "I come from the world of probability theory. I'm an analyst."

"You couldn't find a pattern, but then the third sister came along and you grabbed a few pros and off you went."

"Don't, please. No more."

"He could've taken her any damn time, but he wanted to teach you a lesson. So he chose the night you were there."

A cold silence fell between them. An analyst. An ad-hoc team. Equipment that didn't work as advertised. Who the hell did the thinking?

The wind kept the snow blowing, reducing visibility. Flynn wondered what would come first, the bullet or the bus? Or maybe it would be the tiger.

He didn't like it when his choices were limited to just one, especially when it was bad. Worse, all this flurrying was going to play hell out on the highway. Buses were going to stop in towns and stay there until they could follow plows.

"We need to find shelter. We need to either break into this place or we need to find somebody to help us. We can't stay here."

"The bus is due in forty minutes."

He stood up. "Too long," he said. He gestured toward the highway. "Outside of town, flurries are sweeping that road. So any traffic is stopped wherever it happens to be, and that's where it's gonna stay until it gets plowed out."

"If we miss the bus—"

"You let the sun set on us, we do not survive the night. Period. If the cold doesn't take us, he will. He will not miss again."

She looked up at him. "It's my decision," she said.

He set off, intending to knock on doors until somebody let him in. Who knew, maybe they'd have a truck, maybe with chains.

She caught up with him. Good. He didn't want to see her killed. Whatever she did, though, he intended to survive and he intended to win. This bastard had done enough.

"He's gonna die or I'm gonna die," Flynn shouted into the wind. "But not here, not now. I want my shot at him and I haven't got it. But I will, lady. I will get my shot, and I'm not stopping until I do."

They moved slowly along, huddled shapes in a blowing, frozen haze. They couldn't go far, so Flynn intended to get to the first inhabited house they could find.

Slowly, they passed a bank, its tan brick front encased in ice, its interior dark. Next came a bar, its neon out, its door padlocked.

"Hold on," she said, "don't leave me behind."

He put an arm around her and drew her forward.

"You're strong," she said.

He said nothing. They might be moving slow, but the reality of their situation could not be more clear. They were running for their lives with death by cold close behind them, and closer yet an even more dangerous enemy, who they could not see, let alone fight.

Flynn might not be able to see him, but he was out there, no question, and he intended to end this, and soon.

CHAPTER TWELVE

The house was small and trim, with green shutters and gray siding. It had started life as a double-wide trailer and had been added to over the years. It was set north to south on its lot, so the wind surged down the porch, which was buried so deep in a rippling snow-drift that Flynn had to dig through it to reach the front door. He knocked.

Silence.

"It's empty," Diana said.

"Nope." He pounded.

From inside there came a cry, "Clara! What're you doin' out there?"

The inner door swept open to reveal a man of about sixty in a wheelchair.

"We need shelter," Flynn said. "We need a phone."

"Where's Clara? Where's my wife?"

Flynn felt Diana tense. He said, "We need to get in out of this."

The man rolled his chair back away from the entrance as they struggled in.

"Who the hell are you? You ain't from around here."

"We were waiting for the bus."

"No, that's not the answer. You DEA lookin' for meth labs. Every other house has a meth lab out here. State don't care. They let it go. They have to." He whipped the chair around and rolled toward the back of the house. "Clara! Where in hell is she?"

Briefly, Diana's hand squeezed Flynn's. He was thinking the same thing: maybe the whole town had been raided. Maybe the old and infirm were the only ones left.

"She went out?"

"To the barn, see to the horses. The intercom's down, the cell phones don't work, the landline is down and she's been out there more'n a hour."

"We're cops," Flynn said, "but we're not looking for your meth lab."

"I told you, I ain't got any damn meth lab! None! Natha! Find my girl, you two, you're a damn gift from God."

There was no time to get warm, they went directly out the back. Flynn pointed to the faint trench in the snow that led to the barn. Diana nodded.

"Guns," he said.

"Guns."

"Are you proficient, Diana?"

"I score okay."

They pushed the door open together. "Clara," Flynn called into the dark interior. "Clara!"

A horse whickered, that was all.

The barn was unheated, but the two horses in their stalls had been expertly blanketed. A couple of big electric heaters stood in the center of an area of the concrete slab that had been carefully swept of anything that might catch fire. Their cords led to an orange cable that hung from an overhead socket attached to a rafter. No power, though.

"Clara!" he said again, then, "Oh, shit."

"What?"

"Smell that? That's blood." He looked into the darkness. "Over there." He moved deeper.

A third horse was up against the back wall, deep in the shadows. It lay on its side.

He went to it. Looking down at the maimed animal, he wasn't sure what to make of its condition.

"You ever see anything like this?" he asked Diana as she came up.

"Oh, no."

The lips had been sheared off, the eyes cut out, the genitals removed. A large section of the exposed flank had been flayed down to the bone. Where the rectum had been, there was a neat round wound.

"So you have."

"Only in pictures. Animals mutilated like this have been found for years. None in the context of the kind of disappearances we're investigating, though, not as far as I am aware."

"You know more about this whole damn mess than you're telling me, and I'm getting to really not appreciate that."

"I can't—"

"Yeah, you can, and you will, and you'll do it soon."

Flynn had seen something like this before, too. Some case file. Then he remembered. It was a rural crime down near Alice, Texas. "I saw some of these. Cattle, not horses. A rancher got the hell knocked out of his herd. Two prize bulls and three breeder cows. Fifteen thousand dollars worth of prime beeves. Sheriff thought it was coyotes. We wrote it up as vandalism so the poor guy could collect on his insurance."

He remembered that place. Alvis something-or-other had been leasing that property. He'd run it with Aussie cattle dogs. Good beasts, but not good enough to prevent the loss.

"I have a feeling that the help does most of the heavy work. The kidnappings. But this is him," Flynn said. "Him personally. His help isn't going to be cutting animals like this." He looked toward the rafters, then reached back and pulled his night vision goggles from his backpack.

The upper reaches of the barn were empty. He took off the goggles. "Let's go out the back," he said.

"Three guys are down, remember that."

He said nothing.

This door also slid on rollers, but wasn't as large as the one in the front. Similarly, it wasn't kept up, and it took Flynn an effort to get it to grind open. As he did so, ice showered down on him.

Behind the barn was a mostly bald hill, topped by a few twisted trees. Close in, he could see a faint indentation in the snow. Further out, it was deeper. "That's a buried track," he said, moving forward. He drew his gun.

The further up the hill they went, the deeper and clearer the track became.

"Why would she come out here?"

"She was running. She saw that horse, and when she did, she ran."

As they approached the trees, Flynn felt the same indefinable sense of menace that had saved him in deceptive situations before. "Let's take our time. We want to watch those trees pretty closely."

They were taller than they had appeared from the barn. The snow made distances seem longer, but the trees were under a hundred yards from this end of the barn, and he was soon among them. He was careful, though, never to lose sight of her. He didn't want to lose her, God no, but she wasn't only important as a human being and a fellow officer. Without her, he had no idea who he was working for because she was too secretive to tell him. Probably didn't even have the authority.

In among the trees there was less snow, but every movement brought a fall of the stuff off overhanging branches. It got in around his hood and dripped through his clothes in the form of freezing cold water.

Just beyond the stand of trees they found an area about thirty feet in diameter where the snow had been blown away right down to the grassy hillside.

"Something landed here," Diana said.

He estimated the grade of the hill at a good thirty degrees. "Wasn't a chopper," he said, "not on a slope this steep."

"It must have hovered."

"The pilot is a real expert, then," Flynn said. "Very well trained."

"You think she was taken from this spot?"

"Maybe. Thing is, the snow was blown back from here well after these tracks were made. Hours. If they took her, they took her frozen solid."

"We'll need to tell him she's lost in the snow."

He had his doubts about that. "Maybe."

Flynn turned and headed back through the trees. Diana stayed close.

As they walked, he said, "I don't think we're forming an accurate picture of what's going on here. If you think about it, it just doesn't make sense. Not a damn bit of sense. Some kind of cult group in possession of highly classified equipment, including an exotic aircraft? Hardly seems likely."

"That's what it looks like, though."

They reached the back door. "It's what you've been telling your team. It's not what you know. Question is now, what do we tell this old guy?"

"His wife is lost in the snow. Won't be found till the melt. If then."

He entered the house. The old man sat in his wheelchair. He looked up with the dead eyes of a man who already knows that he's defeated.

"We didn't find her," Flynn said.

"She's dead. Froze by now."

"We don't know that. Could she have gone to a friend's house?"

"She's not in that barn, she's froze."

"There's been predator action in the barn, sir," Diana said.

"Oh, Lord."

"One of the horses has been killed. Looks like coyotes."

"The hell, it's them damn wolves! The Fish and Wildlife owes me for that horse." His face suddenly screwed up. Flynn knew the way tragedy can roll past you at first, then come back and hit you like a boulder dropping from the sky.

"She's still breathing, mister," he said. "Count on it."

Diana glared at him.

"What's she shaking her head for? Don't hold out on me!"

Flynn heard noises on the front porch, the crunch of boots in snow. "She's back," he said.

Diana's eyes widened.

A voice called through the door, "Hey, Lar, I got your thermos refilled, the Katz's're running their genny." Then, "Get this door unlocked, you damn nut!"

Lar wheeled himself off into the front room. A moment later, a tall woman, Montana lean, came striding in on a blast of cold air, snow falling off her boots.

"Hi, where'd you folks stray in from on a day like this?"

"We're police officers," Diana began.

"Well, I got me a horse up in my barn got cut up by space aliens, so you better go up there."

"We've been up there."

"It was them wolves," Lar said.

"Ha! That's what you people told him? Why do cops lie? It's space aliens. We all know it. Been goin' on for years."

"That damn yearling," Lar said. "Too young and foolish to stay away from wolves. Probably didn't even know what they were."

"They took my Bill, you senile old fool. Left the two yearlings just fine. They ain't even spooked."

"What about Jenny?"

"*Your* horse? Nobody's gonna take that ole bag a bones. You couldn't even sell that thing to a glue factory. What's 'is name down the road, that weird beard, offered fifteen dollars. He wanted to make pillows outa the hair." She swung away from her perch looming over her husband, and trained tight eyes on Flynn and Diana. "So what in hell are you doin' invadin' my home, officers? If I may be so bold?"

"Our vehicle failed," Diana said, the very picture of smoothness. "We're looking for a ride into Billings. We can pay."

"You will pay. No question there. You must be feds."

"DEAs lookin' to bust up some meth labs," her husband said.

"That ain't hard to do around here. 'Cept the state police, you talked to them lately? 'Cause they don't share their turf, not to put too fine a point on it." She spread her hands. "I mean, this is not a threat. Far be it from me."

"We're not in drug enforcement."

"Oh. Well, do you do something useful, then? 'Cause maybe then nobody's gonna gut you and throw you out in the snow for your wolves to drag away."

The threat was delivered with the kind of smile that said it had meaning. So this little ole couple were indeed involved in drug operations. He wondered where she had her lab. Probably one of the sheds he'd seen out there. Normally, he would've been interested, just automatically. No more.

"Look, how much is it gonna take to get us to FBI Headquarters in Billings?" he asked.

"Well, let's see. If you tell me why you're here, that's one price. If you don't, then it's another. Which you ain't gonna be able to afford. And, lady, will you please stop thinking about that ridiculous little pistol you got in the right pocket of your parka? In fact—" An impressively quick hand reached in and withdrew Diana's pistol. "Man, who do you work for, you get crap like this as your issue gun? What shit."

She was right about that. An officer carrying a Beretta without a tracking light was not well equipped.

Flynn said, "We're working on a kidnapping. We were overtaken by the storm."

"Who'd kidnap trailer trash? What're they gonna get for ransom around here, twenty bucks and a pair of used boots? This whole town ain't got enough cash to ransom a donkey." She chuckled.

"We tracked the person of interest to Black Canyon City," Diana said. "Then the storm hit, we lost contact with our vehicle and took the bus."

"The wrong way. You're toward Bozeman."

"We were too cold to wait. We had to get on it."

She was quiet for a good minute. She looked down at Diana's gun. "First off, I know you're not a cop, lady. This ain't a cop pistol and here I am holding it and you ain't pissing your pants, which means you ain't gotta file a missing weapon report." She looked at Diana. "Three hundred bucks and I'll take you to Billings. Cash now." She turned her head toward Flynn. "That's apiece."

Flynn could have taken the gun out of her hand and made her eat his own. But he said, "Pay the lady, Ossifer."

A silently furious Diana produced a checkbook.

Clara barked out a mirthless laugh.

Diana put away the checkbook and counted out six one-hundred-dollar bills from what looked to be a narrow stash.

Clara was good at driving in snow, and so the truck clanked along at a steady thirty miles an hour. "Animals get cored out like that around here. Nobody but the poor rancher gives a shit. The cops lie. Insurance company probably pays 'em off, 'cause if it's predator action or act of God, they don't gotta pay, see."

"Space aliens would be what?" Flynn asked.

"God only knows. Whatever, they ain't gonna pay anyway. Bastards."

There was a world of hurt in the way she spat that word. He didn't want to hear the story of her life, though, so he remained silent.

The truck moved steadily along. Flynn watched the road, what he could see of it. He kept an eye on the sky, which was darkening again.

Time crawled. Flynn could almost feel the perp's frustration that they were getting away. Feel his bitter rage. With his trained animal and his fabulous chopper, he had to feel that a couple of dumb cops had no damn business escaping from him.

They arrived in the snow-choked city, finally reaching a recently plowed street where the going was a little better.

After a couple of turns, Clara pulled up in front of an office building, small, on the same scale as all the buildings around here. A small, trim city, the kind of place Flynn favored. Menard with snow.

When they got out, Clara sped off immediately.

"She's glad to be gone," Diana said.

"Probably with good reason."

They entered the building.

CHAPTER THIRTEEN

"**N**obody will have heard of us," Diana said as they went down the hall toward the FBI office.

"What's that supposed to mean?"

She opened the door and went in, Flynn behind her. Two agents and a clerk were on duty, sitting at desks in a single, large room. Along a side wall there were three offices, all closed.

Diana walked up to the clerk and spoke quietly. She produced a small leather folio and laid it on the desk. Inside, Flynn could see a badge and an unfamiliar identification card with a pink sash across its surface.

The secretary stared down at them. "Bill," she called, turning in her chair, "what is this?"

One of the two agents got up from his desk, a tall man in his fifties. He had a tightly neutral expression on his face, the habitual mask that many field officers wore.

Flynn had never gotten much support out of the FBI. Down in Menard, their office was such a revolving door that nobody ever really got to know the community.

Menard was just a way station in the drug wars. The agents who were going somewhere in the organization were all further south along the border.

The first agent took Diana's credential to the second.

"They never know what it is," she said.

"So how does this help us?"

"Just wait."

He watched as the agents, their faces sharp with suspicion, huddled over a phone.

"Who're they calling?"

"It's a nonstandard ID. They've never seen one like it before."

"Because of the secrecy bullshit?"

She nodded. "It's not bullshit, Flynn."

The second agent came striding over. "You can use office two," he said. He handed Diana back her ID.

"That worked, at least," Flynn said as they crossed the room.

"I'm sorry, Flynn, I'm going to need to do this alone."

There were chairs along the wall, and Flynn took one of them. The plaster was thin enough to enable him to hear that she was talking to somebody, but he was unable to make out the words. Once or twice, she raised her voice. He still couldn't discern specific words, but he could hear the emotion in them. She was reporting the deaths of her men.

Her voice stopped. He waited. The silence extended. She came out. Her face was rigid, her lips compressed.

"You reported," he said. "They were not happy."

"They were not."

"So what happens next?"

"Flynn, you're still going to be with me, but very honestly I asked to have you relieved and was turned down on the theory that you're all I have left. So my problem now is that you're clueless and I don't have the authority to bring you up to speed." She glanced across the room at the agents. "We need transport," she snapped.

One of the agents got up and sauntered over. "Yeah? Can I help you?"

"Get us out to Logan."

"Call a cab."

"There's no time for a cab, Delta's about to leave. We need to move right now."

"We have motels. Not up to your standards, I'm sure, but you'll live."

"If you don't want a complaint in your file, I'd advise you to stuff your ego up your ass and do what you're told."

Flynn was as surprised as the agent, who glared at her.

"Right now, Agent."

He jerked his head toward a side door. They followed him down a couple of flights of interior stairs and out to a well-plowed parking lot.

There were two sedans parked in it and three black SUVs, immediately recognizable as federal cars.

"I wanta take my Subaru," the agent said. "Better in the snow."

Once they were in the car, a dense silence settled. Nevertheless, Flynn thought he would try asking the agent some questions that could be useful.

"What kind of crimes do you guys cover out here?"

"Us guys cover the waterfront."

"I mean, specifically?"

"I know I don't have any hotshot National Security clearance, but that'd be privileged information."

An asshole for sure. He kept going anyway. "Any kidnapping cases?"

"Kidnapping? No. Is that what this is about?"

"I can't answer that. My hotshot National Security clearance prevents me."

This brought a slight chuckle. "We had a disappearance four months ago. Not a kidnapping case. The vic packed a bag."

Diana glanced at Flynn, who said nothing.

They pulled up to the departure gates and the agent let them off and sped away.

"Are federal officials always so helpful to each other?" Flynn couldn't resist asking, but he knew the answer.

"Yes."

"So where are we going?"

"Just stay with me."

The airport was small and intimate, a reminder to Flynn of another America, one that still clung to life, just barely, in little places like this and Menard. Steady, settled, and safe—assuming, of course, if you ignored things like the meth industry that drove lots of local economies in poor areas.

Security was no problem, just a single TSA agent with an old-fashioned X-ray device and nobody ahead in line. Not surprising, since Delta to Salt Lake was the last flight out to anywhere, and they had just a couple of minutes to go before the doors were closed. They showed their creds and got their guns passed for hold stowage without trouble. Unlike the FBI agents, the TSA worker accepted Diana's credential without question. He passed his Menard Police Department ID card with equal disinterest.

As they walked down the aisle, Flynn took careful

note of the other passengers. He didn't want a repeat of what had happened on the bus, and he thought they should assume that this perpetrator was capable of almost anything.

He was surprised to identify a Federal Air Marshal three rows behind him. Normally, you found these guys on long-haul flights in big planes. So why was he here? He slid into his seat between a businessman and a kid sealed up in an iPod. The FAM was carrying, which is what had identified him. There was a pistol, small, probably a .38, under the left arm of his thick jacket.

The flight was hot and cramped and seemed longer than it had any right to be. Twice, Flynn went back to the john so that he could pass the FAM. Nothing out of the ordinary, except for the fact that he was there.

Toward the end of the flight, Flynn closed his eyes for a few minutes, waking up when the aircraft shuddered as it began to land.

On the way to the next flight, he commented, "There was a FAM a couple of rows behind me."

"Really?"

"No, I made it up."

"Well, don't."

"Odd that he was there."

"A coincidence, as far as I'm concerned."

"You're sure?"

She stopped. She turned to him. "We are alone, you and I. I know one other person, the individual I report to."

He continued walking easily. Inside though, he was dealing with a major shock. *Only her immediate superior officer?* What in holy hell was going on here?

Their next flight turned out to be to Chicago. They were seated in first class.

"I could get used to this," he said to her. The seat actually had room for him.

"Don't. These were the only seats left. The storm's headed east, and folks want to get in before it closes O'Hare. The flights are packed."

"Why are we going to Chicago? If I may be so bold."

She opened her mouth, seemed about to speak. Remained silent.

"We've got a choice of prime rib or mahi-mahi," the steward said after they took off.

As Flynn ate, he saw that silent tears were running down Diana's face. He said nothing. What was there to say, that it would be all right? It would not be all right, it would never be all right.

Maybe she was going to be relieved or disciplined. Maybe she already knew that. But what was most likely was that she was remembering the men she had lost, and feeling a torment of regret.

"You need to eat," he said.

Listlessly, she took a bite of her fish and chewed.

"Flynn," she said. Then she stopped. He'd seen grief many times, the way it takes a while to hit. Hers had hit. "Flynn," she said again, "you're a good cop and you have some outstanding skills and a lot of investigative experience in our area of concern, but things have changed, Flynn. We're going to need to take a different approach now."

"I'm not leaving voluntarily, if that's what you're driving at."

She closed her eyes and he saw the tears well again, and realized to his astonishment that she was crying not for her lost men, but for him. She leaned toward him. "It's a trap," she whispered. "It's always been a trap and I've gotten you tangled up in it, too."

He added this to the long list of things about this case that he did not understand.

"They feel that you've gotten too deep. You can't be released."

He waited, but she said no more. "Well that's certainly damn mysterious."

"Security is very, very tight and for good reason, Flynn, as you will find. The thing is, there's no going back from this. It's marriage with no divorce allowed. You didn't get a chance to make a decision and that's not fair."

"I made my decision when I walked out on the Menard Police."

She turned to the window. But not for long. Very suddenly she turned back and said to him, "You're going to meet people different from any you've ever encountered."

"And you can't tell me one more thing."

"I want you to prepare yourself for the unexpected. I don't need you gaping like a hick and asking little boy questions."

"Do I do that?"

"When you're in there, you may. This is going to be the strangest experience you've ever had. Beyond imagination."

"I have to admit, I'm curious."

She said no more, and the flight continued uneventfully, a plane swimming in featureless darkness.

Once they'd landed and collected their weapons and equipment, Flynn found that they had a rental car waiting. She drove, and he noticed that she didn't use a GPS. She'd been here before. A lot.

He watched the gray sky and the gray of Lake Michigan, and wondered if there was any way to prepare to face a total unknown.

They'd been on Lake Shore Drive for some time before he understood from reading road signs that their destination was Evanston, just north of Chicago itself.

"I think you need to talk more, Diana. I'm a pro but I'm not a psychic. Narrate this a little bit."

"We'll be there in ten minutes."

"Excessive secrecy and compartmentalization just killed three men. And yet you keep it up."

"I have orders, I follow my orders."

"Following orders is good. But what that means is making them work. Your orders were to stop a dangerous criminal. You didn't make those orders work, so whatever it was you thought you were doing, it wasn't following them."

After a few turns in Evanston, she drove down a street lined with big old houses that looked like they were worth a lot . . . and Flynn became concerned. There were no official buildings around here.

They passed those houses and drove into a less grand neighborhood. Here, there were stark oaks lining the street, and the tall row houses were as dreary as the sky.

They pulled up in front of one of the houses. In the driveway there stood a Chrysler 300. Other than that, the place was silent, the windows dark.

"So where are we? Not your ancestral home, surely?"

"Police headquarters."

"Not a good answer."

He got out of the car when she did, and followed her up the front walk. The air was bitterly cold, tanged with the sharpness of chimney smoke, a gusty breeze coming off the lake.

When she pressed the doorbell button on the jamb, there issued from deep inside the house the faint bonging of an old-fashioned bell.

This was not a police headquarters of any kind, but there was certainly something unusual involved here, because as Flynn had stepped out of the car, he'd seen a flicker of movement from a window in the house across the street.

"Does it bother you that we're in gun sights?"

"You're very observant."

"Always been my problem."

She rang the bell again.

"What're they doing, sending our faces to Washington?"

She glance at him, frowning.

He continued, "There's a camera in the door. Another one between the bricks to the right. Whoever's in there has been able to watch us since we turned onto the block."

"I did not know that."

"Yet you've been here before."

"As I said, this is our headquarters."

He thought, "you look, but you don't see," but didn't comment further. No point. Noted, though, was the fact that her lack of practice as an observer was a liability that must never be overlooked.

The door swung open on a woman of perhaps thirty. She wore an orange jumpsuit and had a plastic net on her hair. Her skin gleamed and Flynn realized that her face was covered with a film like petroleum jelly. On her hands she wore latex gloves.

He was still trying to make sense of this when she

stepped back and let them in. She ushered them into a living room with an old couch, a coffee table, and a couple of easy chairs. A gas log burned in the fireplace.

"Sorry," she said, "we've been working on him."

"Anything?"

Whoever they were interrogating, her expression said it all: they were getting nowhere.

"Flynn, just try to be open. I can't tell you anything about what's going to happen because no explanation would do it justice. I can't even answer any questions, because any question you would have would be unanswerable."

"I know what it is."

"I don't believe that. Tell me what you think."

Flynn said nothing.

CHAPTER FOURTEEN

Two more of the jumpsuits lay folded on the couch. On the coffee table was a silver canister about a foot tall.

"We need to put these suits on over our clothes," Diana said. "And do this." She dipped her hand in the canister and scooped out clear gel. "Put this on your face and neck. Make sure you're well covered. Don't forget your ears."

"What is it?"

"Something that's necessary."

He wasn't objecting. He was here to learn. He slathered the stuff on himself.

"First, you're going to meet the person our agency has managing this case." She paused. "This is a unique person."

He pulled on the jumpsuit, which was supple and light and felt like paper. But it was a lot stronger than paper. Sort of like silk with a paper-like finish, he decided.

Diana slathered herself with the salve and put on an elastic cap of the silken material.

Flynn finished by putting on his own cap.

The woman reappeared. Flynn said, "Hi, we didn't get introduced. I'm Flynn Carroll, Menard City Police, Menard, Texas." He put out his gloved hand.

She looked down at it, then back up at him. Usually, people's faces told him something. Not this time.

"Follow her," Diana snapped.

Shuffling along in his baggy jumpsuit, his face covered with Vaseline that smelled like cinnamon, he followed the woman down the central corridor of the old house, past an umbrella stand and a photograph of a family from about fifty years ago.

"Whose house is this, anyway?"

"A sublet," Diana said. "We found it on Craigslist."

"*Craigslist?*"

"We move a lot."

The woman opened a big oak door at the end of the hall. He followed her into a large room that Flynn guessed must have once been a solarium. It was on the back of the house and full of tall windows, but as dark as a cave. The expansive windows were covered by curtains.

In the middle of the room there stood a man of significant height, six three at least. As they came in, he glared down at them out of eyes sunken so deep in his head that they were like craters. His hair was completely white.

"Sorry to be meeting under these tragic circumstances," he said. "And I apologize for the—" He gestured, indicating the costumes. "I'm allergic to everything." He sighed. "I can't even leave the house."

Slowly, then, he turned to Diana. Some kind of electricity passed between them, and Flynn thought that this was the person she had reported to from Montana. He also thought that they were more than coworkers.

"My name is Oltisis," he said, and at that moment he walked into a shaft of light, and Flynn saw that he had compound eyes, many-lensed like the eyes of a fly.

He sucked breath, but instantly controlled it. Let it out slow. As he did, the face turned toward him. Unhurried. The eyes seemed blank. But they also told Flynn that this was an alien. Okay, that explained all the secrecy.

"I don't surprise you?"

"You do."

"You're very contained, then."

"As are you."

"I'm a cop, Lieutenant Flynn." Oltisis crossed the room in two sleek strides. Flynn saw more than cop in the way he moved, he saw military. Lethal military. This alien might or might not be a cop, but he was certainly a professional killer.

As he sat on a broad leather couch that almost fit him, he gestured toward two wing chairs.

Flynn could hardly tear his own eyes away from that face. The lips were narrow and precise, the skin was as slick and featureless as plastic, and the deep-set eyes gleamed in the thin yellow light that filled the room.

No question, this was not a disguise. He was face to face with a real alien. But he also had a case to deal with. Men were dead. He said, "We need more people, and we need them now. We need help."

Oltisis looked toward Diana. "I put together a cleanup crew to go back to the Hoffman place. Air Police. They're totally out of the loop." His English was perfect. Not the slightest accent.

"Did they find any trace of Hoffman and the daughter?" Flynn asked.

"Doctor Hoffman was in a snowdrift two hundred yards from the house. Frozen to death. Looked exactly like he'd wandered away and gotten lost. Nice touch, he had a bag of garbage with him." He made a gravelly sound that Flynn realized was laughter, but it was bitter, that was very clear. In fact, it sounded like defeat.

"We need to break this case," Flynn said.

"Ah?"

"You look beaten. Sorry."

"And you don't, Flynn."

"Am I a fool, then?"

Oltisis met his eyes with his own glittering jewels. "No," he said carefully, "you are not. Flynn—may I call you Flynn—this is a new kind of police operation. We've got a criminal element operating here and we can't move freely among you. Thus the liaison effort."

"You could surely devise some sort of disguise."

"The allergic response is too deep. We'd need to create human bodies for ourselves."

"So do it. You must be loaded with high tech."

"If one of us is to acquire a human body, one of you has to die."

"I see."

"Criminals steal bodies." He lowered his head. "That's what happened to your wife."

Flynn went silent inside. For the first time, he knew that she was dead. Believed it. Images of her raced through his mind, too fast to track, but of her in her happiness. He swallowed his thrashing sorrow. "Did she suffer?"

Oltisis stared into Flynn's pain, his eyes as blank as a shark's. Flynn thought, "This alien has seen a lot of violence, a lot of death." He continued to question him. "How many other field units do you have? How many officers on your side of the fence?"

"We need more, I agree."

What the hell? Could this be true? "Don't tell me it's just the three of us."

Diana said, "If it gets out that this is happening and not even the aliens can put a stop to it—"

"Jesus Christ, you need a whole damn division on this! The FBI and Interpol, at the least!"

"This gets out, mankind panics and contact gets set back fifty years. No, Flynn, secrecy is essential."

Cops sure as hell couldn't keep secrets, that was true enough, and the public would sure as hell panic, no question there, either. "People need to be warned. Otherwise they have no chance."

"Help us get this cleaned up."

"My wife was kidnapped eight years ago! So how long is it going to take? There are hundreds of people dead. You're wired into the government, you just moved around a unit of Air Police, so put some resources on this or I'm going public." But even as he said it, he knew that it was hopeless. Nobody would believe him, not without this creature in tow, and that was obviously not going to happen.

"You signed a secrecy agreement, Flynn. Don't forget that."

"He's fine," Oltisis said. "He just figured it out."

"But he said—"

"You're on board, aren't you, Flynn? You've seen the problem."

Flynn nodded. Oltisis was so sharp, it was almost

like having your mind read. "I understand the need for secrecy. But there have to be more resources."

"Rebuild your team. I can do that."

"Bigger. And top people. Delta Force operators. CIA field officers. The best of the best. And better equipment. Jesus, you people must have some incredible equipment, not crap like that MindRay."

"That's one of ours."

"Is it a toy, because if that's the best you can do, I have a real problem with your technology."

Again, Oltisis laughed, and this time Flynn got it loud and clear, the cynical laughter of the cop who knows only one truth: every single piece of equipment he possesses is inferior to what the crooks have.

"What're you, fifty years ahead of us? I expected aliens to be, like, a million years ahead of us. But you've got powerful crooks and shitty equipment just like we do."

"Budgets are budgets, Flynn. And we're about a thousand years ahead of you, if you want to know. Among other things, we can manipulate gravity and you can't. But you will. We're helping you speed up your development, because there needs to be an alliance between our species. We're similar and that's rare and valuable. It strange out there and it's dangerous. We need a friend, and so do you."

Flynn said, "You use your connections to get us the best cops and the best operatives you can find, and I am with you."

Oltisis said, "We've been doing that."

"So you came up with a small-town police officer like me. I think I'm a good cop, but let's face it, my skill set is limited because my department's needs are limited. We don't train up supercops in Menard, Texas."

"You have an IQ of two twenty. Did you know that?"

"I did not."

"And you're also highly motivated. We are doing our job, Lieutenant."

"So let's get on with it."

"We have someone in custody."

He was stunned. Then he wasn't. "But he's not the perp we're looking for?"

"No," Diana interjected. "This is one of his customers. My unit got him." She paused for a long moment. "My old unit."

Oltisis said, "He was a thrill seeker. Among us, life is all too predictable. It's one of the major reasons we explore as we do. In any case, he came here, bought a human body and just basically went wild, indulging his every fantasy, and he doesn't have pretty fantasies."

"I thought aliens would be—well, different."

"There's greed and self-indulgence everywhere."

"And the crime committed?"

Oltisis looked steadily at Flynn. "He raped fifty-six of your women, killing forty of them in the process."

"Jesus."

"If he's sent home with the evidence we have, he's going to walk. We have a real problem on Earth gathering forensics to a level our courts accept. In our system, a case cannot be presented until guilt is certain. The only judicial issue is the sentence. We need a confession out of him, Flynn."

"Now, are you saying that this thing—being, excuse me—has *two* bodies, one human and one like you?"

"Let me explain a little further."

"That would help."

"Every living body contains an incredibly dense plasma that bears all its memories, even every detail of its physical form. It's the template, and it's effectively eternal. In our world, doctors can move this plasma from an aged body to a young one. It's also possible to cross species, but it's highly illegal. I could enter a human body. I could live among you. At home, I'm just another person. But here, with my knowledge and my power, I'd be a god."

"So what about death? Do you die?"

"If you wish."

"If you *wish*?"

"When a human dies, your soul will linger on Earth if you have unfinished business here. Eventually, a new body will come along—an infant—that fits it, and you'll enter the new body and return to life. With us, the process is no longer natural. I have a stem cell packet that can be grown into a new body." He gestured toward himself. "If this dies, I can simply move to a new version of myself."

"Will you?"

The face—horrible and strange and yet somehow deeply human—took on an eerie, concealing expression. "You can't have known this, but that's as rude a question as one of us can be asked."

"Rude? I don't get it. Why rude?"

"Let's move on, shall we? Body theft is a major crime, as you may imagine. And when it involves interfering with an alien species, especially a less advanced one like yours, it's actually our most serious crime."

"But the exterior identity—what we can track—that remains the same, am I right? So this guy has a human ID. A human past."

"The process works like this. A person is kidnapped. Then the heart is stopped and the whole body transformed into stem cells, which are grown on a new template. The new body fits the purchaser's soul, and he enters it. The new 'person' won't look the same as the one who was used to construct him. He won't have the same DNA signature, either."

"You can do all that?"

"At home, by law your new body would need to be an exact replica of your old one. But here, well, you don't have body switching yet. So no law and no local enforcement infrastructure. Which is why there's a ring operating, selling my species human bodies so they can live on Earth."

"That's a motive?"

"For marginal types like would-be criminals, it is. They're free here. The local authorities aren't going to catch them on their own, and our police force is hamstrung, obviously."

"So what can they do that's so special?"

"As I said, live like gods. The last one we caught busted the bank at a casino in Vegas, then used predictive techniques you won't discover for five generations to game your markets. Inside of a year, he was vastly rich." He paused. His voice dropped an octave. "This guy wasn't so interested in money, obviously."

"When they're finished, they can go home?"

"If they're ever finished. The one in custody would probably have stayed here for a very long time, maybe across the span of more than one life. You can help us with him, Flynn."

"And what do you want me to do?"

"If the body he's in now were to die here on Earth without access to his dealer, he'd be in trouble. No new body, so his soul would be left to wander until it got drawn into a human fetus. He'd lose his memory of himself entirely. Become, in effect, human. Trapped forever in a primitive species."

"Turn him over to our courts. Let us threaten him with the needle."

"He was careful not to commit any of his crimes in death penalty states."

"Drop him in a supermax."

"He'll escape. But he wouldn't want to be tried in Texas."

Flynn thought about that. Understood what Oltisis was driving at. "Okay," he said, "let me spend some time with him. What's his name?"

"Roger Ormond is what it says on his driver's license."

Diana said, "The identity's perfect. It's been built from deep within the system."

"Take me to Roger Ormond. We'll need to chat for a couple of minutes."

They left Oltisis to his dark office and whatever thoughts a creature like that must have, and have to live with.

"We can disrobe," the assistant said. "Roger isn't allergic."

"What're you going to do?" Diana asked as she pulled off her jumpsuit.

"What Oltisis asked me to do."

"He didn't ask you anything."

Flynn looked at her. "Oh, yeah, he did."

They descended into a cellar that smelled of dust and heating oil. There was an ancient black velvet painting of JFK against one wall, beside it a rusting bicycle. There was also an old portable record player, and in one corner a dust-covered electric wheelchair, its seat well worn. Whoever had lived in that thing was probably damn glad to leave this life.

Across the room, a man sat in a cage made not of bars, but of a sort of shadowy haze that, as Flynn went closer, proved to be a mesh of fine wires. He was under a flood of glaring white light. His eyes were closed, his skin was flushed red, and he was covered with a sheen of sweat.

Flynn went into action immediately. "Mr. Ormond, I'm your attorney. We're going to be getting you moving within the hour."

"Excuse me."

"You've been extradited to Texas."

The face, which had been open and questioning, shut down tight. So he was scared. Good.

"I didn't commit any crimes in Texas."

Flynn remained affable. "Tell them that. I'll stay with you as far as the airport, but after that you're on your own. You'll be assigned legal aid counsel at Huntsville."

"A prison?"

"Guarded by cops like us. Who know the truth. You won't escape. You're gonna die in Texas, Mr. Ormond."

He started to stand up. The cage around him glowed and sparked. He fell back into his seat. "I didn't commit any crimes in Texas!"

"So, Michigan, Illinois, New York."

"I avoided death penalty states."

Bingo. There was the confession. He revealed nothing of the small triumph that he felt. "Well, take it up with your lawyer there. You're moving in an hour."

As he left, the man in the cage erupted, screaming and thrashing. The cage sparked and sizzled.

Oltisis was waiting, his face filling the screen of an iPad.

"Will that do it in your legal system?"

"Oh yes, he's confessed. We'll start processing him off planet immediately. He'll take the full hit."

"Which is?"

Oltisis broke the connection.

Diana said, "They take them out of the body and put them in a sort of trap, is the way I understand it. They don't like to talk about it."

"A trap?"

"It's prison. In this one's case, permanent prison. They'll never let him out."

Flynn thought about that. This plasma they were talking about was the soul. "Soul prison. That's the worst thing I've ever heard of. To be dead, but still in jail."

"I think their name for it says it all. They call their permanent prison 'Dead Forever.'"

They left then, and Flynn could not remember ever feeling so happy to leave a place in his life. The world of Oltisis might be full of wonders, but it also sounded like a kind of hell. No mystery of life. No mystery of death. Imprisonment that could last for eternity. "What do you think of them, Diana?"

She was silent. "Let's do our job, okay. Better to just put the whole thing out of your mind. Concentrate on the work."

They got into the car. "I'll tell you what I think."

"No! I don't want to hear it."

"They've made themselves into monsters."

She started the car and pulled away from the curb.

"Where are we going?"

"I got us a hotel. We'll want to get cleaned up."

"Then what?"

"Once they break it to Ormond that he's been nailed,

they're expecting to get some more information for us about the perp. He'll want to bargain, it'll be his last hope. So we'll get a call from Oltisis. There'll be a second meet."

"That's good and bad. We need the information."

"But you don't want to go back there?"

"Nope."

"Neither do I, Flynn. Neither do I."

CHAPTER FIFTEEN

She'd gotten them a room at a hotel in the loop. They were traveling as man and wife, James and Diana Exeter. Flynn came out of the five minutes he'd actually allowed himself to wash off the oil and the itching that had come from being near the alien. He'd put on some fresh clothes in the bathroom. They were coworkers, not lovers.

He lay back on one of the beds, looking at the new identity pack he'd been given as they left the HQ. "This is well done."

"We're piggybacking on the Witness Protection Program."

He gazed up at her long neck, her full lips, her sad, dark eyes.

"Don't assume they're from another planet," she said. "Don't assume anything about them at all."

"Where would they be from, then?"

She was silent for a long time.

"Hello?"

"Yeah, well, it's damn mysterious, all of it."

"How much does the government know? What about UFOs? Is any of that real? And alien abductions—I mean, the kind where the people get brought back? There's websites, books, claims of millions of abductions."

"We just don't know."

At that moment, he saw something on the ceiling. A light. It moved down the wall . . . toward Diana.

It trembled red on her forehead.

Leaping up, he threw her to the floor. As she screamed, recoiling from what she obviously assumed was an outburst of rage, he hauled the curtains closed. "We're leaving."

"What? Why?"

"You just got painted with a laser."

She started to stuff her backpack.

"No time for that. We're outa here." He confirmed that the hallway was empty, and left the room. After a moment, she was with him.

"Hey," she said as he passed the elevator bank. When he didn't respond, she kept on behind him.

He entered the stairwell and started up.

She stood watching him.

He pointed downward. "Death." He pointed upward. "Life. You choose."

Seconds counted now, so he took the stairs three at a time. After a brief pause, he heard her behind him once again.

He pushed his way onto the roof through a stiffly hinged door, then stepped behind its enclosure, keeping close to the wall as he did so.

"As much as possible, keep something between you and the view. If you have to expose yourself, stay be-

low the level of the parapet. One flicker of infrared
return from up here, and our evening is over."

Somewhere there was going to be access to the elevator bank, there had to be. He could see the elevator's
roof structure, but no outline of a door.

By moving directly toward the back of the building
he could keep the door enclosure between himself and
the view, and still get a look at the hidden wall of the
elevator bank's roof structure.

Crouching, he ran to it—and soon found the opening he needed. He turned to motion to her to follow.

Once again, there was a laser on her. "Drop!"

She stared. He pulled her down. "I need somebody
with field skills!" For an instant, the laser touched the
wall of the building behind the hotel, and then was gone.

"Sorry!"

"Always do what I tell you. Always!"

"Okay!"

He got the hatch open. "We're going to wait for an
elevator to come up, then ride it down. They're on their
way to the roof but they won't find us here, so it'll be a
near thing."

"I screw everything up!"

"Everybody screws everything up. It's the nature of
cop work."

An elevator came up, stopped three floors down,
then continued its cycle. "That'll be them," he said.
"When the car stops, get on it."

"Jesus!"

"Don't look down."

With a loud click from above, the car halted. Flynn
hopped on. Leaping carefully, Diana followed him.

"Now we're going to wait until it passes below

fourteen, then drop down into the cab. When we're there, don't touch any buttons."

From this side, the roof hatch was easy to pull up, and they were soon inside the car. He didn't bother to try to replace the hatch. Their pursuers would know what they'd done. Probably already did. This wasn't about deceiving them, it was about getting just far enough ahead of them to escape.

She leaned against the wall of the descending car. "Thank God."

"If we don't encounter them in the lobby, we need to grab a cab to the nearest El station. We've put them maybe three minutes behind us. If we're lucky."

"And if we're not?"

"We'll need to try another casino."

"Who are they? How did they find us?"

"It's the perp. He undoubtedly followed his client when he was captured. He's probably been watching that house for a while, waiting to see who was going to turn up."

"We have to warn them."

"If we live."

The doors opened onto the ornate lobby.

He could see a second car just passing twelve, on its way down. "Here they come," he said. He wished that he could get a look at them, but there were too many ways to lose control of that situation. He drew her toward the main doors.

He'd tracked people across the plains of north Texas, he'd chased them through the streets and alleys of Menard, and he was reasonable at both things. He could not recall a time, though, when he'd been the runner. The truth was, he had to fall back on spy novel stuff, and he didn't like spy novels. Hadn't read one in years.

"Okay, quick—" He grabbed her wrist and jumped into a taxi. "Water Tower Place," he told the driver. It was the only name that came to mind. He had no idea what it was or where it was. Just something he happened to remember.

"Why Water Tower Place?" she asked.

"Why not?"

"You don't even know what it is, do you?"

"I do not."

"You don't know Chicago at all, then?"

"I don't."

"Water Tower Place is a shopping center in the Loop. That's downtown."

Flynn fell silent. The perp had gone after them first because they were sure to go to ground as soon as Oltisis was taken out. "We need to get to a pay phone."

The mall was enormous and filled with shops. It took a surprising amount of time, but they finally found a public phone.

She made a call and told whoever answered what had happened.

"Let me talk."

She handed him the phone. "You're in immediate danger. You need to get out of there right now."

Oltisis said, "I can't move that quickly. Something has to be prepared, and transport is complex."

"You don't have a fallback prepared?"

There was a pause. "I do not."

"I'd get out of there even if you have to be carried in a bag. There's an immediate threat."

"I'll do my best. I assume we won't be seeing you tonight."

"Have you questioned your suspect?"

"I've just begun. I know that your perpetrator has

human helpers. Ormond's never seen him in person, so he says."

"And you're inclined to believe him?"

"He's ready to open up."

"Get out of there and take him with you. For God's sake don't lose him." Flynn hung up the phone. "Meeting's off, obviously." He looked out along a long, empty corridor. The mall wasn't closed but it was almost empty, and most of the stores were dark.

"We need to hunt up ATMs. We need all the cash we can get. And I assume you have a cell phone?"

"I do."

"Throw it away. First, take out the battery."

They ran the ATM cards until they each had around six thousand dollars in cash.

"Do they ever run out?"

"I don't know. Not soon."

"Too bad this is our last chance to use them."

"*Why?*"

"The cards will be made."

"Bank databases are well secured."

"No they aren't."

It was now pushing eleven P.M., so there was no point in going to an airport. Like it or not—and he didn't like it at all—they'd have to stay in Chicago overnight.

Outside the building, they found long rows of cabs, and more of them at the entrance to the Ritz Carlton that soared above Water Tower Place. Flynn hailed one, and they got in.

"Days Inn," Flynn said.

"Uh, Lincoln Park?"

"That's the one."

"I'll get a reservation ahead," Diana said.

"No cell phones."

"They won't see me."

"How do you know?"

"I'm a hacker. It's what I do."

"A hacker? You have some useful skills, then."

"I like to think so."

As the cab negotiated the sparse traffic, Flynn watched behind them, using what he could see of the rearview mirror. He thought he was dealing with a team of about four individuals with some very good equipment. They had a long-range rifle scope with a state-of-the-art laser sight. The way they had followed their targets, the rifle had to be on a chopper, which had been hovering out over Lake Michigan. Not great marksmanship, though. A good sniper would not have missed.

They also had that animal. Would they be able to make use of it in a city? He didn't see how. They hadn't tried yet, at least.

The Days Inn was in an older building in a neighborhood that was active even at twelve thirty at night. Which was fine. Activity was good.

The cab pulled up and stopped. Diana started to get out, but a gesture from Flynn stopped her. She didn't speak, she didn't turn to him. Good, she was getting the hang of it.

After he'd finished evaluating their surroundings, he said, "Let's go."

They exited into a driving wind. The air had grown noticeably colder. The storm that had paralyzed Montana was getting closer fast.

At the motel, Flynn paid cash. The clerk took the money and directed them to their room. He'd been doing this too long to bother to ask for ID and listen to the bullshit.

The room was stark but clean. Flynn was tired, too. Not a good time for it, though.

The bed was a double, too narrow to avoid the touch of bodies. Silently, she threw off her clothes. She kept nothing on. Her skin shimmered, her curves swept elegantly about as she moved. Steve Glass had been a lucky man.

They lay side by side, as still as two scared birds.

When he closed his eyes, he saw Oltisis, the thin face and deep, dead eyes.

Lights from outside glowed on the ceiling. The distant rumble of a great metropolis in its uneasy sleep lulled them.

Flynn slipped into one of those sleeps that comes so stealthily that they seem more like a state of altered awakening. Diana refocused as Abby, and the dreary hotel room became their old bedroom. The curtains swayed in the summer breeze, the leaves whispered, and Flynn became aware that they were not alone. He thought, oddly, that it was all right that the man was there, that he was slipping his arms under Abby's legs and shoulders, that he was lifting her like a leaf.

He saw the man's face in the moonlight, the intent eyes, the lips slightly parted, the chin a little pointed and yet a little heavy.

And then Abby sighed, and he turned to her but she was gone, and the breeze swept through the room, and a new kind of silence came with it.

He leaped out of the bed.

"What's the matter?"

"Abby!" He ran toward the window. "No!"

She shook his shoulder. And he was back in the bed in the motel room. He hadn't jumped up at all.

"It's a dream I've had before. I see the guy take her."

"Did you?"

"Probably not. We did an Identi-Kit years ago. Posted the Wanted all over Texas. Nothing."

They held each other in the dark ocean of the night, in the unknown. Eventually, they slept again, each clutching the other as a lifeline. Flynn woke before dawn and checked the hotel corridor. Empty and silent. He watched the street for a time, standing back from the window. An old woman in a black coat walked a Collie mix. A bus passed.

He looked back at Diana sprawled on the bed. Circumstances had thrown the two of them together, but he still belonged to Abby. He'd always belong to Abby. For the first time, he found himself imagining her death. Had she known what was happening? And what *did* happen? Was it slow, fast, painful? He should have asked Oltisis. Or maybe not. No, best not.

Finally he sat in the room's threadbare easy chair and turned on CNN, and watched the crawl on silent. A tanker had gone aground in the Azores. A movie star had gone berserk. Ford had a new computer system in its cars.

And *what the hell had just happened*? He was working with a cop from another damn planet, holy God. Secret as hell and the stakes were high. If the criminal elements could be stopped, there would be open contact. Open. Everybody would know. The world would change, and look at that Oltisis, look at the way he was. That had to be the strangest and most wonderful person he'd ever met, and the most sinister. They'd defeated death. What did that mean? Conscious plasmas—is that what we were?

Wonderful. The secret of the ages, and maybe the whole world was going to find out. Maybe we were going to defeat death.

Except for one problem. Small problem. It was that this whole damn thing was going south. Way south. And the worst part of it was, he had no clear idea of a next move. More than anything that had happened so far, that disturbed him.

He closed his eyes, but sleep didn't come, not really. At best, it was the uneasy sleep of the soldier who can see the flicker of artillery on the horizon. Or it was the sleep of the condemned, the mind searching for last dreams that did not come.

In its gradual, stately way, the light changed, dawn rolling in from the east. Diana snored softly. The minutes passed, one by one.

So he was a big genius. Wonderful, he was so glad. Too bad that he had run out of ideas.

CHAPTER SIXTEEN

The glow from the signs outside finally faded into the uniform ray light of a cloud-choked sunrise. When Flynn parted the curtain again, he saw flecks of snow tumbling past.

It was six twenty, meaning that they'd been here for over five hours. They would have to go soon, but she was still sleeping. Her fists were clenched, the blanket pulled tightly around her neck.

When he'd first met Diana, she'd seemed out of her depth and too arrogant to know it, but now she looked small and tragic, lying on the bed all clutched into herself.

"I'm not asleep," she said. She opened her eyes. "Did you sleep?"

"Some. Not a lot."

"Same here. Not a lot."

She got out of bed, indifferent to her nakedness. He was not indifferent to it. She crossed into the bathroom, lithe and perfect, a dancer.

The shower came on. He listened to it, but as he

watched her shadow behind the curtain, he thought of Abby in the shower. She'd liked to sing, Abby. Her voice was a peal of bells.

The shower curtain flew back and Diana came out. "Yours," she said.

When he undressed, she took no notice.

He showered in silence. He was mapping out an exit strategy from Chicago. Keep it simple, make it quick. But where to go?

"I need a laptop," she told him as he dressed.

"We can do that at a Best Buy or a Staples."

"That's numero uno. We also need disposable cell phones. Every time we use one, we need to bust it up and toss the remains. No more than twenty-second calls, and only if absolutely, absolutely necessary. NRO can pull down a cell call in about thirty seconds from anywhere in the world, and we need to assume that our guys are even better."

"Okay, here's my part of this. First, if our friend doesn't get out of that house fast, he's done. If it hasn't already happened. The perp is ahead of him and way ahead of us, and the frank truth is, survival is the issue. So I've been thinking about transportation. What's the safest way to run like hell? Planes are out. No way through security without showing some kind of ID. The train is better. They take cash and we can hide out in a compartment. But a compartment is also a trap, so that's out. Obviously buses are too vulnerable. My bottom line: we buy a car off a lot for cash. There'll be no record of the transaction until the title hits the state department of transportation. So we've got about two days to go as far as we can."

"Then the car becomes identifiable."

"If we're still in Illinois it does. But that's not where

we're gonna be, not unless the trail of that tiger leads here, which I very much doubt."

"The trail of the tiger?"

"I think it's our best shot. That animal has records. Where we're gonna go is where it was last in the hands of its real owners. That's our starting point."

"Let me ask you this. What if we absolutely, completely and totally cannot find the tiger? What then?"

"We go to Plan B."

"Which is?"

"I have no idea."

"Jesus."

"Ninety percent of detective work is having no idea, eight percent is being wrong, two percent is luck. You enter a crime scene, there's a dead guy. His wife, the usual suspect, is alibied and clueless. It feels like there's no next step. But you find one. You take it. Usually small, and usually a dead end. So you feel your way along until you locate another step, if there is one, which usually there is not. That's it. That's being a detective."

"But you solve your crimes?"

"We have a good closing rate in Menard. Better than a lot of places. Mostly you solve the crime because the perp is a moron, which is why this case is such a problem. Our guy is not only better equipped than we are, he's smarter."

Dressed, they went downstairs. In the elevator he said, "We walk in opposite directions on Diversey. You go north, I go south. Get on the first bus you see. I'll get on it, too, next stop. Do not sit together. We both get off at the El."

The doors opened, they entered the compact lobby and checked out. She left while he looked at leaflets. Then he left. He made no effort to case the street. If they were made, there was no point. Escape would not be possible, not a second time.

As he walked, he looked for a bus stop, found one, then waited. In a few minutes a bus pulled up. It was packed, which was all to the good. When he got on, for a moment he didn't see her. Then he did, standing toward the back, deep in the crowd. He grabbed a bar and stayed in the front. They traveled four stops to the El, then he got off, along with most of the other passengers.

He saw her again on the El platform. They didn't acknowledge each other. When the El came, they both entered the same car. Three other people did, too, a man in a gray overcoat with a fur cap on his head, a woman with a blanket-covered stroller, and a girl being led by a Seeing Eye dog. Ordinary people or hit squad?

Farther down in the car, Diana sat reading a paper. That was a nice touch, he hadn't thought of that.

Looking up at the route map, he decided to get off in Skokie. No idea why. It was just a random name. No plan was the best plan.

Stops came and went. All of the people who'd gotten on with them were now off, which was good. Hopeful. Unless they'd been cycled out, of course. Who knew what level of resources they were dealing with? Did the perp have ten confederates or fifty? No way to know.

When the train stopped in Skokie, he got off. She followed. Downstairs, there was a coffee shop. He took a seat at the counter. In a situation like this, it was always a mistake not to eat, so he ordered eggs, toast, and sausage. At the far end of the counter, she ate, too.

She'd probably seen the same dealership from the

windows of the train that he had, but he left first anyway. If there was another one he hadn't spotted, he didn't want to take the chance that she'd go there instead.

It was a twenty-minute walk, and he didn't like the way it exposed them. Nothing to do about it, though.

As he pushed his way into the warm dealership showroom full of gleaming Chryslers, the only salesman in the place appeared, an Indian man with tired eyes and a cranked-up smile.

"I'm looking for something I can drive off."

The salesman sized him up. "Well, let me show you your car," he said. The plaster smile didn't change. The tiredness in the eyes maybe got a little deeper. This man was far from home with a blizzard on the way, and Flynn could see his wife and kids around him, needy ghosts. Most of the world was like this man, keeping on because what else were you going to do? Flynn knew that there would be no savior for Mr. Asnadi.

Mr. Asnadi tried to get him to look at some recent models.

"I got a budget, man. Two grand."

"We can do that. There's a Dynasty—"

"You can do better. What about that Shelby over there?"

There was a Mitsubishi V-6 in the Dodge Shelby, and it was turbocharged. A fast car if you needed it and he would need it, that he knew.

"This is a fine car. We've certified it, you can see. But there's not much wiggle room."

The sticker said three thousand one hundred dollars. There was wiggle room. The way the tires were sitting told Flynn that there was massive amounts of it. The car hadn't rolled in at least six months, and you weren't even going to get a kid to buy an old gray Shelby.

"I'll give you two grand cash now. That's my only offer."

"For two grand, we have this Avenger—"

"The Shelby. Two grand. Or I walk right now."

He sighed. "I have to clear it with my manager."

"No you don't. You're the only guy here. You want to try sitting in a back room drinking coffee while I stew, then come out and bullshit me more? Ain't gonna happen."

"Let's do the paperwork."

Twenty minutes later, Flynn and Diana were driving away. "Beautiful," she said, looking at the cracked dash.

"It's fast and we might need that. Plus front-wheel drive and reasonable tires. It's worth about eight hundred bucks, but I paid two grand to do the deal quickly."

His instinct was to travel, but they went back into the Loop and spent an hour dipping more ATMs. Under no circumstances could they use plastic once they were outside of Chicago.

When they had sixteen grand between them, they headed out Eighty toward Fifty-Five. He wanted to get far away from here as fast as possible, and also out from under the storm, which was fast approaching.

In Joliet, they found a Best Buy. They picked up laptops. She also purchased a hardware firewall. "We leave the wireless connections turned off. When we take these online, it can only be with a wired Ethernet with the firewall between us and the connection." They got a GPS. "We use it only if necessary."

"It doesn't emit a signal," he said.

"Everything emits a signal. Our signals detection units routinely reproduce the images on GPS instruments being used by the Taliban. It's one of the ways we aim our drones."

"I'm an old-fashioned cop, don't forget that. Gumshoeing around asking people questions. So don't let this electronic crap trip me up."

"That's why I'm telling you."

At a 7-Eleven, they got disposable cell phones.

Back in the car, she explained, "Any time we use any phone, the computers or the GPS, anything that connects us to the world electronically, we immediately move on. So don't, like, decide to surf the net before bed or whatever."

"Good enough." When it came to computers and computer security, she was, thank God, clearly in control. "Now I have a question for you. It's time to open up. We're past the bullshit. I know the big secret. So now I want to know if there are any support personnel anywhere who could help us."

"I don't think there's a single soul."

"What about the stakeout team across the street?"

"Garden-variety FBI surveillance unit. Don't know a thing."

"Not very good, either, given that they let a hostile tail pick us up. What about your NSA supervisor? You're not in the office. He must be aware of that."

"Neither are you, and what does Captain Parker know?"

"Point taken." He drove on southward under the deepening sky. Snow blew across the road in writhing ribbons. The car's heater screamed. As he drove, he watched both the sky and the road behind them. The cloud cover looked to be at about two thousand feet, so any chopper that might be shadowing them would stay in the cloud. The road was a different story, the road he could see.

In an excess of caution, he pulled the car off suddenly, tires screaming.

"What's happening?"

He said nothing. Ahead was a crossroad anchored by an Exxon Station, a Jack in the Box, and a Holiday Inn Express.

He pulled into the gas station.

"How about a warning once in a while? You scared the hell out of me."

"We don't need gas. I'm watching our back."

For eleven minutes, nothing else came in off the interstate. Then an eighteen-wheeler appeared, air brakes hissing, and headed for the truck pumps.

"Okay, I think we're clean and we're in an isolated area. Now what we need to do is this. First, we're gonna go online, both of us, and see if we can find any report anywhere of a lost or stolen Siberian tiger. At the same time that we do that, we're gonna put these people in front of us where we can see them."

"Put them in front of us?"

"We're going online flying flags. Wifi. No firewall. Looking for a Siberian tiger."

"They'll find us."

"What they'll find is the motel. We'll be backed off, watching. But first there's another couple of chores."

"Which are?"

"You're going to learn some new driving techniques. A few moves, as much as I can get across in an hour.

And you are damn well going to become proficient with that little popgun you've got."

"I don't like guns. But I'll use it if I have to."

"You will fall in love with it. Worship it. Because right now, Diana, our guns are our gods."

CHAPTER SEVENTEEN

He'd taken them down a long country road and pulled off in a tree-choked dip just beyond a small bridge. "Let me explain this vehicle."

"I'm a good driver."

"This is a front-wheel-drive vehicle. Better for winter, but you're not going to be able to do certain maneuvers. Normally, rear-wheel drive is the way to go, but this has an advantage in bad weather. It's fast, but it also has a lightweight steering pump. This means that the fluid is going to foam if we do tight turns at high speed. Expect the steering to become extremely heavy. Also, rubber brake lines. They could expand and so you need to assume that you could lose your brakes, too."

"So it'll be unsteerable and it won't stop. You'd better drive."

"If I'm incapacitated, you'll have to. Or if I'm done."

"What do you mean 'done'?"

"You got a sixty-six percent casualty rate going so far, Diana."

"I'm sorry. I'm just—" She shook her head.

He changed seats with her, then taught her a few basics, such as how to find the apex of a turn and when to start accelerating out of one, and how to execute a reasonable 180.

On a quiet country road she was barely passable. Under pressure, she was going to forget everything. He didn't even mention the bootlegger's turn. If she needed to execute a maneuver like that, she was already caught, so what was the point?

He gave up on driving and went to handgun skills. They walked a short distance into a frozen field. "You ever fired your pistol? At all?"

"Yes. No. Once. One session."

"The most important thing in pistol shooting is understanding just how inaccurate your weapon is. People are accurate with pistols from distance only in the movies."

"How close do you need to be?"

"With the weapons we're using, a few yards is the outside."

"That's *all*?"

"Targets will be in motion and so will we. You need to get in as close as you can, is the bottom line. A couple of feet, or even a contact shot, is best."

"I did my shooting on a range. There was a trainer."

"The range is a dream world. If you're shooting, your mind is going to be too focused on the act to remember much of anything else. That's what practice is about. When you're under pressure, you'll go on automatic pilot, not lose your head."

"What's the most important thing I need to know, then?"

"Avoid lifting the barrel as you pull the trigger. But

you won't, not entirely, so you need to aim for the largest part of your target that's worth hitting. This is the chest just below the neck. The advantage of this shot is that it does anatomical damage that affects the arms. With a heart shot, your opponent can get off one, maybe two trigger pulls before he's done. Not with this one."

"What about the head? Just shoot him in the head."

"You're going to miss, and once you have missed, you are going to manage the weapon badly. That's what happened to Mike."

"He was highly trained."

"So am I. That's why I know what happened to him."

He kept her shooting until she appeared to be comfortable with her PPK. "Who issued this gun to you?"

"I bought it at Wal Mart."

"It's an okay choice. Just remember exactly how many bullets you have. Count as you shoot. Know, always, whether or not you've got one in the firing chamber. This is absolutely critical, because it is going to take you more than a second to fire if you don't. In an exchange of gunfire, close range, that extra half second is a lifetime—yours."

She looked like she wanted to cry. As they returned to the nameless little cluster of franchises and gas stations, sunset was a dull red streak on the western horizon. Ahead, the black outline of the motel was now dotted with fitful lights. Flynn felt a familiar sadness rolling over him, the great, tragic surge of the human sea, and now, also, the greater sea of intelligent life of which mankind was only a part.

They got takeout at the Jack in the Box, then checked in to the Holiday Inn Express.

He tossed his backpack on the bed, then put the Best

Buy bag down more carefully and pulled the computers out. He ate a chicken sandwich while he checked out one of the laptops.

"It works," he said. He followed the instructions on the desk and was soon online with it. "I've got webcams in my house. I'll just go on my website and click through them all. Then I'm going to surf YouTube looking for video of Siberian tigers."

"If they know what they're doing, you'll get noticed for certain."

"Let's hope."

"I don't quite get this. We're giving ourselves away."

"We want them to come to us in a place of our choosing. We'll be standing off, watching from a distance. When they show up and don't find us, they'll leave. Then we'll be where we need to be—behind them. We'll start calling some shots."

Once online, he stared into his own living room, dark and still. For him, home was the center of his heart, and his loneliness. He did their bedroom, then the kitchen. Finally, steeling himself, he moved to the Abby Room—and just sat there staring, for the moment too astonished to talk. When he found his voice again, he said, "The Abby Room's been torn apart."

She came beside him and looked at the image. "My God."

The walls had great gouges ripped in them, the furniture had been broken apart, the couch torn to pieces, all the photographs scattered. He felt kind of sick, looking at the violence of it.

"Can you rewind?"

He hit the reverse button, and the image began to flicker back. "I've got it set on thirty-second intervals, so it's choppy. It goes back forty-eight hours."

Twenty-one hours ago, there were blurred frames indicating movement. He clicked forward.

In the center of the room, there was a figure. The body was blurred almost to invisibility, but you could see that it was a man.

"It's posed, you know. On purpose. You're intended to see this."

The man ripped down maps, tore up pictures. His fury was extraordinary.

He killed his browser. He couldn't bear to see more. "That's the perp," he said. He tried to fight down the sick horror, but he could not. He choked back his emotions. "Goddamnit. Sorry."

"Everybody in this cries."

"Okay, fine. Siberian tigers. They can't be imported, so the ones presently in the country are the only ones available." He reopened his browser, being careful not to bring up his home security system again. "There is no national database of stolen property. The individual police departments each keep their own records."

"So what do we do?"

"Look for break-ins at zoos and animal shelters that house these animals. The fact of the break-in will be recorded in the National Crime Information Center Database. Although, I don't have a password."

"Not a problem." Her fingers flew. "We have a master access program. It can basically break into any password protected system there is. One with as many different passwords as this one has is gonna be a piece of cake."

He saw numbers flickering across the database's access point. "Okay—one, two, three—"

The entry was allowed.

"That's impressive."

"Give me something hard. The Federal Reserve's master password. Want a billion dollars? I could wire it into your account within fifteen minutes."

"That might be a tad difficult to explain." As much grief as was in her own heart, he was grateful that she was trying to lighten his mood.

She worked through the data. "Here's an animal shelter in Austin, Texas, that was broken into last month. It's reported as a case of vandalism. Chimpanzees were shot. You gotta ask why people do crap like that. And another one. Santa Barbara, California. A lion was killed with a high-powered rifle."

"Nope, if we're on the right track at all, it's gonna be Austin."

"You're sure?"

"They have one of the worst burglary clearance records in the country. A criminal this smart is going to factor that in."

"They logged the chimps as animal cruelty. There are pictures. Ugly. So nothing stolen."

"Maybe and maybe not. Let me take a look." He read aloud, "'Fencing was breached in a large holding area that contained a Siberian tiger called Snow Mountain.'"

"It doesn't say the tiger is missing."

"Say you're a cop. You investigate a break-in at an animal preserve. Of all the animals that are left unharmed, you mention only one in your report. Why?"

"I don't know."

"Neither do I. But I do know that Texas is full of wealthy ranchers who love to stock their places with exotic wildlife. Texas being Texas, maybe you know that the tiger has been illegally taken by such a rancher or sold to one, and you know exactly who did all this—took the tiger and vandalized the facility as a cover—and because of who it is, you have no desire to pursue this individual."

"Is it worth a trip, then?"

"You follow the leads you have."

"I thought we were going to wait here. Try to induce a confrontation. I mean, by now they almost certainly know where we are. I mean, if they have the skill to watch for relevant searches."

"I didn't expect such a good lead. I think we need to run after it."

They were close enough to St. Louis to reach the airport in a couple of hours.

They didn't check out. Why leave behind any more information than you had to? What was the hotel going to do, send a bill?

They were south of the storm now, and the winter sky was vivid with stars. Cars passed now and again, not many though. People were getting their dinner, life was winding down for the night.

He watched the road behind them, but one set of headlights looks much like another, and distances are hard to gauge at night.

"What do you think will happen in Austin?" Diana asked.

"What will happen in Austin is the unexpected."

"If the tiger is gone?"

"Then we're close. The case starts giving up some gold."

"Will they catch us this time?"

He thought about that. "If they don't, it'll be a miracle."

CHAPTER EIGHTEEN

Using one of the throwaway cell phones, Diana had made some calls to airlines and determined that the next flight to Austin wasn't until five forty-five in the morning, so Flynn pulled into a Homewood Suites he happened to see near the St. Louis airport.

Once again, they checked in with cash. There was a stack of *USA Today*s on the counter, and he took one. He planned to look at the weather forecast. Big weather had a tendency to loop down over the country's midsection. If they were going to run into the storm again in Texas, he wanted to know that.

He went into the bedroom, tossed the paper on the bed, and turned on the TV. "Will it bother you?"

"I'm not sleepy."

He could feel a more intense electricity between them. She wanted to take another step, he could feel that. He said, "Outside of Menard, there's an area called the Staked Plain. When I was a boy, I used to ride there, and in the summer of my twelfth year a girl rode with me. Abby." He did not add that they had danced together naked in the grass.

"I'm here," Diana said.

His body went to her and his lips kissed hers, and then his heart kissed her. She was small in his grasp, surprisingly so for someone who occupied so much space in his life. They took their pleasure together then, two people who were tired and confused and afraid, but for this moment were able to find something like shelter in one another.

Then it was over, a memory flying back into the past. They lay side by side in silence. Flynn felt gratitude. He wanted to thank her, but that seemed like another form of rejection. Abby haunted him.

Diana slipped quickly away into sleep. She was soon snoring softly. Flynn envied her the ability she had to drop off like that. For him, night was a prison. He dreaded the feeling of vulnerability that sleep brought. Since the incident, his doctor had explained to him that he was suffering from something called guarded sleep, which means that at some level, you're always awake.

He turned on the TV. For a while, he surfed, watching the Weather Channel, then CNN, then a Judge Judy rerun. Hitler strutted on the Military Channel. On Nick at Night, crazed cartoon figures cavorted.

His nakedness began to make him feel exposed and he put his clothes back on. Cradling his gun, he returned to the living room of the small suite.

For a time, he meditated. His gun lay in front of him, so he also closed his eyes. A few minutes vacation from it would be okay.

Abby whispered his name.

He gave up meditating and went into the bedroom

and got the paper, which was lying on the floor beside the bed.

Back in the living room, he turned the pages, looking for the national weather. As he flipped through it, his eyes rested for a moment on the word "tiger."

He read the brief story, then stopped, too shocked for a moment to move.

He went into the bedroom, shook Diana and said, "Forget Texas, we're going to Vegas."

Diana stirred but didn't wake up.

"Look at this," he said, holding the paper out, then rattling it.

She moaned.

"Wake up, Diana, this is important."

She sighed, stretched, then started to turn over and go back to sleep.

"No, you need to see this."

"What?"

"A tiger is on the loose in a casino in Las Vegas."

For a moment she was absolutely still. Then she sat up. She grabbed the paper and read. "A coincidence?"

"This was yesterday. They'd lost us. My guess is that this is bait."

"It doesn't say anything about it being a Siberian."

"It's not a coincidence."

"If you say so."

"We need to catch the first flight out."

"Flynn, I can understand investigating the place that lost the tiger. But the casino makes no sense. If it's a coincidence, we're wasting our time. If it's not, they'll be waiting for us."

"I see a break in the case. Among other things, casinos are loaded with cameras. Think if we got the perp identified. Think of that."

"It's a trap, Flynn."

"Of course it is, that's the whole point. But we know that. We understand."

They left the hotel and went on to Lambert, driving through the post-midnight world, past glowing fast-food restaurants and dark, silent strip malls.

"Once I watched a rat get cheese out of a trap," he said.

"That's impossible."

"If you're a smart rat it's not. What he did was push the trap along the floor with his nose until it sprung. Then he ate the cheese. We need to approach this the same way, exploiting the unexpected vulnerability."

"What is it?"

"It's unexpected, so I don't know. Yet."

The earliest Vegas flight left just after six, so they spent a few more hours in the next hotel, letting the night wear slowly into predawn. There was no trouble with tickets, and the plane wasn't crowded.

After taking off, it turned into the dark western sky. Flynn looked at Diana beside him. Was she capable? No.

Better question: was he?

Same answer.

CHAPTER NINETEEN

They pulled around the gigantic lion that guards the MGM Grand's porte cochere and got into the valet parking line. Nobody cared, of course, not about a couple of dismal little tourists in a rented Camry. Which was good. A noticeable detective is a bad detective.

He hadn't walked into this building in five years. As he approached the gleaming doors, the old itch came back. He fought it off. You don't start, that's how you control an addiction.

"What do we do now?"

"Find the tiger."

"If it's still here."

"It's gonna be a major production for them to get it out of the building. Security is all over the place, not to mention the press. This place is loaded with cameras, believe me. If security hasn't spotted the tiger being taken out, then odds are that it's still here."

"He could've used the helicopter to take it off the roof."

He thought about that. Then he said, "Possibly, but

he still has to get it up there. Somewhere, some camera will have seen that."

This was the Grand, where the Skylofts had private butlers. How much would it take to convince his butler to help him get the tiger out? A couple hundred bucks would probably do it. Still, could a butler control the cameras?

They passed the huge golden lion in the lobby, heading for Skyloft check-in. They'd booked one, too, top floor.

He could hear the casino and smell the casino. From here, he couldn't see the blackjack tables, but he could imagine the dealers standing behind them, waiting. He'd known a couple of those guys. They loved to see players burn, but they loved even more to see them win. Big wins meant big tips.

He slid the door back and entered the exclusive Skyloft check-in area.

"Reservation for James Carroll."

"Yes, Mr. Carroll! Just a mo—."

The receptionist's smile turned to plaster.

"Get ready for company," Flynn told Diana as the door behind them slid open and a howitzer shell in a black suit came in.

"Excuse me," the shell said, his steel cranium gleaming.

"We're here on official business," Flynn responded. "No gambling."

"Please come with me, Mr. Carroll. And you, too, Miss Glass."

He looked at her in astonishment. "You're booked, too?"

She did not reply.

As they headed toward security, the officer asked, "Are you two a team now?"

"Not really," Diana said.

He led them into a familiar space, scuffed beige walls, no windows, a steel desk and a couple of wooden chairs. Not the sort of room you expect to see in the Grand. It was even more stark than the service areas and the maze of access tunnels that Flynn knew ran under the huge complex.

He thought he might recognize the security chief, but it was a new, short, stocky bullet-headed bald guy. The new howitzer shell said, "Diana Glass. Welcome back. Leaving, I presume?" He looked at Flynn. "And who're you supposed to be, Mr. Carroll, Hecuba's sidekick?"

"I'm a police officer," Flynn said. He pulled out his badge. "Texas."

"Doesn't make a shit here, Mr. Carroll, this is Nevada. The message remains the same. Get out."

"Look—"

"I'm lookin' at a lot of losses between the two of you, now get off the premises or I'll have to turn you over to some real cops, which will not amuse you."

Unless there was a criminal charge, in cases like this the Vegas cops basically just yelled at you. It wasn't against the law to win money from the casinos. It was just annoying to them.

"You have a tiger in here and I know this, and I know how to find it and get it out of the resort."

He heard Diana suck in her breath.

"Your help isn't needed," the security chief said. "We've got eyes on every camera in the structure."

"Why haven't you evacuated?"

"Because we don't think some eccentric high roller is gonna unleash his pet on the guests. We just want him quietly to leave. Like you."

"What hasn't been on the news is why you can't find it, which I know you can't. Or why we can. That hasn't been on the news, either." He flipped his badge wallet closed. "We're not here to gamble."

The security chief came closer to him. Flynn noted that he had a complete set of choppers. Not good with his fists, then.

"Wait here," Choppers said. He left the room.

Flynn looked up at the camera and waved his fingers. "He's gone to get the general manager."

"I really didn't want to come here."

"Are you booked all over town, or just here?"

"Look, in a previous life I built illegal software, okay?"

"For the casinos?"

"Against the casinos."

"All I did was count cards."

"They don't like that, either."

"They do not."

He looked at her with new eyes. From casino hacker to government super spy. "You've had an interesting career."

She smiled a tight smile. "It has been interesting."

The general manager came in. He was not smiling. "I'm told you won't leave."

"We're not here to gamble. We're here to help you with your tiger problem."

"We don't have a tiger problem."

"You have a half-empty casino is what you have. Because of the bad publicity regarding said tiger. That's a tiger problem."

The guy was young, no more than five years older than Flynn, but he had the dead eyes of somebody who'd worked tables too long. Under the flinty, hostile surface was a deeper level of what Flynn sensed was real nastiness. So he had to be beaten about the head and shoulders a little. Not a problem. He said, "Okay, fine, we're gonna leave. But we're also going to let the press know that you refused our help."

"A cop from the beautiful little town of Dead, Texas, and his hacker girlfriend? Nobody cares." He turned his glare on Diana. "Why aren't you in jail? You're supposed to be serving time. Or dare I ask? 'Cause I can see you're carrying heat, both of you. But then again"—he gestured toward a uniformed guard who had quietly entered the room—"so is he."

"I'm not in jail because I cut a deal with Uncle Sam, Willard."

"Willard?" Flynn asked.

"What kind of a deal would the feds cut with a sleaze-ball like you, Diana? You went down for four years."

She pulled out her documentation. "When there's only one person who can do a job, they're gonna deal."

He looked at her ID card. "As if this was real. Please don't bore me. You either bribed your way out or fucked your way out or both. Or you did something to their computers. Probably hacked your own release and just walked."

"Look, Willard, we've been sent here by our bosses for reasons that we cannot tell you to do a job that you are not going to be able to do yourself."

"We've got security patrolling every floor. We've entered and searched every guest room in the complex."

"But you haven't found the tiger or seen it leave the

structure. Not on any camera. So what does that tell you?"

"LVPD SWAT are standing by."

"Hordes of cops in black Darth Vader outfits. International media attention. That would not be good."

"Whatever, I fail to see what a card shark and a jailbird hacker are gonna bring to the table."

"Go the SWAT route. Or let us do our thing. Nice and private. You see the tiger, then you don't."

"Do we get an ID on the shithead who brought it in?"

"I guarantee the tiger. The shithead if we're lucky."

"And what does this cost?"

"Not a penny. We really do work for Uncle Sam." He looked at Diana. "She's been scared honest."

"That would be false. So let me put it this way. If this fucks up in some way—if it turns out to be some sort of bass ackwards scam, I'm not bothering with the cops. I'm gonna just go ahead and brass you two until your faces are but a memory."

"You beat up ladies now?"

Willard focused on Diana. "I saw this 'lady' here toss an armed man twice her size fifteen feet into a glass wall."

"I've only seen her geek side," Flynn said.

Willard stared at her for a while. "That was her geek side. Don't even get me started about her skill at ripping marks."

Her face was scarlet. She did not reply.

A long sigh from Williard. "What do you need to get started?"

"Smart move," Flynn said.

"Nope, it's a case of curiosity killing the cat. Why would a big-time hacker team up with a small-time counter? I'm fascinated."

"Let's roll some videotape."

Willard took them to the security complex, which Flynn saw was fitted with state-of-the-art cameras watching the gaming area. Every corridor on every floor was also covered. "Any penetration into the rooms?"

"Not legal."

"Detectives, maybe? Police investigation?"

"It happens, but nothing's going down at present."

He introduced Scott Morris. Flynn saw a graying former cop, probably a retiree. Sincere, capable, dedicated. "Scott supervises the system. He'll give you what you need."

"I have all the incidents edited together," he said. "This is the first one that was noticed." He touched a button, which froze an image.

They were looking at a blur stretched along the floor line in one of the access tunnels. Diana said, "You can tell what that is?"

"I can tell that it isn't supposed to be there."

"Could be a big cat," Flynn said.

The security officer returned the camera to real time. The shadow was now gone.

"What was it then?" Flynn asked.

"Nobody could figure it out, so it got kicked up to me. I did a little work on the image, but it's unresolveable."

"What's the refresh rate on these things?"

"Eighteen fps."

"So whatever it is was moving really fast."

"Faster than a man can run."

"Where's that tunnel?"

"Right under us, actually. Access to the lion habitat is through there."

The MGM Grand's lions were a world-famous tourist

attraction. When he was here gambling, Flynn had passed by the habitat often enough. Even the floors were glass, so it was going to be a hard place for a tiger to hide.

"Street access? Is that where they bring the lions in from the ranch?"

"Yeah, there's access out onto Tropicana. A couple of hundred feet."

"Let's see the best image of the tiger that you have."

"This is from the tower. Sixteenth floor. Three twenty this morning."

The animal came down the hall, stopped, and looked up at the camera.

"My God," Diana whispered.

Brilliant eyes sparked in a sea of gray-orange fur. The animal's face seemed almost to smile. Then it slowly turned around and, switching its tail, ambled down the corridor and around a corner.

"Next camera?"

Scott Morris pushed another button. "This is all there is. A blur again."

"It displayed itself intentionally," he said. "And it's still here. And not alone." He asked Scott, "Do you cover the Mansion? With cameras?" This was an exclusive facility behind the Grand itself, reserved for high rollers and people willing to pony up $5,000 a night for accommodation.

"We cover the whole facility."

So there would be no reason for the perp to prefer the Mansion over the Skylofts, and perhaps a good reason to favor the lofts, because he would have arrived the same way he'd arrived at the Hoffman's, from above, using that high-tech aircraft of his.

In any case, MGM was going to know a lot about

the people who stayed in the Mansion. You didn't just walk in, you had to be invited.

"What about the roof of the tower?"

"There's time lapse video of all roof areas. We've examined every foot of it."

"How long is the delay?"

"Sixty seconds."

Easily time enough for someone to land, drop the animal and its support crew, and leave. Working at night, staying below FAA radars, using that soundless helicopter or whatever it was, it would have been easy.

"What we need to do is concentrate on the top floor of the tower, not the roof, the roof cameras are too slow. But I want to look at every inch of interior footage."

A few minutes later, Flynn was watching one camera, Diana the other. "You're looking for a blur," he said. "They know the frame speed of the cameras, so the animal is moving fast."

"It's that well trained? Tigers are hard to train." Morris said.

Flynn said nothing.

It took three hours, and during that time neither of them saw a single sign of anything unusual. Butlers and room service waiters came and went, guests came and went, but nothing else happened.

"Like I said, it's still here," Flynn said.

"Which surprises me," Diana replied. "If it's bait. Wouldn't they have exposed it, then pulled it out as soon as they could?"

"Gotta let the fish swallow the bait, then you can set the hook. That's what we're doing now. We're swallowing the bait. Next step, the hook will be set."

"How will it be done?"

Flynn thought about that. "We shall see."

"Look, it's not in this complex," Morris repeated. "I'm sorry."

"If it's not anywhere you've looked, then it has to be somewhere you haven't. I suggest we start at the point of entry and we move through every space where the animal has been observed."

"And?"

"We shall see."

"Flynn," Diana said, "that's just blatantly taking the bait."

"A smart fish wants to get the fisherman to go home. So he plays a game with him. He wants to frustrate him. He takes the bait, but he's careful. He's not greedy. He nibbles. So the fisherman up there thinks, 'have I got a bite or is it just the current?' Finally, he hauls in his line and finds a clean hook. This happens a few times, and the fish is finally left in peace. Full, too."

"So he leaves and we get nothing. Stalemate."

"Oh, no, he's gonna get something."

"What?"

Flynn made a gun gesture. "The fish, in this case, is gonna follow the line right back to the fisherman in his little boat."

"Flynn, you'll get killed."

"Somebody will, most likely."

"Remember Montana. The animal is extremely dangerous, and whoever's behind it is even more so."

Flynn said nothing.

CHAPTER TWENTY

The lion habitat was immediately beside the security area, and it took them only a few moments to reach it with their latest minder, a young guy called Josh who apparently thought they were celebrity guests looking for an insider's tour.

He nattered away about the facility's history and its considerable prowess as one of the most popular exhibits in Las Vegas.

The walls and floors were clear glass, so it was easy to see the lions, but not entirely. There was a small area where they could stay out of view.

There was a crowd in front of the habitat, and a line full of kids formed up along the wall. It was a happy situation, calm and orderly. No problems here. There were cubs in the habitat, and the children were eager to have their pictures taken with them. Farther down the corridor, more people were filing into Studio 54. The casino was humming, too, and a show was letting out of the Cirque de Soleil's KÀ Theater.

This was a chess game with no board and more than

one expert opponent. Or perhaps it was better to say it another way: a chess game with the perp and some other kind of game with the tiger, played by tiger rules, whatever they were.

He asked Scott, "Did you check the whole habitat?" He knew the answer, but he wanted to hear it from the man who had done the work.

"What's there to check? Six lions, two cubs, glass floors, end of story."

Obviously, Scott was not aware of how the habitat was laid out. Flynn went to the door. "I need to enter the space," he told their minder.

The man blinked. His expression of surprise said that it wasn't a frequent request. Finally he said, "No."

"It's okay, Ricky," Scott said.

"Don't we need a release or something?"

"I need to do this right now."

Scott spoke into his radio, then listened. Willard, no doubt. Flynn waited. At a nod from Scott, Rickie unlocked the heavy door and stepped aside.

"Hey," the trainer who was handling the animals said, "You know what you're doing?"

"I need to see into the enclosed area."

"There's nobody in there. We're all out here."

This guy was tight with his lions, which was good. It meant that he could control them. Flynn was fast enough to deal with one lion, but six would be a definite problem, and lions weren't like tigers, they worked in packs.

The public was now aware of his presence in the enclosure and was watching him. He moved through the visible space, then took a few steps up into the hidden area.

It was exactly as he expected. He called out to the trainer, "There's another animal in here."

The trainer's head turned. "*What?*"

"Back in here. And I don't think it's a lion."

The man came to Flynn. "That's empty. It has to be."

Flynn moved a little deeper into the dimness. "Get security over here."

"This is impossible!"

"Look for yourself," Flynn said. "Carefully."

"Jesus, you're right. What is that?"

"We need somebody who's able to work with tigers. And this one is very damn smart."

The trainer had taken out a small LED flashlight. The yellow of the tiger's eyes reflected back. "What the hell . . . how did that get in here?"

"We need to get it contained."

"There's tigers at the Secret Garden in the Mirage. Is this one of their animals?"

"No. But they have experts, for sure."

"Yeah, Siegfried and Roy. *The* experts."

"Aren't they retired?"

"If they're in Vegas, they can advise. Plus, the Mirage has a good group of trainers. It's a top-notch operation."

One of the lions roared, then another. From outside there was excited babble, kids squealing.

"They've been restless as hell, and this is why. How long as that thing been in there?"

"That's unclear."

Behind them, Ricky opened the access door. "You guys okay?"

Immediately, there was a stirring from within the enclosure. "Close it," the trainer shouted.

The lions erupted, roaring and striding, and at the same moment the tiger emerged. It was easily as big as two of the lions put together.

It fixed its stare on Flynn.

"It knows you. Is this your animal?"

Flynn said nothing.

The tiger came into view of the public, causing an immediate round of applause. The next second, it leaped, and Flynn had never seen anything quite like it. The movement was smooth and swift and covered a good fifteen feet.

As the tiger slammed into Ricky, he went down with a surprised grunt.

"Holy God!" the trainer shouted.

From outside there came a confused babble, then an eruption of screams.

Perhaps because of pack instinct, but also due to curiosity, the lions followed the tiger through the door.

"Goddamnit!" the trainer shouted.

"Stay cool, we've got work to do," Flynn said. He grabbed Scott's radio. "The animals are in the casino," he said on the emergency channel, "you need crowd control and all the wranglers you can get."

He followed the trainer out into the broad hallway between Studio 54 and the casino. The lions were close together, moving down the center of the hall toward the casino, and the large crowds still exiting KÀ were parting like the Red Sea. But not all of them. An elderly lady who looked like a pile of bags with a face clapped her hands and confronted them, smiling happily. "Oh, how cute," she gushed.

Another voice shouted, "It's an act," and there was a smattering of uneasy applause.

"Oh, God," the trainer moaned.

Security was pouring into the corridor from both directions. Then a little boy with a toy ray gun burst through the crowd and took a firing stance. The next thing Flynn knew, he was spraying the lions with a super-soaker.

They remained silent and still, shaking their heads, annoyed by the water, unsure of themselves.

"It's not gonna last," the trainer shouted back at Flynn.

"I know it."

A guard appeared with a gun.

The situation was three seconds from trample panic. "Don't fire that," Flynn shouted, "don't let people see it!" The guard holstered it and stationed himself in front of the lions and spread his legs and arms, attempting to block their progress.

Now other people joined the old lady, attempting to attract the lions to them. One man succeeded in petting one of them.

"Lay off," the trainer shouted, "don't confuse them!"

"Folks," Flynn said in his most commanding voice, "we need you to back out of here. Nobody run, just move out of the corridor, please. Stay away from the animals."

The old lady was lifting the dewlaps of a lioness and shrilling at her husband to take a picture. Flynn's warning did not stop her. Then a man with a cigar in his hand burst around the guard, roaring and thrusting it at the lions.

One of the them charged this sudden movement. The old woman was knocked over.

In three strides, Flynn moved among the lions, then past them. Quickly, he confronted the man with the cigar, lifted his arm and shook it out of his hand, and twisted the arm back behind him. Then he took the guy's legs out from under him, whirled him around and pushed him away. He turned to the old woman and drew her to her feet. "Put her back together," he said to another security guard who had just come up.

The lions, now afraid, began running. More screams erupted. Flynn's trained ears counted ten sirens immediately outside the building, just beginning to wind down.

"Call your pros," he shouted to Scott. "Right now!"

"It's been done!"

Willard burst onto the scene. "SWAT's deploying."

Flynn took off after the lions.

They invaded the casino, moving fast. Their fear was escalating fast. At this point, they were highly likely to lash out at anybody who confronted them.

This was a huge space, and most of the patrons still weren't aware of what was happening. But then one of the lions jumped up onto a blackjack table and roared. Nobody could mistake that sound, and every head in the casino turned this way. Then the rest of them ran deeper into the room, and were lost to Flynn's view amid the high-roller slots. Roars and cries of terrified surprise followed immediately.

"Stay with this animal," Flynn shouted to two guards. "Send SWAT into the slots with nets, not guns. No guns, do you get that?"

"Yessir!"

He also ran toward the slots, vaulting the nearest row of them and landing in the lap of a spectacular young woman. Her chips scattered, mice on the run.

People were jumping up from their machines, shouting, flapping their hands at the lions, trying to leave the area.

Flynn knew about as much about lions as he did about tigers, which was just enough to know that they were efficient killers, but would only attack for food or in self-defense. For them, violence was a tool, and right now what he needed to do was to convince them not to use it.

"Clear the area," he shouted into the panicking crowd. "The police are on their way. Just take it easy, back out, don't make sudden movements." They slowed down, clustering, getting quiet. "That's it, that's right. Now just back out. Security will escort you to safety."

In moments, fully equipped SWATs appeared, and they had animal control nets. There was going to be some roaring and some resistance from the lions, but basically this was over.

Diana came up beside him. "This is what the perp's been waiting for. His tiger's going to take us out somehow, and right now."

"He's going to try. Listen, I need you out of here."

"No way."

"They must not take both of us. So you get out of here, you get in the car, and you drive, Diana. You drive far."

He spotted the tiger. It was making its way behind the high-roller slots, moving fast, staying low.

"The perp could be leaving the facility about now. You go out to the front and make a note of every vehicle that pulls away."

"He'll use his chopper."

"In broad daylight? He's gotta have permits, he's got to get clearance to use the helideck. No, he'll use a car and this is a chance to see him or see somebody who works with him. Get some basic detective information." The tiger disappeared from view. The animal was going somewhere. It would be picked up, and Flynn intended to still be alive when that happened, and to be there.

"You come with me," Diana said.

"The tiger's going somewhere to be picked up. If I'm there, I can call in support from the local cops. Maybe round up some of these people."

"You will not survive this, Flynn."

"Go!"

She turned.

"*Now!*"

She left.

Flynn trotted to where the animal had been, but there was nothing there. He looked ahead and saw an access panel. Loose. It must have gone through, and it must have been helped, otherwise the panel wouldn't just be loose, it would be open. Smart as the damn thing was, the tiger didn't have hands. Fortunately.

As he slid the panel aside, he reflected that he'd seen the tiger's face more clearly this time. He'd had the uncanny sense that a person had been looking back at him through the eyes of an animal.

On the other side of the panel he found an access area that led to a forest of ductwork. It was a ventilation management shaft. The interior was unlit.

This was the moment when he needed to nibble the bait, not swallow it. The smart fish also had the discipline to defeat his own eagerness, and that was not easy, not when you were as hungry as he was.

CHAPTER TWENTY-ONE

He stood waiting for his eyes to get used to the dark. His night vision was decent, and this was always preferable to a flashlight. He could use his night vision equipment, which was still in his backpack, but it projected infrared and that would not be wise. For all he knew, tigers could see into the infrared, or this one could.

Soon, he was able to make out the shapes of ducts. There was light coming from his left. Also, on the floor, smears in the dust that could only be tracks. Instead of hiding, this tiger had gone toward the light, and that was very damn strange, especially because light changes the hormone mix in the human brain but not in the brains of predators. More visual information makes our other senses less acute. Could the tiger sense this, or somehow even know it? Or was it just a coincidence that it was going against its own instincts in such a way that gave it an advantage, but would look to most human pursuers like a mistake?

Flynn made his way under a long series of ducts, skirting the lighted area, moving as swiftly and silently as he could. He listened for any and every sound, and soon began to hear noises coming from the deeper dark. He stopped moving. Stopped breathing. Closed his eyes to concentrate on his hearing. Finally, he cupped his hands over his ears and turned slowly. As he did so, he was gradually able to make out a voice. Then that it was a female voice. Then that it was the voice of a child.

"Wee Willie Winkie runs through the town, upstairs and downstairs, in his nightgown . . ."

Incredibly, what he was hearing was a little girl telling a Mother Goose story.

"Rapping at the window, crying through the lock, are the children in their beds . . . are *you* in *your* bed, Jerry?"

He got his gun into his hand and went down on his stomach, drawing himself forward slowly enough so that the sliding sound was barely audible. As he moved ahead, the little girl's voice grew steadily more distinct. Also, he began to see flickering light, very dim. A candle?

The voice continued, "Hush-a-bye, baby, mommy is near, hush-a-bye, daddy is near . . ."

There came another voice, even smaller, hardly even articulate, whimpering.

"Hush . . . hush." The little girl was comforting an even smaller child.

Using the voices as a guide, he felt his way along, soon discovering an iron hatch that was standing open. As he felt the edge, he could detect neat slices in four heavy lock tongues. This door had been cut open, and not by any tiger, no matter how clever it was.

This was the work of the perpetrator or his people, the first overt sign of their presence he had found. So his instinct had been right. It wasn't just the tiger under here. Somebody with a powerful tool was here, too, and not a blowtorch. The edge was absolutely smooth to the touch. A torch would have left a much more irregular surface. No, this had been cut by a very good blade—as a matter of fact, no blade Flynn had ever heard of.

Could this be their lair? Was that the real reason they were in Vegas? Maybe he'd overestimated their cunning, and blundered into their most secret place.

He told himself, no, don't make that mistake, that's nibbling the bait too hard. One more like that, and you taste the hook.

From the beginning, he had known that he would come to this point. Maybe the child wasn't even real, and maybe something else was happening entirely. He was in a labyrinth, after all, a real one. Who could tell what the truth of such a place might be?

It was an easy step through the door, whisper quiet sneakers on hard concrete. As he stepped through, he felt the thickness of the wall. It was a good four or five inches of steel reinforced concrete. So this was an access hatch, not intended to be opened often, if at all. But what was it for? What was this space he was now in?

The little girl was now silent, but the candle still flickered. As he moved toward it, he became aware of dampness underfoot, and at once understood. He was in the city's storm drain system, and that hatch was not a hatch at all, it was a gigantic relief valve. An enormous structure like the Grand would be served by massive risers from the city water system. If one of them burst, this and other valves up and down this outer wall could be opened to let the water out into the drainage system.

But what in the world were children doing in a storm drain? Were they runaways?

Flynn had been born helpful. It was part of who he was and a big part of why he'd become a cop. Even as a kid, he'd rendered aid whenever the situation arose. When it came to putting bad people in jail, Flynn's motive was protective, not vindictive. He didn't care so much to punish wrongdoers as to keep innocent people safe.

He was in a tunnel perhaps fifteen feet high and twenty wide. The candle, guttering now, was a hundred yards further on. As he drew closer, he began to make out a bed, then a table against a wall, then what amounted to a small room built entirely inside the drainage tunnel.

People lived down here. They were raising children down here.

He walked into the tiny area. There was a mattress set on a rusty box spring, with two children sleeping on it. A tattered paperback of Mother Goose lay near the hand of an exquisite little girl, her blond hair a tangled mess, her face in sleep like something one might see through a keyhole into heaven. Cuddled beside her was a snatch of brown hair, all that could be seen of the smaller child she had been reading to.

Standing on the far side of the bed, just at the edge of the light, was the tiger. The eyes bored into him, but not with lust for the kill or even with hate. There was something like a frown there, not much of an expression really, but Flynn thought that it communicated clear meaning. The tiger's face was not angry. It was not murderous. The tiger's face was asking a question: "Who are you?"

Flynn had a shot—not much of one, but he could safely fire across the kids and maybe hit the animal. Moving as slow as oil, he raised the Glock. Quite calmly, the tiger watched it come up.

If he hit his target, the shot would be nothing short of a masterpiece. He breathed deep and set his feet.

The tiger disappeared as the shot blasted out, the noise rocking the tunnel, then echoing away in a series of thunderous slaps. Distantly, there were shouts, "shot fired, shot fired," then the thutter of feet running in the thin water that filmed the floor of the tunnel.

Other people lived down here, obviously a whole community. They were the kind of people who knew the sound of a gun when they heard it.

He had not hit the tiger. The tiger was gone.

The little girl lay with her eyes opened, her lips twisted back away from her teeth as if she was in pain. Her eyes were fixed on him. In the hand that had held the Mother Goose was a flying Taser. It was armed. The LED was glowing. A C2 like that could fire its electrodes twenty feet.

He realized that he had swallowed the bait, taken it deep into his gut. And now, in the form of a Taser in a child's hand, came the hook.

As he shifted and dropped, she fired. He felt one of the electrodes hook into the sleeve of his jacket, then the floor seemed to turn into the ceiling, and he knew that she'd hit her mark.

In training, he'd taken Taser hits. He knew to expect the confusion and the out-of-control muscle spasms that followed, also the way sounds became tinny and the world distant.

Somebody was there, a dark figure standing over him. "What you doin' down here, topsider, you lookin' fer little girls." A blow hit his back. "That yo sweet, topsider?"

The effect wore off enough for Flynn to pull one of the hooks out of his clothes. He fought to respond to the voice, but could only manage a gobbling sound.

"You done good, Becky," the voice said. "Now we gonna kill us a topsider."

Flynn had been tricked into getting himself killed by a completely unconnected party for a reason that had nothing to do with anything.

"No," he managed to croak, "there's an animal down there." It came out as a series of gobbles.

"Zap him again, Becky." The man pulled a switchblade out of his pocket and snicked it open. "Gonna start with your balls, you piece a shit."

Flynn managed to suck a breath. "Animal in here! Dangerous!" He fought to get an arm up. Even though the little girl was standing on the trigger, there was no second pulse from the Taser.

"You're the goddamn animal."

Flynn pointed. "There's an animal back there in that tunnel!"

"What?"

"I'm a police officer. I was driving an animal away from your kids."

"You're a cop? Down here?"

Flynn had recovered himself enough to raise both hands. The Glock lay before him on the ground. "Swear."

"Shit a friggin brick, what the hell're you doin' down here? Cops don't come down here."

"To warn you . . . an animal—big cat—escaped from the Grand. In the tunnels."

"Jesus. Becky, you seen it?"

She shook her head.

"She ain't seen it." The blade reappeared.

"She was asleep."

At that moment, a light shone the tunnel, bright, a professional-quality flashlight. It moved closer, coming down the same shaft that Flynn had used.

"You're a lucky man," Diana said. "I thought I was gonna find meat."

"What in fuck's name is going on around here?"

"You watch your trap around those kids, buddy," Diana said to the guy.

"My kids are my business."

"Well, you better get 'em outa here until the SWATs track down that tiger."

"You're kidding."

"You heard me. This officer probably saved their lives. 'Cause the animal went right through this tunnel."

"I saw it," Flynn said. He pointed. "Just there. Which is why I fired my weapon."

"Come on," Diana said. "SWAT's coming down the tunnels and we have work to do."

Flynn was perplexed. What had just happened here? Instead of the perpetrator's goons, Diana had shown up. It wasn't surprising that she'd ignored his request and followed him, but still, something was wrong.

As they made their way back toward the Grand, she said, "We misread this situation totally."

"It looks like it."

"This had nothing to do with us. They were on one of their missions."

"Oh?"

"During the confusion, while the entire staff chased the tiger, which you can be assured will not be seen anywhere near here again, the assistant manager of the resort disappeared from her office without a trace."

Flynn did not reply. What could he say? What could either of them say?

When they had emerged back into the now-closed casino, she said, "There's worse."

"Hit me."

"Flynn, there's been a fire in Chicago, a bad one. A gas explosion leveled four row houses. Seventeen people were killed."

He stopped. Looked at her. It was dark, but not so dark that he couldn't see the shock in her face, or share her stunned horror.

"Oh my God, they got him."

She nodded. "Flynn, we're on our own."

CHAPTER TWENTY-TWO

The assistant manager's office was neat as a pin, except for the exquisite antique snuff box the Las Vegas detectives had found, which turned out to contain cocaine. They had also discovered that her credit rating was through the floor and she had a long string of dismissed cases that the Grand wouldn't have been able to see on her record before she was hired. The publicly available part of it showed only a traffic conviction.

Flynn breathed the room. Felt it. He noticed a curtain that had been pulled abruptly, but that was all. It looked out onto a distant view, so it was unlikely that somebody had been concerned that the window was under incidental surveillance.

According to the available tapes, she'd left the office when she'd gotten the alarm about the problem with the animals. She had never arrived on the scene.

"What is it?" Diana asked.

"What it is, is nothing."

"You sense something."

"You know, I'm not really thinking about this office.

I already know that we're never going to find Elizabeth Starnes or Gail Hoffman or Abby or your Steve or any of them. What I can't get out of my mind is that tiger. I saw its face again."

"And?"

"It was intelligent, Diana. Like a person. It was like seeing a person wearing the face of a tiger."

"You wondering the same thing I am?"

"A human mind put into the body of an animal. Yes I am. You could see curiosity. Like it was wondering who I was."

"Feline curiosity?"

"Like it was asking me if we really needed to be enemies." He shook his head. "I think it's part human, and I have to wonder if it would change sides."

"We'll never get close enough to it to find out. Especially with Chicago gone. We need help."

"You gotta have contacts above that level. Who does Oltisis report to? Did?"

She shook her head.

"*What?*"

"I was seconded to Oltisis. Sent to him on an origin-blocked order."

"What the fuck is that?"

"A legal order that comes from a code-protected source. You can verify the code, but not identify the source. Could've been anybody. Most likely some agency that's so classified even I've never heard of it." She paused. "Or them."

"Why are they so damn secretive?"

"If the alien presence is revealed and the public goes nuts about the disappearances—"

"Yeah, yeah, but this goes deeper than that."

She sighed. "I know it. Mirrors reflecting mirrors.

No damn end to it." She paused. "The thought has crossed my mind that the bad guys might be in control at home. It could be that the ones helping us aren't the police at all. Maybe they're dissidents or revolutionaries or something."

For a moment they were both silent, each contemplating the enormous stakes involved, and the mysteries they faced, and the responsibility they bore.

"We have to just keep pushing," Flynn said, "and hope whomever Oltisis reported to catches up with us."

"That would be true."

Flynn continued, "They did Miss Starnes during the day, so no helicopter."

Willard had become more cooperative. The company very badly wanted to find and prosecute the people who had caused the mayhem. The LVPD already had a blizzard of warrants out for them, not to mention a massive hunt for the tiger. They weren't looking for Elizabeth Starnes, though not very hard. Given cocaine use and the kind of police record that would belong to a clever junkie, the resort was just as glad to be rid of her. In any case, it looked more and more to the police as if she'd walked out on her job, not been abducted. In other words, the old story.

Flynn and Diana had been given a small office in the security area, and computers with access to the property's floor plan, its registration records, even the casino information.

They both worked the records, looking for things that didn't add up, and in the back of both of their minds there remained the same hollow thought: we're alone.

Flynn traced Elizabeth Starnes's movements, picking her up in a stairwell, then again in the main lobby.

There, she met an elderly man. She greeted him with what looked like professional courtesy, then walked out with him.

"Go into her family history," he said. "See if she has any older relatives."

"Her father lives in Crescent Manor. Charles Starnes. He's a slot machinist."

"A picture?"

"DMV probably has one." Her fingers flew across the keyboard. "Got it."

"That was a couple of seconds."

"Fast hands."

"No wonder Oltisis wanted you, you're a friggin' genius."

"Always been my problem," she said tightly. "Makes you think you can get away with any kind of shit. If that hack I did on the Grand had gone down the right way, I'd be in Tahiti now, not a worry in the world."

"Tahiti'd get old, be my guess."

"No older than catching car thieves and pushers."

"Yeah, as screwed up as this is, it's better."

They laid the driver's license photo side by side with a blowup of the face of the man Elizabeth had met in the lobby.

"It's close," she said.

"It's a maybe. Let's talk to the father."

"We lose time."

"A little."

"What do we gain?"

"You never know."

Leaving the Grand, Flynn thought that they were entering a new and far more dangerous world. How had the baddies ever taken out Chicago?

"You did warn them in that call?"

"Absolutely. Oltisis said he was aware of the problem and all over it."

Flynn said nothing.

As they walked through the port cochere, past the line of parking valets, Vegas was gold with late sun, the neon just gaining definition against the blazing western sky. Looking toward the mountains to the west, blue now, he thought of the tiger on its strange journey, and what it had seen and what it knew.

They were alike, him and the tiger, two hunters. The only difference was in their choice of prey.

Diana sat beside him in the car, her hands folded in her lap, her face as pale as a cloud, her eyes hard and quick and scared. The eyes of the hunted.

"Where were you in prison?"

"Lesbian Island."

"But you're not one."

"I was put there, okay? End of subject. I do not wish to talk about old lives that are dead."

"After I lost my wife, I left Menard. Couldn't stop going. I'd dip in here to hit a few casinos for money."

"You counted good enough to get booked. That's impressive."

"I have a trick memory." His mind was a warehouse full of file cabinets, full of details that he could never escape. "I recall every hand I ever played. And not just cards. I can tell you about the breeze on the night of August 14, 1997. I can tell you about the T-shirt Abby wore on June 11, 2006. You name it, I've got the details."

"Details suit a detective."

He turned onto Thirtieth. "I guess. At least I don't need a GPS. Saves a little money."

"What if you've never been there before?"

"I've seen a map."

The father lived in a single-family home on Langdon, a short street that dead-ended into a condo complex. They pulled up in front and got out of the car.

"It's empty," Flynn said.

"You're a mind reader, too? Do you have a cape? Some kind of leotard?"

"Yeah, I have a leotard. Asshole Patrol."

She knocked on the door. As he expected, there was no answer.

She said, "You're sure this is going to be productive, because now we've got to look for him."

"If it wasn't him at the Grand, then we have a picture of a member of this group, so yeah, it's going to help."

"He's not here and we'll never find him."

"Let's go back to the car."

"And go where?"

"Nowhere. Wait."

"Wait?"

"What a detective does, mostly."

They said little, and that was how he preferred it. You chatted during a stakeout, you missed things. It was all about focus.

The sun went down, the sky to the west raged with the light of the strip. Bats darted past the car. The air turned cool, then cold. Diana rolled up her window. "I hate the cold," she said. Her hand went to her neck. He knew that she was remembering the Hoffman stakeout.

It was nine twenty when a man came walking slowly down the street.

"It's him and don't get out of the car until he enters the house and closes the door. If he's gonna run, you want him to start from a confined space."

"Why would he run?"

"No idea."

He was old and stooped and used up. Whatever he'd had, Vegas had taken it. Flynn watched him go up the walk, enter the house, and close the door.

"Okay, now."

They got out of the car and followed him. Flynn put his hand on his badge wallet. The big star on his badge was a giveaway for Texas, but if he flashed it fast, maybe the guy wouldn't notice. Diana's credential would likely work better.

He knocked, then again, then the door was drawn open. Mr. Starnes stood there in a black undershirt.

"Yeah?"

Flynn did his badge. "May we come in?"

"You're cops so it's about Lizzie. I'm finished with her. Whatever she's done, she's done. Not my problem."

"When did you last see Elizabeth?"

"Dunno. Three years? Five? Last time she showed up high. Sick of it. Sick of her."

Flynn thanked him and returned to the car, Diana following.

"You hardly asked him a thing. I think he knew something."

"He knew nothing and he's not the man she met in the lobby."

"Oh. Is that good?"

"It's good. Now we have a face. A real face, of somebody we know is involved, maybe the perp himself."

She followed him to the car and they headed back to the Grand.

"With a face," he added, "we have a shot at finding a name."

"How would we do that?"

"The old-fashioned way. We get the picture fixed up as clear as the computer genius can make it, then we hand it out to the staff. We show it to maids, bellmen, valets, anybody who might be able to help."

"What if he doesn't have an identity?"

"There'll be something somewhere. There always is."

"You know that? Despite how careful they are."

"I know it."

They returned to their small office. Willard came in. "I'm getting my hotel fixed. Nobody can figure out how that hatch was cut. You guys got anything for us?"

"Not our lookout," Flynn said.

"But you're government. You've got resources."

"Report the kidnap to the FBI. Get them involved."

"No, thank you. I've got the LVPD to worry about already."

"Then don't ask."

"Don't ask? Fine. I got a front office that's about to wring my neck and your only fucking response is *don't ask*?"

Flynn sighed. "If we told you, we'd have to kill you."

"That bullshit line. Is that from a movie?"

"No doubt. Look, tell your front office that it's classified and it's all under control and they will never hear from us or the asshole with the tiger again. Or the tiger."

"I hate the government so much I'm even afraid to vote Republican," Willard said.

"Get out."

He left, slamming the door behind him.

"You were nice."

"Thank you."

As Diana passed the image through a software photo processor in her laptop, it became clearer and clearer.

"It's a disguise."

"How can you be sure?"

"The hairline's too perfect. The face is too tan. Likely, it's makeup."

"One that you can see in a picture, but that Elizabeth Starnes bought from three feet away? I don't think so."

"For whatever reason, she wanted to buy it."

"Well, it doesn't help us, Flynn."

"There's more information out there."

Parking valets at places like the Grand sometimes remember things, so their first stop was the port cochere.

The encounter in the lobby had taken place just after noon. He'd already looked at a list of the Grand's shift patterns, and the shift that was on right now would have seen anyone who left at that time.

He said to Diana, "I need you to fade while I do this. Unless these guys think I'm a private dick, they're going to clam up, and PIs don't roll with beautiful assistants."

"And cops do?"

"Question marks do, and that's what they don't like."

She stalked off down the port cochere. Traffic was light, so there were six valets waiting. He wasted no time, he knew the drill.

"I need some help," he said, holding up the picture.

Eyes moved toward it. Brains calculated. Flynn knew the question that these guys were asking themselves: could this asshole be stripped of a c-note with a lie? He headed that one off at the pass. "I know the man's name, that's not the problem. What we need to know is if he was in a Hertz car."

Interest dropped a little. Not a divorce case, so less money was going to be involved. But then again, Hertz was a big outfit.

"We don't like our cars getting boosted," he continued, "so anything you know." He rubbed two fingers together.

One of the guys took the picture and looked at it. "This wasn't a rental car," he said.

"You closed it out?"

"I worked a double shift today. I opened it, too."

Flynn watched the other guys. No trace of a suppressed smile anywhere. "So, okay, what've you got?"

"Nightlights Limo both directions. Two passengers inbound, three outbound."

Another of the valets sighed as if he was a tire losing air. The fool had just given up the money.

"That's one of them in the picture," the fool added. Then he fell silent.

Not a fool, then. Pretty good at what he did, actually. "Okay, so give."

Silence. Not a gesture, not a sound. He'd been doing this job for a while. Discreetly, Flynn showed a hundred-dollar bill. The guy rubbed his cheek with three fingers. Was the Grand this strict about this kind of tipping? He hadn't thought a casino would be. Live and learn.

Flynn played the game, rubbing his own cheek with two fingers.

"See 'em," the guy said.

He took out two hundred-dollar bills. They changed hands.

"That's the second passenger in the picture. Obviously not the lead guy. The boss was wearing about five grand, one of those suits where the guy's name is woven into the pinstripe."

He fought down his excitement. "And the name was?"

"Morris. In the pinstripes."

"Morris looked how?"

"He looked rich is how."

"Give me a description. Hair, eye color, anything you remember."

"He stayed well back in the car. I'm guessing at five eleven, say. Full head of black hair. Suit and tie, unusual around here. You're looking at a film star, sort of, but old-fashioned. Am I helping you?"

"Names?"

"Morris in the pinstripe. And he might have said 'Jay.' Might have said that name."

"Like he was talking to somebody or about somebody?"

The valet shook his head.

"Anything more you can tell me?"

"Look, we're deep into this and obviously it has nothing to do with Hertz, so I'm gonna need another couple of memory sticks."

"Anybody else got anything, now's the time." He put his hand on his breast pocket where he kept his wallet.

Another of the men said, "I put number two back in the vehicle. One of our managers was with him."

"That we know."

It took a hundred-dollar bill to get him to go any further. "The guy who went and got her was well dressed."

"This was Jay?"

"I didn't hear that. He thanked me for opening the door, that was it."

"And your manager? How did she act?"

"Drunk. High. Couldn't tell. Not walking the walk, that was for sure."

That was all they knew, so Flynn walked out of the port cochere and back into the hotel. Diana caught up with him in the corridor.

"I have good descriptions of two persons of interest. And a couple of names. Last name of Morris. And Jay. Somebody named Jay was with him."

"Can you find them?"

He considered that. He had descriptions. He had the name of the limo company they'd used. "Yeah," he said, "I can find them."

CHAPTER TWENTY-THREE

The least impressive vehicle Starlight Limos offered was a stretch Mercedes 300, and that's what Morris and company had used. It didn't take long to identify the driver, a part-timer called Ronald Brewster. The boss gave him up for twenty bucks. He lived in a weekly rate motel off the strip.

"On an approach like this, you need to follow procedures that I'm sure you aren't familiar with."

"What sort of procedures?"

"When a cop knocks on a door, anything can happen. So you stay behind me. Don't try to engage at all. Just stay out of it."

"I'm here to do my work, just like you are."

"Yeah, fine. This isn't your work. You're here because you're safer with me than alone. With me, you might live. Without me, you won't."

They walked around a swimming pool full of brown water that smelled of dead chemicals and drowned rats. A half-inflated Batman toy floated in it. The exotic orange mildew on the chaise lounges could have come from another planet.

It was dark now, and some of the rooms showed lights behind drawn curtains. Most did not.

He'd probably been in motels like this hundreds of times over the course of his career, sometimes to convince some guy not to push some girl through a wall, sometimes to arrest him for doing it. The Tara in Menard was the same sort of place, where sleazebag lawyers took their nooners and people went to live out their final acts.

He ran his eyes along the roofline, along the balconies, looking for threats. It was possible that they'd finally broken through a significant barrier on the case. For the first time, they were actually investigating real, solid human beings. In all likelihood, they'd never been expected to get this far. So the strikeback, when it came, was going to be sudden and hard.

"Why are we standing here?"

"I'm looking for something."

"May I know what?"

"Danger."

That silenced her.

"You make a move in a place like this, everybody thinks you're coming for them, and they all generally have reason to think that. Knock on the wrong door, you're liable to get blown away for nothing."

"And the right door?"

"You're likely to get blown away for a reason. Let's go."

Brewster was downstairs, in room 103. The lights were on.

"Wouldn't it have been safer to call ahead?"

"Then the lights would be off, because Mr. Brewster would be gone." Here and there, Flynn saw a curtain part. Here and there, lights went out. There was a rasping click from two doors down. "Somebody in 121 racked a pistol," he said. "Be aware of this."

He knocked on Brewster's door.

Silence.

"Mr. Brewster, we're PIs. We need a little information."

Silence.

"I got a c-note for you, you open the door."

Nothing.

"Okay, I'll push it under the door. You still don't want to talk, you can keep it." Then, to Diana, "Gimme a hundred-dollar bill."

She handed him the cash. "I hope this is worth it," she said.

He slid the bill under the door. "There's more where this came from, buddy."

"*No*," she whispered.

"Five minutes, Mr. Brewster."

The silence extended.

"Nobody there," Flynn said.

"You're sure?"

"The place isn't breathing. Look, I'm gonna pop the lock, so stand away from the door. If there's gonna be shooting, this is when."

"But the man with the gun is two doors down."

"Exactly." He gave the door a slightly harder knock. "Come on, Mr. Brewster, there's money out here, but it can't wait forever." With his free hand, he slid a credit card into the doorjamb. "They make these easy, so cops can pop them without damaging the premises."

When Flynn opened the door, a cloud of smoke came out—crack smoke. "Not good," he said. Then he saw the body. "We have a problem."

The face was purple, the fists clenched against the throat.

"Is he ill?"

The man had been murdered, but this was no time to get into that. "Back out."

"But—"

"Do it now!"

She remained rooted, staring. He took her by the shoulders and pulled her out. He pulled the door closed until the tongue of the lock clicked. There would be little evidence of their presence here, unless the next door decided to yap them to the locals. Hopefully it was some paranoid, not a cop-talker.

"Is he asleep?"

"Get to the car."

They crossed the courtyard. Once they were in the car, he said to her, "The man was dead."

"My God."

"They made it look like he popped himself on crack. He didn't."

"You know that? How?"

"Trust me."

Unless they were very lucky, the two of them were made and this time they were going all the way down.

"What does it mean?"

"They were cleaning up a loose end. We're the other one."

"Why not just blow us away?"

As he drove, he glanced at her. "I like to think it's because we've been a little too slippery for them. But that guy hadn't been dead for fifteen minutes, so they're moving fast and we're their top priority, you can be sure."

"What do we do next? Do we need to get out of here?"

"Ever been to Phoenix?"

"No."

"You're going. Right now. Phoenix, Salt Lake, wherever we can get to fast."

He drove to shake a tail, but he doubted that it mattered. They'd have a box on the car, no question.

"What are you doing?"

"Driving fast. Hoping to live through the next few minutes."

"Is somebody following us? What's happening?"

He saw an underpass and headed for it. His chief concern was overhead surveillance.

"Why weren't we in this much danger an hour ago?"

"I think that the tiger was meant to kill us. Me, at least. For whatever reason, it didn't. Doing this guy was cleanup. He'd seen too much and heard too much. Now they're probably frantic to get us. We've slipped through a few of their traps. No more. And we need to ditch this car right now. We're taking a bus."

"No buses!"

"A city bus like in Skokie. Couple of miles. So don't bark at me."

"I don't bark!"

"We're going to steal a car and find a small private airport and steal a plane."

"Come on."

"Or we're done. Understand, even though we can't see them, they are right on top of us and if we make a single wrong move we are dead. They haven't been baiting us or playing with us. They've been trying hard to get to us, but we've had a lot of luck. That has to run out. Maybe already has."

"We shouldn't have come to Vegas at all, then."

"We have a face. We have two names. It was worth it."

She fell silent, which was just as well, because he had to think.

He saw what he needed, a restaurant. "We're going in," he said. He repeated, "Stay close."

It was a seafood place, Christie's it was called, a low building looking like a mushroom in the middle of a sparsely occupied parking lot. A big neon trout danced in a pan on a tall sign near the building. They got out of the car into a faint scent of hot cooking oil. The sign buzzed and flickered.

"May we help you?" the hostess asked as they crossed the plant-filled entrance hall. It was late, close to closing time. Her plastic smile could no longer conceal the exhaustion in her eyes. How many jobs did she work, he wondered.

She guided them to a table amid a sea of tables. A waitress, Susan by her nametag, came and slid them menus.

"Go toward the ladies' room, the kitchen will be back there. Keep going through it, when you reach the parking lot, stay out of sight. I'll be there in a couple of minutes in a vehicle."

Without a word, she got up and headed to the back. In a moment, he followed her. As he exited into the lot, he saw her standing in shadows near the restaurant's Dumpsters. He wondered how close this thing was actually cut at this point. If he kept her with him, would that slow him down enough to make capture certain? He couldn't forget the way she'd frozen at Brewster's place. On the other hand, she'd had the presence of mind and ability to follow him into the tunnel.

He decided that he didn't care, he needed her. And it wasn't just to work this case. He needed her for reasons he could not put into words. She had a right to live and be safe. He wanted to make sure that happened.

He spotted a Ford about ten years old. He went to it and quickly popped the door lock, then entered it and worked under the dashboard, feeling along the wiring harness for the right leads.

The car came to life and he drove around to Diana.

"This isn't a good idea, Flynn, I have to tell you."

"It's the only idea. Everything else gets us killed."

"If we get caught, we're car thieves. Nobody has our backs. Remember that."

"Use one of the throwaways to track down a small general aviation airport somewhere in the area, closed at night, big enough to have a few planes parked there."

"Searchlight Airport," she said immediately. "Seventy miles south off Ninety-Five."

"You just happen to know this?"

"It's in New Vegas. The videogame."

"You play videogames?"

"I play with videogames. Crack them. Fool around with them."

"There'll be planes on this field? Flyable planes?"

"I have no idea, but I know it's there."

As they headed down Ninety-Three toward the turn onto Ninety-Five, he saw the Boulder City Municipal Airport. Plenty of planes, but it was also a busy facility, visibly active right now. The only way this was going to work was if they took a plane off an unmanned airport and stayed low and well outside of traffic patterns and radar coverage. Driving a hot car wasn't going to work, because they were too likely to get stopped. If the Menard City Police had onboard computers that automatically ran every plate they saw, which they did, the Nevada State Police certainly did, not to mention the LVPD. A stolen plane, on the other hand, was even better than a stolen boat. It wasn't expected. Homeland Security or not, there was little infrastructure to stop them. Plus, planes sat on general aviation fields for a long time. Until the pilot reported it, there wouldn't even be anything in police files. Add to that the fact that they could manage some serious distance, and it was the best option, no question.

Once they were on Ninety-Five traffic thinned out. Soon, the nearest vehicle was miles behind them. The only lights overhead were stars. Not that this meant much. If you had a silent helicopter and kept it below the radar ceiling, you could turn out the lights and the FAA would never know. But he had gained some confidence in his ability to lose them. Between Chicago and Vegas, he was now convinced that they'd been further behind them than he'd thought.

Still, there were loose ends. There always were, and one of them was bothering him a good deal.

"Let me ask you this, Diana. You're aware of bioactive tracking devices?"

"Sure. We put them in people like Rangers and pilots who're flying into hostile territory. They're injected under the skin. They're the size of a grain of sand."

"Were you ever given one?"

"Not to my knowledge."

"But it could have been done without your knowledge?"

"During a physical or something, maybe."

"How effective are they?"

"The signal has to be picked up by a satellite. You need the codes. If you know what you're doing, you can basically pick one up from anywhere in the world."

He did not like to hear that. "I don't think an unknown cop like me would have one."

"You're hardly unknown. First off, you're part of a classified database that contains every detail on record about every US citizen with an IQ over 190. You've been in that database since you took that IQ test in high school And we watched you for three months before we brought you in."

"What the hell is a database like that used for?"

"We watch for math skills and logic skills. The intelligence community eats geniuses like candy. We're addicted to them."

"So now I know why you got recruited. But why not me? I'm reasonable at math."

"The Abby Room stopped any recruitment track you might have been on."

"I wanted to rescue my wife."

"It was evidence of obsessive behavior, the curse of the very bright."

"I am obsessive. Damn obsessive. And cursed, of course, or I wouldn't be here doing this, I'd be in Menard and I'd still have Abby and be living the life I was born to live."

"If she hadn't been kidnapped and you hadn't gone off the deep end, you'd be working at NSA or someplace like that right now, and you'd be very happy and very well paid like I was. Like me and Steve were." She fell silent.

"You don't have a Steve Room, but you think it'd be a good idea."

"I will have a Steve Room. I like the idea of the Abby Room. Comforting."

He thought about that. "The hell with it," he said, "sometimes I hate the world. I hate life."

"Join the damn club."

He wished he had some way to definitely tell if either or both of them was trackable. "What frequencies do implants operate on?"

"Ours are FM. High on the band."

"But addressable?"

"If you know what you're looking for, sure. An ordinary scanner held close to the body will pick up the signal."

"We'll stop at a Radio Shack tomorrow." He did not add, "if we live." "Would we be able to remove them?"

"Size of a grain of sand, usually lodged in deep tissue. We'd have to dig them out."

"Nice."

When they reached Searchlight, there was not much to see. A single casino, like a ship lost in a black ocean. Worse, they had to drive up and down the highway four times before they finally found the tiny, weathered sign that marked the airport.

He turned onto what proved to be a dirt track.

"I'm sorry," she said.

"No, it's good. As long as there's a plane, we're good."

"An airworthy plane."

"A flyable plane."

He didn't bother to tell her that it had been years since he'd flown anything. His license wasn't even up to date. And he hated landings.

There were no planes visible, but there was a large hangar.

"I wish we had that thing we flew into Oregon. What was that?"

"Provided. No idea except that it worked."

"It was a damn fine airplane." He got out of the car and approached the old hangar. A lizard rushed out from under his feet as he shuffled through the sand.

"It's locked up tight," she said.

He didn't bother to respond until he discovered that she was exactly right. The lock on the access door was a good one. Not only that, it was new.

"Drugs are probably moving through here," he said as he examined the mechanism. "This is going to need brute force." He returned to the car, opened the trunk, and took out the tire iron.

"What if it's alarmed?"

"It'll be a bell or siren so who's going to hear it?"

"Maybe somebody lives nearby."

"It's your airport, Diana, you tell me."

"Go to hell."

As he worked the tire iron into the doorjamb, he said, "Sorry, that was uncalled for."

"It was."

He gave the tire iron a shove, hard, with his whole body.

He needed to be less harsh with her. She was out here for Steve the same way he was for Abby, and it was just as tough for her and it hurt just as much.

The door sprang back on its hinges. Warm air came out, sweet with the scent of aviation fuel.

"I was right," he said.

"About?"

"It's an active airport. There's planes in here." He stepped in. "Two of 'em."

They both shone their flashlights into the cave-like

blackness, revealing the fuselage of an elderly single-engine plane, with another standing in the deeper shadows.

"This one's a Cessna 172," he said. "No rear window, so it's probably pushing fifty."

"Fifty what?"

"Years old."

"And the other one?"

"You don't want to know. This is the one that might work. It can take us about seven hundred miles."

"Is there any gas?"

"Oh, it's ready to fly. They both are. These are drug planes. They move coke and hash, high-ticket stuff. Lightweight. They'll have usable avionics. Though I wouldn't try playing with an iPad while landing in a storm."

He went over to the plane and shone his light in. "There's a Garmin GPS in the dash, which is good."

"It looks awfully run-down."

"It's junk. They stick a Garmin in these things and spend nothing else. These planes go in all the time, or get impounded by the DEA. So they're expendable. So are the pilots. Let's get the hangar door opened."

He went over to the old wooden door and popped off the padlock with the tire iron. He handed the iron to her. "Keep this."

"Sure. Why?"

"In case anybody shows up. Keep watch. Let me know if you see any lights. This is a drug stop, so there could be security. Silent alarm." He got in the plane and switched on. The avionics lit up immediately and he began to not like this. He didn't like things that were too easy. Always an angle somewhere, something not seen.

An old plane is even easier to wire than a car, but it has to be done from under the cowling. He didn't need to, however. He found the key in the glove compartment.

The engine fired up immediately. This thing had been flown recently. It was probably scheduled to do so again, maybe even later tonight.

He called to her, "We're in good shape, get in."

She came over and clambered into the co-pilot's seat. She strapped herself in.

He throttled up until the plane rolled out onto the sand apron. Typical of the region, it was an east-west runway, sited to catch the prevailing winds. Not much of one, though, basically the desert floor denuded of weeds and cactus. He headed the plane into the wind. Once he took off, he'd turn east.

There was a car on the highway, moving fast, maybe heading here. He ran up the engine. The plane began to move forward. There were no lights. He was just guesstimating the position of the runway.

As they began to roll faster, plant life thudded against the wheels. The whole airframe shook. The speed crawled up, but not fast.

"Is it going to take off?" Diana yelled over the squall of the engine.

"I have no idea!"

CHAPTER TWENTY-FOUR

The drag of the sand slowed them down, and they kept trundling along, hitting cacti and slamming into tumbleweeds until it seemed as if they were going to go all the way to the Pacific without leaving the ground.

"Make it take off!"

"I'm trying!"

He watched the speed creep up to fifty-five knots, then sixty, then hang there, remaining maddeningly fifteen knots under rotation speed.

Without warning, the ground was gone, and he realized how this airport worked, which was really, really badly.

"What's happening?"

"We just taxied over a cliff."

"Oh God!"

"I agree."

The stall horn started bleating. His only choice was to drop the nose into absolute darkness and hope that the ground was farther away than he thought.

"What's going on now?"

"We're either gonna die or we aren't."

The airspeed indicator shot up to sixty-five and he felt the wings begin to bite. At seventy, the stall horn stopped. At seventy-five, he pulled the stick back, rotating nicely into a clear night sky.

"We've lived," he shouted to her over the rising blare of the engine.

"Barely."

"That would be true."

He'd taken off into the west and climbed to two thousand feet while getting the feel of the airplane. It had been a long time and he was more than unsure of himself. Worried that he might become disoriented, he kept his eyes on the instruments, not even glancing out the windshield. At least, at this hour and in this place, his chances of colliding with another airplane were too small to calculate.

He kept climbing, heading west. Eastward there were mountains, and he wanted plenty of altitude before he approached them.

At five thousand feet, he commenced a slow turn. Any higher, and he risked running into a monitored airway. He didn't have any idea of what the established flight paths might be, or where they were. He didn't want to blunder into approaches to larger airports, maybe at Bullhead City or Lake Havasu City.

"Where are we? Why do we keep turning?"

"We're heading into mountains. I'm gaining altitude."

"Dear God."

"You're a worse flyer than me."

He was actually relaxing a little, at least for the moment. Unless their pursuers were able to track them personally, this was going to prove a decisive blow to them. It wasn't as good as getting behind them, but at least when he landed this airplane, he would know that they had lost him.

The Garmin showed the highest peaks below them at thirty-five hundred feet, so they were safe here, and safe, also, from the DEA, the Border Patrol, and Homeland Security. DEA was interested in night flights by small aircraft, but their primary concerns were movement northward from the Mexican border and low-altitude flight.

"Do we know if we're dealing with any exotic technology?"

"We know so little, Flynn. Almost nothing. For example, why did they send only one cop, and what are his capabilities? His limitations?"

"One limitation we know."

"What?"

"He got his ass killed."

She turned to the window. "I've thought that he might be the only good guy. Their Dalai Lama or whatever. And the rest of them are all . . . Christ, I don't even want to think about it."

He hoped that she wasn't going to add a morale problem to her difficulties with field skills. Low morale was as lethal as a gun.

The tiny cabin shuddered, the engine howled, blue flames glowed in the exhausts. He kept them at cruise, a steady hundred and forty miles an hour. Two hours out, they were north of Seligman, Arizona, and he was not liking the feel of the air. To maintain his heading, he was having to crab the plane northward more and more. The wind was picking up. Worse, there was continuous lightning on the northern horizon, and it was getting more distinct.

The plane bucked like a frightened horse, the creaking of the airframe audible even above the engine and wind noise.

Diana was now slumped forward. Flynn knew what her problem was, but he didn't see any airsickness bags.

"If you can, feel in the seat pocket behind you. There might be a bag back there."

She did it and found one, and none too soon. In seconds, she was heaving into it. He opened the vents and cold air poured in, a mix of the scents of exhaust and desert night.

The heavy weather was bearing down on them fast, but he couldn't turn south, not and expect to thread through the higher mountains around Flagstaff. He needed to stay between Flagstaff and the Grand Canyon, basically, or he was going to crash this airplane.

"There's a light," she said. "Below us."

"What kind of a light? Is it moving?"

"Steady. Not a strobe. Moving, yes. Getting bigger. I think it's coming up."

He doused his running lights, then dimmed the cockpit as deeply as he dared. At a minimum, he needed his artificial horizon and his compass.

"Where is it now?"

"Gone. It went out."

"Went out? What's that supposed to mean?"

"That it is *gone*, as in disappeared. Jesus Christ, why do I have to spell everything out?"

He pushed back a flare of anger. They were getting on each other's nerves. "Let's not fight," he said.

"This is a goddamn nightmare!"

He flew on. There was nothing else to do.

When the light didn't reappear and nothing else

happened, he restored his instrument lighting but left the running lights off. They'd been in the air now for two hours, and he had another three hours of fuel left. Like so many of these drug wagons, this plane had been modified to fit larger tanks.

"We can make El Paso," he said. "We'll land at Sunrise Airport. I've flown in there."

"We can't rent a car without identifying ourselves."

"That's not the plan."

"I don't want to steal another one. It's too risky."

"That's not the plan, either."

"So we buy?"

"We can't buy."

"Then what? I don't get it."

He said nothing.

The storm now behind them, they flew into a gradually spreading dawn, and he was relieved to finally see the horizon. As the plane began to feel like a more solid platform in the sky, the sense of disorientation that had dogged him from the moment he'd taken off faded.

The light that Diana had seen coming up was also gone. What it might have been they would never know. The sky is a big place.

The landing at Sunrise was surprisingly easy. He squawked their approach and got immediate clearance. They hit the runway with a single bounce, then Flynn throttled back.

"That worked well," Diana said. She sounded ready to kiss the ground.

"The Cessna is a forgiving airplane."

He pulled out one of the disposable cell phones and dialed a number.

"Hey, Miguel." He shifted into Spanish. Diana's face immediately reflected the predictable suspicion. "*Com-*

padre, I'm at Sunrise and I've got an airplane some-body on the West Coast probably wants back. It's on the apron in front of the old Bellanca hangar. The bo-gus on it is NT273, it's a Skyhawk."

"What're you up to? I thought you quit the cops."

"I did. Private enterprise now."

"Anything there for me?"

"An airplane."

Diana interrupted. "What are you saying? What's going on?"

He closed the phone, pulled out the battery and the chip, and crushed it between his hands. "A friend's go-ing to pick us up," he said.

"That's off the reservation, damnit. *Way* off. And you know it."

"Nothing's off the reservation anymore. He will pick us up, he will take care of the plane, he will get us where we need to go."

"You can't have involved the El Paso police."

"No police."

"Then—oh, Christ, not a gangbanger?"

"He's honest. A good guy."

"You've tangled us up with the drug trade. Flynn, this is not a direction for us." She opened her door. "Come on, we need to get out of here."

He climbed out, also. They needed to get away from the plane anyway. The way it had been hidden, it could well be on some DEA list.

"Miguel and I went to grade school together. When we were six, he beat me to a pulp. Put me in the hospi-tal. Last year, he did ten years on a case I worked. We're good friends."

"He did ten years last year?"

"He blew his way out."

"Good Christ!"

"Not with explosives."

"But he's an escaped convict. You can't get an escaped convict involved in this."

They walked into the lobby. Flynn eyed the sandwich machine. He was definitely hungry.

"He got off for good behavior."

"Who shaves nine years off a ten-year sentence for good behavior?"

"It was very good behavior. I thought you'd be comfortable with an ex-con."

"Don't throw that in my face, okay? I wasn't guilty."

"Neither was Miguel." He put some money in the machine and got a ham and cheese sandwich. "Avoid the pimento," he said.

"No food," she muttered. "Later."

"That's right. Sorry."

Miguel had gained so much weight that the only reason Flynn recognized him when he finally ambled in was that there was nobody else coming through the doors this early in the morning.

"Hey, buddy."

"Thanks for the plane, man. That's gonna be some useful hardware."

"No problem. You better get a paint job on it, though, I think it's probably on the list. Not to mention its former owner."

"You movin' stuff? You on the sweet side of the law at last?"

"I'm still honest."

"The plane tagged?"

"Don't know. Could be."

"We'll find anything like that."

"I need clean transportation. Car or truck."

"I got a Range Rover, good VIN, good plates, not a problem."

"Done, let's go get it. We're on a schedule."

He gave Diana a long look. "Man, I'd like to see her work a pole."

"You would."

"The truck's gonna set you back. Not much."

"Yeah, it's gonna set me back one airplane."

"You come in here with a hot airplane and expect a clean truck in return? Man, that ain't right."

"Neither is dealing in stolen goods."

"You aren't a cop anymore. You tell me that, it's gonna stand up in court. I know the law."

"Eddie is still a cop, and Eddie still doesn't care for your ass."

The negotiation was starting to take too long, but Flynn could not betray his urgency. He just wished he believed that he could get away from their opponent, but he did not believe that. Maybe they were out of his gunsights right now, but he doubted that it would last.

Finally, Miguel said, "The plane is a good trade."

They headed for his house, where the Rover waited. Diana was silent, furious at Flynn for letting an outsider so close.

Flynn wondered how long it would be before the perp and his friends showed up in Miguel's life, and extracted from him every tiny bit of information he possessed.

"Where you goin'? Or should I ask?"

"See Mac."

"*Mac?* Ain't nobody shot him yet?"

"Mac dances too fast."

"Where's he keepin' himself these days?"

Flynn laughed. "That I'm not gonna tell you. The

plane is worth four times the truck. That's enough for one day."

"I wouldn't sell Mac. Mac's my friend."

"Everybody's your friend, Miguel. That's why you have no friends."

Twenty minutes later, they were heading out of El Paso in the Rover. Across the Rio Grande stood the dirty hills of Juarez, a most dangerous city, but bright in the light of dawn.

Flynn thought it would be nice to be in Juarez right now, hiding in a small hotel somewhere, deep in the city's maze of streets.

Even there, though, it would just be a question of time, wouldn't it? From now on, it would always just be a question of time.

"Who's Mac?" Diana asked.

"MacAdoo Terrell. The worst person I know and one of my oldest friends. Maybe the worst person in Texas, which is saying a fair amount."

"MacAdoo Terrell and Errol Caroll?"

"Mac and Flynn. Our parents died before we were old enough to kill them. At least Eddie got a decent name. He was the third member of our gang."

"And why are we going to see the worst person in Texas?"

"Because we need a friend."

CHAPTER TWENTY-FIVE

Where the Rover had come from, Flynn hoped he would never know. It had the feel of death about it. Why he knew that, he couldn't really say, but he knew it. It was his cop sense, he supposed, which had been in overdrive for a while now.

They were a few miles west of the little town of Iraan, pronounced Eerie-Ann in West Texan.

"We'll turn north on Three Forty-Nine," Flynn said. "Mac's got fifteen thousand acres of hell and good hunting up there."

"What's so bad about this guy?"

"What isn't? He won't show himself right away, incidentally. When he does, it'll be a near thing for me. He's got any number of reasons to want me dead, and we don't have enough money on us to do more than get him to think about changing his mind."

"A lot of people don't like you, Flynn. Casinos. Your boss."

"Eddie Parker? We grew up together."

"Well, he seemed pretty sour on you. Why does this guy hate you?"

"First off, Eddie has been pretty sour since we were about five. Second, I put Mac's brother on death row."

"And he can't blow his way out?"

"Not so far."

"It strikes me as foolish to expose ourselves to more danger than we're already in."

He turned onto Mac's road. It went back three miles, and it rode like it hadn't been spread with gravel in a good long while.

"Shouldn't we get our guns ready? Mine's in my backpack."

"I know where your gun is." He took his out of its shoulder holster and laid it carefully in a cup holder. "They won't do us any good."

"I just do not see why we'd come to some criminal lair or hideout or whatever it is."

Flynn saw Mac's shack huddled down in its draw, a ramshackle mess but topped by a very large, very clean American flag.

"See that? That's why."

She shook her head. "A crook wrapped in a flag is still a crook."

He knew that Mac would already have the truck in the sights of one of his superb rifles.

"There are gonna be dogs," he said. "Don't get out until Mac calls them off. They'll tear you to pieces." He pulled a little closer to the shack and the dogs immediately swarmed out from under it. They were Mac's own special breed, Weimaraner–Pit Bull mixes. Loyal, fast, lethal. If a bullet was going to stop one—and that was the only thing that could—then it was going to have to be well placed. Their wide heads, huge jaws, and yellow-gold Weimaraner eyes made them look the part of the hell-hounds that they were.

As soon as the truck stopped, they swarmed onto the hood and began clawing at the windshield and leaping against the doors and windows.

"My God, Flynn!"

"Just stay cool. They can't get in."

"How do you know that?"

"Armor glass. It'll take two or three blasts from a ten-gauge shotgun to knock out one of these windows. Dog teeth can't do it."

Mac was on the porch, standing back in the shadows, so still he was hard to see. He had the same ability to remain motionless that his brother did, and his father had in his time.

Slowly, his cupped fist went up to his lips. In it, Flynn could see something silver. "He's using his dog whistle."

An instant later, the dogs scurried back under the porch. Flynn rolled down his window.

"Hey, Mac."

Mac walked toward the truck. "You got a shit of a lotta nerve comin' out here, Carroll."

"I need some help."

"Oh, well, good. Allow me to accommodate you. Who's my rape victim?" He leaned into the window and said to Diana, "After I blow this shitbag's head off, we're gonna party."

"I didn't drop the big one on Weezy," Flynn said. "The jury did that."

"You put him in the same courtroom with them. Chained to the fucking wall."

"Your brother is obstreperous."

"You want a cup of coffee, come on in."

As they entered the shack, which was all gray boards,

split shingles, and tin on the outside, a luxurious bach-
elor pad unfolded. The ample living room was paneled
with exotic woods, a collection of stag, lion, rhino, and
elk heads decorated the walls, and a brilliant black and
yellow tiger skin lay before the big stone fireplace.

"Well, asshole, you came at the right time," Mac
said. "Cissy!"

Flynn held in his shock as Cissy Greene, Governor
Greene's oldest daughter, came sliding out of the kitchen.
Cissy was not underage, not quite, and she was as ripe
as a woman ever can get, her curves florid, her face
glowing, her lips beckoning moistly. How in the world
this very bad man had hooked up with her he could
hardly imagine, but here she was, big as life and a lot
prettier than her pictures.

"Cissy, this here is Asshole Flynn and his boyfriend.
What's your name, son?"

It was cruel and it wasn't true, but Diana went red.
"I'm actually a woman," she muttered. "My name is
Diana."

"Oh, the goddess Diana herself, my goodness, I am
honored! No wonder you appear so ferocious. Meet
Actaeon up there." He gestured toward the magnificent stag head.

"I thought I had him torn apart by his own dogs,"
Diana snarled.

"Hell no! He lived through that and came to Texas.
Where else? I got that sucker from one mile. *One mile*,
girl! Not my best shot, but decent." He smiled. "The
reason you-all are lucky is that Cissy here is a terrific
coffeemaker. Just drop the grounds in her mouth, pour
in boiling water and make her gargle. Personally, I can
pack a bullet a lot better than I can make a cup of java."

He gestured at them to sit, and Flynn and Diana

dropped down onto the magnificently soft leather couch. It was light tan, and Flynn thought better of asking him what it was made of. The Nazis had done lampshades and gloves. Mexican drug lords were way past that.

"Is that a tattoo," Diana asked, fingering a faint shadow in the surface of one of the couch pillows.

"Guy was a bandito. Low-grad South Texas bangers. Assholes."

Diana jumped to her feet.

Mac directed a frank gaze at her. Flynn could see that he was taking in her beauty. "If I saw you naked, would you have me torn apart by my own dogs?"

"I'd whip your sorry ass myself."

"Oh! Upon my word, Flynn my love, I see the attraction now. Coffeemaker can't keep me in line, but I'll bet goddess here keeps your ass good and red."

"Mac, we're not on a social visit. You're the best gun I've ever known, and the only person I know who's hunted tiger. I have a job for you."

"And if I do it, you'll get Weezy a reprieve?"

"No can do. You'll get a hell of a tiger skin, though. Better than this scrawny tourist rug."

"'No can do?' You worthless sack a shit. Sometimes I really wonder why I bother. I'm too damn affable, that's my problem. So I'm tellin' you right back, 'no can do.' But I am curious. Since we aren't in India or Siberia, what tiger?"

"We'll get to that."

"Not today we won't. 'Cause you just decided to get the fuck out of my house."

"Let me ask you this. Are you a patriot?"

"Shit, I knew that was gonna come up! Goddamnit, every cop who comes out here pulls that same card out of his hip pocket. Dubya has hunted this sliver of mine, my friend. A saint who got his ass handed to him by the negro."

"This will be the most patriotic thing you have ever done, Mac. Because what is at stake here is America. Our land and our people as we are now. So, if that matters to you, now is the time to face the fact that Weezy killed all those nuns because he's a total wacko and is best left to his fate."

"Is that it?"

"That's it. That's my play. Except I know why you've latched onto Cissy Greene. Obviously."

"Your boy has got fine card moves," he said to Diana. "He won a lotta money out here at poker, before civilization set in. Jesus God, you put Mexicans in the sheriff's office and whaddya get. Screwed is what!" He gave Flynn a long, sad look. Flynn knew that he was thinking about his poker game. When a wealthy rube sat down at his hallowed table, he soon discovered that he couldn't get up until he lost. Then he was kicked on the ass and told to go home.

"You want some Blue Label?" he continued. "I got a coupla cases I could let you have. Finest scotch in the world."

"Why offer me a bribe now?"

"Not a bribe. Sealin' a deal. I feel good, 'cause I'm gonna do good. Although savin' America and shootin' a tiger surely can't be played outa the same deck of cards."

"The tiger's just a first step. We have to get past it to get to what I really want."

"Okay, mister police, so your idea is I start by killin' an endangered species. Then what? Weezy leave some nuns behind?"

"You did it, didn't you? Weezy's taking a fall for you."

The convent had been on land wanted by Reich Development. The Sisters of Mercy would not sell, and it was soon being rumored that Reich had put a bounty on them. At the time, Eddie had thought Manny the Torch was going to be coming over from Dallas, so that was who the department was watching for. Then Weezy had showed up and blown them all to kingdom come. He'd imploded the building, and very professionally.

Because he'd come across as a nut case, the suspicion that it was a contract killing had never been followed up. In the State of Texas, though, nobody could be crazy enough not to get the needle for detonating nuns.

As always with Mac, the waters ran deeper than they appeared. To understand him, you had to read the eddies and whirlpools.

His face, previously throwing off smiles like confetti, had grown careful, the lines around the eyes tightening. His physical stillness had also returned, and Flynn knew that this could still go south real fast. Way south. He thought about his gun out in the car. He imagined Diana trapped under this monster while Cissy squealed and hit at him with her curling iron.

"You're a clever man, Flynn Carroll, I'll give you that. Now what more do I have to do?"

So he was going to let it pass—for the while, anyway. "We're gonna have to go on the hunt of a lifetime, you and me. At some point, we will be tracking the most incredible tiger on the planet. Not a half-starved tourist tiger concerned only about its mange. Eighteen feet of pure Siberian fury, and as smart as we are. At least."

Mac's mouth had dropped open. His eyes went

kind of glazed. He said, "If you weren't the straight-est shooting cop in Texas, I'd tell you to your face that you'd lost your mind."

"The tiger is only the front door. Behind that door is hell, Mac. The real thing. Might as well be."

"We're gonna be tying a knot in the devil's tail?"

"In a manner of speaking."

"So what's our next step, Detective Carroll?"

"Me and Diana, we're in danger."

"I don't like this, Mackie!" Cissy shrilled.

"Send her home, Mac, she doesn't need to be here."

"She can't go home. Her daddy got caught in bed with the damn secretary of state again and the missus has cleared out of the Governor's Mansion."

The secretary of state was Charles Forte. A guy. "Well," Flynn said, "boys will be boys. But at some point, we will have to go places where Cissy cannot follow."

"She shoots pretty good."

"I can outshoot you," she said, her baby fat wob-bling prettily.

Flynn would get back to that later. "We need to use your computers now, Mac."

"My computers are off limits to the po-lice."

"They're also unhackable. The most anonymous damn computers I've ever encountered. Everything proof."

"This I gotta see," Diana muttered.

"You're not gonna see much, son."

"Quit calling me that!"

"I can let you open a browser. Nothing else."

Flynn knew that Mac's computers were vitally im-portant to a big part of his business. The Texas Rang-ers had discovered that they were connected to a server farm he owned in Thailand, and were probably responsible for sending out billions of spam emails a day. His hackers in the Philippines used the system to do a brisk trade in government secrets, stealing from one country to sell to another. But never America, not Mac's beloved America. Or probably not.

His favorite scam, though, was to wait until a big shipment of drugs was moving up through the region, then tip off the DEA for a reward. His going rate was ten percent of street value. It was a perfectly legal business, but risky—which was where the guns came in. As often as not, the DEA guys found all the mules and guards involved with the shipment dead, shot from a distance with a high-powered rifle.

"This is interesting," Diana said, calling to Flynn from the computer room. She had begun to work, with Mac hanging over her like a morbidly fascinated vulture.

Flynn went in. "Where's Cissy got to?" He didn't like these people where he couldn't see them.

"Coffeemaker's making coffee," Diana said.

"I have no secrets from my lover," Mac said.

"Yeah, you do. Among them that she's a hostage."

"She can walk outa here anytime she wants."

"She's gonna walk into Iraan? Thirty miles? Cissy's in your clutches so you can get a pardon for Weezy, am I right? Does she know she's a hostage?"

"Maybe, but she doesn't care. In fact, she starts coming as soon as the big bad evildoer just brushes past the subject of sex. She's your classic con hag, rich, bored, and hot as oatmeal. There was a bunch of Tri-Delts out here from UT trying to outhunt their boyfriends. I cut her outa the herd."

"There's a Jay Elder on the board of directors of the Texas Animal Rescue League," Diana said.

"Could be a hit. This is the place near Austin?"

She was silent, working. "Jay Elder is an attorney, in practice twenty-three years. He's got property around Lake Travis west of Austin. He's also got a Louis C. Morris on his client list." She tapped a few more keys. "Interesting."

"A Louis Charleton Morris died thirty-seven years ago. An infant. So we know that our guy is wearing an alias, and he's fortyish. Fits the picture."

"Man, you are good with those suckers," Mac said, "whatever the hell you're doing."

"I am good, son," Diana replied. She clicked a couple more keys, and paper came out of the printer. "Jay Elder, Louis Morris, the animal group, and a satellite view of the facility."

"I'd pay for your services," Mac said. "A lot."

"They'd cost more than you have. Whatever you have." She turned off the laptop, then turned it over and examined the base. In a moment, she had a black oblong object in her hand. She swung it high overhead and smashed it to bits on the desk. Gouges of mahogany flew.

"Hey hey HEY, what the hell? What the hell did you just do?"

"Nonsecured computer used in a classified operation. Hard disk has to be destroyed. Legal thing, son. Sorry."

"Damn you!" He came at her.

Flynn saw that the rage in his eyes was damn serious, and he stepped between them. "Hold off! Just hold off!"

Mac stopped, but that was going to last maybe five seconds.

"Jesus, Diana!" Flynn said.

"He's got a backup system."

"It doesn't fucking work!" he shouted.

"I fixed it. All of your stuff is on it, none of mine. If I'd left traces, you'd draw federal interest. You don't want that."

"Anybody ever gets me, it ain't gonna be a fed."

"It'd be a drone strike." She took out her credential. "Ever seen one of these?"

Mac looked at it. Now he shifted his eyes back to Flynn. "What kinda crowd are you running with, buddy?"

"It's a long story. Suffice to say, if you help us, there will be credit earned. Significant credit."

"Flynn, if it don't involve saving Weezy's life, it don't mean a thing to me. That's my little brother, man!"

"Don't keep hitting me with that, you've got the governor's daughter strapped into your guillotine and we both know why. Weezy will not take the needle."

"As long as she stays by my side. But since when does a twenty-year-old do anything for more than a couple of long farts? Soon's I run outa horse, she's gone."

"Mac, don't reveal a crime to me."

Mac spread his hands. "So, okay, let's go tiger hunting."

CHAPTER TWENTY-SIX

They'd taken a suite at the Four Seasons in Austin on Mac's dime. They were using one of his laptops and any calls were made over one of his cell phones. His security was the best.

Mac and Cissy had ordered up champagne and caviar, fried wontons, Snickers bars, the list was long. She was pleading to invite friends, and Flynn thought it wise to let that happen. With them would come grass and crack and X and coke, and for Cissy a useful oblivion. In anticipation of the fact that they would be separated, a friend of Mac's, Giorgio Budd, had appeared.

Cissy and Giorgio bickered in the living room. He was a masseur, but she didn't want a massage. Flynn could hear them from the bedroom he and Diana had made into an office.

"So come on," Giorgio wheedled. "I can do it through your clothes, it's nice. Daddy no see."

"Yeah, but daddy touch."

"No, no, no boobies, baby. Just let daddy do his thing."

She yelled, "You're too icky, okay! It'd be like being touched by the Pillsbury Dough Boy, get it? You need to meet my dad. He'd love you."

"He's a stinkin' Republican. I don't massage no stinkin' Republican."

"You could bite off his dick. You'll get the chance."

Mac sat in the window of the bedroom they'd made into an office.

Flynn said to him, "That's going well."

"If she bolts, Giorgio has orders to tie her up and stick her in a closet."

"Don't tell me these things, damnit!"

Mac's window overlooked the Colorado River and a sunny view of South Austin beyond. "I got a bad feeling," he said. "I had a good feeling. Now I got a bad one."

"It's gonna be a piece of cake."

"No, Flynn, it isn't."

Mac had good instincts, there was no question about that. Excellent. Flynn had not told him of the casualties so far, and he wondered why not. He should warn the guy, obviously. And yet he didn't.

He liked Mac, who was, as he claimed, an affable man. But he was also an extraordinary engine of human suffering. That's what crime is—the infliction of human suffering for financial or other gain. God only knew how many lives Mac's scams ruined in a week, not to mention his more murderous activities. Of course the DEA and the Rangers let the shooting of drug mules and cartel gunmen happen. Scumbags killing scumbags, nice and convenient.

"I've got the whole area mapped out," Diana said, "from the Animal Rescue to Jay Elder's ranch compound near Lake Travis. There's a house, a barn, a couple of outbuildings, a dog run and kennel. Active."

"What took you so long?" Mac asked. "You coulda gotten that off Google Earth an hour ago. We need to get out there, get a feel for the land."

"Mapped to three feet, in real time," she continued. "Google Earth doesn't do that."

"You guys can recognize faces from space, can't you? Read license plates?"

"Very yesterday, but yes."

"What can you do now? Read minds?"

"Classified."

"Cool word, son. Must make you feel important as hell."

It was already pushing seven, and the sun was starting to set.

"There's something strange," Diana said abruptly.

On the screen of the laptop she was using was a wilderness area. Right in the middle of it was what appeared to be a small village, made of logs and expertly camouflaged.

"It's in the middle of a wildlife preserve. Strange place for a village."

"Any signs of life?"

"I can't be sure. There are paths, obviously."

"What the hell does this have to do with the price of bread?" Mac asked.

Diana said, "It's two miles from Jay Elder's ranch house. And look at the buildings—there's been an effort to camouflage them. Quite skillful. You wouldn't see this for what it was on a Google satellite map. And as for Google Earth, their trucks stick to roads."

Mac peered at it. "Boy, I can even see individual branches in that camouflage. From way up there."

"Mac, we can determine your rate of hair loss by watching your bald spot. Face it, if you weren't useful, the feds would've crushed you like a bug a long time ago."

"You'd be surprised at how good I am."

"They're better. Now, let me see. I can switch to another lens—here we go."

The image changed to infrared. Nobody had to ask about the change. Both Flynn and Mac knew infrared very well.

"Hm," Diana said. "No obvious heat signatures. Flock of deer, eleven does and a buck, about half a mile away. That glowing dot is probably a buzzard looking for supper. Nothing dead, though, not big enough to spot, anyway."

"Corpses are cold," Mac said.

"Rot is hot, son. This system is sensitive enough to pick up the heat of decay."

Flynn said, "Maybe it's an old hippie place. Commune. Austin was a major stop on the Hippie Highway."

"Old paths would be more vague. These are sharply drawn. People use this, but I don't think they're there now. And they don't have pets. No sign of any dogs or cats."

"You wouldn't happen to be able to spot a tiger with that thing, would you?" Mac asked.

"I would but I haven't."

"Shit, then, what am I supposed to hunt?"

"You don't understand," Flynn said. "The tiger isn't where it's supposed to be, penned at the Animal Rescue League. It's the only Siberian tiger presently missing in the United States. It's called Snow Mountain, it's seven years old and it has had a number of legitimate exhibitor owners, specifically two zoos and a circus. Apparently it was sold along because it ate a hell of a lot. It's about forty percent larger than what's normal for the breed. It was collected by the Texas Fish and Wildlife from an abusive situation, so the record says. Of course, records lie."

"And it's here in Texas—specifically near Lake Travis? Or not?"

Diana said, "Jay Elder is here because he was at his law firm yesterday. But he's just back, interestingly enough, from Vegas."

"How do you find things like that out?"

"Classified, son."

"Quit that, okay? I'm sorry I insulted you. Son."

"You are sorry, son, I agree there. Now, take a look at the Elders place. Tell me what you think." She shifted to another image, this one of a ranch house in a small compound of buildings. There were three trucks parked near the house, two of them Cadillac Escalades, and the third a van with blackened windows. The van's side door was open, and it was possible—just—to see a bit of the interior.

"There aren't any rear seats," Flynn said.

"Nope, and look closely." She blew the image up to a blur. "Isn't that a barrier behind the front seats, like the kind you see in taxis? See that white there, across the top—you can just see the dashboard beyond it, so that's clear. But below, it's a featureless blackness. If you were transporting a large animal, you might use a van like that, especially if it had a touchy disposition."

"He's touchy all right," Flynn said. But then he remembered the expression on the cat's face in the storm drain, almost—was it kindness? A sort of kindness? "Touchy and complicated."

"I have two images here. The van pulled up. Then this one, the van with the rear door opened. About seventy seconds between them. I'm hoping we can find some residual heat in the second image."

Mac said, "Do the DEA boys have access to stuff like this?"

"Classified."

"I think I might retire," Mac said.

"Don't do that, Mac," Flynn said, "you'll kill my dream."

"Which is?"

"Collar of a lifetime."

"Fuck you, Flynn."

"Double back."

They both chuckled, remembering their young days in the streets of Menard, getting up to no good together. "Fuck you" and "double back" was essential dialogue of their youth.

When they were ten, they'd been like three brothers, him and Mac and Eddie.

"Too long, Buddy," he said.

From the living room came a peal of female laughter. "She's discovered that Giorgio's a eunuch," Mac commented.

"Oh, come on," Diana said. "There are no eunuchs."

"He was cut by a sultan so he could be trusted to massage the ladies of the hareem."

"Holy shit, who would consent to that?"

"I don't think that 'no' was an available answer. He made some money, though." Cissy laughed again, wonder in her voice. "When he can't get what he wants, which is to touch their beautiful bodies, he does show and tell. Works the pity angle. She'll be on his table shortly."

"Guys, this has processed up nicely."

Flynn saw the same image on the screen, except this time there were a few extra blurs. "What are we looking at here?"

She pointed to a ghostly smear. "That's a man. The computer's telling me he's six two and fairly heavy. Likely a real bruiser. Now, here's the interesting one. Right there by the open door. The computer doesn't know what that is, but it's definitely a valid infrared signature. A minute or so before this photo was taken, something warm moved through that space."

"They just let a damn tiger out to roam the effing night?" Mac asked.

"Looks like it," Diana said.

"It can't be smart enough to risk that. What if it eats a kid?"

"It'll go out and take a deer, be my guess. Stay out of sight, come home at dawn."

"Damn hard to credit."

"Mac, this hunt is gonna be the challenge of your life."

Mac smiled, just a little, deep in his face. "You know, I think I'm gonna take my nice warm girl into the master and get myself prepped."

"Don't drink anything more. Don't get fatigued."

"First off, I've only had three bottles of that flat-assed Dom Perignon they sent up. Plus sex before a hunt helps my concentration." He went off into the living room. "Girl! Get offa that thing, you're gonna get your ass laid right now." A moment's silence, then, "Come on, little man, you can quarterback."

Chrissy, Mac, and Giorgio went into the bedroom, and soon what they used to call "sounds of revelry" in Flynn's frat house at UT were heard. He wished he had Mac's courage to still live as a boy, but he could never be as careless with lives—his own and others—as Mac was.

"Would you please go close that door?" Diana asked him.

Fine by him. Envying Mac's kind of freedom wasn't healthy.

"I've picked up a couple more traces," Diana said when he came back. "Here—" She pointed to what looked to Flynn like a slight white discoloration in the image. "And again." The next discoloration was even fainter. "It was moving south-southeast." She looked up from her work. "Flynn, I think the damn thing is on patrol around that house."

"Ideal for Mac. If it's following a set pattern, he'll figure that out. The man could track a ghost in a snowstorm."

"That's going to work both ways."

"There'll be two of us, and neither one's going to do what Snow Mountain expects, which is to assume he's dumb." He paused. "Diana, do you know anything about combining human and animal genes? Would that be the reason the damn thing is so smart?"

"You have to assume so. Or maybe it's a mix of ours, tiger, and who knows what? Think about it. If they could be from anywhere, they could *bring* anything."

"I'm wanting to give Mac some idea of what to expect. He understands that this is a real smart tiger, but how smart he doesn't understand."

"If he gets eaten, I have to tell you, I don't personally have a problem with that. But that's just me, of course."

"Friend of my youth. Plus, I see a future for him on our new team."

"How could he possibly survive a security check?"

Flynn said nothing.

The sun was well down now, the lights of the city glowing, the river a black ribbon. Flynn could even see a few stars, but that wouldn't last. The moon was rising in the east, full and fat, a big Texas moon.

He began methodically assembling his equipment, his own personal night-vision lenses, his new pistol—one of Mac's .357 Magnums—and his other essentials, a handheld GPS, a backup compass.

She slid his MindRay into the backpack.

"No."

"You were using it under pressure in adverse field conditions."

"All field conditions are adverse."

"We can't leave this thing in a hotel room."

That stopped him. Surely she didn't expect to come with them. "Diana—"

"I know what you're about to say, and don't even think about it. You absolutely need me in the area."

"No."

"I can operate a command post in the car. I'll be looking at satellite data as you work."

"Do it from here. We both have cell phones."

"It's too much of a risk and you know it. You'll be lucky to have an hour before they detect you. Maybe less. If cell phone calls are popping out there, way less."

He couldn't deny the truth of that, nor the fact that the information she could provide would be extremely valuable, even essential.

"We can use the same radios we used in Montana. I've got yours, mine, and Mike's in my backpack. They are low power and the encryption technology makes them sound like backscatter. No scanner in the world will even identify our transmissions as signals."

"In this world. Maybe we failed in Montana because alien technology was in use against us."

She was silent for a moment. Then she said, "The value outweighs the risks. If you get detected, I'm going to see them coming. And what if I nail down the location of the tiger? That could happen."

He looked at her. She glared back at him, the determination and defiance if anything increasing her attraction.

"Good enough," he said, "let's get studley back in his pants and do some hunting."

CHAPTER TWENTY-SEVEN

As Flynn and Mac headed off into the thick brush, Flynn looked back at the truck. They'd parked it off the road near a little place called Balcones Springs, where they'd pulled the truck up into a brushy area along a disused road, but one that was high enough to provide the low-power radios a useful platform. Nearby was the Balcones Canyonlands National Wildlife Preserve, as difficult an area to walk as the Texas Hill Country offered. It consisted of nearly forty square miles of steep-sided hills, gnarly ravines, cactus, and cedar. The only nearby water of any significance was in Lake Travis itself.

They were still two miles both from the strange little village and Jay Elder's ranch house, and about equidistant between them.

Flynn touched the "transmit" button on his radio's earpiece. A moment later, there was a brief burst of static, then another. Mac and Diana, acknowledging.

"That satellite stuff has me spooked. How does she gain access?"

"Dunno. It's not a password, that I do know. Something more esoteric."

"What if this guy Elders has access to the same feed?"

"He doesn't."

"You know that?"

"If he did, why would he be doing something as risky as using guard animals—the tiger, for example. Or the dogs."

"I get your drift. It's just that my bad feeling is getting worse, man." He looked down at his GPS. "The last place she picked up the tiger was eighteen hundred yards due north." He put the GPS in his pocket.

"Best turn it off."

"It goes off by itself."

"Until it does, it radiates a signal. Not much of one, but it's there. I know from experience with what we're dealing with, we need to be real, real careful about signals."

"What are we dealing with, Flynn?"

The question lay there, unanswered in the dark between them. "How much have you figured out?"

"That this is some kind of classified government deal. That this animal is really weird. What is it, something that escaped from a lab?"

"Something that was created in one, that we know. Whether it escaped or was sold on or exactly what happened isn't clear." He did not tell Mac why they were actually going after the tiger, to get at the extraordinary criminal behind it. It wasn't that he didn't want to. He didn't know how.

They moved through the moonlit hills with the swift precision of men whose lives had unfolded in places like this. The land around Menard was much the same:

dry, mean, and hard. It was the sort of land that looked inviting from a distance, but would give you maybe two days if you got lost in it—assuming that you didn't get snakebit or slip and fall down a bluff. By the third day, you'd be too crazy with thirst and weak from struggling in the terrible land to do anything but stagger until you dropped. Observed from a porch on a high bluff on a summer evening, though, the land smiled like a saint.

"Guys, I have a new trace. A thousand yards north northwest of your position."

Flynn pressed his transmit button to indicate that they'd heard her.

In flat land, it would have been a possible shot, but not in these cruel little hills, just high enough and steep enough to tax a strong man.

"We need to split up," Mac said. "Let's angle in, maybe five hundred yards apart. First one gets a shot, takes it."

"Absolutely do not get out of sight of me. *Do not*."

Mac frowned, shook his head. Beneath the rim of his Stetson, his face was in deep moon shadow.

"Come on, let's move ahead. You see a shot, take it."

Separated by fifty yards rather than five hundred, they slipped softly through the moonlight, each man concentrating on his own silence. The north wind grew stronger, hissing in the cedars and sighing in the live oaks, making the autumn grasses dance. There was that note of sadness in it that colors so much of nature. Far to the north, the same clouds that he and Diana had seen from the plane were putting on an electrical display as they rolled across the featureless plains of Texas.

They both carried Weatherby Mark V Deluxe rifles chambered for .300 Weatherby Magnum cartridges.

The boat tail spire point bullets they were using were forged in Mac's own shop, by a master bullet maker called Carlos Gons. Gons's bullets were famous in West Texas for being the finest that money could buy—assuming you were friendly with Mac, of course.

A skilled sniper could use these rifles and these bullets to shoot extraordinary distances. But not in this terrain and not at night. Here, they were looking to get within three hundred yards of the quarry, and to do that they were going to need to surprise it.

Flynn had considered just going in to the ranch house with some serious ordnance, but he now needed to investigate that village, also, and that was not going to happen until the tiger was gone.

Mac stopped. He pressed his transmit button twice, looking for a report from Diana. A single flutter of static came back: "no joy."

But Mac still didn't move. He raised his night vision binoculars to his eyes. With this moonlight, you didn't need night vision goggles, but the binoculars were useful for looking into shadows and pulling in distant detail.

There was a sound, then, soft but unmistakable. It was the chuffle of a tiger and it could not be more than fifty feet away—but not in the direction Mac was looking.

They were about to take a hit.

"Back to back."

"What? Why?"

He said to Mac, "Back to back."

"What's going on?"

"It's here." He touched his radio. "Diana, it's within fifty feet of us. Do you see it?"

"I don't—no . . . standby—oh God, Flynn it's in

those cedars to your left. Flynn, it's going to pounce right now!"

Flynn fought down the impulse to run. Unlike the situation when he'd faced it with the Glock, one of these rifles would bring it down immediately.

"You heard?"

"Oh, yes." Mac examined the cedar thicket with his binoculars. "Where the hell is it? Ask her again."

He pressed his transmit button. "We need coordinates."

"It's in motion away from your position. Flynn, something about the way it moves causes it to just leave traces. I can hardly track it. But it appears to be going south, toward the lake. Moving fast. Now it's gone. No—stand by." A pause. "Lost it."

"Okay, take a breath. It's trying to lead us, looks like."

"Into a trap?"

"Away from the village. Away from the ranch."

"So we ignore it."

"If we do that, we fall into whatever trap's been laid for us."

"So let's follow it."

"Then we fall into a different trap. We've been outmaneuvered."

"Man, I'm hunting a tiger, here, not a damn werewolf."

He thought he now needed to tell Mac the truth. But how? This was a man who had absolutely no idea about aliens, except for the illegals who worked his and every other ranch in swarms. Employers called them grad students.

Diana had said that the government didn't actually know what they were. And that was after sixty years of watching them. So how the hell did he explain them to Mac?

Maybe he didn't. Maybe what he needed to do was to just put Mac where he could do some damage and hope for the best.

"Let's head for that funny little village," he said.

"Not the ranch?"

"That's the head of this snake. I'm looking for the heart shot."

"Flynn, I'm always looking for the heart shot and the high card. But just before we go charging off, *where the fuck is my tiger?*"

Flynn hit his radio. "Anything?"

A burst of static was her only answer.

"Verbal, please."

She came back, "It's well south of you now, probably close to the lake."

"Then nowhere near the village?"

"No. No way."

He said to Mac, "We'll find it at the village."

"But she said—"

"Come on." Flynn began moving cautiously forward. Mac stayed close. They went down a long draw, then up onto higher ground, skirting one of the weathered limestone hills.

"What're we expecting?"

"No idea."

As they moved slowly ahead, the village came into view, in the form of a number of structures that appeared almost Polynesian in design, low buildings open at both ends, with peaked roofs and elaborately carved lentils.

"What the hell?" Mac muttered.

Diana sent a burst of static, then spoke. "It's come

out of no damn where and it's heading directly toward you. I've got a clear view, it's running fast. According to the computer, you have three minutes."

"We could take cover in one of these," Mac said. "Set up an ambush."

Flynn went closer to the nearest one. The wood was dark, the carvings were hard to make out in the shadowy moonlight. Wind blew through the thing, which was open at both ends.

He thought maybe that it was an alien village, right here on earth. Was it the only one? Did anybody know? They were just so damn uninformed about the whole thing. Hopefully there was somebody somewhere with good information, because a village—Flynn was no expert, but to him this looked like some part of an invasion.

He risked a light, shining it into the interior.

"Empty, looks like," Mac said.

They took a step in.

"My God, it stinks in here," Mac said.

It was a milder version of the smell in Oltisis's office. Flynn took another step forward, moving deeper.

"Flynn?"

He turned around.

"Is there something behind me?" Mac asked.

Ten feet behind Mac, right in the center of the village, standing absolutely still, was the tiger. It had taken no more than a minute to get here.

Its eyes were on its prey. As in Montana, the animal had outmaneuvered them. Flynn could not get a shot off at it without hitting Mac, and it was so close to him that it could tear him to pieces before he even finished turning around. On the other hand, the moment the animal jumped onto Mac's back, Flynn would have a kill shot. So this wasn't a quite a checkmate for the tiger. It was a double check.

"Mac, come to me."

"Man, that smell—"

"Nice and easy. Do it now."

Mac's eyes became tight steel in the moonlight. His face closed down. As his finger slid over his trigger, he came a step closer. Silently, the tiger shifted, keeping Mac between itself and the gun. What an expert it was. It had thought at least five moved ahead.

Mac took another step, and the tiger remained behind him. But it knew that he could bolt at any second. So could it—and it did, just as Mac entered the structure.

"Where was it?"

Flynn did not answer him. He was watching in astonishment and growing horror as the darkness behind Mac continued to deepen. Silently and in some unknown manner, the apparently doorless opening was closing.

He ran past Mac, but it was already much too late. Where the rear opening had been was the blackness of a wall.

The tiger had not thought five moves ahead or eight, but ten, twenty, maybe more.

What it had done was elegantly lethal. It had coaxed them into a man trap.

CHAPTER TWENTY-EIGHT

Flynn reached up and touched his transmit button. "Diana? Come back."

Silence.

Mac said, "That thing is smarter than me, Buddy."

"It's brilliant."

"What is it, Flynn? It can't be a tiger. It just looks like one."

"I don't know, Mac. I just don't know."

"My flashlight's dead."

"Mine, too."

"And the radios. And my GPS."

Flynn found his in his pocket and pulled it out. It had been off, but when he pressed the toggle, nothing happened. "Same here."

None of the electronics worked.

"Goddamnit, what have you gotten me into, man?"

"I thought we could handle this."

"Well we can't."

Suddenly Mac was in his face, his breath full of sour fear. "Flynn, for God's sake, what in fuck is this about?"

There was nowhere to begin. "What I think is that maybe if we can make our way to the wall, we can get out of here."

"The fuck, we're trapped, man!" Mac fired his rifle, the report shattering in the confined space. He fired it again, straight up, and in the flash Flynn saw him, his eyes glassy, his face a glaring mask of fear. Again he fired, and again Flynn saw him. This time his lips were pulled back, his eyes were glaring almost comically, but there was nothing funny about the transformation—the visible disintegration—of this man.

"*Mac!*"

Again he fired, and this time Flynn saw something behind him, a figure standing with its legs spread and its hands on its hips. Its mouth was an oval complication of spiked teeth.

Not an animal. Not like Oltisis. But not human either . . . not quite.

"Cool it!"

Again Mac fired, and this time Flynn saw in the flash that there were figures all around him.

"Shit, they got my damn gun!"

Flynn tightened his grip on his own.

"We're not gettin' outa here, man!"

"Stay cool, there's always a way."

"Fuck, oh, *fuck*!"

"We're not done," Flynn said.

Mac began babbling and weeping. Anybody who gets scared enough reveals an inner asshole, was Flynn's experience. Mac was no exception.

Slowly, Flynn turned around. Behind them, there had been another door, so maybe it was still possible to get over there.

Porting his rifle, he moved forward. There was the

softest of flutters against his cheek. Lurching away, he cried out with surprise.

The rifle was gone from his grasp. Incredibly.

His first thought was to draw the Magnum, which was still under his shoulder. He stopped himself, though. Whoever had taken the rifle would surely take it, too.

"Fuck, they got my Mag, man!"

Flynn didn't respond. He kept his arm tight against his shoulder holster.

There was a book of matches in his pocket, kept there for whatever emergency might require them. Would they still work? He had no idea, he'd been transferring them from pocket to pocket for months. Moving as slowly and quietly as he could, he reached in, felt his keys, some change, and then the matches. Crouching over them, he pushed the cover open, tore one out and struck it. There were sparks, but no light. Again he struck it, and this time it flared, sputtered blue, then caught, a tiny yellow flame.

In the light it gave, which was not much, he saw Mac, now lying on the floor. He was surprisingly close by. "Mac, get your ass up."

There was no response.

"Mac!"

His eyes were open but staring blankly. Flynn recognized this as a state of extreme shock, like a man lying on the roadside beside the twisted ruin of his car.

Just at the edge of the flickering pool of match light, there was movement.

The match went out.

Frantically, he fumbled another one between his fingers, struck it and held it up.

Standing over Mac was one of the creatures. It looked

up at him with eyes so large that they were like great, plastic buttons, sky blue and swimming with tragedy.

The match went out. Flynn lit another.

Mac groaned. He lifted himself up on his elbows, he saw what was standing over him and started to roll away, and at once the thing began striking him with a nasty little sap, which caused him to throw up his arms in defense of his face, and to scream a gargled, quickly stifled scream.

Now Flynn did draw the Magnum, holding it in both hands, bracing it in front of him.

Another of the things jumped toward him.

The Magnum was gone, taken with such extraordinary quickness that Flynn had no chance to react. One instant, his hands were hard on the gun, then next they were empty.

He backed away, then he turned and blundered across the small interior space, in the process upending what felt like furniture and causing something to screech in anger—more than one something. In fact, the space seemed to be filled with these beings, five, ten, who knew how many?

This was their home.

He came to the back wall. Feeling along it, he attempted to understand what is was made of. From the outside, the building had looked like nothing more than a loose construction of dried branches. In here, though, it was slick and hard, cool like stone.

He kept feeling along the wall, seeking some kind of hinge or latch or some sort of opening.

Across the room, he could hear Mac screaming, and could hear the screams becoming more and more muffled, as if he was being enclosed in something.

Until he was also helpless, Flynn realized that they intended to contain him, not risk attempting to overpower him.

This told him that, while they were faster, he was stronger. Also, they either didn't want to kill him or didn't have effective weapons of their own.

Understanding that they were treating him like a rampaging animal gave him some room for maneuver. Not a lot, because, just as was true of a cop facing a knife-wielding drunk, there would be conditions that would force them to risk attempting to overpower him.

He mustn't try to fight them. He mustn't be destructive. He continued feeling along the wall, until he came to what seemed to be an intricate mass of twigs and branches woven together.

The Russian boar he caught on his place up in Tom Greene County never understood the trap. But he was human, surely he could understand.

Methodically now, he felt among the twigs. The structure had been wide open at both ends.

Twigs. Wood. He had matches. Could he set it on fire? No, they'd put a stop to that the same way he would if a drunk with a knife started trying to use it.

They were close around him now, but why didn't they get more violent? What were they waiting for?

In one of Mac's gun flashes, he had seen a beam about six feet up, and above it what appeared to be loose thatch. Thinking that he might be able to break out that way, he raised his hands upward and felt for purchase. Holding on with the tips of his fingers and pushing with his feet, he went up the wall faster than he had expected—or than they had, because there was an immediate rush of scurrying below him, and rough, guttural whispering. His fingers throbbed, but he kept climbing until he felt the beam.

Long, pealing cries rose, full of complicated, haunting undertones, like the wind on a winter's night, like somebody crying in the dark hills of childhood, like wolves howling.

What was really going on here? How were these people—or things—connected to Oltisis? Could it be that there were two species of alien on Earth?

He swung out onto the beam, and immediately saw before him two of the creatures. In the next instant, the closer of them leaped at him, screaming and clawing.

As he pulled it off, the second one slammed a sap into the side of his head and he fell from the beam, forcing his arms up to protect his head as he fell. When he hit he rolled and bounded to his feet. One of the creatures was crushed and broken beneath him, writhing and screaming with a warbling banshee madness. Lightning-fast hands grabbed at him.

One after another, he pulled them off, but the pummeling saps kept coming until finally what felt like a sack of iron slammed him in the right temple.

Then the dark.

CHAPTER TWENTY-NINE

Something hit Flynn in the forehead so hard his eyes flashed. Still, though, he didn't wake up completely. He tried to turn over, but something else scraped his shoulder, preventing him

When he opened his eyes, it didn't help. This was absolute dark. Again he tried to sit up and again he slammed his head.

His lay still. His temple throbbed, his forehead ached, his shoulders were compressed and the air was thick.

Twisting, he raised his left hip until he could free his arm. He felt upward—and encountered a ceiling not even a foot above his face.

So this was no floor he was lying on. He'd thought himself in some sort of tight crib, but this was not a crib. The ceiling could only mean one thing: he was in a box.

For a moment, he was out of control. He kicked, he hammered at the lid, screams burst out of him.

No. Keep your head. Right now, your mind is the only weapon you've got.

This was what Abby had experienced. Steve. All of them.

Poor damn people, above all, poor *Abby*.

He pushed at the top of the thing. No give whatsoever. Steel? Thick wood? What did it matter, he wasn't going to break out, it was far too strong.

Panic hit him again, causing him to start gasping, causing his stomach to twist against itself and his heart to fly.

No, *no*! You *will* go silent inside. You *will* slow that heart rate. You *will* stop that gasping.

Okay, breathe evenly, let the heart rate drop, focus the mind. No matter how hard it is, do it.

He visualized an open space. Dark but open.

The air was thickening fast but still breathable. So far, no frantic waves of suffocation were overwhelming him. Yet.

Keep the breaths even but shallow, don't move unless absolutely necessary.

All right, let's get our bearings. You're in what appears to be a coffin or a box.

First thing you need to know is, have you been buried alive or are you still aboveground?

He had fallen to the floor, fallen on one of the creatures or aliens or whatever they were.

What he had to do now was change his situation or, if that wasn't possible, face it. If he'd been buried alive, he was going to die here. It wasn't pretty, but he'd damn well died in a good cause. On the other hand, if he was aboveground, maybe there was a way out.

The air was getting very bad very fast. He felt along

the join between the lid and the sides of the box. Seamless. Might as well be welded closed, and maybe it was.

Long ago, he had reconciled himself to the idea that death might come to him during the course of his work. But not now, not before he had gotten to the man who had killed Abby.

He inventoried himself for tools. He was still fully dressed, so maybe he still had some of his possessions.

The rifle and the pistol were gone, of course, but he could still feel his wallet. Only by raising his shoulders and wriggling his hips could he manage to push his hands down into his pockets.

Frantic surges of air hunger coursed up and down his body.

He got his right hand into the pocket, and to his surprise it closed around his pocket knife. It had been with him since high school, and contained a blade, a fingernail file, and a small scissors. As he scrabbled at it, attempting to get it out, he tried to think what he might do with it.

It was then that he noticed that the air hunger was getting less. He was beginning to be able to breathe again.

That could mean one of two things—either his twisting and turning was opening a crack somewhere, or somebody on the outside was introducing oxygen into his air supply. He remembered something about the Chinese doing this during some distant war, perhaps Korea. The objective was to so terrorize the victim that he became open to brainwashing.

If this was torture, then they were out there watching and listening. They had a use for him and needed him to be so broken that he would follow their orders.

So what needed to happen in here to get them to open the lid?

The answer was clear: once they were sure that he had completely lost it, they would bring him out.

He began having trouble breathing again. His mouth opened, he gasped, but he also remained totally still.

Finally a surge of need went through his body that was so intense that it made him kick. His chest heaved, he sucked air through his open mouth. Tormenting urgency swept his body.

He cried out, he slapped the lid, he threw himself from side to side, he wailed.

And the anguish receded a little. His head cleared. He was still breathing frantically, he heart hammering, his chest pumping, but it was getting less.

He forced himself to calm down. So it wasn't that he was opening a crack somewhere in the box by pushing against it. Somebody was indeed out there, and they were intentionally torturing him.

His breathing was labored now, but no longer terminal.

Once he had completely panicked and completely despaired, he was going to be taken out.

Fine, he would deliver the panic they were looking for. It wouldn't be hard, he was nearly there already. He knew that what at first would be an act would quickly become actual terror, because his screaming would flood his body with adrenaline.

He uttered a groan.

Soon, the air was getting stale again.

Another groan, but this one turned into a scream, and that opened the subconscious gate that he'd been holding closed with all of the inner strength he possessed.

There came boiling up from his dark interior a gigantic, roaring explosion of sound. He hammered, he kicked, he raged, he bellowed.

No escape.

Tears came. He found himself sobbing like a child.

His idea that he was being tortured was a fantasy. There was nobody out there and the coffin was underground. He had been buried alive, and everything else was just rationalization and wishful thinking.

Another scream burst out of him, then another and another and another. He smashed his head against the lid until he was reeling with pain, he clawed and screamed until his nails bled and his voice broke. He collapsed into the suffocated, gasping sobs of a dying man.

He lay, spent but still panting and ever more frantically. He began to float away on a lurching, tormented sea.

Again the cries came, so hysterical that they sounded like somebody else, an unknown version of himself, possessed of vast rage and fear and a hunger for life that was stronger by a factor of a million than the strongest love or terror he had ever consciously known.

His lungs churned, his tongue lolled, his hands began to weaken, and the clawing turned to scrabbling and helpless slapping at the unyielding lid.

There came a ripping sound. Then a click. Then light flooded him and air as pure as dew.

He writhed, he uttered choked sounds from a place in his mind so deep it had no words, he saw only the glare of the light and then, within it, a shape.

The shape focused.

A face stared down at him, softly intent, the eyes as pale as snow. "Hello, Flynn."

Flynn gasped, frantically sucking air, unable to stop himself. As relief washed through him, he realized that he'd been just moments from death in there. Much closer than he thought.

He recognized the face immediately. But the security camera had lied. The oddly plastic skin and the too-perfect hairline were not a disguise. This was not a human face, but something that had been made to look like one.

"You're Morris."

An arm like a piston thrust him back down into the box.

"Yeah," he said, "you can call me that. It's a name on a suit, put there to confuse the garbage." His lips lifted away from his teeth, as if in a smile. "I've got an offer for you, and I'll kill you slow if you don't do my little job for me. Is that understood?"

Flynn said nothing.

"All right, if that's the way you want it, fine." He put his hand on the lid.

"What's the job?"

"Too late, Flynn. You're done." He murmured something to somebody out of sight, but Flynn heard it: "Take him out and bury him."

With an earsplitting crash, the lid came down.

Flynn hammered at it, he couldn't stop himself. "Don't do this! Jesus, let's talk, come on!"

The box scraped and Flynn felt his weight shifting. He was being moved.

"For God's sake, give me a chance!"

He had thought that he had been broken. But now he discovered that he had not yet understood what that was.

As they maneuvered the box, he could hear grunting.

Who was it? Not the creatures from the village, surely. No, there was a murmured word in Spanish. People, then. Henchmen.

He thought that you could not be more deeply a traitor, than to betray mankind itself.

The box lurched so far to one side that he rolled over, then was hurled back as it hit something with a dull, hard thud.

He'd been slid, then dropped into a grave.

"Listen to me! For God's sake!"

And what will you do, little man, he asked himself? Will you, also, trade your species for your life?

There was a crash. Another. Then more and more. Dirt was being shoveled in. They were doing it for real this time, and the air was getting thick fast, and this time it would not be refreshed.

He bellowed, he kicked, he hammered at the lid, he rocked from side to side trying to break open the coffin.

The sound of dirt being shoveled in ceased to crash against the lid. As it got deeper, the sounds became more muffled.

This was it. He was now underground.

He went to another level of terror, one far beyond where he had been before, deeper yet, more raw than anything he had ever known. It was a savage, blind animal fear that caused him to scream like a desperate infant, slicing away layer after layer of toughness and strength and hard-won inner composure, leaving in its wake a panicked, shrieking rat.

Where had he gone wrong, what had he said or hadn't? There had been no bargaining, no time.

"Give me a chance," he screamed. He hammered on the lid, he kicked. "For God's sake *what do you want me to do?*"

There was a sound.

He froze. What was that? He listened.

It went in and out, in and out, and he thought it was the whisper of breathing.

"*Please!*"

"I want you to do what's needed, that's all."

The voice was in his ear, *right* in his ear, so close, so intimate that instinct made him attempt to turn toward it.

"Then tell them to dig me out! I'm smothering fast!"

"You will do the work I have for you."

"They're still filling the hole, tell them to stop!"

"I have work for you."

It was a choice. *The* choice. Die here like this or do the monster's work.

There could not be a traitor more profound. But if he died, there was no chance at all that Abby's destruction would ever be avenged.

"All right!" he shouted, "I'll do it!"

Nothing happened. He waited, sweating it out.

His heartbeat grew rapidly more irregular, his mouth lolled open, his tongue hung out, and his breaths came faster and faster, more and more uselessly. He was breathing his own breath.

"You will do this work?"

He tried to answer.

"I can't hear you."

A gasped whisper: "Open . . . open . . ."

The digging stopped.

"Open . . ."

There was light all around him, and air flowing like grace into his very soul. His body flushed with relief and his head swam as his blood reoxygenated.

He hadn't even been underground.

Morris chuckled. He reached down and drew Flynn to a sitting position.

Flynn looked at the box he had been confined it.

"Not a coffin," Morris said. He was a man of about six feet, dressed in jeans and a T-shirt, a weathered Stetson on his head. "Coulda been used as one, though." He lifted Flynn under his arms. "Still shaky?"

"No."

"You lie like a child."

Flynn took quick stock of his surroundings. He was in a barn, its big door open wide to a sunny morning.

"Come on, let's get you something to drink. I got Coors, Lone Star, Shiner."

"Just a cup of coffee."

"Nah, you want a Shiner." Morris snapped a finger at a man standing nearby, who Flynn recognized as Jay Elder. He sauntered over to a dark blue cooler and opened it. As he reached in, ice rattled.

"Sounds good, doesn't it?"

"I have to admit that it does." He estimated that he was forty feet from the door. He couldn't bolt, though, not yet, because Elder was coming back with a frosty longneck.

The animal in him wanted that beer in the worst way.

"Flynn, you gotta understand that you're all mixed up. We're the good guys here! That thing you met in Chicago, that was evil."

"Okay."

Elder arrived with the beer. "It's gonna be a new era for mankind," he said. If he thought that he wasn't evil, he was a fool.

He took the bottle. Shiner is a rich brew, and he could

smell the sweetness of it, and practically taste the cold relief it would bring to his throat.

"Go ahead," Morris said. "You've earned it."

He lifted it toward his lips, calculating carefully, moving slowly to buy time. A quarter-second delay, a wrong half-step, and he was going to end up back in that coffin, this time for good.

Using all the strength in his arm and shoulders, he reached back and swung the bottle into the side of Morris's head.

The bottle exploded with a wet *crack* and foam and glass sprayed across Morris's head and face.

He stood there staring. He didn't even blink.

Flynn cried out in shocked surprise—under the coating of skin there must be steel or something.

Then Morris made a sound of his own, a low growl that reminded Flynn of the voice of the tiger.

He broke and ran. He was thirty feet from the door when Elder, thin and wiry and quick, leaped at him. He was light but fast as hell.

Not fast enough, though, to avoid a punch, a solid blow to the chin, which lifted him two feet and hurled him backward. He landed on the barn's dusty floor.

Morris roared, and Flynn knew that he was hearing rage from another world.

What must it be like, to produce minds as fine as Morris's, but so filled with rage? Or those things in the village—were they part human? Why were they so sad?

The universe is a dark place.

The last thing Flynn heard from Morris as he ran out the door into blazing morning sunlight was a roar—as it changed into laughter.

He had an inkling as to why. It was all part of breaking his will. They'd done it during the Inquisition, done it in Nazi Germany, done it in the Soviet Gulag. The technique was to let a prisoner think he had escaped, then, just as he touched freedom, drag him back.

So his aim was clear: he needed to go farther than they thought possible.

He ran across the barnyard and vaulted its weathered wooden fence. Without looking back, he knew from the silence that Elder and Morris were not following him. This meant only one thing: somebody else was. He thought it would not be the tiger, not in broad daylight, and not as close as this to the heavily developed shoreline of Lake Travis.

From somewhere nearby, there was a sudden burst of barking. An instant later it was silenced.

His heart seemed to twist against itself, his throat to twist against itself from sheer terror.

One of the outbuildings they'd seen had been a kennel.

Dogs were a problem. Big time.

Too bad he'd lost Mac, Mac knew dogs and knew them well. As he ran, he continued to listen, but the dogs were no longer giving voice.

So, were they also smart, maybe as smart as the tiger?

He had to force himself not to run wildly.

This was going to be hard. It was going to be very, very hard.

CHAPTER THIRTY

As he ran into deeper brush, Flynn inventoried. His only weapon was the pocket knife. He had no compass, no cell phone, and no GPS, only the knowledge that he was running in a generally southerly direction.

He did not hear the dogs, but he also did not believe for a moment that he was beyond the perimeter of the trap Morris and Elder had set for him.

He knew that he was leaving a scent trail. Worse, the harder he tried to get away the more he sweated, and the stronger it was getting. His effort to escape was making him easier to catch.

To break his trail, he needed to get to water. He needed the lake, but how far was it? More than a mile, certainly, and this shore was not developed, so he wasn't going to be stumbling across any roads.

They'd chosen their location with characteristic skill. Being near a large city and a population in constant flux around the lake gave them access to plenty of genetic material—if that was even what they were after—but they were also isolated enough for them to keep them-selves well hidden.

He forced himself to move more slowly, to tend his track as best he could, to reduce his visual and scent signatures.

The sun was strong, and he was sweating ever more heavily. He was exhausted from his ordeal and so de-hydrated that he was beginning to struggle with mus-cular control.

Then he heard something—a quick rustling sound to his right. The instinctive reaction was to turn away, but you can't escape a dog like that. He is going to be faster than you are, and you cannot hide from his nose.

Flynn's hands were good enough to give him a chance to stop maybe one of them, but probably not for more than a few moments. So he turned toward the sound, and charged into the cedar thicket that the animal was sliding through.

He screamed, he couldn't help it—a short, sharp cry, instantly stifled. The dog was black except for the face, which was long and lethal-looking, but as pink as human skin. The eyes were green. They were entirely human.

Immediately on seeing Flynn, the dog turned away, careful not to expose its nose to his fists.

His gut frothy with disgust, Flynn broke off the as-sault, leaped out of the thicket and continued running.

Behind him, he could hear complicated, guttural sounds as the dogs communicated among themselves. They were fanning out, preparing to outrun him and capture him in a pincers movement.

A steep hillside appeared ahead. Forty feet up, the limestone emerged as a cliff, and in that cliff there were a number of low openings. Caves.

Could be good.

But no, no way. They were deathtraps. Even if they were large—huge—the dogs would gain an unbeatable advantage. They didn't need light, he did. Worse, the damp air of a cave was an ideal carrier of scent.

So he continued following the terrain lower and lower, until at last he came to water—or rather, a dry creek bed. Still, though, it led downward toward his only hope.

It began to be possible to discern the voices of individual dogs, as they muttered and growled among themselves.

As he got closer to water, the plant life grew more dense, and the thickening stands of cedar were getting harder and harder to move through.

The voices of the dogs stopped.

He thought, "they're coming in for the kill." Maybe he should have gone for the caves. Maybe he should have done a lot of things, chief among them not moving ahead with this until contact with some sort of headquarters had been reestablished. He'd gotten Mac killed. God only knew what had become of Diana.

Now there was silence around him. But why? He turned around and around, wishing he could somehow pierce the glowering stands of cactus and the dark cedar thickets with his eyes. What was the holdup? He must have some advantage, but what could it be?

He looked up the long rise he'd just descended. Then he turned a half turn. Nothing there but cedar. Another half turn—and winking through the choking underbrush there was a metallic gleam.

Metal, hell, that was water. Of course, the dogs had already scented it. And he saw one of them, just for an instant, a black flank gleaming with tight fur. It was moving quickly, staying low behind a stand of cactus on his right.

He saw their problem: he had a better run to the water than they did. They'd stopped here in hope that he wouldn't see it before they could maneuver in front of him.

No longer concerned with being detected—they knew where he was to the inch—he hurled himself wildly ahead, throwing himself into the foliage between him and whatever water was below him.

There came a chilling sound, the furious rattle of a snake. They were common in the Texas hill country, with its ample supply of small animals and the warm rocks that snakes needed to gather energy.

He knew the risk, but there was no time to stop and deal with it. He threw himself against his side of the stand of cactus, tumbling away from the fat, bristle-encrusted pears, feeling them piercing his shoulder and flank.

He was falling then, dropping through resisting, scraping masses of cedar, dropping further, stopping, clawing himself free and falling again.

Breaking free, he fell ten feet, maybe more, through clear air. Enough to shatter limbs if he hit wrong and he was completely out of control.

He landed on his back in clear, cold water and heard its silence as he sank, and saw above the sun dancing on its surface. He also saw the snake hit the water, a good eight feet of writhing fury.

Stretching himself out, blowing to reduce his buoyancy, he kicked his way deeper. Close by, the silence was profound, but he could hear a distant buzzing of engines. This wasn't a stream, it was the lake itself.

He heard splashes behind him, at least a dozen of

them. The dogs had lost a small battle, but that had only sped them up. His one advantage was that he could hold his breath, which was not so easy for a dog. But they were going to be faster.

He'd been winded before he fell, though, so he had to surface right now.

The instant his head broke the water, he both gobbled air and turned and turned, trying to see what he was up against. A quick count revealed the hideous heads of twelve sleek animals speeding toward him from three of four possible directions.

Immediately in front of him, not three feet away, was the snake. Sweeping his arms, he backed himself away from it. It raised itself up, using water tension to force a good three feet of its length above the surface. It couldn't strike, at least. To inject its venom, it would need to be close enough to dig its fangs into his skin.

Sucking breath after breath, he twisted around and used the one ability that he had that none of these animals, not the snake or the dogs, could equal. He could hold his breath long enough to dive deep. And once he was underwater and too far from the dogs for them to see him, they weren't going to have any way of determining his location.

He swam as deep as he could, passing over a drowned tree, characteristic of Texas's many artificial lakes. He'd pulled more than one drowning victim out of such trees on Lake Menard.

Even as he went to the surface for air, he could hear the tireless churning of the dogs getting louder. He didn't bother to turn and look at them when he broke the surface, that would eat a good second that he couldn't afford to lose.

Again he breathed, again and again, saturating his

lungs with air even as the dogs got louder. Then he saw, turning out of an inlet about a quarter of a mile away, a power boat. It swung in a graceful arc, remaining up on plane, its wake spraying behind it. Nobody would come out under that much power unless they were on a mission.

Between the dogs and the boat, he had been very neatly trapped.

Again, he dove deep, but this time did not double back toward the dogs. They were smart enough to anticipate that. They would move from line abreast to a deeper formation, and surround him and tear him apart the moment he surfaced.

The sound of the oncoming boat got louder.

He had to surface, and when he did, he saw a figure on the front of the boat. It was Morris, and in his hand was a long-barreled pistol. Some kind of a target weapon, accurate at distance.

The boat was coming fast, its wake foaming white.

He dropped beneath the surface.

The trap was sprung. Here, he ran out of options. Here, they dragged him out of the water and took him back, a thoroughly broken man.

There would be more torture, until he'd been to death and back many more times.

But why? What was it that Morris wanted him to do?

Now the boat was circling above him. As soon as he surfaced, he was going to be within range of both the pistol and the dogs.

Looking up at the hull, he could see that the twin props were on shafts that extended out behind the craft, which appeared to be about forty feet in length.

He swam upward and, as the boat swept over him,

he resurfaced in its prop wash. As he sucked air, though, one of the dogs piled into him.

He went back down, leaving the snapping jaws and churning claws behind.

Then he felt something unexpected—a current of warmer water.

This could mean only one thing, an incoming stream. He swam toward it, keeping as best he could in its warmth. No matter what, he had to remain submerged until he was in the mouth of that stream. If he went up to grab even a single breath, he was caught.

To conserve his oxygen, he forced himself to do the opposite of what instinct was screaming for him to do. He forced himself to slow down.

Moving carefully, he began to be able to see the limestone bottom rising. He was swimming up a small canyon. With just inches to spare, he passed over the skeleton of another drowned tree, this one with the stark remains of what had been a stone house below it.

The bottom rushed up, and then he was swimming in three feet of water and there were flashes in his eyes, and he was going to take another breath, and it was going to be water.

He breathed. Breathed again, deeper. But it wasn't water, he had come up into the bed of a stream no more than ten feet wide and just three feet deep.

He lay flat on his back, letting its water sluice around him, allowing just his face to break the surface. He didn't want a single molecule of odor to reach those dogs, nor a single sound, and he didn't want his body heat to be detectable, much less his image.

He remained as still as possible, just pushing himself along with his heels, doing it inch by inch. Eventually, the stream would have a bend in it. Only when he was around that bend and invisible from the lake could he dare to move more quickly. Even then, he would stay with the water.

He came to a deeper pool, the water crystal, the limestone glowing tan. Around him, birds sang. He slid deeper, waiting there with just his face exposed, minimizing the chances that his scent would reach the dogs.

Finally he moved again, slipping around a turn in the narrow creek.

All was quiet. He hadn't even stopped the birds. He raised his head and listened. Distantly, the boat's engine screamed. Good, they were operating a search pattern.

Finally, carefully, listening to every sound and watching every shadow along the banks of the stream, he eased himself to his feet.

He froze, watching and listening. There was no sound of movement in the thick brush that surrounded the creek. He crossed to the far side, then climbed a bluff until he could see what turned out to be part of Lake Travis, a mirror of the sky dotted with sails. Small white clouds flew overhead. Nearer, the boat was now stopped. He could see the dogs on board, sitting in a group on the fantail. As they worked to gain scent, their heads turned first one way and then another.

Obviously, they weren't picking up his scent, but they did not stop trying. Then one of them went to the rail. It stood, nose to the wind. Another joined it.

His heartbeat increased, he barely breathed. It was time for this reconnaissance to end, so he moved back into the water, and then quickly up the creek, which was as shallow as a few inches on this side.

He went a hundred yards, then climbed the bank and pushed his way through the brush. The ridge he had descended was about five hundred yards ahead and perhaps a hundred and twenty feet high. Somewhere beyond it was the ranch headquarters where he'd started.

A single bark, low and shockingly close, told him that he'd made a fundamental mistake doing that reconnaissance, and the trap he'd entered was already closing.

Only two alternatives were left to him, either to do something that they wouldn't expect, or something that they couldn't counter—or, for that matter, both.

One thing that might throw the dogs off would be if he backtracked along his own scent trail. He was wet now, leaving less odor behind. They might be tricked. They might lose him.

The only problem was that doing this would return him to the ranch.

Had that been the real plan all along, to induce him to go back to the compound and be captured where he'd started his escape?

He looked carefully along the ridge, then at the cactus and tufted grass below it.

Tracking is a skill that involves not only careful observation but also careful visualization. To keep a trail, you need to not only read sign, you need to be able to discipline your imagination to see the path as the person you are tracking must have seen it.

Doubling back along the lakeside, he returned to the bend. Beyond this point, he knew that it would not be safe to go. To reduce his scent further, he submerged himself completely. Then he left the water and went across toward the bluff, crossing his own trail about sixty steps later.

Turning, he looked back the way he had come. Not surprisingly, he had left a clear track.

He scanned the terrain ahead. Were they hidden somewhere, already aware of him, already waiting in ambush?

Backtracking as carefully as he could, he climbed the ridge. He would risk the dogs noticing the movement.

He could not do the safe thing, which was to keep going out to the road. He had to determine if there was any way to help Mac, assuming he was still alive. Or Diana, for that matter. If it had been him in the Rover, he would have come in to provide support as soon as communication failed. She would have done the same, and since she hadn't, he had to assume that she was in trouble, too.

They might both be trapped in boxes somewhere, or under some other type of torture, or slated to be broken down into component parts or whatever was being done to people.

Doubling back, he made for the ranch compound. If they'd left it unguarded, he might gain some useful intelligence. Who knew, maybe he'd event turn it into a win.

Still, he had to be damn near conservative. If he lost his life, who knew what would happen then? Maybe there wasn't anybody else left. Maybe the whole operation would fail. For sure, it would be a catastrophic setback.

Atop the ridge, his own sign was quite clear, a swathe through the tall grass that looked like it had been put down by an elephant. The dogs, all nine of them, had crossed the clearing line abreast. Their tracks were straight and light. They had worked to minimize their sign.

Moving ahead, but not so fast that he would raise

his skin temperature and once again intensify his scent, he worked his way back. Soon he saw, through a thick stand of cedar, the shape of a building. He went closer, slipping deep into the cedar thicket, stopping when he came to its border.

The place was silent. No sign of movement. There was the barn, a new shed nearby, and the small rock ranch house. Under some live oaks fifty yards away was the kennel.

The barn doors were still open, the interior shadowy.

He watched some mourning doves pecking in the small patch of grass near the house. These were flocking birds that fed on the ground. They were sensitive to nearby movement and would fly up at the slightest sign of disturbance. He waited, but they continued to feed in peace.

Morris could not have left this place unguarded, so its empty appearance had to be a lie.

He stepped out of the cedar and strode quickly to the barn. On the floor toward the back stood a long silver box, open, the interior lined with black plastic. His box. There was oxygen equipment nearby, a green canister lying on its side, some tubing disconnected from two nipples on one end.

He forced back the impulse to hammer the thing to bits.

Under the pecan tree by the house, the doves were still pecking at nuts.

Mac and Diana were not in the barn.

He stepped out and moved away from the structure. Turning slowly around, he listened for anything that might help him. His hearing was good and it was very quiet, but the silence was total. By now the dogs would be breathing heavily, but he didn't hear anything that suggested their approach. Fearing the tiger, he looked, also, along the rooflines.

He dared not go close to the house. The dogs would hear the doves rising from a long way off. They would know what it meant, too, no question.

He looked toward the shed. There was a padlock on the door, a new one. His picklocks were gone, of course.

No matter how carefully he listened, only the cooing of the doves disturbed the silence of the place.

Could they have actually left him an opening? Maybe they'd never considered the idea that he'd be so foolish as to return to the compound.

He went to the shed, moving carefully and methodically. The lock was a good one. He could not force it without tools. Behind the shed, though, he found a low roof with a trapdoor in it. A storm cellar. Not surprising, given that one of the most powerful tornadoes ever recorded had touched down a few miles north of here.

He bent down, grasped the rusted iron ring in the center of the trapdoor, and pulled it up.

It was dark and silent and it felt large. Hill Country ranches didn't have big underground chambers, just root cellars, and usually not even that. So this could be something constructed by Morris.

He wanted to call out to Mac and Diana in the darkness below, but to raise his voice was far too dangerous. As he listened, he thought he heard a faint pulsation, like a big pot boiling.

He wanted to go down the ladder, but that was beyond the limit of responsibility. He was here to make best efforts, not throw himself away.

For a long time, he listened to that sound. Boiling,

he thought, definitely. No voices, no sound of movement.

As he left the shed, he heard a sound coming from the direction of the ranch house, high and sharp, that certainly was not doves. But what was it? Not a voice . . . or was it? Perhaps not a human voice.

And then he heard another sound, just the slightest edge of a yap, quickly stifled.

He saw movement at the house, a door opening.

Even so, the doves did not move, which meant only one thing: they were not normal doves. They were another deception, and a very clever one indeed.

At the same moment, one of the dogs appeared at the edge of the compound. It came across the field at a trot, its tongue lolling, its eyes intent on the house. It went up to somebody hidden just inside, and as it did the person crouched down to greet it.

It was one of the creatures from the village. In the sunlight, its skin was yellow-gray and its eyes seemed, if anything, more deeply sad than they had in the gloom of the structure. He could see a shadow of humanity there, but also something else. Was it a mix of a creature like Oltisis and a man?

Maybe, but it couldn't walk the streets, not by a long shot, not like Morris could.

The high-pitched sounds became a strange, musical cooing, joined by the dog's voice, a group of vocalizations more complex than any ordinary dog could make.

They were taking pleasure in one another, these two misbegotten creatures, a dog with a man's eyes and this . . . thing. The dog licked the creature's hands and it smiled, its teeth jutting out of its mouth like blades.

More dogs appeared, and then the snarl of engines as two four-wheelers burst out of the brush.

Flynn faded back toward the far side of the compound, trying to keep the shed between himself and the danger.

When he was back in the brush and somewhat concealed, he turned and ran toward the road he and Diana and Mac had come in on.

As far as he was concerned, the secrecy was over. Without Diana and Oltisis, he had no official recourse. So he needed to bring some level of policing authority into the situation, and damn the secrecy. Let the secret get out. Better that it did.

Problem was, he also knew that the cops wouldn't do anything serious unless they had evidence of a crime, and so far he couldn't offer much. Certainly not enough to enable, say, the Travis County Sheriff's Office to get a warrant to enter onto the ranch property. No judge was going to approve a warrant on the basis of what would sound like the ravings of a lunatic. The fact was that he wasn't going to get any police action out of a claim that there was a village full of aliens on some rancher's property—unless they tossed him into the state hospital over in Austin.

Even if by some miracle they did move, it would not happen overnight, and this needed to get done fast. The only thing that might work against the kind of power and intelligence he was seeing was speed.

There was only one answer: he had to come back here with serious firepower, and fast, and he needed to kill them all.

CHAPTER THIRTY-ONE

He sat hunched over a beer at one of his college haunts, a place called the Scholz Garten in central Austin. He'd come here because it was deep in the inner city, and Morris and Elder might be cautious in a populated area.

He sat at his old table in the far corner of the outdoor beer garden. Across from him was Abby's chair. It was late in the afternoon, the shadows were long, and the memories of her were as raw as blood.

Once he had reached the road, it hadn't taken him long to find the spot where the Rover had been. It was gone, but there was no sign of anything unusual, such as tire marks that might indicate a sudden departure. The truck had remained in place for some time. He had even been able to make out scorch marks left where the catalytic converter had touched some grass.

As he sipped beer, he searched gun classifieds in a local rag. He was looking for a very specific weapon, a Heckler and Koch MP5. If he could find a dealer with a Federal Firearms License and the weapon in his inventory, he was hoping he could obtain it and let the paperwork float along behind the transaction. To own a fully automatic machine gun in Texas, he'd need to get a sign-off from a local honcho of some kind, but he was figuring that could be accomplished with a donation.

He went to the pay phone, dropped in four quarters and phoned a guy called Joe Harris in a little town called Lost Mill, who advertised a selection of weapons. He had no HK in stock, but he thought he could get his hands on one pretty quickly.

"How fast?"

"Well, I could get it brought in here—let's see—how about seven?"

He would need to carry it around, so he wanted concealment. "Does it have the CIA case?" This was a briefcase with a trigger in the handle, a nice piece of equipment.

"No CIA case. Those things are hard to come by."

"Don't I know it. So I'll be around at seven to take a look."

After he'd reached the highway, he had hitched and walked until he got to a place called Four Points, where he'd found a bus and taken it into Austin.

When he'd rented the car he was now driving, the clerks at the Avis station had been concerned about his appearance. He looked like a tramp with an improbable amount of cash, and the cash was mysteriously damp. He'd used his real credential, and the police identification had reassured them, fortunately, just enough to get them to give him a car. The use of cash would keep the rental record at the station until the car was returned and the completed transaction processed.

He didn't want to show the gun dealer his real pass, for fear of spooking him, and he couldn't meet him looking like he was headed directly to the nearest 7-Eleven to commit mayhem, so he planned a first stop at a motel to clean up.

Everything was so very normal, the Texas sun starting to set behind tight little clouds, traffic passing on Congress Avenue, up the street the improbably immense state capitol building looming over the city. All was quiet—but Texas streets could be deceptive, as he well knew. There had been some notable crimes committed in this city, some textbook crimes. A classic story of police action against a sniper had unfolded at the summit of the University of Texas tower back years ago, which was still studied as a model of how to respond to such an emergency, and, for that matter, how not to. A cop had died investigating the sound of gunshots. The lesson: don't expose yourself until you know where the shots are coming from.

He drove south on Congress, then took First Street to Interstate Thirty-Five. Harris was just the other side of the line in Hays County. Between here and there was a Super Target, and not far away, a motel.

As he drove, he automatically kept his rear under surveillance. Once on Thirty-Five, he stayed well below the speed limit and far to the left, letting the traffic pass him like a river. Texans are not slow drivers, and nobody hung with him.

He knew that the gun was going to cost a lot. He would need to bring cash, which meant a visit to a bank. When he'd dipped the special ATM card earlier, though, it was dead. He visualized some bureaucrat deep in some Washington cubbyhole canceling the cards as soon as contact was lost with their holders. Nobody would ever stop to think that this might leave them in the wind. Budgets trumped lives, always.

Fortunately, there were Frost Bank branches here. This was his bank in Menard, an old Texas outfit, and he was going to need to make a substantial withdrawal from his personal savings. He had about thirty grand on deposit and he'd have to get it all. It was already a quarter to six. He watched for a branch.

As he drove south along the highway, he saw a Wells Fargo, and somewhat later a Frost Bank sign. He pulled off the next exit and doubled back.

The branch was small, but when he handed over his withdrawal slip, the clerk didn't react with any surprise. This was agricultural country south of Austin, full of farms and ranches and basic businesses like rock quarries. There were going to be a lot of illegals working, and that would mean cash payrolls.

"Hundreds, please," he said. Bigger bills were faster to count and took up less space. He carried the money out in a brown paper bag, got into the car and stashed it under the backseat.

His next stop was Target. His clothes were done, and in any case, they'd been touched by those creatures out there—God knows what they had done to him while he was unconscious—and he wanted them off his body. He wanted a long, thorough shower, lots of soap.

In the Target, he headed for men's clothing. He passed a mother with her two girls looking through racks, a clerk stocking a shelf with radios, a couple of guys searching for T-shirts, and he found himself at once loving them as he had never been aware of loving his fellow man before, and also feeling oddly distant from them.

He understood the origin of Diana's inner distance. It was having secret knowledge of a larger world that did it. They were innocent, he was not.

He found the camouflage sweats he needed, and then the black sneakers. A ski cap and mask were harder, but he eventually dug some up in a sale bin. He also got a white shirt and some slacks, and threw in a dark blue windbreaker, the thinnest one he could find. He planned to buy a pistol off Harris as well.

In the checkout line, he waited behind a family who was buying a gas grill and had a lot of questions about it. The wait was hard.

Finally, he left the store and crossed the parking lot to his car. The details of the world were in sharp focus, sounds, movements, the expressions on people's faces, even the feel of the asphalt beneath his feet. It was how he felt just before walking into a domestic dispute, which can so often turn out to be a more dangerous situation than it seems. More cops were injured and killed on domestics than on any other type of run.

Given his plan, he did not expect to survive his return to the compound, and, frankly, he was beyond caring. If there was an afterlife, he'd be with Abby. If not, then not. The only thing that mattered was that everybody at the compound also came out dead.

He reached the motel at six twenty. He checked in and went quickly to his room. This was a point of vulnerability. He was unarmed, so if they were following him, this was an ideal time to take him.

He threw his bag of clothes on the bed, stripped and showered with the curtain open. He was focusing down very tightly now, concentrating his thoughts on the unfolding mission, preparing his mind and body for action.

Once he was cleaned up, he drove to Joe Harris's operation, which consisted of two double-wides on a bare lot in bleak scrubland south of Austin.

The first thing that came to his mind was that the setup wasn't straight. The double-wides had the barren look of crook places.

Harris had dogs behind a chain-link fence, which frantically announced themselves as Flynn walked up the uneven flagstones leading to the first trailer. This was about the point, when he was in a uniform, that he would've unsnapped his holster.

At least they were just ordinary dogs.

He knocked on the flimsy door.

"Yo."

"I'm Flynn Carroll, I called about the HK."

The door opened onto a man who looked like he'd been inflated and then rubbed with beet juice. Even a mustache that would've caused a sensation in Dodge City failed to hide train-wreck teeth when he smiled.

Flynn recognized it as meth mouth, the dentist's dream.

"Well, come on in," Harris said, his accent deceptively softened by the south. But this was not a soft man.

Flynn stepped into the dim, smoke-choked interior. An air conditioner screamed as if in its death throes, doing little more than jostle the sweaty air. The chrys smoke was almost dense enough to induce a transfer high, and, in fact, Flynn took a slight hit from it. Felt good, which was bad. Drugs and high-intensity action are mortal enemies. When quarter seconds count, as they would tonight, you need to be spotlessly clean.

An HK in pristine condition lay on the Formica table that filled half the kitchen area.

"I assume you can show the cash, 'cause she can't go outa here on no check or nothin'."

Flynn noted that there had been no mention of paperwork or identification. He also took note of the Diablos tattoo on Joe's arm, and of the fact that he was wearing a small pistol on his right ankle, maybe an AMG Backup. Not very accurate, but in a confined space like this, who cared?

"It's in my car," Flynn said. "How much're we lookin' at?"

"I'm thinkin' about twenty-two thousand dollars, sir."

"That's strong."

"You look at 'er. She got class, a lotta class. Plus this fella, it turned out he had—lemme get this here—" He brought up a black plastic briefcase. "This is just dead on for the CIA case."

It was a good briefcase, no question there, the trigger mechanism solidly constructed.

What he had in the car was exactly twenty-two thousand two hundred dollars. He decided to see just how crooked this crook was.

"I need to take the gun with me. Can we let the paperwork float?"

"You plannin' some kinda score?"

"I have a buyer. Kinda on the warm side."

"*Cucuracha*?" It was slang for a cartel enforcer.

"Big enough to cook and eat."

The guy looked into Flynn's eyes, looking for some kind of sting, no doubt. In Flynn's experience, guys like this always ended up trusting plainclothes cops more than they did their own damn mothers, they were that stupid.

"I'll tell you," Joe finally said, "I don't know if you

noticed, but the governor's kinda stopped carin' who does fed paperwork and who don't. I mean, you ain't gonna go shoot up the capitol, I hope. 'Cause that would be embarrassing." He chuckled. His eyes never left Flynn's. "I see you in there, you little shit pussy. Your *cucuracha* ain't around here, is he? You're gonna sell this thing cros't the border, ain'tcha? Gonna get some Border Patrol killed, probably. I don't think I can do that."

It was an opening gambit. Soon, the price would be thirty grand. Flynn didn't really care, because he had decided that he wasn't going to be a buyer today. He was, however, leaving with the weapon.

"I'm not in the business," he said. "I don't bargain."

"What are you, then?"

"I don't want to lie to you. I'm gonna put you on your ass and take your gun."

"*Wh-a-at?*"

"I don't want to. But this HK is hot and I'm not gonna pay anything close to that kind of money for a hot gun. Anyway, I'm probably pretty hot myself, so I kinda think we were made for each other."

A hand meaty enough to be a filling meal started for the ankle holster. Flynn reached across the table and bumped Joe's ulnar nerve against his humerus. The hand flopped and Joe yelled.

Still without getting up, Flynn aimed a blow at the middle of his chin, thrusting upward as he connected. There was a crack and Joe's head pitched back. He fell over in his chair, crashing against the sink hard enough to bring more than a few filthy dishes down with him.

Flynn stood. One thing he had learned from watching bad guys screw up was never to waste time in a situation like this. Do what you have to do and get out.

He looked down at Joe. He'd be in slumberland for ten minutes, maybe a little less.

He laid the HK in the case and made sure all the magazines were full. There wasn't time to toss the place for more rounds, so what was in the three thirty-round magazines had to be enough.

As far as a carry weapon was concerned, he didn't see any pistols in view, so he contented himself with taking Joe's AMG. It was chambered for the .380 ACT round, which was good. This round gave it better stopping power than the more common version, which was chambered for a .22 round. There were also a few of these out there that could accept a .45 cartridge, but the accuracy was really poor. The combination of the pistol's fixed barrel and the ACT round's low breech pressure offered an outstanding mix of accuracy and firepower for a compact pistol. Ole Joe did indeed know his guns.

Leaving the trailer, Flynn made it a point not to hurry. There were bound to be eyes on this meet, no question. He couldn't afford to raise suspicion, otherwise every cracker inside of three counties was going to be here in minutes. Forget the cops, these guys were way more dangerous than the law. You messed with Diablos, you dealt with Diablos, no police need apply.

His next step was clear. He would return to the Lake Travis area and await darkness. Then he would move on Morris and his people and his animals, and what would happen would happen.

A machine gun is a good weapon. Used correctly, of course, and he knew how to do that.

As he drove, he considered his chances. On balance, he thought that Morris had not expected him to return to the compound. It hadn't been a trap at all, but a mistake. So he could be outsmarted—once, anyway. Maybe, then, twice.

He had one objective and one objective only: waste Morris and all who were with him.

CHAPTER THIRTY-TWO

He had planned his return to the property as carefully as he could using Google maps and satellite views he examined on a computer at a copy shop. The house and the barn appeared on the satellite view, for example, but not the shed, the village, or the kennel. Diana's images had been real time, of course, but Google satellite photos averaged about two years old.

This meant that the dogs and the creatures in the village were all recent additions. Ominously, then, they were in the process of expanding their operations here. But it also meant that there had to be vulnerabilities. Something wasn't properly guarded. Some plan of defense was flawed. The question was, would he be able to find that flaw?

One thing was certain: the whole operation—compound, village, all of it—would be carefully guarded now, and in depth.

He had waited until nine before setting out. He wanted as much time as he could get prior to moonrise, which tonight was at eleven twenty-six. But he also didn't want to arrive any earlier than he had to. He'd used the time to find stores where he could put together a new rig.

In his backpack was a pair of fairly decent night vision binoculars with an infrared light source. In addition to the AMG backup and the HK, he was now carrying two Tasers and a good combat knife.

He had considered blowing the whole place to kingdom come, but you are not going to be able to buy the necessary explosive materials without tripping all kinds of alerts. It was one thing to get hold of a machine gun of a type used by the drug cartels and readily available on the black market, another to buy explosives that Homeland Security took an interest in.

Before he left, he'd located on the map a new spot to leave the rental car, and as he drove down the main road, he ran his plan mentally, dwelling for a moment on each phase, making certain that everything was as well thought out as possible.

He'd worked the maps carefully, and took a different approach to the ranch. He didn't want to park anywhere near the place they'd left the Rover. For this reason he drove not past the ranch, but down to the little marina that was in an inlet about a mile away. He had hit upon the idea of playing two cards at once. He could conceal the car and also disable the boat, which was almost certainly kept there.

He parked in the marina's lot. There was a snack shack still open, and he strolled in and bought a Coke, then, as if he owned the place, ambled down to the single floating dock. It was not difficult to recognize Morris's boat, a forty-foot twin built for speed. He stepped aboard, then slipped in under the protective canvas. Wiring a boat with two engines to deal with would be an annoyance, but he didn't need to start it. He pulled up the engine cover of the port Chevy and quickly removed the distributor cap and tossed it overboard. For good measure, he ripped out the gas line. He repeated the performance with the starboard engine.

Bon voyage, bastards.

It would be a long trek up to the ranch compound, and it would take him closer to the village than he'd like, but the steepness also meant that getting back down here fast was going to be a lot easier.

Returning to his car, he opened the rear deck and methodically equipped himself. He wore the knife in a sheath on his left hip. Easier to reach with his right hand. He tucked the AMG into the ankle holster he'd taken off its owner. The night vision binoculars went around his neck, with the fully loaded magazines in two big fanny packs. He carried the HK naked. If he had occasion to carry the machine gun in population, he'd use the case, but there was no need here. Dressed as he was, any cop was going to see him as a threat anyway, so there was no real point in hiding it.

As long as he could, he kept to the road for ease of movement. Once he left it, though, he rolled on the ski mask. White skin was easy to see even on the darkest night. Of course, with night vision equipment, he would still be easy to spot. Not to mention the animals. The dogs' noses worked all the time, but the tiger's eyes were going to be a lot better in the dark.

He had bought some copper screen at Home Depot, and had fitted it into the crown of the dark blue cap he was wearing, so he wasn't worried about a MindRay. They might have something better, but there was nothing he could do about that, or any equipment of extremely advanced design, for that matter.

His assumption was that, one way or another, he was certain to be detected. The question was, how close could he go and how much destruction could he cause before they dropped him? And they would do that, no question. He was here to kill, and therefore also to die.

He thought he had at least an even chance against the tiger, as long as he could see it in time. With his armory, he could take the dogs, but any use of his guns would obviously end all surprise, so if they came out, he planned to fade back, then return later.

His pace was steady, the road empty. The eastern sky glowed faintly. The moon was on its way.

He reached the point where the road bent slightly to the right, and as he came around the curve, he heard a sound, low, not quite an engine noise, but also not natural. Not the tiger or the dogs, so probably a machine of some sort.

Barely breathing, he slid into a cedar thicket at the roadside. Slowly, the sound grew louder. It was a motor noise. Carefully, moving just as he would when he was stalking somebody very smart, he raised the binoculars to his eyes. He looked up the road. Nothing. And yet the sound was becoming more detailed. Something very quiet, and therefore probably closer than it seemed.

It was ratcheting now, like nothing so much as large insect wings.

Then he saw it, flying right up the center of the road as methodically as if it was a miniature drone, a four-inch wasp, black with yellow stripes on its abdomen.

No wasp flew like this and no wasp was this big, not even in Texas.

Almost certainly, it was a drone. The Pentagon could make fake insects, he'd read about them being deployed as spy cameras in Afghanistan. But this was beyond that, this was an actual, living creature that was also a machine.

Continuing directly down the center of the road, it flew slowly past.

He remained still, not moving the binoculars, not moving anything.

The creature made a slow circle above the center of the road. It hovered, facing the thicket. Flynn stopped breathing. It was a calculated risk. His stillness would make it harder for the insect's compound eyes to detect him, a fact he remembered from high school biology. Assuming that it even had compound eyes. Who the hell knew, maybe it could see the head of a pin at ten miles.

It came closer, hovering, its yellow legs folded beneath its abdomen. As any country Texan would, he recognized it as a Cicada Killer, a big, normally benign wasp that was common in the region. Big, but not the size of a jumbo shrimp, which this thing was going to top by a good half inch.

As it examined the thicket, the head moved from side to side, but not with the mechanical seeking of an insect. No question, it was under intelligent control.

The thing maneuvered into the thicket, its head now jerking quickly from side to side. So it was indeed using compound eyes, and therefore it must be a genetically modified wasp, not a machine made to look like a wasp. It was, in effect, a living camera, and whoever was watching through those eyes was trying to overcome their limitations with rapid head motions. The result was a horrifyingly odd and unnatural spectacle, a wasp moving its head as if it was on a spring, all the while flying with bizarre deliberation.

It came closer. If he made the least motion, he was going to be seen. The operator was obviously already suspicious or the thing wouldn't have stopped to examine this particular thicket. In any case, Flynn was soon going to have to move. In another thirty seconds, he'd have to release his breath, and when he did, he would be detected.

Slowly, its wings humming, the wasp drifted among the branches, moving more skillfully than any wasp should. It came closer to him. Its head vibrated. It came closer yet, so close that he could feel the air of its wings on his cheek.

Then it was silent. Where had it gone? He waited. Had it flown away?

A tickling began, first on his cheek, then on his temple, then a scratching on his eyeball. It was on his face, crawling there, and now not only could he not breathe, he could not blink, not once, not while the tiny claws tapped his watering eye and the head vibrated, buzzing more faintly than the wings had, and the mind behind those eyes, perhaps in the village, perhaps at the ranch, tried to understand what they were seeing.

Over his head, then, there came a sudden flutter, loud, then a great, rattling clatter and the Cicada Killer's wings snarled and it buzzed away. For an instant, Flynn was confused. Then he realized that the creature was chasing a cicada that its presence in the thicket had just disturbed.

Living machines had their limitations, it seemed, insofar as they remained true to their instincts.

Breathing again at last, he reached up and rubbed his tear-filled eye.

Then he thought, "Did the thing go off chasing the cicada, or did it make me and fly away for that reason?"

The ranch was another world, where technology had entered animals and changed their deepest natures. Not only the tiger and the dogs, but also that snake, he felt sure, had been altered. Also, the doves, which was why they hadn't flocked when there was movement in the house. They had been another trap, continuing to feed and express no alarm as the dogs silently approached. All the while, though, someone had been watching through their eyes, and sending information back to the dogs.

He slipped out of the thicket and into the clearing behind it, which was now glowing with the light of the rising moon. He was moving way too slowly, he had to pick up his pace.

He remembered as a boy lying on the plains side by side with Abby, her hand slipping into his as the moon rose, and glowing above them, the cathedral of the Milky Way.

The mystery of the stars. The tragic face of the creatures in the village. Morris smiling like a doll smiles. The eyes of the dogs, green some and brown and blue— full of humanity and the savagery of animals.

The tiger, curious, sorrowful, and brutal.

By dead reckoning now, he moved toward the compound. He remembered telling Diana "Love your gun," and it was truer now for him than it had ever been before. The metal of it vibrated under his hands with a secret life. The trigger longed to be pulled. The gun was a life changer, an engine of evolution. The gun was holy, it was god in metallic form. The gun was freedom.

A flashlight, maybe, flickered on the path ahead.

As he looked, he also listened to the rustlings of the night, seeking for the sighing movement of a new hunter slipping through the tall grass.

When would he see the tiger? When would he see the dogs? Or would another snake seek him out, a big copperhead, perhaps, as swift as a shadow?

Before him was a long rise, and beyond it a glow. The compound, it had to be. There was nothing else out here but the village, and it didn't show lights.

Binoculars or not, the house was just an indistinct shape. But there was more movement between it and the barn, people going back and forth. How many was he contending with, five or ten? More?

He wondered if the humans involved here were really traitors to their species, or were they themselves in some way under control?

If he thought he had a choice, he would not be here, not with all these unknowns involved, any one of which could destroy him.

In the corner of his left eye, there was the flicker of a swift shadow, but when he turned it was gone.

That was the only evidence he needed. That had been a dog and therefore he had run out of options. His plan had been simple. Rush the place, spraying it with machine-gun fire, all the while seeking to target Morris.

Now, getting to the house was going to require another approach. At some point, any rush was going to be stopped by the animals.

To his left was the long white bone of the caliche road that he had just left. To his right, a clearing full of stands of prickly pear cactus and cedar. Night-blooming flowers filled the air with fragrance.

Something caught his eye—not a movement, but a shape that did not fit the terrain.

In the clearing, standing so still that he almost hadn't seen it, was the tiger. Incredibly, it was not a hundred feet away, close to its ambush range. As always, it had stalked him with almost supernatural skill.

He didn't move. It didn't move.

Three seconds passed. Five.

He couldn't kill it, not without the noise of gunfire reaching the house.

Its long body was low to the ground, but he could see it clearly, almost flowing like a liquid as it edged closer to him.

Unlike at the Hoffman place, there were no trees here to use as a backstop, just these gnarled stands of cedar, and the cat would be at a definite advantage inside one, able to make its way among the branches much more easily than he could.

A nearby sigh drew his eye to the tiger again. Incredibly, it was now less than ten feet away. It had come on him much faster than he had anticipated, even with his knowledge of its skills. Moving slowly, he slid the little AMG into his hand.

He could not see it anymore, but he could hear its breathing, deep and slow, completely calm, no tension in it at all. Still without moving a muscle, he attempted to determine the direction the breathing was coming from. Behind him? Possibly. Possibly also off to the left. In fact, since he was right-handed, his left rear would be his most vulnerable spot. Probably, it had even factored that in, it was that smart.

A nervous finger kept touching the trigger on the little pistol. Once again, they were at what was becoming a familiar impasse. His only survivable situation was if his first shot was a head shot. At night, with a fast-moving target and a small, short-nosed pistol like this, it would be almost all luck.

There was a faint sound, perhaps an intake of

breath—and he realized that the tiger wasn't behind him anymore at all, but now concealed in the cedar directly ahead.

This time, it had outmaneuvered him. The battle of wits that had begun in Montana was over.

The tiger had won.

CHAPTER THIRTY-THREE

He braced the pistol. There was a streak of movement, the sound of big paws skidding in dirt—and then the frantic blowing cry of a deer.

The tiger had run right past Flynn, moving so suddenly and so quickly that he wouldn't have had a chance to get off even a single shot.

Flynn watched it as it busied itself devouring the deer it had just brought down. The creature had died at once, and the tiger now lay on the ground gobbling into its entrails.

There was no question in Flynn's mind but that the tiger had seen him and had definitely known that it had a chance to take him.

He recalled that moment in the storm drain, the curiosity in its face, and the sadness.

The tiger had self-awareness, and the tiger apparently did not like the situation it found itself in. "Slaves are dangerous, Mr. Morris," he thought to himself. Good.

He didn't plan to push his luck, though, so he left it

to its kill, fading quickly back through the cedar thicket, then heading due east toward the highway. He was glad that he trained himself in the skills of orienteering and dead reckoning. He didn't need a compass to make sure that he didn't accidentally close the distance between himself and the house instead.

As he walked, the ground rose slowly, until he had a huge view of Lake Travis, dotted with the lights of boats. Very faintly, he could hear music echoing across the waters.

He had to win this battle this night, that music must never be silenced.

Now he was directly behind the house, and about half a mile out. He understood, though, that he was looking at an unknown world full of unknown creatures—insects that were really observation platforms, snakes infused with extreme aggression, human-dog mixes, the tiger, and who knew what else? What of the creatures from the village? Nothing would prevent them roaming these hills at night. They had overpowered him so easily that if he so much as spotted one from a distance, his only choice was going to be to blow his cover by killing it immediately.

Never standing to full height, slipping quickly from cedar thicket to cedar grove, he moved as quickly as he could.

When he once again reached the caliche road, he paused to see if he could gain any additional information from remaining entirely still for a time. He backed into a stand of cedar. It would somewhat cover his scent, should the dogs come around, or the tiger decide that he was, after all, to be attacked.

Using the binoculars, he reconnoitered up and down the pale strip. No animals in evidence except an armadillo about a hundred yards away, snuffling for grubs along the roadside. Or was it only that?

Armadillos gave dogs a wide berth, so maybe it was an indicator that they weren't nearby. More likely, though, it was like the doves, a subtle deception. So it probably meant that the dogs were indeed nearby.

There was another noise, but this time it was more rhythmic, not the hum of wings.

He stepped out into the road, hesitated, then reached down and felt the ground—and felt a vibration. He pushed the binoculars to his face, and saw, just nosing around a bend in the direction of the highway, the glittering grillwork of a car with its lights off.

It was too late for him to jump back and too late to move carefully enough to conceal his tracks. He leaped ahead and rolled into the brush. Then he froze. The car had a full view of him now, and movement attracts the human eye, especially in the dark. Even under conditions where a man can't see a boulder ten feet ahead of him, he can pick up movement.

As the car approached, he remained absolutely still. He was looking at a GMC Acadia, black, moving slow enough to avoid kicking up dust in the dry roadway.

Was this another attacker? Some sort of outlying patrol?

A shaft of moonlight rested on the driver's face as the vehicle crept past. Flynn saw a woman's hair, some kind of a sweatshirt, and a face with a distinctive, immediately recognizable profile.

He lay there in the ditch, his mind racing. *Diana?*

But no, it was impossible. She had recruited them all, she had created the team. But it was a very special team, wasn't it, consisting exclusively of the few police officers who had complained to the FBI that the abductions were real.

They had all been slaughtered, all but one.

Had it been another deception, designed to silence the few people who had realized what was happening and were equipped to do something about it?

Still puzzling it out, he rose from the ditch and faded back onto the far side of the road, into the land that belonged to the state wildlife refuge.

From his experience as a detective, he knew not to draw conclusions until the facts came into focus, and they weren't in focus now. In fact, they had just gone out of focus—way out of focus.

He had never known that it was possible to feel this isolated and alone.

He also knew from the bitter anger that he felt that he had begun to love Diana—not that she had replaced Abby, but that, as this ordeal went on, he had been finding a place in his heart for her.

But who did she love? Who was she, really? Cut away all the promises and all the claims, and what was left was an ID that she admitted was false.

He put some distance between himself and the ranch, crossing a limestone hill, stopping only when he reached a bluff. Far below was the lake. This was the bluff where he'd seen the caves. Were they of any use to him now? Maybe, but the chance of getting trapped was too great.

He had definitely been observed by the tiger and possibly in other ways, so he could not risk remaining on this side of the ranch. Also, he needed to regain his pace. The moon was already well risen, the land flooded with its glow. The more he hesitated, the more his danger increased.

Even so, this whole side of the property was now compromised. He had no choice but to descend the bluff, go back across the road near the marina, and climb up to the ranch from the other direction.

If he was fast, this might work.

He clambered down, intending to double back and make his way along the lakeside until he reached the stream, then cut through it and return in his earlier scent trail.

When he was about halfway down, there was a flash from below. It wasn't bright but it was followed by a familiar electric crackle that surprised him so much that he almost lost his grip. Struggling not to fall, he turned to look down—and saw, incredibly, that the entire clearing at the foot of the bluff was filled with the creatures of the village with their great, stricken eyes. Four of them had Tasers, and a fifth had something that from this distance was far more dangerous. This was a rifle, probably one that he or Mac had brought into the village.

Laden with the machine gun, the heavy magazines, and his other equipment, Flynn nevertheless had only one maneuver. He had to climb back the way he had come.

Immediately, a rifle shot rang out. It was wide to the left, perhaps fifteen feet away and low. Knowing as much as he did about shooting, Flynn knew to move toward the impact point, not away from it. And indeed, this caused the shooter to miss again, this time by five feet to the right.

If he was lucky, this would work one more time, maybe two. The shooter was small, therefore clumsy with the rifle. But with unknown capabilities. He increased his speed.

Another shot struck the limestone, this one close enough for him to feel a spray of shattered stone against his cheek. The shooter was either brilliant or very poor, to be trying for a head shot.

Another shot, and this time Flynn felt the heat of it. Limestone fragments from the bluff stung his neck.

The next shot would make it.

He reached the lip of the bluff.

Pulling himself up with all his strength, he rolled onto the top as two shots in quick succession slammed into the limestone just below him.

The shooter had found his target, but an instant too late.

They were racing up the bluff with the ease of creatures made to climb.

He ran, speeding toward the road. He was desperate now and he knew it. His only hope was to make it back to the marina and get to the car. But they could flank him easily, and there were the dogs and there was the tiger, and Diana out there, who could be extremely dangerous, as much as she knew about the way he thought.

The car. Now. His last chance.

CHAPTER THIRTY-FOUR

He stayed off the road itself, leaping stands of cactus, darting around cedar thickets, stumbling when he came upon a concealed draw, then picking himself up and continuing on.

He ran hard and far, passing through the silent countryside with the swiftness of a deer, quick but vulnerable.

He couldn't hear a sound behind him or around him. It was as if he was entirely alone. And now he had to add a new concern, which was the silent helicopter. Now that they were certain he was here but no longer sure of his location, it might well become involved.

He reached the marina, which was closed and dark. He rejected the idea of taking one of the boats. Even if he had time to wire it, they would then know where he would appear next, somewhere along the lake.

His car was the only one left in the hard-dirt parking area. He ran to it and got in. As he inserted the key in and started it, he looked up and down the road, seeing no movement.

An explosion shattered the air, and for an instant he thought the car had been bombed. But it was a rifle bullet. It had shattered the windshield. The shooter was in the brush fifty feet away.

He threw the car into gear and floored it. As he accelerated, the little car fishtailed wildly in the dirt of the parking area. Fighting to regain control, he pressed the gas pedal and it leaped ahead.

Dust churned up behind him as he sped along the marina road. His plan was now to violate all the rules. Instead of running from this impossible situation, he intended to rush the house and just shoot until they got him.

But the moment he turned into the ranch's road itself, the black GMC that Diana had been driving appeared, blocking his progress.

Hauling on the steering wheel, he turned into the pasture and went slamming through a mass of cactus so large that his tires spun in the pulp.

A second later, the truck was behind him, its grill filling his rear window.

As he maneuvered through the pasture, he fumbled the backpack open and worked the machine gun into his hand. To stop the vehicle chasing him, he needed a perfect burst. He levered the gun to semi-automatic mode.

Was he about to kill Diana?

He put the thought firmly aside. This was work, feelings came later.

The truck kept close, so close that he couldn't see the windshield. The driver wasn't a fool, he probably knew that if Flynn got a shot at it, he was a dead man, and also that Flynn wasn't going to waste bullets firing into the radiator.

A series of cracks, nicely measured, resulted in his own rear window being blown away. A powerful round was in use, sounded like a .308, probably a NATO round. Blow his head right off.

He swerved around some cedar, then skidded into more cactus, then plunged down into a draw. Behind him, the GMC blasted through the brush, pushing dense cedar aside like it was grass.

Again there was gunfire, and this time Flynn felt the whole car tremble as it took the shock of a round penetrating the trunk.

So they were going for the gas tank. Smart enough. He still had no shot.

Something had to be done, or he was going to lose this thing right here and right now. He drove on, unable to determine a productive course of action.

Then he saw water, then again, ahead and to the right, the lake, its surface far down another bluff.

Okay, here was a maneuver for him. He got the HK into the backpack and opened his door. Now he was driving fast along the bluff's edge, doing forty, fifty, the car shaking itself almost to pieces. Outside his door, the cliff fell away.

This was going to be a very damn close thing. Very close. He didn't often bother God with his crap, but he bothered God now. A lot.

He spun the wheel to the left, causing the Cruze to literally go into tumbling flight. As it did, he dropped out of the open door and onto the cliff's edge.

The car went spinning into the lake.

He let himself fall and keep falling, breaking his plunge as best he could. Finally, he was sliding, then some roots and a loose boulder temporarily stopped him.

Far below, the car struck the water. Nothing left but a red trunk, then the night blue of the lake, the car gone forever.

He looked up, and saw five feet above him another of the caves. Yesterday's deathtrap was today's refuge.

As the truck snarled back and forth on the ledge, Flynn clambered into the cave. How well did they know him? If Diana was involved, they would be certain that he hadn't been in that car when it struck the water.

A moment later, he had his answer. It came in the form of gravel dropping down past the mouth of the cave.

So they knew their man.

The air coming out of the cave was cool—too cool, in fact, for this to be a small place. Back there somewhere was a very large cave indeed. Limestone tends to cave out over time, and this was old country.

He took his binoculars out of his pocket and saw, stretching away behind him, a substantial cavern. Its ceilings were cracked, there was rubble everywhere, and the only access to deeper areas was through a series of openings that looked like real traps, the kind of places that would never let you find your way out.

No time to lose, though. As somebody dropped down outside the mouth of the cave, he plunged into the opening with the strongest breeze, and found himself squeezed tight as he forced his way along.

Confined spaces were never pleasant, and he had been sensitized by that damn coffin, but he kept pushing, dragging the backpack behind him, one of its straps around his left ankle.

He came out into a larger space—and saw all around him huge, glaring eyes. His heart practically exploded out of his mouth, but he choked back the scream as he realized that these were not living creatures but paintings of the gods of some forgotten tribe of Indians. They were beautiful, tall, staring balefully, their arms pointing toward the ceiling—where, when he raised his head—he saw a magnificent representation of the night sky.

Scraping echoed through the cave as his pursuers started down the shaft he'd just come through.

He headed deeper, walking, stooping, running when he could, not really keeping track of his movements. He could get lost in here, no question. But no matter what kind of twists and turns he took, he always heard behind him the scrape of their footsteps, and their quiet grunting as they negotiated the next narrow passage.

No more than one or two of them, he thought.

He smelled dry grass—just a whiff of it, but it was there. That bit of air had come from the surface. So there was another entrance ahead.

Sucking air, painting the way ahead with infrared, he was soon moving steadily upward.

Behind him, the sound of their scrabbling had grown louder.

A glow ahead, then a faint voice from behind shouting at him to stop. He did not stop. Then there came the crack of a shot. The bullet was wide, but not very. He ran away from the sound and toward the glow— and found himself clawing his way out through a big stand of cactus, clawing and pulling at it, and forcing his body out to the surface.

Ignoring the torture of a thousand needles, he came up through the cactus—and saw, not fifty yards away, the truck. As he trotted toward it, he could hear that its engine was still running. He didn't wait, he ran toward the vehicle, putting every single bit of strength he still possessed into the sprint.

The truck was empty, so he now had two choices. He could take the truck and head back to the highway and get the hell out of there. Or he could rush the ranch compound with it.

He turned the truck toward the house. His job. His battle.

He did not see the two figures in the road behind him, did not see one of them yank an old Stetson off his head and hurl it to the ground in frustration.

CHAPTER THIRTY-FIVE

He stopped just out of view of the ranch to check his weapons a last time.

The HK was in good shape, and you wouldn't expect a weapon this durable to have any problem with a little fall down a cliff. All the magazines were there.

He stuffed the AMG into the pocket of his jeans and transferred the extra machine-gun magazines to his belt. Not the most secure way to carry them, but it was what he had. His most critical moments would be during exchanges. He'd trained with an HK and knew that he could pull and set two magazines in just under three seconds. Good time, but maybe not good enough.

He pulled the vehicle forward until he could see the compound. The house appeared quiet, the lights out. Beyond it, the barn was also dark. To every appearance, the place had been abandoned.

He took deep breaths, cleared his mind, and concentrated his attention on the world around him. He saw, just for an instant, some camouflage in motion about two hundred yards away. Somebody was in among a stand of mesquite, using the mottled shade as cover against the moonlight.

If he'd seen them, they could see him. He put the truck in gear and began moving toward the house. He drove quickly. There was no way for him to know whether or not they had realized it was him in the truck. He also didn't know how many people here were capable of putting up a defense, let alone what form their weaponry might take, except that it would be exotic and it would be devastating.

He took the HK in his left hand and steered with his right. He passed the house, heading toward the area beside the shed that covered the entrance to the underground chamber.

Methodically, as he prepared himself, he tried once again to put aside his policeman's confrontation training. He could not announce himself. He had to just do this.

He got out of the truck and held the HK ready.

As he'd driven across the compound, there had been no movement from either the house or the barn.

Something hit him in the right shoulder with such force that it spun him around. A flash of pain shot down his chest and up his neck, but he regained his balance, turning to face the direction the blow had come from.

There was no nearby cover. He looked farther, and there, in the shadows of a cedar thicket, he saw a darker area that a careful observer could see had a human outline. He must be using some sort of stun weapon.

Just briefly, Flynn squeezed the HK's trigger. It blared out a burst and the figure sank. Just that quick. That impersonal.

Four shots, so twelve still in the magazine.

He moved closer to the shed, preparing for a reaction to his burst of machine-gun fire. But nobody moved in from the perimeter and the house and barn remained quiet.

He considered going down the ladder into the storm cellar, but decided to explore the shed first.

The door was unlocked, so he pushed it open.

This was probably an old well house. Before entering, he looked up at the grandeur of the sky. This was probably the last he would see of the world. He hoped that there was some sort of afterlife. That was all, hoped.

He entered the shed. Again, absolute quiet. There was an old stove pushed against one wall and a wooden trapdoor in the floor. Beneath it, there had to be opposition. That was fine by him. Just as long as he got to Morris, he didn't care whether he survived or not.

He lifted the ring, then hefted the door slightly. It wasn't barred from below. No, this was obviously the path they wanted him to take. The guy in the thicket had probably been out there to incapacitate him with the stun gun and carry him down.

When he pulled it up, the door made no sound. Well-oiled hinges, lots of use.

He climbed down the old ladder to what had once been the root cellar, then took a narrow spiral staircase, much newer, that led deep.

The closer he got to the bottom of the narrow space, the stronger the odor became of blood and burned flesh, of burned hair and another stench that cops come to know. It doesn't have a name, but it's the smell of things that have gone horribly wrong, that clings to places where violence has taken place. It's made up of sweat and blood and shattered lives, mixed together as the odor of fear.

The room glowed with soft fleshy light that came from the walls themselves. It was not a normal room, not a human room. Like the village, like all the rest of this place, it was an outpost of another world.

There was also a sheen of blood on the floor, and the stink of the place was so powerful that he had to fight hard not to gag.

Again, he heard the distant pulsation. He began moving toward it.

Machine gun at the ready, he went deeper. The pulsation became more and more distinct. Now it didn't sound so much like a boiling pot as a thumping assembly line.

Ahead there was a figure, short, quick, dressed in black, opening a box of a familiar kind.

A moment later, something that looked like a glowing fireball sizzled into existence immediately above the body inside the box, which was a young woman, very pregnant. She was motionless but she did not look dead or even asleep.

Certain insects, he recalled, paralyze their prey so it will remain fresh for use later.

Her face was in shadow, but when he saw it clearly, he was confronted by such beauty that he gasped.

Immediately, the creature in attendance turned toward him, its movements snapping fast, like those of a quick snake.

There was a flash and for an instant Flynn saw in black outline the skeleton of the young woman and the skeleton of the baby inside her. The fetus moved its hands toward its face in surprise.

The light filled the room with a brightness like thick, glowing milk.

An instant later, the light was gone and his eyes were

dazzled, and someone was standing in front of him. He felt hands on the machine gun and knew that in a moment it would be gone.

He didn't wait for his eyes to recover. He didn't wait for anything. He pulled off a burst and the creature flew backward, its arms flailing, its mouth and eyes wide with surprise.

Four more shots. The magazine was now half empty.

He stepped into the fight, moving quickly to aim the gun at a second creature. Had it been fully human, its face would have been the sort that cops see late at night, a whore's face, worn and tired and profoundly lonely. As it was, the great blue eyes were not only sad, they were tired. Also uncaring. He thought that it didn't care whether it lived or died.

Flynn did two shots, no more needed, and the figure flew backward into the wall, then slid to the floor.

He went to the young woman, whose eyes were now so glazed that he feared the worst for her. Working quickly, he performed CPR, but he couldn't get a pulse.

Light glared from behind him. As he threw himself to the floor, he turned into its glare.

"It's over," Jay Elder said.

If you have a gun, best to let it do your talking. Flynn depressed his trigger and the last burst on this magazine brought a brief shout, then Jay Elder disintegrated.

Replacing the magazine as he rolled, Flynn pushed the table over, creating a shelter for himself behind it.

Immediately, a stun weapon smacked the table, causing it to jerk back into his face. Four more of the creatures from the village rushed him. Another burst took them out.

Silence fell. The air was thick with the sickly stink of

cordite, the powerful reek of blood, and a strange odor, the same cross between sulfur and cinnamon that had filled Oltisis's space.

When there was no more fire directed at him, he took out his small, powerful LED flashlight and aimed it around the darkened room.

Elder was on the floor, his chest a mass of blood. Lying against the spiral stairs was one of the creatures from the village, also dead. In front of him there were the remains of at least six more of the creatures.

Flynn pulled out the empty magazine.

There was a whisper of movement in the dark.

A light came on, and suddenly he was face to face with the narrow, gleaming face of Morris. "Don't reload, Flynn," he said, "this is finished."

Flynn said nothing.

"You've cost me," he continued. "I can still make some use of her, but not much. And the infant is already sold along, so that means a refund. I don't like to do refunds, Flynn."

"What in hell does that mean, sold along?"

"I'm just a businessman trying to make something work in an out-of-the-way place that happens to contain some nice genetic material. This is a mean little planet and it's dying. I want to get some of what it has to offer before you're all gone. That's all."

"But it's a crime where you come from, doing this. That's why your cops are after you."

"In some parts of our world, it's a crime. Not in all."

"You've turned yourself into something that can live freely on Earth. And you're struggling making more. That's why your helpers look like that."

"They aren't 'helpers.' That's a work gang, nothing more. When they're used up, they'll be terminated."

They were slaves, as Flynn had suspected. He realized why they'd been made to appear so strange. It was so they couldn't walk the streets and therefore couldn't escape.

The ability to manipulate life had created a whole new type of crime.

"What are you, Morris? You're not like Oltisis, are you? Not the same species?"

"Consider this a living costume. It's not pleasant and, thankfully, it's temporary. But to answer your question, I've been a lot of things in a lot of places." He gestured at the carnage around them. "This is costly. You're going to have to pay."

"What happened to my wife?"

"Your wife?" He looked over toward the dead woman. "That's your wife?"

The realization that he had not the slightest memory of Abby made Flynn's anger flare.

"You will go where she has gone," Morris continued. "Or you will die right here, right now." As he spoke, he slipped a rod into in his hand, blunt and black and thick. It's end glowed like a coal. He waved it toward Flynn.

Searing agony. The machine gun flew from his hands as he grabbed at his chest, tearing the cloth away from his burning skin.

But he wasn't on fire.

The HK clattered to the floor.

"If I put a charge in you, you'll feel that pain for hours, until you die of exhaustion. Or you can come with me." He sighed, and Flynn knew it as a player's sound of satisfaction, a sound that comes when the trump is laid down or the queen trapped.

CHAPTER THIRTY-SIX

Inside himself, Flynn fought for balance. He had to restore his mission, so he had to get past this checkmate, and he would. The only checkmate he would accept was death.

Morris said smoothly, "It's not going to happen your way, Flynn. It's going to happen my way."

Flynn eased his foot toward the machine gun on the floor.

Morris kicked it away. "You need to understand that you've never come unhooked from my line." He gestured vaguely. "The life you have known is over."

Flynn still had the pistol in his shoulder holster.

"The pistol, too. You can't win, Flynn, I'm sorry. I'm smarter than you are." He glanced around the room. "I oughta just burn you, you bastard." The stout little device in his hand hissed and its spark grew brighter. Morris smiled. "Fascinating, isn't it? Come on, we're going over to my factory."

Morris directed him to ascend the stairs. He was

caught, no question, but he concentrated on every detail as it unfolded. He needed not only to get an opening, but to see it. He'd watched many a fugitive miss a wide-open path to safety.

Outside, moonlight silvered the world.

"Get in," Morris said, gesturing with his weapon toward the GMC. "Elder was a good man. Making off-the-scale money. I can pay at that level, you know. Gold. You join me in this little, insignificant business I have going here, Flynn, and you'll be a billionaire in a year."

Flynn said nothing.

"I'm just sayin', Flynn, the money is serious."

As they entered the vehicle, Morris was careful with his weapon, keeping it constantly ready. "At home," he said as he started the car, "the equipment is better."

"Where is home?"

Morris didn't answer for a moment. He began driving across the grounds, heading out into the brush. "You know, I don't think I can explain that to you. It'd be like explaining this car to a chimpanzee. Can't be done."

Flynn thought, "So the truth is, it's somehow vulnerable." He would not forget Morris's inadvertent admission. If he lived.

They drove along a rough pasture track to the village.

From this perspective, the structures were really amazingly well camouflaged. They appeared to be a few piles of brush, the sort of thing left behind when cedar is cleared. Only from overhead could you see that it was organized around a central path.

Flynn had been watching Morris carefully, looking for an opening. So far, there had been none.

"Now, what's going to happen to you in there is that

the contents of your mind—all of your experiences—are going to be taken out for sale to people who don't have the rich opportunities that life on Earth offers."

It probably wasn't bullshit, but he couldn't say that he understood it.

"Your body will be dissolved and reduced to recoverable stem cells, which will be sold on the black market." He laughed a little, and in that laugh Flynn heard a very human sound, the glee of a psychopath. He regarded Flynn with wide, avid eyes.

"Why are you telling me this?"

"You've caused me extraordinary trouble. I won't deny it." He smiled his soft, haunted smile. "I just want you to know how it's done. What was done to your wife."

A searing flash exploded into the car and, absolutely without warning, half the village burst into flames. Instinct caused Morris to whirl away from the blast, in the process dropping his weapon.

Instantly, Flynn reached out and grabbed it, and by the time Morris had looked back, it was pointed at him.

Morris's face told his story. He was horrified and he had no idea what was going on. Neither did Flynn. Opening the door with his free hand, he backed out of the vehicle—and found himself three feet from the tiger. From inside the truck, there came a sharp burst of laughter. Morris began to get out the other side.

Flynn's problem was that he had no idea how to use this weapon. It was a featureless black cylinder, and the end was no longer glowing.

In the firelight, the tiger's eyes flickered. The face was not angry, it was not cruel. Instead, he was seeing that same questioning expression. Very softly, he said, "Help me."

Morris came around the car. Another of the weapons was in his hand, and the tip of this one was glowing.

Frantically, Flynn shook his, twisted it, squeezed it until his fingers went numb.

Morris held his at arm's length.

Flynn stared helplessly at the red tip.

He was hurled backward, falling against the tiger.

But the tiger backed away. Then Morris was on top of him, slamming his face with the fury of the mad. He'd seen it before, he'd felt it before. Guys on angel dust fought like this. Crazies.

From above, there came a powerful wind, sweeping up clouds of dust and causing the tiger to crouch, then turn away.

There was a snap and a deafening roar and the other half of the village burst into flames.

Snarling, Morris leaped to his feet. He raised his weapon. The red went to white, then to iridescent blue. But he didn't point it at Flynn, he pointed it overhead.

Flynn looked up to see a shape not fifty feet above them. It didn't make a sound, but it was visible in the firelight. It was the silent helicopter.

The weapon glowed brighter. The base of the helicopter began also to glow. It swerved away. Morris followed it. The helicopter began to smoke.

Flynn was getting to his feet, but then the tiger finally decided to charge, and he was forced to roll aside, throwing up his arms to defend his face.

The tiger went right past him, it's immense bulk flying through the air with startling ease.

It hit Morris directly in the chest, causing him to

plunge fifty feet across the compound and crash to the ground. His weapon flew off into the night. But he was immediately back on his feet. "Snow Mountain," he said, "do *not*!"

The tiger stared at him.

Overhead, the helicopter began to work its way lower. The remains of the village burned furiously, ringing the scene with dancing flames and casting terrific heat.

Wobbling, the chopper reached eye level. A voice called out, "We can't figure out how to land this damn thing!"

It was Mac. Sitting beside him was Diana.

The chopper went up, disappearing into the night sky.

Flynn saw that Morris was on his feet. Snow Mountain was close to him. He wasn't attacking, but he wasn't doing anything else, either.

Flynn dodged into some shadows, trying to minimize his exposure to Morris.

The wind from above returned. Got stronger. The chopper appeared in front of him, wobbling uneasily at eye level.

Diana peered out. "Flynn, you're a pilot, what do we do?"

"Draw the cyclic toward you!"

Mac yanked it into his stomach and they lurched away into the dark, then came rocking back.

Mac yelled, "That didn't work!"

"Reduce power!"

"Got it!"

"Move the cyclic back, *barely*!"

They were hovering now.

"Reduce power more."

They dropped to an altitude of about four feet. He could reach out and touch them. The chopper wobbled, began drifting into a slow spin.

In seconds, they would lose it. He saw the truck moving. Morris was getting away.

"Jump," he shouted, "do it now!"

But the chopper shot up into the sky. The truck was quickly disappearing into the dark. Then the helicopter reappeared, nose down, dropping fast. Not the right attitude for a chopper, not this close to the ground. But Flynn could do nothing. They were going to pile the damn thing in.

At the last moment, it lurched. It spun on its axis. Once again, it hovered at an altitude of ten feet.

"See, the bastard won't land! It's got a fuckin' mind of its own."

It did, Flynn knew. Somewhere in there, a sophisticated crash avoidance system didn't like Mac's piloting.

"Jump or die, damnit, both of you! Do it NOW!"

Something dropped out. Flynn recognized it by its shape: it was a shoulder launched urban assault weapon.

Where in the world had Mac come up with a thing like that?

He'd probably never know.

The chopper was still at about five feet. Shielding his eyes with his forearm from the hurricane of dust it was producing, he ran forward.

"It'll take off again," he yelled, "*jump*!"

First, Diana leaped out. She tried to roll off the kinetic energy but did it like she'd seen in movies, not the way that worked.

Mac dropped down, rolled expertly, and danced to his feet.

As he came out, Flynn dove into the cockpit and pushed the collective all the way to the floor, causing the rotor blades to lose lift. The chopper dropped to the ground. He turned off the ignition switch and the engine quit.

"That sucker's alive," Mac said. "And it don't like me." He was caked with dust.

Flynn could no longer see the truck.

Diana hobbled to her feet. The dirt in her hair made her appear to have gone gray.

"Sprain?"

"I'm fine!"

Mac produced a Magnum. Diana had one, too. Good.

Diana dug another Magnum and an iPhone out of her backpack. "Take these."

Flynn took them. "Safe to use the phone, I wonder?"

"Right now," Diana said, "all he has is that truck. His money, my friend, is gone. His life is gone."

"You hacked him?"

"To the bone. If he has cash in his pocket, that's what he has."

At that moment, the ground shook. Soon, more flames could be seen flickering through the trees.

"He just did the compound," Flynn said.

"Then he's a total bum with nothing but a busted car. 'Cause he ain't even got any insurance policies. Somebody canceled 'em. And his deeds. They're gone from the county record office. Plus the electronic back-ups. Sometime later tonight, that truck's gonna run out of gas and he's gonna be walking. That'll be what he has. Feet."

The hell with that, he had his life, which was not acceptable.

Flynn ran toward the helicopter.

CHAPTER THIRTY-SEVEN

Gathering up the UAW, he told Diana and Mac, "You two stay here, get away from the village, do back-to-back defense. Shoot at any and all movement and expect that tiger to come around at any time. But don't drop it unless it charges you. The tiger is conflicted, and that might be valuable down the road."

He got into the pilot's seat and restarted the engine. As soon as it ran up, he loaded the rotor with lift and rose into the sky.

The lights of structures that lined the lake shot past as he worked the foot pedals to bring the chopper's yaw under control. At the same time, he looked toward the ranch, hoping to spot the truck in the glow of the fires burning there.

No joy. The truck wasn't near the compound, and beyond fire light, the land was dead black.

He took the chopper into an uneasy hover, then leaned out of the open door with the UAW on his shoulder. Its sight was light-sensitive, and he soon spotted the truck bouncing through the brush, heading cross-country toward the main road, rather than going anywhere near the ranch's driveway or the smaller road that served both it and the marina.

He began working the helicopter closer. He was no expert with its controls, though, and it was a struggle.

The UAW had just one rocket in it, so his first shot would be the one he got. The Magnum wouldn't be useful, just noisy, so the rocket was his chance.

Working the cyclic and the collective, he dropped down and moved closer to the truck at the same time. It was invisible to the naked eye, but easy to see in the sight, and the closer he got, the more the crosshairs converged. But then he would overcontrol the chopper or undercontrol it and the whole process would need to be repeated.

He had just two hours training on helicopters. He hadn't even soloed. Still, this commercial-military hybrid was relatively easy to fly, and he was beginning to be able to close in nicely when the whole airframe started shuddering, the collective came up on its own and the engine went to full throttle.

The chopper went up so fast it was like being in a high-speed elevator. Flynn was normally almost silent, but this caused him to cry out with surprise.

The autopilot had taken over. It was probably controlled by Morris down in the truck.

The altimeter was winding up at breakneck speed. As he watched, he went through two thousand feet.

Okay, think. He was not going to overcome this situation using manual control. At best, the battle that would ensue between him and Morris and the autopilot would crash the chopper. He surveyed the instrument panel. No obvious autopilot override.

There was one thing he could do that had to work. Also, though, it might kill him.

He took the UAW up and sighted in the speeding truck, but the sight didn't even activate. Far out of range.

So this was it. He was down to one choice, and it was a really bad one.

He checked his straps, then reached down and twisted the fuel shutoff valve, stopping the engine. The warning horn sounded as the wing went into autorotation and the ascent stopped. The autopilot was still controlling it, though, and as soon as Morris realized what he'd done, he would try to crash it, no question.

Working quickly, he flipped circuit breakers, hoping to kill something crucial, like the autopilot's telemetry. Turning off its power supply wouldn't matter. Autopilots have backup batteries.

As he flipped more and more switches, the instrument lights went dark, then the instruments themselves ceased functioning.

He was now on straight visual in a dead black night, with only the distant lights along the shore, and those of the various fires below, to orient him.

Once again, he brought the UAW back to his shoulder. As the chopper lost altitude in uncanny silence, he searched for the truck.

It was moving at breakneck speed, not a hundred yards shy of the main road. Flynn didn't care whether this bastard's bank accounts had been hacked or not, or what had happened to him. He needed killing.

As the chopper continued to descend, the truck grew in the UAW's sight, until finally the crosshairs began flashing yellow.

A few more feet. He dropped the chopper's nose. Maybe they would die together. Fine, he didn't care.

The crosshairs moved closer and closer together. Then, very suddenly, they were red, and in the center of their cross was the truck.

He fired the rocket, which left the tube with a ferocious roar and a kick.

He tossed the tube behind him out of the way and concentrated on piloting the chopper, which was now rapidly losing altitude.

A blinding flash of white fire announced the end of the truck, and Flynn roared, "Abby, baby, Abby baby, I love you!"

He couldn't bring her back, but this was the end for the evil bastard who had destroyed her, and that felt damn wonderful.

Police procedures didn't matter. Morris was not human, therefore the only law that applied was the law of jungle, and Flynn did that kind of law as well as any of the criminals he so despised.

Using the cyclic, he got the chopper aimed straight toward the dying fires of the village. As he came in, he heard both Magnums being discharged.

Adjusting the collective to decrease lift on the rotor, he dropped down as fast as he dared, hitting the ground approximately a hundred yards from the village.

His jaw snapped, a flash went past his eyes.

The helicopter became still. His ears rang from the shock of the impact.

Before moving, he checked himself: hands okay, arms, feet, legs. If he was going to go into a firefight with impact injuries, he wanted to know where he was impaired, and what it would do to his effectiveness.

He jumped out of the chopper and approached the

village. To the west, huge flames still gushed up from the ranch compound. Further south, a smaller glow marked the position of the truck.

Diana and Mac came out of the underbrush.

"I thought you crashed," she said.

"No. What were you two firing at?"

"The tiger's out there."

"Has it charged?"

"You can't ask us to take a chance like that!"

She was right, but he was also relieved when, very suddenly and in absolute silence, Snow Mountain appeared. His stripes were such perfect camouflage in the flickering firelight that it almost seemed as if he had materialized out of clear air rather than walked out of the shadows.

He came closer. Mac readied himself to shoot again.

"No," Flynn said.

Broken only by the crackle of flames, the silence the tiger brought with him was as strange as a cry from a distant world.

Flynn reached out and laid his hand on the lion's head—a small human hand lost in the fur of the immense animal.

"You could sell that thing for a damn fortune," Mac said.

"Don't even think about it."

The tiger looked off into the dark.

Flynn was relieved that Diana wasn't the traitor he had thought her to be. "We're a good team," he said.

Snow Mountain turned and slipped into the darkness.

Mac ran after him. "Hey!"

"Leave him be, Mac."

"I don't get my skin or to sell him to a zoo or nothin'. Shit!"

"He's got his own demons to deal with, that one does."

"He's part human, isn't he?" Diana asked.

"Be my guess. And who knows what else?"

"What'll happen to him?"

"He'll roam the land, make some kind of a life for himself." He looked off in the direction he had gone. "That's the loneliest creature in the world."

A cathedral silence settled, as they all contemplated together the plight of Snow Mountain. In the distance, a dull explosion echoed from the direction of the compound.

"How did you ever get out?" Flynn asked Mac.

"I had to do a good bit of killin,' tell the truth. Is that murder, doin' those little gooks?"

"There's no law to cover killing aliens, if that's what they are. There will be, but not now."

"Well anyways, it was self-defense."

He thought of what had been happening at the compound, of the fate of the captured. "It sure was. I thought you were a goner."

"I was acting."

Flynn recalled that he'd been a terrific Dracula in junior year at Menard High.

But for the crackle of fires, everything was quiet.

Mac looked from one of them to the other. Slowly, a smile came into his face. "Have we won?"

Flynn noticed that Diana's hand had slipped into Mac's. For a moment, he felt shock. Disappointment. Then he forced it back inside. He'd been lonely for a while, so he'd stay that way. Fine. Abby was with him and she had no plans to take up with some damn crook.

He reflected that whole worlds can change in a moment on the battlefield, and that had happened here.

He smiled back at the two of them. "Right now, we've won."

Above the sirens, because it was so close, there was a sound that made Flynn freeze. "Back to back, brace the pistols!"

Dogs came leaping and snarling in at them from every direction at once, their bodies speeding like liquid fire, their teeth flashing, their human eyes filled with human hate.

With the care and expertise of a man, one of them grabbed Flynn's throat with its long claws. Its mouth opened and it was slashing with its teeth when he blew it in half. For a moment, the jaws continued snapping with shark-like fury, then, its blood gone, it dropped away like a stone.

Behind him Diana's shot went wild. As she screamed and another dog leaped on his back, he turned and blew off the head of the one attacking her, then killed two more at her feet.

All the while others piled on him, until their weight staggered him and he fell forward between Mac and Diana, then forced himself to turn into the ravening pack that was on his back, and fired four more times, taking all of them out, leaving them in pieces on the ground around him.

Then they were gone.

Mac hung his head.

Diana sat on the ground covered with blood and sobbing.

Flynn said, "There are eighteen. We did twelve. The others won't try again."

Diana dropped her pistol into her backpack.

"Unless we disarm ourselves. You love your gun, remember."

"It's too hot to hold."

"It'll cool off. Mac, you okay?"

"I'm alive."

"We're done here," he said. He could hear pumpers churning over at the compound, but great masses of smoke were still pouring skyward, lit by the fires in the underground chambers.

"Those guys gotta be wondering what the hell was going on out there," Mac said.

"Probably think it was some kinda drug factory. Probably figure it belonged to you."

"Me? I don't have any penetration into Travis County. I'm way west of here, buddy."

"It's time for us to go on down the road," Flynn said. "Morris and his operation are done."

As the three of them walked out to the highway, Flynn saw that Mac and Diana were still hand in hand. In silence, Flynn walked on ahead.

Once they were on the road, Mac directed them to the parking lot of a closed strip mall. The Range Rover was there, pulled up behind a dry cleaners.

"Backup transportation," Mac said. "We stationed it here last night."

Last night seemed like a thousand years ago.

Moths and bats swarmed around the floods that lit the parking area. In the far shadows, a young couple necked in a convertible. Music echoed in the distance.

"I thought we'd go on over to the Oasis, knock back a few," Mac said. "Sounds like there's a band goin'."

On the far distance, Flynn heard country music, the wail of a violin, the frantic twitter of a mandolin.

He preferred blues to bluegrass.

They drove to the bar, which overlooked the lake. In the parking lot, though, Flynn hung back. He'd seen a taxi rank, cabbies trolling for kids too drunk to drive, and smart enough not to.

He watched Diana and Mac disappear into the lights and the crowd. He'd thought she was his, and it was going to take him time to get easy with the truth.

This battle had been won, but there was a war going on, and they needed to be prepared for whatever might come. They needed a bigger operation, more and better-trained personnel, more equipment. More of everything, and better.

He got into one of the cabs. "Take me into town. Motel 6 be fine," he said.

The driver worked in silence, which was good. To Flynn, silence was home.

The cell phone buzzed. He looked at the number, did not recognize it.

"Yeah?"

"Flynn, where are you?"

"Kicking back," he replied. "Catch up soon."

"You don't want to celebrate?"

"I'm good."

"Flynn—"

"Diana, you be careful. I know Mac well. He's a professional criminal and he breaks hearts for fun."

"Flynn, I love you."

"I love you."

Silence fell. Extended.

Finally, Flynn added, "But you want him."

"He wants me."

Pretty as she was, she was too hard along the edges to have been wanted very much in her life. Mac went for powerful women, though. He enjoyed demolishing them.

"I'm here," he said, "and you're gonna want a shoulder in the end."

"Mac is a lovely man, Flynn, that's what you can't see."

"If you say so, Diana."

He hung up as the driver pulled up in front of the Motel 6's tiny lobby.

He checked in with his own credit card, a small but sweet satisfaction. In the room, he flipped through the channels. Nazis, cartoons, girls, the usual late-night stuff. Still, he left it on in the background. The mutter of artificial excitement relaxed him.

Toward three, he decided that sleep was not in the cards for him tonight.

He pulled on his jeans and a sweatshirt and went out into the parking area, then up onto the shoulder of the empty highway.

He walked, listening to the rhythmic whisper of his shoes on the tarmac. When an eighteen-wheeler thundered by he didn't vary his pace or even glance at the drama of its passing, so deep had he gone into his thoughts.

His memories of this extraordinary experience followed him as shadows in the wind. Whatever happened, he was going to stay with this thing. In the end, whatever these creatures were, he would banish the bad ones from Earth, and create conditions that would enable the others to share the richness of their minds openly with mankind.

Flynn Carroll walked as he henceforth always would, with his secrets buried in his silence. He walked his own path, but not alone. Abby was there by his side. He chose to believe in the prevalence of the soul, and that she was, as are all decent people, part of the essential goodness of creation, of which he was soldier, servant, and ally.

In the silence of his heart, he embraced the people he had loved, and those he had lost. The moon had set, and the Milky Way in its majesty spread across the great vault of the sky.

He paused, looking up into the vibrant beauty of it all, and imagined other eyes and other minds perhaps returning his gaze, and thought on the richness of the weave of good and evil he had touched, and what dark secrets must still be undisclosed. Had Morris been the only criminal of his kind? Were there more, as yet unsuspected, or would there be? And what of the alien police? If there was more crime to fight here, would they be willing, this time, to send enough support? And if not, then how would he proceed on his own?

He walked on down the dark highway, alone and content to be alone. His battle was won, and that was good. A good feeling.

A meteor flashed in the sky, then descended in blazing grandeur.

Or was it a meteor? He stared along the horizon where it had fallen, looking for some new glow or some other hint that it had been, perhaps, a conveyance from the deep beyond.

Nothing glowed, though, and no more meteors appeared.

Fine, then he would go on down the road, and see what might develop. The questions, however, of who these creatures were and where they had come from and what their true motives might be—these questions had not been fully answered, not in his opinion. He had wrecked the enterprise of one of their criminals. But the greater mystery that they represented had not been solved.

But that was tomorrow's problem. Today's had been solved. Whoever they were, their good guys now knew they had a friend here on Earth, and their criminals that Flynn Carroll was somebody to be reckoned with.

Turn the page for a preview of

Alien Hunter: Underworld

· · · · · · · · · · · · · · · ·

WHITLEY STRIEBER

*Available now
from Tom Doherty Associates*

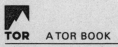

TOR A TOR BOOK

CHAPTER ONE

As he did every morning, Flynn Carroll was going through police reports on his iPad, reading them quickly. Then he stopped. He flipped back a page. As he re-read, his eyes grew careful.

He didn't look the part of a careful man. His appearance—ancient chinos and a threadbare tee—was anything but. Duct tape repaired one of his sneakers. His hair was sort of combed; his beard was sort of shaved. But the stone gray eyes now stared with a hunter's penetrating gaze.

In two respects, the report was right in line with the others that were of interest to Flynn. A man had disappeared, in this case two days ago. This morning he was discovered murdered in a characteristically brutal and bizarre manner. What was different was that the body had been found very quickly. Usually, corpses were located days or weeks after the murders.

Not only was this a case for him, it represented a rare chance. The killers would generally do two or three or more victims over a period of a few days. The first body would rarely be found until at least two or three more killings had been done. There had been no other disappearances or characteristic murders reported anywhere in the area. If this was the first in a new series, it represented both a major change and perhaps a major opportunity.

The change was that this victim wasn't an anonymous homeless person picked up off the street. This was a citizen with an identity and people and a place in the world. The opportunity was that the killers might still be operating in the area, and Flynn might have a chance to get them.

He unfolded his lean frame and got to his feet, striding off between the rows of consoles and neatly dressed technicians who manned the command center.

As he passed one of the linguists, he asked, "Got any new messages?"

"This week? Two lines."

He stopped. "And?"

"A complaint, we think. They seem to be saying that you're too brutal."

"Me? Me personally?"

He laughed. "All their messages are about you."

They'd been asking their counterparts on the other side for six months for more information about these killers. All they had been told was that it was a single, rogue band. From the amount of activity Flynn guessed that it consisted of about seven individuals.

Another of the techs sat before a strangely rounded device, beautiful in its gleaming darkness, but also somehow threatening, a glassy black orb that seemed to open into infinity.

Flynn went over to him.

"Jake? Got a second?"

The man was intent on his work, peering into the blackness. Within this small, very secret working group hidden deep in the basement of CIA headquarters in Virginia, this device was known as "the wire." It provided communication with their counterpart police force. This other police force was headquartered on a planet our experts had decided was called Aeon, the government of which was eager for open contact with mankind. Supposedly.

The problem was—again, supposedly—that they weren't entirely in control of their own people. Aeon, our experts had decided, had evolved into a single, gigantic state, but it was free, and so, like any free country, it had its share of criminals.

Flynn's take: let's see this place before we decide what it's like. Nobody had ever been to Aeon—unless, of course, the people who had not been killed, but had instead disappeared without a trace . . . like his wife, Abby.

"Let Aeon know we've got another murder."

"Yessir."

"And if there's any response, anything at all, get it translated on an extreme priority basis."

As far as Flynn knew, only one alien—a creature that looked human—was responsible for the original crimes, which had been the disappearances. These new crimes—all killings—were being done by things that looked, frankly, alien. They weren't the "grays" of popular imagination, with their huge eyes and secretive ways. Flynn had never encountered one of those creatures. Apparently they weren't from Aeon. With such a big universe, so incredibly ancient and complicated, who knew what they really were or where they were from?

The ones he was trying to take off the map were wiry creatures with narrow faces and blank shark eyes. They had four supple fingers and long, straight claws that could also be used as knives or daggers. They were biological but not alive, he didn't think, in the same way that human beings are. Their rigid determination and ritualistic, unvarying murder techniques suggested to him that they must be robotic.

He did not hate them. His objective was to clean up the alien criminal element on Earth so that the public could safely be informed that contact was unfolding. To the depths of his soul, Flynn wanted open contact.

There was one exception to his dislike of killing them. The first alien criminal known to have arrived on Earth had called himself Louis Charlton Morris. His used a highly sophisticated disguise that gave him human features that were regular and spare. His hair was brown, his lips narrow but not cruel. His expression was open, even friendly. If you encountered him in a dark alley, you wouldn't think you had a problem. You'd also be just as wrong as a person could be, because Louis Charlton Morris could do far worse than kill you. He could take you into the unknown and do to you there whatever he had done to Abby and so many others.

There had been a police officer here from Aeon, until he was killed. He had two legs and two arms, and a face with lips that were somewhat human, but the eyes were those of a fly. He could not expose himself to our atmosphere, and had worked out of a hermetically sealed office in Chicago.

Disguising oneself as Morris did was, it seemed, so

illegal that not even a cop could get a clearance to do it. Since Oltisis's murder, though, they had apparently changed that policy. No replacements had showed up, however.

Flynn's theory was that the killers belonged to Morris. They were something he had created and were being used to get revenge.

Flynn's previous life as a detective on the police force of the city of Menard, Texas, had hardly prepared him for this work. Have your wife taken right out of your marriage bed in the middle of the night, though, and you're going to change, and change a lot. You will go on a quest to find her, or find out what happened to her. To serve that quest, you will learn whatever you need to learn, and do whatever you need to do. You will push yourself hard. You will not stop.

He walked across the room to a door marked only with a plastic slide-in sign: "Director." On the other side there were more desks, more computing equipment, more quiet, intense men and women. Saying nothing, moving with the supple energy of a leopard, he went through into the inner office.

"I've got one I want to move on right now."

Operations Director Diana Glass said, "Okay, what are we looking at?"

"Town in Pennsylvania. Guy disappeared yesterday. He's been found. First report from the area."

"They could still be there."

"That's what I'm hoping. There's a strange kicker, though. He's a neurologist. Doctor Daniel Miller."

She raised her eyebrows in question.

"It gets more interesting. He worked at Deer Island."

"On the cadavers?"

"Possibly. There's a neurobiology unit there." He paused. "So maybe he hit on something somebody would rather we didn't know."

"Official Aeon would never do this."

"You sure?"

"Maybe it has to do with his work, but I also think a citizen was involved to make sure you'd come. It could be an ambush, Flynn."

"Probably is."

"How did it go down?"

"He went out on a mountain bike. When he didn't return at sundown, his wife called for help. The bike was located at dawn. The cops brought hounds, but his scent was only on the bike."

"But they found the body anyway?"

"In a wetland a few hundred feet from his house. Same condition as the derelicts. Lips cut off, genitals and eyes dissected out, drowned." So far, more than twenty homeless people had been taken off the streets, mostly in the northeastern US, brutally and bizarrely mutilated, then drowned in the Atlantic and returned to locations near where they'd been picked up.

"We need some advice from Aeon."

"And how are we going to get that?"

"The two police forces, working together—"

"Don't even start. There's one police force. Us. Ever since Oltisis, Aeon's side has been all smoke and mirrors."

"For God's sake, don't do any more killing."

He locked eyes with her.

She looked away. "The other side objects more strenuously every time you kill another one, Flynn. They want them back."

He said nothing.

"They have laws just like we do! They want these creatures back for trial and punishment."

"No they don't. They're not creatures."

"That's a matter for debate."

"You haven't fought them. I know when I'm dealing with a machine, believe me. No matter how high-end its brain is."

"They don't want them killed. Bottom line."

"If they want them back, tell them to damn well come and get them."

"If you're wrong about what they are, you're committing murder."

"We're disabling machines, not killing people. Anyway, this is our planet. So, our laws."

"Which don't include blowing away perps like—" She hesitated, unsure of how to continue.

Flynn knew exactly how. He said, "Like they're broken machines and cannot be stopped in any other way."

"Aeon is far in advance of us technologically, Flynn. Far more powerful. When they complain, we need to listen."

"'Aeon' consists of messages translated from a language we barely understand, coming from some place we can't even find, that will not send a replacement for the one policeman they did give us, or even explain what they think happened to him."

"Oltisis was killed in Chicago, not on Aeon."

"And what about a replacement? Or, God forbid, even two. Or fifty? Why don't they send us a whole team of detectives and a nice chunk of SWAT? Seems the logical thing to do."

"They regard this as a small problem. One we can handle ourselves. They haven't sent support out of respect for us."

"Have you ever told them the truth?"

"What truth?"

"That only one person is able to even get near these critters? I need support, Diana. The risk is just incredible."

"We have messages that specifically forbid you to kill, as you know. You've got to promise me you'll abide by them."

"So what do I do? Bag them up? Drag them off to a supermax?"

She sighed. She knew perfectly well that they could not be contained.

"Over the past nine months, I've done four. If Aeon's telling the truth and this is a rogue band, maybe I can wrap the problem up on this mission. Finish the thing."

She leaned far back in her chair, her long blond hair falling behind her, her green eyes, so deceptively soft, filling with uneasy calculation. Her face, an almost perfect oval, took on an expression that Flynn knew all too well. When she was twenty, it must have been a soft face, sweet with invitation. Her journey to thirty had been a hard one, though, during which she'd seen death and done some killing. Her face still said angel, but now it also said soldier. Hidden behind that cloud of Chanel was a woman with a tragic secret, which was that the blood of some of her own cops was on her hands. He knew she was as haunted by members of their original team who had been killed by Morris and his group as he was by Abby's disappearance.

"Losing you would be a phenomenal disaster. In fact, we can't afford that risk at all anymore, not until we've trained up a bigger unit. Which gets me to something I haven't wanted to bring up, but I'm going to have to order you to stand down on this one."

For a little while in the dangerous period when they were tracking Morris, the two of them been together twenty-four hours a day, sleeping in the same room for mutual protection, and they'd gotten to be a thing—sort of, anyway. They had wanted each other, but he had not been able to dismiss Abby's ghost. Their affair had been an act of desperation, which had faded when the threat had become less. With her sitting in the boss's chair and him married to a ghost, he considered it entirely over.

"Time, Diana. I've gotta move."

"You heard me."

As he walked out, he called transportation and told the operator, "I want to be in Mountainville, PA, in best time."

Diana came up behind him.

He walked faster.

"Flynn, at least wear the rig."

The rig was designed to record his moves, to be used in a training film. "Nope."

"Unless you wear it, we can't hope to teach others. You can't work alone forever, Flynn."

"Fine. Hire Mac." Mac Terrell was an old friend from Texas. He'd worked the Morris case with them. He was among the best sniper shots in the world, if not the best, and Flynn could use a sniper in this.

"You know I can't."

"No rig. Forget the rig."

She hurried along, working to keep up as he strode out of the command center.

"Flynn, please!"

He stopped. "The rig contains electronics. As I have previously explained, when I wear it, the electronics will be detected, and therefore, I will fail to engage the perpetrators. Of course, they may well engage me, in which case, I'm done."

"Do not go out there."

"I could end this!"

"Flynn, it's a trap and you're completely buying into it. I don't get why you don't you see this."

"If you know you're entering a trap, it's not a trap, it's a mistake on the part of your enemy. So I'm gonna walk into their mistake and they don't make many, and I will not lose this chance."

"Flynn, will you grant me one favor? A small one?"

"I'm not gonna wear the rig, but yeah, something else."

"Come back alive."

"Fine. Done. Good-bye."

This time, she stayed behind. He passed through the two departments that concealed the command center, went to the transport hub, and got in the waiting SUV.

The driver was silent. Flynn was silent. Usual routine. He spent the drive to Dulles looking at satellite views of Mountainville. Frustrated by what he was seeing, he texted Logistics, "Throw me something better than Google Maps."

'That's all we have. Not a strategic location.'

He punched in the tech's phone number.

The answer was immediate. "Sir?"

"Get to the Pennsy Department of Geology or whatever they call it over there. You want a map that details any isolated watercourses within two miles of the house. Mountain streams, that type of thing. Any that are spring fed and absolutely pure. And any caves, crevasses, rocky areas, especially near the good water. You want a map that shows all of that. You got it, you call me. Make it fast, it's as urgent as they come."

He put down his phone, then returned to the Google map. Steep hills, lots of cliffs, which meant exposed climbing. For them, the best terrain. For him, the worst.

The car dropped him at general aviation and he strode quickly through to the waiting plane.

As he entered the cabin, he asked the pilot only one question: "How long?"

"An hour and sixteen minutes."

"Get me there in an hour." If this had any chance of working, he had to be ready by sunset. Maybe the aliens would be there one more night. Not two, though. Never happen.

"Sir?"

"I know the plane. It can do it."

"It'll risk the engines."

"Do it."

Once they were airborne, he called the unit's FBI liaison officer. "Flynn here. Get the body out of the hands of the locals immediate. Standard procedure, autopsy and record, then freeze. Provide the family with stock ashes in an urn. The local cops are to be told that this is a terrorism matter. If they talk they're gonna be spending the rest of their lives inside. Obviously, make certain there's no press."

"Got it," the liaison officer said.

The engines howled. The pilot was running them as ordered.

Flynn watched the land slide past far below, the trees tinged with autumn, little towns nestled in among them, America in its quiet majesty, her people in their innocence.

He wanted things to be right for them. He hadn't been able to protect Abby, but he could protect them, at least a little, at least for a while.

As always at such moments, he wished he had Mac with him. They'd grown up together but gone down opposite paths. Mac was a criminal, more or less, so tangled up in being a DEA informant and massaging the drug cartels, you couldn't tell at any given time which side of the law he was on.

If Flynn missed anybody besides Abby, it was Mac. He'd helped wreck Morris's operation just like he lived his generally illegal life, with skill, ease, and pleasure.

His extensive criminal record made him a security risk. So no clearance, which meant no job despite the fact that he'd been effective and, unlike most of the others who had worked on that case, lived. Morris had been running his operations out of a ranch near Austin, Texas, complete with bizarre intelligence-enhanced animals and human accomplices.

Flynn slid his hand over the butt of his pistol. What success he'd had—the killing of four of the things so far—came from one central fact: he had become very, very fast with his weapons. None of the trainees he'd been given so far had been able to come even close.

It wasn't too surprising, given that a man could practice for a lifetime and never learn to shoot a pistol as fast as Flynn could. He'd always been good with a gun, but in the past few months, he had reached a level of proficiency that was, frankly, difficult even for him to understand.

The engine note changed, dropping. The plane shuddered, headed down. Flynn looked at his watch. Fifty-four minutes.

He hit the intercom. "Thank you."

The reply was a burst of static. The pilot was probably thinking about who he'd have to deal with if he'd blown his engines.

From the air, Mountainville appeared to be little more than a few stores and some houses tucked in among a twisting range of dark hills. The single-strip airfield wasn't manned. The plane could land, though, and that's all that mattered.

The place looked the picture of peace, but Flynn knew different. Somewhere down there, a man had endured what was probably the worst death a human being could know.

Also down there, he had reason to hope, would be his quarry.

The plane bounced onto the runway and trundled to a stop, its engines still roaring. He got out and crossed the tarmac to the car that had been left for him. As per established procedure, the vehicle had been dropped off by the regional FBI office. Nobody was to meet him. What Flynn did, he did alone.

He tossed his backpack into the trunk, then got behind the wheel. For a moment he sat silently preparing himself for whatever might come. Then he started the engine.

The hunter was as ready as he could be. He headed off toward Mountainville, and whatever might linger there.

Learn more of Flynn Carroll's past in

They Did Not Know

· · · · · · · · · · · · · · ·

A never-before-seen short story by

WHITLEY STRIEBER

On the night that all of their hopes and the lives they thought lay before them began to unravel, Flynn Carroll and his wife, Abby, decided to go horseback riding in the moonlight. But in the weave of things, perhaps it wasn't really a decision at all. More a call. An order, even, at least for him.

Abby mounted Serena, floating up into the saddle in a flash of jeans, one elaborately decorated boot gleaming in the last glow of the sun. She and Flynn had cracked a Lone Star in the kitchen of his parents' ranch house, passing it back and forth as they walked over to the barn and saddled Serena and War Chief.

As they rode out, Flynn's father arrived from branding, in his pickup. He got out and came hurrying over to the barn, head down, gray distinguished hair flying in the south wind that sweeps Texas on summer nights.

"Son, you don't want to night ride."

He was right. It would be dead dark on the prairie.

"We'll walk 'em, Dad. It won't be a problem."

"Flynn—"

His father still thought of him as a teenager. Flynn was thirty, married now two years. "Dad, it won't be a problem."

"You come back with a broke-leg horse—"

"We won't." Flynn mounted, looked down at his father. "We won't," he repeated.

"Why do it on a hellion like War Chief?"

"He's here."

"Well, yeah, none of the hands are gonna ride him unless they have to."

"I like WC."

"I guess I see that. You're both so damn stubborn."

Flynn didn't like coming out here. Being rich had always set him apart, and the Two Bar was very rich. He and Abby lived in a small house in Menard. He had joined the police force. But tonight—well, he knew exactly why he wanted to come. They had made a decision, the two of them, and it was right that they come here to fulfill it.

"Come on over to the house, I'll show you the branding log. Pretty good day, son."

"When we get back, Dad."

His father's reply was a silence that Flynn knew was filled with sadness. They had argued fiercely over his decision to leave the Two Bar. His mother had begged him. There had been tears, there had been bitter anger. Still, his father never stopped trying to interest him in the ranch. It was among the last of the great Texas ranches, two hundred thousand acres of ranchland, farmland, and oil rigs. The family's wealth was fantastic. Flynn made $36,800 a year as a recently promoted detective in the Menard City Police Department and was very happy. His dad was worth at least a billion dollars, maybe more, and was not very happy at all.

Of course it was all crazy. What Flynn was doing. Was it rebellion? A desire to find something of himself that didn't belong to the Two Bar? That's what Abby thought.

Now, as they walked their horses into the deepening evening and their long shadows stretched out behind them, he saw her smile at him out of the edges of her eyes.

"You be careful on WC," Flynn's father called. "He'll throw your ass, he gets half a chance." They had left the corral and were heading out into a vast natural prairie, this time of year studded with flowers and rich with their perfume.

"WC can't throw me."

"The hell, that horse could throw Jesus Christ and the twelve goddamn apostles. Shit. Sorry, Abigail! Sorry!"

"Eleven goddamn apostles," Abby called back. "Remember Judas was a Judas." Her father was a hard-shell Baptist who'd brought his family out from Abilene ten years ago because of a schism in their church. Abby had left his rigorous beliefs behind, but Harry Carroll didn't really grasp that. He still saw the tightly pious little girl who Flynn had fallen in love with when they were thirteen. In fact, she had strayed so far from her childhood beliefs that she was barely welcome in her father's house.

They rode on.

As it became obvious that they were definitely heading out, War Chief whickered angrily and tossed his head. Outbound, he'd sidle along snorting. He'd try to nip Flynn or scrape him off on one of the scrubby trees. But on the way back, they'd thunder across the land, a lurching giant on a flying horse.

"Let's go up the north way, get over that draw where the flowers're so thick."

She laughed a little. "Why go way up there?"

"Well, why don't you just hazard a guess."

She laughed more. They'd kissed for the first time on one of those long hills this time of year. They'd been fourteen, dating for a year. She'd had eyes like the sky, lips like roses light as air, skin as pale as a cloud.

Now, things were different. There mission was more serious than a kiss. Now, it was the right time of month. Once she was pregnant, they would not ride again, not for a long time.

He wanted the baby conceived here, on the Two Bar. He wanted to do it lying on the land, embraced by the earth of it, by the life of it.

Once their child was born, he thought he'd probably return to ranching. He just needed to find out first if there was anything else in him.

When they were about half a mile out, Abby called out, "Race you!"

Flynn made WC rear, the horse's one trick. If anybody but Flynn tried it, WC would tumble them out of the saddle and head for the barn.

Abby took off, Serena's hooves spattering dirt as she soared away into the lingering evening.

"Darn, no fair," Flynn shouted. He snapped his reins. WC picked up his pace, working into his gut-pounding trot. Flynn had first sat on a horse at age three, but WC knew how to cause even a good rider pain.

A quarter horse like Serena takes off like a Ferrari in heat, and she was three lengths ahead of WC inside of half a minute.

"You go, girl," Flynn shouted.

"Eat dust, dude!" Serena and Abby plunged ahead, surging into the last whisper of light. Bouncing along behind her, Flynn just laughed. He knew his horses, and he knew that Serena would tire soon. Once that happened, she could not be forced, not if you respected your animal, which Abby certainly did.

WC was now sort of sidestepping. Slithering.

"Your horse trying to put out a campfire?"

"My horse is trying to neuter me!"

"He better not!"

He finally got WC going and they were off again, but this time Serena didn't take off like she had at first. She was past that quarter-horse burst. WC had become aware of the competition and was finally thinking about galloping.

The wind rushed past, the first stars wheeled above, the Big Dipper and the Great Bear. Scorpio ranged across the firmament. The western horizon was deepest red, blood on the edge of the world.

They swept across the night, young and in love and in the fertile dark. And were watched.

They could never have imagined, in their excitement and the running night, that they were being observed by somebody at once as far away as eternity and as close as a breath.

Or perhaps that wasn't entirely true. Perhaps he should have realized it, for nothing about Flynn Carroll was as it seemed. First, that wasn't his name. Second, he was already married, although not under the law of this land.

The watcher measured the flashing patterns in their brains, listened to their tumbling blood, comparing what it saw to patterns that had been etched in secrets deeper than man may know.

The watcher was aware that they would sense the danger that it brought, and so stayed well downwind of them. Humans can smell danger, they just don't know it.

Flynn reined in WC. "Evening star," he said, pointing to the strip of green that had replaced the blood in the deep west. A jewel lay there, silver against the last glow.

"Venus," Abby said, "Venus this time of year."

He dismounted. She was a lithe girl, graceful and cheerful and as mysterious to him as the sky, and as grand. The elegant logic of her curves made him long to hold her, to reenter the balance that was their delight.

She looked like something you'd see in heaven. She smelled like sea foam. As she swung gracefully off her mount, her hair floated around her.

He said, "Know where we are?"

"The ridge. The flowers."

"Exactly where."

"I can't see a thing."

"Yes you can. You see those boulders over there?"

She drew close to him. "What did you bring me here for, you naughty man?"

Gently, he leaned down and kissed her on the neck.

He drew her down into the mat of flowers. They swam in their perfume. The air shimmered with the music of crickets.

"Flynn, we're out in the open."

"The horses won't care."

"What if your dad rides out?"

He turned her face to his and kissed her. For a moment, she was stiffly unwelcoming, her churchly modesty causing her to push at his chest. When the kiss went deeper, she finally sank into it.

Venus rode low in the west, chasing the sun. The gibbous moon was rising in the east. Somewhere in the dark, coyotes called to one another.

They lay back, side by side. He would have her naked, but he would take his time.

"What're those?" she asked, pointing to a triangle of stars.

"I don't know. Not a constellation."

The watcher was now close enough to feel their heat and smell their breath. It saw not only their young bodies but also the dark fates that had already been written for them, part of the mystery to which all belong.

Flynn said, "I was going to spout that poem you love, but I forgot it all."

"'I went out to a hazel wood because a fire was in my head, and cut and peeled a hazel wand and hooked a berry to a thread.'"

"I can't memorize worth a damn."

She sighed. "It's so pretty here," she said.

She took his hand and laid it on her chest. He felt the sweet softness curving under the cotton of her blouse. "Squeeze that," she whispered. "I like that."

Instead, he lifted himself up and began unbuttoning the blouse. He opened it and, recalling their backseat days, reached around to unsnap her bra.

"They're moving," she said.

"What?"

She sat up and pointed. "Those three stars. They're moving."

The watcher stopped. Drew back. They must not become afraid, they must not leave, not now. Time was of the essence, and if it ran out, then this complex effort would all have to be repeated. The watcher was not alive, but it was intelligent, and it would do whatever it must to fulfill its mission.

"I want you," Flynn said.

"I've never done it outside."

"Abby . . . " He kissed the cream of her naked breasts. His hands went to the button on her jeans.

She laughed again. "You are so dirty."

"This is beautiful. It's pure."

He drew down her jeans and she lay naked in the night, an angel glowing in the flowers.

He raised himself on his elbow. His heart was bounding, his whole body opened to every detail of the moment. He was aware, with sudden clarity, of the world around them, the sleepy horses grazing nearby, the night wind filling the air with the scent of the flowers, the nearby snuffling of some night creature, the heat of her and the scent of her, musk and gardenias and sweat.

He looked down into the gravity of her face, seeing in it the religion of life, and then he laid his lips upon hers again and was at once lost in the taste of her and the tentative flicking of her tongue and the rising of his heat, his member now a sword, questing ferociously, making his own jeans into a drum skin.

Then her eyes were looking past him. In passion, he thought, but her breath shuddered and her throat worked, and then she tore away from him. In his fright and surprise, he leaped to his feet.

"Sorry," he shouted. "Sorry!"

Then, and to his complete amazement, she screamed. She grabbed her temples. Her eyes were white terrified pools in the dark. He stared down, watching her, not understanding.

"Abby, I'm sorry! I'm so—"

She took another breath, opened her mouth, and started to scream again. He clapped a hand across it.

"Abby, it's okay, we'll go home, we'll do it at home." He glared into her face, willing her to come back to herself.

Her nostrils dilated, her eyes bulged—and he understood that something was strange here. He could see her face too clearly. But why, when it was so very dark?

He whirled and looked up into the strangest thing he had ever seen.

To the west there were three bright stars in a row, stars that were not present in any constellation. Overhead, instead of the soft glow of the Milky Way, there was a riot of stars in a million colors, a sweeping massive horde of them, gold and yellow, blue and red, silver and green, more stars by far than he had ever seen before, so bright that they lit up the land brighter than the moon.

Where there had been grass bobbing with flowers, there were long creepers, thick masses of them. Their leaves were pale and feathery.

He leaped to his feet. They were in a vast field of waving plants, long tendrils in the night wind, which brought a sweet scent that pierced Flynn's heart with an entirely unexpected nostalgia, but also gripped his blood with icy claws.

On the ground, Abby gasped and sobbed, choking. He went down to her and put his hands under her arms and lifted her. She trembled in a way that reminded him of some gentle little animal, a quail desperate in his hands that he had caught in an Indian snare as a child.

Then, above the whipping ocean of leaves, he saw a figure. It was a stocky darkness, little more than a shadow. But it was there, and now it was moving, edging toward them. It was the careful stalk of a hunter.

The lives they had been living a second ago had become, in the tiny drop of time it had taken for this change to occur, something that belonged to deep memory and the emptiness of ages.

The way she huddled against him, his dear little bird, he knew that she felt it, too.

The figure was now quickly coming closer, and Flynn somehow knew that it was coming for Abby. In an effort to conceal her, he drew her down, but she stiffened, frozen like a mouse under the gaze of a snake. He whispered, barely a breath but full of wild intensity, "*Down!*"

She came with him and they were two rabbits crouching.

Something was buzzing now, the sound of a fly, but enormous, close, then torn away by the wind.

Then it was there, right in front of them, its cobalt-blue work clothes gleaming in the strange starlight, its face that of a pinched frog, its eyes two bulging, expressionless domes of insectoid lenses.

It was a fly the size of a child.

Abby fell to her knees, spread her arms, and looked up to that mad sky.

"Abby?"

"That's a demon, this is hell!"

A female voice said, "Not really, sweetie."

Flynn turned toward the new—and so familiar—voice.

"Flynn, come with me."

The voice was indeed familiar, but the face was in shadow. Not only the voice, but the place. "Don't look so damn confused. You're where your soul was born."

Abby was still on her knees, her hands now clutched together, her head bowed. She was praying hard.

"Listen to her calling on her gods," the other woman said. She came closer. She was beautiful in the night, with dark, flowing hair and skin like cream.

"Who are you?" Flynn asked, and was instantly washed with the most powerful sense of loss that he had ever known. It struck him and lifted him like a great wave into its surging grip.

Her face was . . . so very, very dear. And this place, the shimmering, waving fronds, the three stars—he loved this place terribly, with his blood, with his soul, which now felt as much a part of his body as his skin and his humming heart.

"You tell me who I am."

"I—I'm sorry."

"Tell me!"

He looked down toward Abby. "She's naked. Don't leave her like that."

"You took her clothes off."

Flynn was at a loss. He did not know this place, and yet he loved it. He did not know this woman, but her face was palely familiar, and her dark hair as it flowed in the wind was a lovely and haunting thing to see. Desire, until a few moments ago wrapped up in Abby, scalded him with unexpected intensity.

"Flynn," came a tiny voice from below. "What's going on? Where is this place?"

"Don't you dare tell her," the woman hissed.

"But I—"

"You're under orders just like the rest of us." She gestured with a slim arm toward the crouching Abby. "This is so dangerous, this whole situation."

And then came a great thunder in him, the crashing roar of recognition. Memory flooded in, memory so strong and so complete—but so entirely unexpected—that he gasped from it and reeled away.

Then he locked eyes with her, in the wind and the shadows of a racing little moon. He reached a trembling hand toward her. She did not move.

"Something's wrong, Diana."

"You can say that again. And thank you for remembering my name."

She took his wrist and drew him away. Hearing the rustle of their departure, Abby shrieked and leaped to her feet. She came bounding after them, leaping through the rough fronds.

Diana, who he knew now was his wife—his real

wife—threw back her head and laughed, the sound at once as raucous as the voice of a crow and as dear as the giggle of a lover.

Abby flung herself at Flynn, her hands grasping frantically. Flynn watched, all his passion gone. She was just an instrument, part of his mission. Or so he told himself. When dark blue figure carried Abby away, her shrieking became an awful, despairing cry.

"Don't hurt her," he said to Diana. "I'm the one you should be angry at."

"I'm not angry, I'm jealous."

"Don't hurt her."

He watched Abby disappear into the darkness, struggling and crying out, tearing helplessly at the thing that gripped her in its thickly gloved hands.

Diana kept moving.

Finally, he followed her. He didn't see a choice. As they went up a long rise, Abby's cries faded into the nasty, hissing wind. The closer they came to the crest of the hill, the brighter the sky became, until, as they mounted it, a view exploded into Flynn's consciousness that swept everything else away: his fear for Abby, his confusion at what was happening, his questions about Diana—all of it—in a tide of memory as keen as a cold blade and as sweet as a summer song.

Before him there spread a vision of lights, and he at once knew that this was the great city of his birth and his upbringing and his soul's deep home. This was the Aerie, known across the land of Aeon as the City where the Truth Is Known.

Home.

She had stopped. She had turned to him. She stood

with her arms tentatively open, a tall silhouette against the blazing lights of Aerie and the magnificent drama of Aeon's sky.

He went to her in silence, and in silence they embraced. He felt the warmth and soft scent of her, this woman who was so many things more to him than any woman on Earth is to any man. Still, though, Abby was there in his heart, dear.

Arm in arm now, they went along a familiar path, to their home and office, Social Police Division 211, the headquarters of the Police Protective Unit that was tasked with keeping criminal elements from exploiting Earth.

He was an officer. He was on mission and had been recalled.

He did not have a good feeling about this.

He followed Diana through the contemplative quiet of the central office. As he did so, the faint, dry-straw scent of the air, so familiar, the sounds of quiet conversation between man and machine, the soft footsteps as officers went from one station to another—all of it combined to induce a flood of memories.

He'd become a policeman on Earth because he was a policeman here. He'd taken form in the Carroll family because he would one day need a great deal of money. His childhood was in the record of the state of Texas and in the memories of his earthly parents and friends, but he had actually come in just two Earth years ago.

Earth was in terrible danger. His job: protect them.

In this work, you could not take such memories with you, but you could take your orders, so deeply encoded that only a few police specialists could extract them from your unconscious.

"Have I gone off mission, Diana?"

She walked faster. He saw her fists clench.

He passed the Earth Unit, where operators at observation stations watched for smugglers attempting to reach the planet. Outside, he knew, there were forty more such stations, each dedicated to another primitive planet, to preventing it giving up its wealth of genes and souls to criminals intent on selling them to underground scientists, slavers, wealthy thrill seekers, and whomever else might want them, whether for experimentation or entertainment, or to build them into brilliant robots.

"I don't want you to give her a baby."

"I thought—"

She turned on him. "Remember who reads you." Her voice was quiet, but her eyes were stunned with hurt. "Your feelings for her are agonizing to me."

His heart opened to Diana, the real love of his life.

"You know it's on mission. The baby is on mission."

They turned a corner and headed for Diana's private suite—their suite—where their marriage had been consummated, where they had chosen Earth work, where they had embraced for the last time before he began his tour.

In the middle of the large, comfortable room, Abby floated in an Isolate, her open eyes empty. The flickering lights of medical analysis touched her smooth skin.

Diana walked up to her. Gazing at her, she put her hands on her hips. "Incredible," she said. "She looks like an angel."

"A baby would endanger her? Is that why we're here?"

As she floated there in perfect nakedness, shimmering with the blue light of the device that held her, he could almost believe that her soul, incredibly pure, had appeared on the surface of her body.

"She's perfect," Diana whispered.

"Then you understand."

"It's starting. On Earth."

He felt an awful sinking of the heart, and yet with it came excitement. This was his work, why he was a policeman here and a policeman there.

"We're married. We want a baby."

She came to him and stood before him. Her face was flushed, her eyes fixed with anger. She drew back her right hand and slapped him hard.

Instinct almost caused him to strike back, but training stopped him—training and love. She turned away, plunged to her desk, and dropped down behind it. "I'm so sorry." She shook her head. "Pardon my lack of professionalism."

Diana didn't have a baby with him; of course she was jealous. He felt it, too, the hollow cold truth that he might not come back. That his real wife might never bear their child.

"When I'm there," he said carefully, "you know . . ." He gestured vaguely. They could not take memories of Aeon with them. Undercover cops like him lived and worked in total amnesia. If they remembered themselves, they were vulnerable to an enemy that could read the mind.

She stood again and came to him.

He took her in his arms and felt as she pressed herself against him a rush of memory and a rush of love.

"You want the child?" she asked. Then, very softly, her voice a burr of misery. "With her?"

He held her more tightly. "I want our child."

"No," she said sharply. "Violation of the mission." She gazed at him. "What's it like?"

"When I'm there, I'm Flynn Carroll, wondering why the hell I'm giving up a billion-dollar ranch for a little, tiny police job."

"Billion what? I'm sorry, I'm not tracking."

"Their measure of wealth. The obscure corner of earthly life I happened to enter turned out to be incredibly wealthy."

"I did not know that. So your life there must be very pleasant."

"I gave it all up to be a cop. Nobody can figure me out. Frankly, neither can I. Not when I'm on Earth."

She came to him, and when she drew close he felt in her embrace a haunting, beloved memory of Abby. He would never tell her this, though. Never.

"Love, do your best. I'll have to watch every detail, remember that."

He kissed her and felt her vulnerability and her anguish, and shared it.

She broke away then and went to the window. Sunrise was not far off, and the eastern sky was a strip of pink, one of the moons hanging there like a pearl.

"The Moon of Love," she said. Then, bitterly, "Can a moon mock you?" She whirled around. "She's a cover, nothing more. Which you seem to want to forget."

"As I must. As you know."

"She could be in danger."

"I know it."

"And the child."

He knew that, too, and it made his guts crawl. What was worse, back on station, all of this would be forgotten. "What would you have me do, love?"

She went back to her desk, her place of authority. She had brought him here to warn him. Were there also orders? Her hands, fisted, lay before her. "Mission Control regards them as expendable."

As far as the police department was concerned, Abby and the baby she and Flynn were going to have were a cover. They were bait.

"They will be taken," she whispered. "Inevitably."

Agony. Agony in his heart. But the whole human species and its chance to evolve and join the chorus of conscious species in the universe depended on this mission, and therefore on such sacrifices. He said, "I know."

"I'm sorry I brought you here. I apologize."

"You had to. We both know the regs. If I'm going operational, this is the only way to tell me." His consciousness would forget, but not his deeper self. There, the hard, quick, brilliant police captain would remain hidden, waiting to take the lash to whatever smugglers presented themselves.

Hand in hand, they walked down to the transport, a formation known on Earth as a wormhole. Diana pressed their code into the heavy door and they entered the confined space of the transition chamber. The transport position shimmered before them, a darkness beyond the end of darkness. In this universe, there are many walls and many openings in those walls. On Earth, places that are closer than a hair seem more distant than the farthest star. Here, where the truth was known, such a traverse as this was just a short step, nothing more, but through a system that had taken a thousand years to create, a truly extraordinary triumph of the mind.

"Has she been sent?"

"She's back. They've got her lying right where they found her. She's just about to awaken."

"I love you, my wife."

Diana squeezed his hand.

He took a breath. He stepped forth, into the strange, empty coldness of the transport. There was the familiar hollow rush, then he staggered out into the night and the flowers of the Texas prairie.

She lay there, as pale as a cloud in the sea of white dots that covered the night prairie. Far to the east, Earth's own moon was just rising.

He lay down beside her and gazed up at the strangely empty sky. Earth was an outlier, orbiting a star at the extreme edge of this galaxy.

As his memory faded, he clung for a last sorrowing moment to Diana. Then he turned to Abby. Her eyes were open, gazing into the sky.

His last memory of home winked out.

Abby said, "Flynn? Are you awake."

"Mm?"

"It's three. *Three*, Flynn!"

"How can it be three?" he said. He thought, *We've been here half the night and I never did it.*

"We must've been tired. Plus, WC took off. We've gotta double on Serena now."

"Forget the horses."

"We need to get home; what'll your folks think?"

"That we're out here being bad. Which we are." He drew her to him . . . but as he felt her warmth and the curves of her, he also felt from deep in his heart something he did not expect and could not explain, which was a cold, gripping sorrow. It seemed like an echo from a long ago time, some tragedy that he had long forgotten, but that now returned to him, in this moment when new life was about to be made.

"You're shivering," she said.

He kissed her, and as he did, he entered her. "I was cold. Now I'm not."

Their bodies crossed a bridge of stars, the stars of hope, the stars of new life, the stars of the miracle that is mankind.

When they were done, they lay back side by side. He raised her hand to his lips and kissed it. She turned and clung to him.

"Aren't you cold?"

"I love being naked with you like this."

"Well, I'm cold."

He got his windbreaker, which lay beside them, and put it over her. He stared up into the stars.

"I wonder if there's anybody up there," he said.

"God, I guess. Somewhere." She took his hand and laid it on her belly. "Somebody in here," she said.

"We can't be sure."

"I felt it. I felt the exact moment."

He lay there in wonder not only at the beauty of his

wife amid the stars and the flowers, but at the mystery of life itself, and the new life that she seemed so sure now lay within her.

As the moon cleared the eastern horizon, they mounted Serena, Flynn sitting behind Abby and holding her around the waist. He leaned against her, inhaling the straw-sweet scent of her hair, pressing tight against her softness and her warmth. Gently, quickly, he kissed her neck. She giggled, a happy music.

Something inside him seemed to call to him, the voice of some unknown observer, stern and deeply sad. "*Danger,*" the voice said, and was gone.

But there was no danger, not here in this familiar place.

They let the horse walk as slowly as she wanted, through the bright moon shadows.

On this perfect night, the world was wonderful.

"I'm happy," he said.

"Then why do you sound sad?"

"I'm not. Far from it."

As they rode, Flynn became aware of tears drifting down his cheeks. Drifting at first, then pouring. It was as if somebody he could not see, who lived inside him, was experiencing this lovely night as a tragedy. They rode on toward the distant lights of the house, and the whispered warning faded, and then the sadness.

Flynn kissed her neck again, and she arched her head and reached back and laid a hand on his cheek.

They unsaddled Serena and WC, who they found predictably standing at the barn door. Hand in hand, they crossed to the silent house and crept up the back stairs to Flynn's boyhood room. On the way, Abby tickled him and they stifled laughter, and in his own he heard once again that mysterious note of sadness.

The night passed, stepping softly into dawn, and they came downstairs to a sizzling ranch breakfast. Flynn's mother and father twinkled at them, but nothing was said of the late hour of their return.

On distant Aeon, Diana wept for the man she loved, working tirelessly to protect him and his earthly wife and their coming child.

Or was she protecting them from Mission Control's plan, which was to use them as bait? Other eyes saw, other, darker minds wondered just who this seemingly innocent man might really be, and drew closer, and looked closer.

And then they knew.

Another deep-cover cop had been exposed—or rather, a subtle trap in which he and his earthly wife were the bait had been sprung. Soon the criminal band that was now evaluating Earth would conclude that he was indeed a policeman from Aeon and take steps to neutralize him.

By so doing, they would reveal themselves, the long game would grow shorter, and, if all went well, they'd be mopped up and the people of Earth would be left alone for a little while longer.

Over the next weeks and months, the movements of Abby and Flynn were observed, their associations researched, their every breath and every heartbeat recorded, along with the heartbeat of the infant sleeping within.

In a world so far away its home star could not even be seen from Earth, Abby and her infant came up for sale in an auction room that somebody from Earth would have seen as a sort of heaven, palatial and blue.

It was not a heaven. It was a place where souls were bartered, as evil a place as exists.

Figures watched her terror, just as butchers on Earth watch the terror of cattle, and with as little emotion. Others discussed her genes and the baby's rich stem cells.

The bidding was quick, just a gesture here, a nod there. In the end, the two of them went for a sum large enough to satisfy even the greediest smuggler.

They would be broken up for their DNA. Probably.

On the day that she was sold, Abby, all unawares, made Flynn a chocolate pie. On her belly, there was a mark, red and hardly sore at all, where a long needle had been inserted. The infant, rich with new cells, was now labeled, as was the mother.

They were free Americans on one planet, property on another.

All was done, then, but for the waiting.

Late some nights, a car would drift past the house. Far away, Diana would watch it and wonder. Who was in it? Why were they there? Was it from Mission Control, perhaps some part of it she did not have access to? Or was it something else entirely—a sign, perhaps, that the trap was working?

The car was followed, but went nowhere important. Abby and Flynn lived their lives and slept their sleep, and the world rolled on.

Not forever, though, and not for long. Their life together soon would end, and his life alone would begin, and with it the quest that would come to define him, to find the woman he loved, to rescue her, to return her to their house of perfect love.

Diana would watch and weep inside for the husband who had forgotten her, but she would continue to serve the mission, duty before love.

In the great vastness of the universe, worlds begin and end every day. Somewhere eyes are being raised to the sky for the first time and somewhere for the last time, always. But in the heart, in the house of love, tiny events are enormous events, such as the loss of the one you love.

Flynn lost Abby and Diana lost Flynn, and the universe went its heedless way. But not for them, for them the losses were so vast that they were almost unimaginable.

Duty kept Diana loyal to the mission, and she tried not to hate the man she loved, watching him search for this other woman, this simple human creature who, after all, had been nothing but a bit of bait. That, and her own husband's new and eternal love.

ABOUT THE AUTHOR

WHITLEY STRIEBER is the *New York Times* bestselling author of more than twenty-five books, including the legendary bestsellers *The Wolfen, The Hunger, Communion,* and *Superstorm,* all the bases of movies. His book *The Grays* is also being made into a film. His website, Unknowncountry.com, is the largest of its kind in the world, exploring the edge of science and reality. You can learn more about Whitley's books at www.strieber. com and follow him on Facebook and Twitter.